Laura Daniels was ... degree in English Lite... ...as a director of a London publishing company, and is now a freelance editor and writer. She is married to an American, and they live in a Kentish village on the North Downs. She also writes crime novels under the name of Amy Myers.

Her most recent novel, PLEASANT VICES, is also available from Headline.

Also by Laura Daniels from Headline

PLEASANT VICES

The Lakenham Folly

Laura Daniels

HEADLINE

First published in 1995
by HEADLINE BOOK PUBLISHING

First published in paperback in 1996
by HEADLINE BOOK PUBLISHING

10 9 8 7 6 5 4 3 2 1

ISBN 0 7472 4927 X

Typeset by
Letterpart Limited, Reigate, Surrey

Printed and bound in Great Britain by
Cox & Wyman Ltd, Reading, Berks

HEADLINE BOOK PUBLISHING
A division of Hodder Headline PLC
338 Euston Road
London NW1 3BH

AUTHOR'S NOTE

Lakenham and Bishopslee villages are fictitious, though set in the Darenth Valley and North Downs of Kent respectively, and in Florence the complex of the Basilica of San Lorenzo has been extended to encompass fictitious buildings for the purposes of this novel.

For their invaluable help to me during its writing, I would like to thank Peter Gent, Robert Goodwin, Laurie Hoffman, John Hope, Dr Nicholas Penny, Sheelagh Taylor and Adrian Turner; any errors stem from me and not from their painstaking care. As usual, the encouragement of my agent Dorothy Lumley of the Dorian Literary Agency, and of my editor Jane Morpeth at Headline, has spurred me along the route from start to finish, and to them my heartfelt thanks.

Chapter One

'Who's there?'

She stopped, then wondered why. There was nothing, save the known and familiar: the gate just yards away, the path and home. She wasn't even particularly late this evening, although it was already dark. The job had sounded interesting but turned out to be routine. An archaeologist requiring help home from the site with his booty had prosaically materialised as a rather dull man with two large suitcases. What had she expected? A Roman urn slung over one shoulder and a mummified corpse on the other?

And just what fantasy was flitting through her brain now? So much for the image of a practical 'rely-on-me' Gemma Maitland. She clutched the torch slightly more firmly. The Granada was safely locked up in the garage; she had only to cross the lane, and within seconds she'd be in her personal garage, otherwise known as her cottage, Waynings. She reminded herself that for her night held no terrors – not now anyway – and the wall that seemed to loom between her and her microwaved supper-to-be was not only invisible but non-existent, the effect of a long tiring day and lack of sustenance. The insidious tentacles of night for once had had their way, but the practical chances of thieves, rapists and murderers lurking in the bushes could be discounted. After all, the reason she'd chosen Waynings was that it was right at the end of the row of four old cottages and next to the woods. Her garden seemed an extension of the forest; the tall, large bushes were well-loved shapes, their fresh spring greenery made mysterious by the dark, which was lightened only by the glow of her torch and the single lamp above her front door. Hurst Lane could boast no street-lighting of its own.

'Right. Forward the Buffs!'

For some ridiculous reason, she shouted this out loud, secure in the knowledge her neighbours were away; but her war-cry confirmed what her brain was struggling to deny. Something seemed to be happening to the back of her neck. A distinct attack of the prickles that had nothing to do with the rough wool of her jacket. Nonsense. It was only the reminder of a May evening that winter was not far behind.

The bushes on either side of the path stirred gently in the breeze. No rapist leapt out on her, but nevertheless her footsteps quickened. A sudden rustle in the bushes made her stifle a scream, then a laugh as Launcelot leapt out and yowled in feline reproach for his delayed supper. Ancient cats of ten years should not be expected to have to forage for themselves in the forest. Then she saw Launcelot's attention was not on her; he was staring intently into the bushes at the side of the path – not in contemplation, but with ears alert, body tense. The hunter might be old but he never forgot. If she bent down she would see a bird, a rabbit or a mouse, wouldn't she? Gemma swallowed. Of course she would. After all, she was no shy maiden; she was fully trained in self-defence – she had to be in her job. She was thirty-seven, no longer a little girl afraid of the unknown, of wolves that might leap from the forest to seize little Red Riding Hood. She knew the dark. She had stretched her arms to welcome it these past eight years, and now it was her friend. She had only to put her hand into that bush to prove it so.

But what if someone reached out to touch it from within?

Launcelot yowled again. A whiff of a spicy, pungent scent brought by a sudden breeze hit her. She hurled herself at her front door, unlocked it, almost tumbled inside and slammed it shut behind her. No longer a friend, the dark swallowed her. She fumbled for the switch and light flooded the hall.

'Just as well I didn't marry an Eskimo,' she tried to joke to herself, ashamed of that lurching heart. 'Let there be light.' Ritually she rushed round the cottage turning on every switch, even the light in the hall cupboard. Only her bedroom did she leave in darkness, forcing herself to cross to the dormer window. She looked down into the garden and laughed in relief at her own stupidity.

'I won,' she said for some reason, opening the window to gloat, full of confidence again in the familiar. A barn owl screeched as she leaned out over the sill, breathing in the sharp mysteries of the eerie world of night. Over there was the Charing to Canterbury road, marked by the occasional hum of traffic; to her left was the country lane leading to it, which passed through the sprawl of the small village of Bishopslee. Little light from the village penetrated as far as Waynings.

'I'll get a security light fitted,' she told herself not for the first time, as a small dark shape suddenly moved and scuttled across the lane. She watched it until it disappeared into the blackness and then drew her head back in, her hand poised to draw the curtains.

'*Daisy, Daisy, give me your answer do* . . .'

Floating, note by note on the night air, came the sound of a whistled tune. A man's whistle, surely, uncommon enough nowadays; the sound chilled her, disembodied, impersonal, threatening. A poacher? Badger-hunters? No, neither would make more noise than they had to. Whoever it was, moreover, had nothing to do with her. And yet she did not seem to be able to move. Was it louder, was it receding? It seemed to stifle her, drum at her ears, threaten with its very ordinariness.

'*I'm half crazy* . . .' Frozen, she stood there, irrational in terror, gazing out into a world in which she could see nothing, until at last the sound died away. Only the silence remained to mock her.

'Lakenham House. But Grandpa, why?' Gemma broke off, somewhat bewildered. Why there of all places to celebrate a hundredth birthday?

General Maitland smiled. 'Humour me, my dear. Old men have strange ideas.'

'Not you.'

'Time marches even faster than generals.'

'There's some reason, isn't there?'

'A whim.'

It was Gemma's private fear that the hundredth birthday would prove too much of a milestone. She knew that sometimes such an event was too much for even the most stalwart of fighters, and she and her grandfather's guardian angel (his housekeeper, Mrs Plummer) were determined to keep him with them as long as possible. She

4

suspected, however, that he intended to indulge their whim only as long as it suited him. She visited him here at Tenterden as often as she could. She had no other family – not close, anyway. She'd lost Bill; and her father, Grandfather's only son, had been killed in Aden in the early sixties; her mother had married again and lived in America. Death wasn't going to snatch her remaining family a moment before it was entitled to. Tough, though small and frail with years, her grandfather maintained a bright-eyed interest in life like that of a man half his age. Damped down they might be, but the fires within him could still surprise her. As now.

'Wouldn't it be more sensible to have a smaller celebration in Tenterden?' Why on earth had he chosen to accept Charles Lakenham's unexpected invitation to a party at Lakenham House, which would involve a drive of over thirty miles each way? It wasn't even as if it were Thomas Lakenham, his old friend. He had died fifteen years ago; this was his son, Charles, the fifteenth Viscount Lakenham, now a man of sixty, who, in order to pay for its upkeep, ran Lakenham House as a retirement home, and had moved with his wife Maria into one wing. Now their family had grown up and moved away, it provided ample room.

'Certainly it would. But I am determined upon Lakenham House. Take me please, Gemma.' There was no hint of the supplicant in his voice, nor did there need to be.

'Of course, Grandpops, but can't you explain why?' Then she knew. 'It's something to do with the Lakenham Set—'

He interrupted her quietly. 'I would like to accept this invitation, Gemma.'

Message received and understood. Hers – in this case

at least – not to reason why, but to carry out the General's orders. No wonder the poor devils facing him at Alamein hadn't stood a chance, she thought, amused.

The Darenth river valley looked quietly pleased with itself, as indeed it had cause to do, in its June plumage. There was very little water in the river, and she recalled reading of the public concern over the continuing drought in Kent with increased demands on it. Today there was a mere trickle compared with the river Samuel Palmer had painted last century. She could remember what it looked like in full spate from her childhood, distant memories of the gurgling stream, a summer afternoon, and a jamjar full of sticklebacks. Quite a few houses had sprouted in the meantime, mostly on the outskirts of the villages, but once away from them the valley looked as peaceful and timeless as ever. She glanced in some concern at her grandfather; he was already looking a little tired. Or perhaps he just had something on his mind other than his hundredth birthday? Perhaps the latter, for it was he who had asked her to turn off the main road to drive through Shoreham village before they reached the turning that led to Lakenham. She was glad she had brought the BMW today; it was her personal car, a present to herself three years ago, and used for high days and holidays – and 'special' jobs. The Granada, one of three that her business owned, was ideal for most runs. Bishopslee Cars had grown out of the small taxi service run from home which she had started after Bill had died. Correction – a year after Bill had died.

Everything had changed with his death; her life kaleidoscoped, tossing her mercilessly about; if it had not been for Grandfather she would not have landed so gently or so quickly – if at all. It had been her own impulsive instinct that made her throw up her career as a tax accountant, and she had not regretted it. What was the point of throwing everything into the race to the top of the tree if fate sawed through the roots that gave you life? The race had done Bill no good. Nor her. He'd died of a heart attack at thirty-four, leaving her a widow. Without the child they'd planned to have 'one day'. Her hands tightened on the wheel as a surge of loss – familiar but rare now – gripped her. A year after his death, as her capital drained away and her life-force with it, Grandpops had stepped in and sorted her out. In essence he had put it to her: there are only three options in battle – go on, back or stay where you are till they get you. Which way are you heading?

'Not back.' Not to the life she'd known with Bill.

'Here then?'

Here there was anger, too much drink, desperation, and something inside tearing her apart. 'No.'

'Then create your own strategy and *advance*. Work out the tactics as you go.'

She had smiled, unconvinced, but almost as soon as she'd moved to Bishopslee from St Alban's, someone to whom she was giving a lift to hospital mentioned that the village had a crying need for a taxi service. A month later she was in business. Two days later she cut the long dark hair that Bill had loved into a shoulder-length page-boy style, threw out the business suits for neat trousers and jackets, and made a date to see an old schoolfriend for lunch. A year later she took an office in the village and an assistant. Three years after that she took on another assistant, invested in technology, widened her scope. The description Gemma Maitland, special assignments, sounded good, was good. Not precisely hush-hush stuff for MI5 or 6, but just interesting jobs both for her and her staff as couriers, investigators of everything from ancestors to old pictures, and more or less anything that needed a car and ingenuity. The taxi work remained her bread and butter.

Word of her reliability and high success rate quietly spread to the City, then throughout the Establishment, and her assignments increased. A year ago they had been forced to invest in 'The Girl', otherwise known as Kirsty. Kirsty had little interest in life outside her social horizons, which extended for a diameter of ten miles, and the boutiques of Canterbury and Ashford. But she had one priceless gift. She was a genius at booking appointments, which Gemma assumed had developed through the expertise she showed at juggling her social life. Gemma had made a joke about it once. Never again. Her social life was to Kirsty a very serious matter. She was, after all, nineteen and getting on a bit, she pointed out.

The BMW glided through the dotted houses that made up the hamlet of Lakenham, a collection of cottages originally built for workers on the Lakenham estate, and now lived in by those of neighbouring Shoreham, Lullingstone or Eynsford.

General Maitland shifted slightly in his seat as the green BMW turned in through the gates of Lakenham, and Gemma turned the wheel slightly as the drive twisted towards the house, a large, seventeenth-century, William-and-Mary red-brick mansion. Lakenhams had lived here since the house was built, though there had been a couple of wobbles in the direct line, when the title had passed to remote cousins.

'A retirement home,' grunted the General, as she

stopped the car in front of the house. 'The old lord, Thomas's father, would have turned in his grave. A great one for tradition he was. Nothing shall be changed. His wife had to fight to get a bathroom installed, let alone electric light. What would he have thought of all this, eh? But where does tradition get you? They're all dead now, and their timeless tradition has died with them through no fault of theirs.'

'This is your birthday, Grandpa,' Gemma reminded him gently. 'No talk of the past. What did you used to tell me? A good general always looks forward.'

'You'll have to speak up. My hearing's not too good.'

'Nonsense. You heard me very well.'

'Did I? Perhaps I did . . . perhaps I did.'

'Maitland, you bally rotter, did you hear what I said? A toast for the future. A toast to the British Empire on which the sun never sets, God bless her. A toast to England – may her cricket-bats never rot. A toast to the twentieth century and the New Renaissance . . . Why aren't you drinking, Maitland? You're with us, aren't you?'

Thomas Lakenham leapt on to the table, and solemnly poured the contents of his silver goblet over Maitland's unsuspecting head. 'There, I've christened you in claret. That'll wash your cynicism away, old chap. You'll see. We'll be making the same toast here in eighty years' time, in the 1990s. You'll wonder why you ever doubted us, Reggie.'

Charles Lakenham had aged since Gemma had last seen him – she hadn't attended his father's funeral, so she supposed it must have been at some function at which he had accompanied his father before that. She remembered the beam, and the round, pleasant face. Now he had broadened out and his hair was grey. He rushed up to them, bowling a wheelchair with great dexterity.

'Delighted you are with us, sir. A great honour.'

'Damn it, Charles, if you think I'm getting into one of those contraptions to enter my own birthday party, you've another think coming,' the General told him amiably as they shook hands.

It took time, but her grandfather made it in on his own two feet. All the same he sank down thankfully in the comfortable leather armchair that Lakenham had thoughtfully placed with one or two others on a slightly raised area at one end of the large reception room. Gemma was glad of that, for it meant people would approach singly to speak to him, not crowd him in. Her heart sank at the look of the room. There must be at least a hundred people here. Not only had all her grandfather's cronies from the regiment been invited – youths who had served under him in World War II and now were old men themselves (though no doubt to him they appeared young striplings), but in addition to some family friends and cousins whom she vaguely recognised, there were a great many people she had never seen before. At least half of the number present. Residents of the home, she supposed, for they could hardly be turned out for the day. And some might be staff . . .

'I deduce you must be one of Miss Nightingale's young ladies.'

She turned round to find a glass of champagne being waved invitingly beneath her nose by a tall lean man of about forty. The high forehead and glasses made him look serious and ordered, but the light brown springy hair seemed to suggest a life of its own. Moreover, there was a humorous twist to his mouth that looked distinctly promising. She decided she'd investigate – cautiously.

'Wrong war alas,' she laughed. 'My career didn't get going till World War I.'

'Is that why they started Rose Day? In your honour?'

'Sorry to disappoint you. I'm General Maitland's granddaughter, not Queen Alexandra. Gemma Maitland.' She put out her spare hand.

'Paul Shane. I see you're wearing a wedding ring though. Divorced?'

'Widowed,' she said briefly.

He said no more. Wisely. It was her business why she had reverted to Maitland. It had been part of the new life, the advance forward into no man's land.

'Do you live here?' she asked politely.

He grinned approvingly. '*Touché*. You, me and the beautiful blonde over there doing the Sharon Stone look-alike must be about the only folks under seventy. No, I'm not yet a resident. I'm Philip Shane's grandson.'

'Of the Lakenham Set?'

'Of course.'

Gemma searched her memory. Though her grandfather never spoke of them (or perhaps because of it), she had done her own private research. It had not been easy tracking down odd references in books, but she had managed to glean quite a bit about the later lives of members of the Set. 'The banker?'

'Yes.'

'And in the Royal Naval Division in the Great War?'

'The *Great* War! That's a severe case of jargon.'

'Sorry. It's being close to my grandfather that does it. He always calls the first war that, even though he went

11

through both. Not to mention a few minor ones as well.'

'He's a splendid man. I've enormous admiration for him.'

'Have you met him?' she asked, surprised. Her grandfather led a retired life nowadays.

'For his achievements, I should have said. Such sloppy phrasing ill becomes a solicitor. Though I did meet him too – at the late Lord Lakenham's funeral. I talked to him for some—' He broke off as Sharon Stone swept up to them, swinging a mass of golden hair. 'Gemma, meet Anne Masters. Gemma's the General's granddaughter, Annie.'

'Brill,' she said, casting an offhand but genuine smile at Gemma.

Gemma was slightly surprised; she was more used to incomprehension or positive hostility from younger generations when her grandfather was mentioned. They were pacifists, was often the line – as though her grandfather weren't a pacifist too. It was what one did that made the difference. No right-thinking man welcomes war, he had ingrained into her when she was a child.

'Julian Grenfell,' she had once thrown at him, eager to impress with her knowledge. ' "And he is dead who will not fight/And who dies fighting has increase".'

'There are those who find fulfilment in war without necessarily having sought it. It does not affect my argument.'

'Are you a descendant of the Lakenham Set too then, Annie?' Gemma asked now, chiefly of the back of the blonde head whose owner seemed, to her amusement, intent on staking a prior claim to Paul. Flattering to be regarded as competition!

'Oh yes.' Annie shot a look at Paul that puzzled

Gemma. She supposed they must have been talking about the Set before she arrived. 'I'm the great-grand-niece – or is it grand-great-niece – of Jack Holland.'

'The poet? One of the other two VCs? He died in the war, didn't he?'

'Yes. He was married and had a daughter, but she passed on without issue, as they say. I'm the result of Jack's brother.' She grimaced. 'To tell you the truth, I've never been too interested in all this family stuff. But it's suddenly got rather exciting, hasn't it, Paul?'

'You could say that.' Paul didn't seem disposed to comment on why this should be so.

Am I missing something, Gemma wondered? Or was she simply being cut out by a young blonde? The said blonde needn't worry if so. Gemma's advance into no man's land after Bill's death was literally the case. There hadn't been any men in her life, not seriously, since he died, and so far as she cared, there needn't be ever again. That part of her life was over. It led to nothing but grief. Victorian ladies of old flung themselves into the unknown as an antidote to grief, and in her own way she had done the same. And succeeded admirably. Young Sharon Stone could have her conquest. She almost said, 'Bless you, my children,' as she slipped away – rather to Paul's annoyance, she noticed with a small spurt of pleasure, which she quickly suppressed.

It struck her that it was an odd party. Superficially everyone was chatting, her grandfather was talking ani-matedly to one person after another, the noise-level remained high. Yet somehow there was some sort of tension around, not quite usual in a relaxed birthday party, even a hundredth one. Also there seemed to be a rather odd mix of people, if you studied them. Charles

Lakenham hand-picked his residents, so he must be a man of far-ranging tastes.

Who for instance was that overpainted, overdressed woman – surely she knew that high-pitched, overloud voice? It was trained, professional, overpowering in ordinary conversation. Wasn't she an actress? Yes, it was the woman who played those aristocratic comic parts on TV. Slight in figure, very old now, but the voice remained easily identifiable, even if the name wouldn't come. And who on earth was the small weaselly-faced woman over there? She must be in her eighties; she looked as if she had worked hard all her life, and was still doing so. She couldn't be a member of staff at that age, so she must be a resident. Yet her clothes didn't suggest she could afford the prices Lakenham House must charge. Perhaps the Social Services paid her fees? No, surely this would be a completely private home.

Now she was beginning to bring her 'professional nose' into play. She realised that the people who lived here must be in that group at the far end, not talking, but close together as if in mutual support. Near them, there were several people who looked ill at ease. She wandered over to talk to one of them, an old man sitting rigidly in his chair, as if buttressed against the world. Former army, she decided, from the moustache and set of his back. So much for her professional nose. He turned out to be a retired banker from Brentwood.

'Are you a resident here?' she asked politely.

'No.'

'You're not another descendant of the Lakenham Set, are you?'

It was meant light-heartedly, but he stared at her as though she spoke gibberish. She was about to leave, rebuffed, when at last he answered.

His reply was unexpected. 'No, I'm an orphan. Drew's my name. Stanley Drew. Banker. Ex,' he added, almost unnecessarily. He must be about eighty. And a bachelor, she decided, though more cautiously this time, from the appearance of his clothes. Or widower. She was about to give up, when Drew decided to be forthcoming. 'It's all been a bit of a shock, you see,' he confided. 'After all this time.'

He *was* a widower. He must be talking of his wife's death. He could hardly have just discovered he was an orphan. He did look as if he'd had a shock.

'You look rather white,' she said, concerned. 'Would you like me to get you some tea?'

'It's my heart. I have to take things easy.' There was a certain amount of pride in his voice.

'Of course. Tea.' She procured a passing waiter.

'Two please,' Stanley murmured.

'Two?'

'Lumps.'

'Oh.' She watched as he stirred the tea, wondering whether her hands would be as gnarled in forty or fifty years' time.

'It's not every day you hear,' Stanley offered lugubriously, 'that you might come into a fortune.'

'Have you? That sounds wonderful news.'

'If they all die first, that is.'

He seemed to have his eye on the room in general. Feeling she had dropped like Alice into a crazy wonderland, Gemma speedily made her excuses to escape. He didn't seem to mind, and at least he looked more cheerful. Probably plotting a mass murder, she thought. Poor old chap. Then she saw Charles Lakenham beckoning her to the platform, and she hurried to join her grandfather. Time for speeches. Ah well, she'd sat through enough at the regimental reunions. This one ought to be relatively painless, at least.

Charles Lakenham beamed at his guests, obviously in his element now. 'I don't know how many you've been to, but this is the first hundredth birthday party I've been to . . . I'm sure you all know that, as a captain in the First World War, Major-General Sir Reginald Maitland was awarded the VC. You may not know what for. A German machine-gun emplacement was firing at his company while they were pinned down in no man's land. Advancing under fire, he managed to wipe it out, and then returned, crawling back across no man's land, stopping to bring a wounded private with him although still under fire from neighbouring guns. In the Second World War he commanded a brigade in North Africa and Sicily, then went out to the Arakan. You all know what happened to the Royal West Kents at Kohima . . .'

Gemma's attention began to wander. Too much champagne, probably. Her grandfather was standing up to it splendidly; he was impassive during the eulogy – he'd had much practice – and the earlier signs of tiredness had now gone. But at Charles Lakenham's final words, his head jerked up.

'The toast is: the last and most distinguished of the Lakenham Set.'

He hated that, Gemma realised with amazement. Why was he so reticent about any mention of the Lakenham Set? Or was it the words 'Most Distinguished' he objected to? Of the original twenty members, only eight survived the First World War. Who was to say, her grandfather would argue, whether their achievements were greater or less than his own? What might they have accomplished had they lived?

Reginal Maitland stared at the cake in front of him. It was huge, for it bore a hundred candles. The lights in the hall were dimmed; everyone was waiting for him to blow them out, waiting for the moment when he would truly feel a hundred years old. He saw a hundred flickering lights, a hundred regimental colours borne proudly into battle to be uselessly extinguished one by one. 'The lamps are going out all over Europe; we shall not see them lit again in our lifetime.' Foreign Secretary Grey's famous words on the eve of war in 1914. Could Grey have averted war if he'd acted sooner? If he'd been a different sort of man? Probably not. If nations were hell-bent on war, they might be temporarily swayed, as at Agadir, but never totally deflected. In the end the lemmings would get what they wanted. Death, destruction, disaster.

General Maitland blew gently, watching as the candles went out. He worked swiftly at first, then, as he neared the end of his task, a careful watcher would have observed that the last twenty were extinguished ever more slowly. One by one, counting over in the memory of a hundred-year-old man: Anthony Manders-Wright, of the Honourable Artillery Company, wounded by a whizz-bang at Hooge, blown to kingdom come on St George's Day 1917 on the Black Line at Gavrelle. That Moaning Minnie had snuffed out the life of potentially the best prime minister of the century. Daredevil Jack Holland, VC. Shot down in his Sopwith Pup over Arras the day after he won the VC on a lone patrol over enemy lines to carry out a recce on the German reinforcements, and made his way back badly wounded to impart his information, after taking on three Fokkers. What remained of one of the great poets of all time? A handful of verse quoted in every anthology of war poetry. But think what might have been.

And on and on until there were only eight candles left. Eight who survived the carnage. Private Alyson, stretcher-bearer in the Royal Army Service Corps, awarded the VC for rescuing three wounded men under fire in no man's land. One of the casualties was Manders-Wright, who died in his arms. The General blew the candle out slowly. Young Maggers, 4th Rifle Brigade, given the MC for his role in the heroic counter-attack at St Eloi. Heroic? Men were heroic, not attacks or counter-attacks. He survived – survived so well he went out of his mind ten years later. Quite suddenly one day, sitting in the garden. Was that a better or worse fate than that of young Dukey? Always in trouble with his father. Who-ever heard of a duke who painted namby-pamby pictures of flowers? Young Dukey got the MC at Ypres. He survived the war too – but he brought the yellow mustard gas he'd got at Ypres out with him. Never one to cause a fuss, he died quietly in 1936, just before he'd be called upon to succeed his father. Much better his brother should succeed instead. He killed himself, of course – or did his father do it for him? Not that he'd given up painting in his illness. It was just that his paintings weren't of flowers any more. They said he was mad too. His father had him locked up. At home of course. No public fuss. Some said nowadays the Cenotaph ceremony was merely a glorification of war. To those that were there, it was the opposite; a reminder of its horrors, *lest the world forget* . . .

Only three candles left now. Philip Shane, dear Philip, always the joker. Always laughing. He didn't laugh much after Gallipoli and Passchendaele. He thought he'd joined the Navy when he volunteered, and found himself fighting on land in the Royal Naval Division. His jokes stopped altogether in 1918 and he became a banker. He died in his seventies and even that seemed a lifetime ago now. Even Thomas had been dead fifteen years. Carefully, the General blew out the last-but-one candle. Thomas Lakenham, the leader of the Set, the all-round Renaissance man, the golden-haired Sir Philip Sydney of his day: sportsman, artist, scholar. Poor Charles hadn't inherited his father's grace of manner or his gifts. Good-hearted but dull. Well, sometimes it happened that way, skipping a generation. He'd been surprised when Thomas stayed with the Scarlet Lancers after the war. Thomas had gone to war a dreamer, an idealist. He joined General Gough's brigade, just back from Ireland and the heroes of the Curragh Mutiny which so nearly brought about civil war. The artist had gone to war, and a soldier returned. He and Thomas both chose to stay in the Army. But when Thomas retired, he'd taken his seat in the House of Lords, and gone back to painting, as though he'd been doing it all his life. And then he too died.

Maitland stared at the remaining candle, near its end now, and sputtering. He was the only one left, the only one who knew. Who understood what they had wanted. *They*, not him. He hadn't heard, hadn't wanted to hear. Now he owed it to them to listen to their ghosts, to light the flame of their lives again. And he knew now he had to act, and act quickly.

He did not blow the last candle out, but watched it as it spurted a last flare before it too was extinguished.

19

★ ★ ★

The lights went up. The General was aware of the cheers, that it was time for him to speak and he had nothing yet to say to them. Not to this generation. It was with the past he needed to communicate. The sight of Gemma's expectant face, however, gave him strength to rise to his feet.

He made a joke, carefully culled from his long experience of after-dinner speeches. It wasn't very good – they laughed too heartily. Perhaps he was wrong. He should try to make them understand. But it was hard after a lifetime of silence.

'Nowadays the Lakenham Set would be called privileged. It would not be a compliment. But we knew ourselves to be so, and it was a responsibility we took seriously. We had a duty to our family, to our servants, to those weaker than ourselves. We also had a duty to the future that we never questioned. We believed in ourselves, in England, in the shining glory of the future . . .'

He stopped, realising from blank, but politely attentive faces, that he was getting nowhere. How could they understand? But if they did not, how could he atone? He had said '*we* believed'. Only now did he know that to be true, and somehow he must make it come true.

He switched smoothly with the effortlessness of long experience to safer topics, and sat down to a storm of applause.

He sat for a moment before he asked, 'Charles, before I leave, I'd like to see the Folly.'

'Of course.'

'That's where the Lakenham Set used to meet, isn't it?' Gemma broke in excitedly. 'I hadn't quite taken in that it was near here. Oh – *I* remember. I came here once as a child, and there was a place like a castle, or so it seemed to me. Was that it?'

'It sounds like it. The Folly stands on the far side of the grounds. We'll find the going rough, sir. It hasn't been kept up. And it's probably unsafe structurally now.'

'Don't you go there?' Gemma asked, surprised. Surely he must take an interest as Thomas's son, especially with all the hoo-ha about the Set.

'It needs money spent on it. The occasional TV documentary on the Set doesn't pay for it.'

'Then why don't you sell – or leave it to English Heritage or the National Trust?'

He looked startled. 'Well, it's not mine to sell, is it?'

'Charles—' the General began, but Gemma interrupted him.

'Surely your feelings about not breaking up the estate should come second to the preservation of—' She broke off. 'Why are you staring at me like that?'

'Do you mean to say you've not told her, General?'

'Told me what?' Gemma demanded.

He did not answer.

'Good God,' Charles continued unbelievingly. 'Do you mean she still doesn't know about the lottery? About the tontine?'

'The *what*?'

'No,' the General replied at last. 'There was no need.'

'No *need*?' Charles spluttered, as she looked questioningly from one to the other.

'*Was* no need. Now there is. Gemma, you will take me to the Folly.'

'We'll all come,' Charles said eagerly.

'No. Just Gemma, if you please.'

21

The Lord Lakenham in residence towards the end of the eighteenth century had been to the minds of his neighbours somewhat eccentric. Instead of devoting himself to the pursuit of the true country pastimes – hunting, politics and the prompt collection of rents – he dug holes. He also set off on extensive trips on the Continent, long past the age when a grand tour might have been appropriate. Moreover, he was deemed suspiciously fond of books; the volumes in his library had a distressingly well-read look about them which ruined the set of the binding.

His lordship's holes had a purpose, however. They were dug in a quest for pottery. A chance find of a shard of red-glaze, the discovery that a neighbour's foxhounds' kennels, erected on the ruins of Eynsford Castle, had rotted in parts to reveal some interesting old tiles (which like the china were identical to some he had seen on his travels), sent him scurrying to his history books. A report that a labourer, in driving in a post on neighbouring land, had struck something flat and solid which looked uncommonly like a piece of the coloured, painted stone he had seen in mosaics in Italy, convinced him. The Romans had not merely forged a path from Deal to London along the route of Watling Street, but spread out and colonised. Where more likely than his own beloved Darenth Valley, pleasant, fertile, sheltered?

Unfortunately the owner of the land where the mosaic had been discovered obviously did not share the same interest in classical remains, for there was no further excavation. Baulked of the pleasure of proving himself right, the then Lord Lakenham thereupon decided to build his own Roman monument; he would re-create what might well lie beneath its foundations. After all, where one Roman building existed, so might others.

They might even lie all along the valley. But what kind of building was it? A temple? A theatre? No, probably a house. As he had little idea of what a Roman villa built in Britain might have looked like, he built much in the style of one of the grand buildings of ancient Rome, imposing, columned, porticoed, with a roof devised as best he could.

Before he could attend to its interior decoration, however, he died, and the building remained unused for fifty years until his grandson took a hand. He had no interest in antiquities, but much interest in getting away from his wife. He therefore spent a lot of money on 'improvements'. To his predecessor's 'Roman' architecture he added pinnacles, castellations, the odd tower, a chimney or two for modern comfort. He decorated and furnished it as he would his own study and library: heavy, solid, comfortable. The Folly was a large building and boasted many rooms, several of which he turned into bedrooms.

The next Lady Lakenham, recognising the illicit purposes to which it had no doubt been put in the past, closed the Folly down. The next opened it up again for the use of her sons. The eldest was Thomas, fourteenth Lord Lakenham, who inherited title and estate in 1912. While up at Oxford, Thomas fell in with a group of young men, like-minded in aspiration and high ideals, and the Folly was an ideal meeting place during vacations. Though sports were not ignored, the focus of the Lakenham Set was artistic; poets, musicians, artists, they believed wholeheartedly that the world (Europe) was poised on the threshold of another renaissance in science and art. By the long hot summer of 1914 they were all about twenty-one years of age. One or two had gone down the year before, some had a year still to put in until finals.

The Lakenham Setters were accustomed to meet at least thrice yearly at the Folly. But 1 August 1914 was to be their last meeting.

Gemma bumped the wheelchair over the sloping lawns that ran down to the River Darenth, regretting the high-heeled sandals and light-coloured flimsy dress she'd put on for formality's sake. Her grandfather was far from heavy to push, but it was tiring work, even before she got to the edge of the wood in which the Folly was buried. Curiosity – and her grandfather's silence – drove her on. Would it be the same magical place she remembered from her childhood? Or had memory, as so often, played tricks?

'Turn right here, Gemma.' Her grandfather pointed along an overgrown path.

'I'm not sure—'

'Nonsense. Just use me like a battering ram.'

All very well, but brambles were stubborn and they were both scratched by the time they'd pushed their way through to the centre.

'There.' There was triumph in his voice.

The wood was not as thick as she'd imagined. It cleared into what had obviously once been a fairly large formal garden, its shape still vaguely recognisable, despite the undergrowth. Here and there a weather-worn statue peered through foliage, and a stone seat in an overgrown arbour faced the building, marking the garden's boundary and backing on to what was now an impenetrable tangle of undergrowth and woodland. But this was not what Gemma saw as she looked up from her preoccupation with manoeuvring the wheel-chair over the uneven ground.

She saw the Folly.

Even her dim childhood memory had not prepared her for this. Crumbling, weatherbeaten, and magnificent, the pinnacles and columns of the Folly stared proudly out in their ivy shroud. Enormous, a dinosaur even when it was built, now it seemed unbelievable as it sat in its own disused garden. The paving of its terrace was cracked, the columns of the portico looked as if only the ivy held them in place. It was a British Museum built in a village, a Colosseum built in Harlow New Town, a Balmoral in a jungle.

'Come, we'll go in.'

'Go *in*?' she echoed helplessly. 'How?'

He rose to his feet, oblivious of her words. His hands trembled as he sought her support. 'There,' he whispered, as his past rose up before him. 'The steps.'

'You wait here,' she told him eagerly. 'I'll clear the way.' Indeed, when he pointed she could see now the outline of steps to the terrace, and hardly noticed the damage to hands and dress as she beat the way open with the help of his walking stick. The steps were there, made of rough, huge stones, and she was sweating and scratched by the time she returned to him. He did not notice, far away in the past, but clung to her arm as she helped him up the steps.

'Won't it be locked?' she asked as he limped towards the door, with his stick.

'I have the key. We all had one. Charles remembered that.'

She took it from him. It was massive, solid and rusty, but amazingly the lock still worked; it had not rusted to

the point of unusability. The door itself resisted, however, swollen with the years. He leaned past her, pushing
impatiently. Creaking, it swung open, and the last of the
Lakenham Set slowly entered.

Chapter Two

He seemed so unmoved. It couldn't be so, of course. Gemma was finding it hard enough to choke back her own emotion, and she was an outsider. The stillness that emanated from him was because in spirit her grandfather was far away, in an age that passed nearly eighty years ago. The time-machine in which he had travelled had set him down in a familiar land, peopled with old friends whose voices were raised with the shouts of youth. What lay around her was not frozen in its cocoon of cold and damp, but alive with vivid memories.

'I think, Gemma, I shall sit down.' It was an apology for age. Gemma helped him to one of the leather chairs in the main reception area within. Reception area? Strange words for what lay around them. From the outside the Folly was a crazy mish-mash of Roman, modern and Gothic architecture. The interior was doing its best to follow suit. Beyond a colonnade of pillars inside the door was this huge rectangular lounging area; above it obviously the second storey. On its far side, however, was a large semi-circular dining area, which looked on to open farmland beyond a curtain of trees. To her amazed eyes it looked like a distorted Pantheon tacked on to the villa – there was even the hint of a mosaic floor under the heavy rugs. The dome above it lacked the disporting gods and goddesses it cried out for, though whether they would have approved the décor beneath them was doubtful. It was clear the mid-Victorian owner had master-minded the heavy, comfortable chairs and table, mahogany book-cases, and stuffed birds who stared indignantly from their oval glass cages. Antlers guarded every doorway. But even this was not what held Gemma's attention. This was no museum-piece of a home where soul was gone, leaving only the outside trappings. This was more like a glimpse into the *Marie Celeste*. This was yesterday's home.

'Thomas never came near the place if he could help it. I guessed so, and Charles confirmed it,' said General Maitland, as if realising what she was thinking. 'Someone comes to clean once in a while, a minimum of heating is maintained, but nothing has been touched. All is as it was.'

Chairs were still scattered untidily around, as though their occupants had but lately rushed hurriedly from the room. Glasses and decanters (these at least were empty) lay waiting to be used; a small cupboard door swung open revealing half-empty pipe-racks; cigar-boxes lay open on a dresser. Victorian ashtrays could be seen strategically placed. An *Illustrated London News* still lay on an occasional table. The atmosphere was so strong that Gemma almost felt she had only to stretch a hand to grasp that of a blazered student stepped from the pages of *Zuleika Dobson* or Rupert Brooke. Stretch a hand? When had she last had that thought? Then she remembered uneasily her irrational panic of a few weeks ago. Irrational? Maybe, but all too real. '*Daisy, Daisy, give me your answer do . . .*'

'Did you cook here too?' she asked hurriedly at

random, seeing what was obviously a kitchen to one side. Almost she expected to see the mouldy remains of a half-eaten meal on the huge oak dining table, but there were not, merely a large bowl of elderly dried flowers.

General Maitland shook his head. 'I fear we were not so liberated in those days. Food was brought from the main house. Old Josh—' He broke off and began again, as if the memory was suddenly too vivid to express. 'Old Josh brought it, and chafing dishes kept it warm. Old Josh's son became Thomas's batman,' he told her matter-of-factly, watching her as she explored the room leading off to the left of them.

She laughed, jerked out of uneasiness. Of course, what else would a crazy enthusiast for Roman antiquities provide but a bath-house? Even a hypocaust, probably. One end of it looked into what resembled a miniature Roman arena, brick steps leading down to a large circular area on which probably in mid-Victorian times a tin tub had been carefully placed. By 1914 it had acquired a new role, with bookshelves, books and chairs, leaving the arena as it was. A masculine den if ever there was one.

'May I go upstairs?' she asked, interest now truly captured.

'Be my eyes, my young legs, Gemma. Indeed, in one of the bedrooms you may perhaps find some property of mine still in the wardrobe. Would you look?'

She hurried up the wooden staircase, which creaked ominously once or twice, but refrained from disintegrating into a pile of sawdust. A corridor ran the width of the building with doors leading from it. Dark and smelling of damp, it sported Phil May prints, interspersed with yellowing Beardsleys. She opened the door of the central bedroom cautiously, as though she might find behind it the ghost of a twenty-year-old youth, indignant at this intrusion of the future, then laughed at herself for such whimsy. She of all people, known for her practicality. Whimsy had gone the way of fairy tales, and romance vanished with Bill. The bedrooms looked out over the dome of the Pantheon, and they too looked as if their occupants had only recently departed. At one end was the bathroom, sporting a smart cast-iron enamelled bath complete with shower and douche, all enclosed in decorated wood.

She peered into the last bedroom; to her surprise the bed was still made up – surely that pillow even bore the indentation of a head? Somewhat uneasily, feeling she was trespassing, she turned her attention to the wardrobe, for this might be the room her grandfather had indicated. Its door had stuck with damp and she had to pull hard at it, afraid that she might pull the whole mahogany monstrosity over. Eventually it yielded to her tug, and mustiness assailed her nostrils. But she had struck lucky – she supposed. There were old clothes in here. Surely Grandfather couldn't have meant these old once-white trousers and blazer, however? Why remember *them*, or was it just a quirk of memory casting up the inessential, while the essential lay deeper? She searched the other bedrooms, but though all of them had books and magazines lying around (a collector's paradise), none of the other wardrobes revealed anything.

'Is this what you meant?' She ran downstairs and displayed her trophies doubtfully to her grandfather.

'Yes.' He reached out his hand to take them, then turned them over in his hands as though by their touch alone the past was brought alive. 'There had been a tennis party that afternoon at Lakenham House. Thomas held them frequently during the summer, and we all joined in.'

'Just men?'

'Oh no.' He laughed. 'Naturally not. We were twenty-one, after all. Of course there were girls.'

'One girl in particular?' She had seen the sudden moistening of his eyes.

'Perhaps.'

'Ellen, I've suddenly decided to love you for ever. Shall you object?'

Ellen Shane considered his question gravely. 'Are there many girls you're intending to love for ever, Reggie?'

'You're absolutely the only one at present. So it must be true love. Shall we breathless throw ourselves on the windy hill, laugh in the sun and kiss the lovely grass?'

'I don't think we or Rupert Brooke would find Thomas's rose garden very comfortable for throwing ourselves on.'

'You must give me a rose. If there's a war I can wear it in battle.'

'Very well, but roses fade. How about a handkerchief as well to wave at the enemy, so he knows you're coming? I've only used it once today.'

Reggie Maitland dropped to one knee as she ceremoniously installed the pink rose in his buttonhole and pressed the small lace-trimmed piece of white lawn into his hand. Reverentially, he placed it in the breast-pocket of his blazer. 'I shall sleep with it under my camp-bed pillow every night.'

'Along with all the other girls' handkerchiefs?' A

pause. 'Reggie, will there be a w—?'

Quickly he stopped the word with a kiss. 'Don't say it, Ellen, not here. Not today,' he told her huskily, then, taken by surprise at his own feeling, he stared at her and her blue eyes reflected his own astonishment.

Nothing so sensuous as the far off pit-pat of tennis ball on racket, distanced by the warm sun of a summer's day. Nothing so sweet as Ellen's lips. Nothing so sweet as first love.

His hands painfully searched through the pockets of the blazer.

'What are you looking for?' Gemma asked him gently.

'I left them here by mistake. Or was it a mistake? It was as if I knew—'

'Knew what?'

'That nothing lasts. Nothing.'

'Did you not see her again after war broke out?'

'Oh yes, I saw Ellen when I came home on leave in '15. Then she became a VAD. After that our time together had to be snatched out of the jaws of war, and all the sweeter for it. But war had the last laugh. It gave and indirectly it took away.'

'What happened to her?'

'She died in the 'flu epidemic in 1918. I married your grandmother five years later.' His hands at last found what they sought, and he drew out a handkerchief. A withered rose petal fluttered to the floor. He stared at it, then quickly pushed the handkerchief back.

'How did you come to leave the clothes here?'

'Because of what was to happen that evening, all twenty of the Set stayed that night in the Folly. We talked far into the small hours, then tumbled into beds or chairs wherever we could find room. We were bursting with excitement, good port and the confidence of youth. It was the climax of that long hot summer of 1914.' His voice changed, brisk now, the general in command. 'In that corner, Gemma, you will find a book propping up a chair leg. Would you fetch it?'

Taken by surprise, she could not instantly find it and his sudden impatience was almost tangible. She dropped to her knees, once more regretting the light-coloured summer dress as she grovelled under the armchair to which he was pointing. It was under the back leg and, as she tugged at it, the chair tilted with a crash.

'It was this book began the whole thing.' General Maitland took the red-bound volume which had been liberally nibbled by insects.

'What whole thing?'

'The Lakenham lottery.'

'The Great Tontine?' *Thomas Lakenham shouted with laughter as he snatched the book from Jack Holland's hands. 'Standards slipping, aren't they, old chap? From Voltaire to Hawley Smart? They didn't know your scurrilous tastes when they awarded you that First.'*

'Give it back, you bounder.' Jack leapt amiably in pursuit of his reading matter. 'Don't you realise it's a valuable contribution to the literature of our times? If it hadn't been for Hawley Smart, there'd be no Sherlock, no John Buchan. Hawley was the Giotto of the English literary renaissance.'

'No use, Holland. We convict you of the ultimate sin. Triviality.' Philip Shane leapt on the table, snatched up a white napkin and placed it sorrowfully

over his fair hair. 'We sentence you to be taken hence to suffer death by boredom. You shall read all Maitland's essays on medieval history at least ten times.'

'Objection, me lud.' Reggie sprung on the table at his side. 'My essays are a rattling good read.'

'Overruled,' Thomas Lakenham shouted.

'I call the first witness,' Manders-Wright called out gravely, hands on the lapels of his dinner-jacket. Then he rapidly removed them, and seized a kitchenmaid who had incautiously ventured into the room to set dinner. She screamed as he swung her up on the table and jumped up beside her, keeping a firm hold round her waist. 'My witness will testify that this villain Jack Holland was so engrossed in The Great Tontine *that he failed to kiss her, though he had ample opportunity.'*

'I never kiss her,' said Jack sanctimoniously. 'She—'

'Point proven, me lud. He's a cad.'

'I was about to say,' Jack intervened with dignity, 'she's always too quick for me, aren't you, Mary?'

'Nonsense.' Reggie Maitland grinned and held up his arms to jump her down as Anthony relaxed his grip. The girl did so, and Reggie promptly seized her and planted a kiss on her cheek.

'Your case is lost, sir,' cried Philip in delight. He jumped down, took the offending book from Thomas and disappeared agilely through the window, hotly pursued by Jack, then the rest of the Lakenham Twenty, save for Reggie.

Reggie strolled through the front door, and watched as nineteen young men howled and whooped through the gardens. He had planned his tactics, and they were not complicated. He waited till Philip headed in his direction, swooped to meet him, snatched the book and disappeared with it back into the Folly.

When the Lakenham Set, taken by surprise, caught up with him, there was no sign of it.

That might have been the end of Reggie Maitland, since the Set now scented new prey, but Old Josh appeared to save the day.

'Dinner is served, gentlemen.'

In a few moments The Great Tontine *was forgotten as discussion ranged from Marie Lloyd to the Fauve school of painting, from Sigmund Freud to Nijinsky, Marconi to Marx. Anything. Everything. Save war.*

'Why not war?' Gemma asked.

'The dinner table was sacrosanct. War and politics were for the port. You must remember that this was Saturday 1 August. War was not certain until 11 o'clock on the Tuesday evening. Incredible though it sounds, up until Sunday, even Monday perhaps, for most people the burning question of the hour was not a possible war on the Continent but Ireland, which was on the point of civil war. The Government was desperately trying to push through Home Rule against the wishes of Ulster. In March the British Army in Dublin under Gough refused to obey an order to march against an Ulster loyal to the crown, and in the end the Government was forced to yield. It survived in power, so in July the Home Rule Bill came before the Lords, who were determined to wreck it. The King stepped in, but when he too failed, there seemed no alternative to civil war, and gun-running had begun with a vengeance. But there was an alternative – it was provided by Germany and the Austro-Hungarian empire.'

'War? Rot, Anthony. Look at this,' Thomas cried, waving the new Illustrated London News, *as they lounged after dinner, the port decanter circulating rapidly.* 'Last Sunday they were shouting "Hoch, England" outside our embassy in Berlin. Not "to blazes with England".'

'Last week was an age ago,' Anthony observed sagely.

'Determined to look on the black side, aren't you? Try looking on the port while it is red, old man,' Philip Shane advised him. 'The Continent will always look after itself. The Tsar is just bluffing. He may have mobilised, but that's only to show what he thinks of Herr Kaiser. He can't afford not to rattle a few sabres after he did his Nelson's blind-eye act over our chum Franz-Joseph's gobbling up Bosnia and Herzegovina. Anyway, if the Kaiser wants to take on Russia, he'll leave France alone, won't he?'

'Ever heard of the Schlieffen plan?' asked Reggie quietly.

'You academic types! If it came to a fight, the Kaiser won't even spare a glance westward. He'll go all out against Russia.'

'Which will bring France in under their alliance,' Anthony pointed out.

'Which will bring us in,' Reggie contributed.

'Not if half the Cabinet has anything to do with it,' Manders-Wright said wryly.

'If Belgium's neutrality were threatened, everyone

would stand behind Asquith.'

'Even the Kaiser isn't idiot enough to invade Belgium,' Thomas commented – unwisely.

'There's a hole in my bucket, dear Charlie, dear Charlie,' sang Reggie and Philip in unison. 'Ever heard of the Schlieffen Plan, dear Thomas, dear Thomas . . .'

'Rubbish,' Thomas fought back stoutly. 'Look here.' He rushed back to the dining table, followed by the other nineteen.

'The decanter is the Kaiser, Moltke is the salt-cellar and his beloved Schlieffen Plan is this ladle.'

'Gentlemen,' moaned Josh helplessly, trying to rescue his dirty dishes and cutlery but unable to fight a way in through the dinner-jacketed backs poring over the field of battle.

'The essence of the plan depends on the German right sweeping through Belgium into France, having captured the railway junctions at Liège.'

'Conquering France leads nowhere. Look—' Lakenham moved forks speedily in the direction of Russia represented by the cheese-board.

Above the cries of 'Nonsense', and 'Well done, sir', came the sound of the gong crashing out. Instant silence for at least two seconds.

'Gentlemen, kindly return to your port,' Josh announced firmly.

'By Jove, he's a point,' roared Jack, rushing back to the port decanters, the others stampeding after him.

'You're a regular John Barleycorn, Holland,' called Reggie.

'Who?'

'Jack London's alcoholic memoirs. Out this week.

Surprised you haven't read them, with your highbrow tastes.'

'I believe literature is like port. If it isn't encrusted with age it isn't any good.'

'What about Brooke?' shouted Shane.

'Cambridge man. Out of the running.'

'Meredith?'

'Jury still out.'

'Shaw?'

'Won't stay the course.'

'What about this new chap James Joyce? His Dubliners, *reviewed today. "Sordid, unillumined, circumscribed . . . but unfortunately he has the touch of genius." There's a review for you,' said Reggie wistfully.*

'I'll wager you we won't have heard of this James Joyce in twenty years,' declared Jack.

'Twenty years? We'll all be dead. We'd be over forty.' Thomas clapped a horrorstruck hand to his brow.

'Your widow can pay out, then. A fiver on James Joyce or not. Speak, gentlemen.'

'Done,' cried Philip.

'Reggie?'

'Definitely not.'

'No faith in your own judgement?' Thomas mocked.

'I promised my father,' Reggie informed them virtuously, 'that I'd leave off the gambling after I came into my pile last birthday.'

There was an immediate chorus of shocked disapproval, perhaps at such extreme demands or perhaps at Reggie's acquiescence.

Thomas came up with Solomon's solution. 'Wager a fiver you won't break it, Reggie. Your father would approve of the morals of that.'

Reggie thought this over carefully, then shook his head regretfully. 'No – I say, steady on, you chaps—'

He was grabbed bodily by his fellows – or as many of them that could lay hands on him – and carried back to the dining table. The large bowl of flowers was solemnly emptied of water, and filled even more solemnly with claret. Reggie was then hoisted on to the table, and upended with his head in the bowl, gurgling in red wine.

'Drowned in a butt of claret,' shouted Shane in high glee. 'Poor old Maitland. He didn't deserve to die so young.' They stood with respectfully bowed heads as Reggie spluttered.

'Take the wager?' yelled Jack, his face materialising next to Reggie's.

'Glug-gles.'

'And that was all the Lakenham lottery was?' asked Gemma, somewhat disappointed, though she hadn't known quite what to expect.

General Maitland smiled. 'No. But it planted the seed for what was to happen. Very shortly, in fact. Patience, my dear, patience.'

'This fellow Joyce might be part of a new movement,' Thomas suggested, lighting a cigar and puffing contentedly.

'Sordid, the review said.' Reggie sipped his port complacently.

'A new way of thinking. We can't see the plan yet,

of course. Perhaps it won't be obvious for a hundred years or more. Everything round us is changing, heaving, as if it was about to come to life, itching for rebirth. You must feel it too. Look how much has happened in the last hundred years. We've leapt from trembling at the name of Napoleon to being able to fly through the air. We've got telephones, electricity, radio waves; industry is booming, the Empire prospering. Not only have the Wright Brothers come along in America this century, and Grahame White over here, but Almroth Wright has made tremendous breakthroughs in medicine; we've got motor cars — we're unstoppable.'

'Wright is a good name. When I'm Prime Minister,' Manders-Wright informed them seriously, 'there'll be no more Alfred Austins for Poet Laureate. It will be Sir Jack Holland, OM; the President of the Royal Academy will be Thomas Lakenham—'

'Hear, hear,' Lakenham cried approvingly, pouring him a port, 'and Maitland here can be the Boswell of the Lakenham Set.'

'The Set,' cried Philip, holding his glass aloft. 'To carry the torch of England's glory through the twentieth century. Art, science, we've conquered so many fields—'

'But not ourselves,' murmured Maitland quietly. No one took any notice, if they even heard.

'We're privileged to come from the best families, with centuries of tradition behind us,' said Thomas quietly, seriously. 'It's up to us to lead, to train, to spread education, to inspire. We should do it, and we shall. Nothing can stop us. What is it, Josh?' he broke off impatiently.

The old man was standing at his side with a note borne upon an ornamented salver. 'The footman brought it from the house, sir. It's a telephone message for Mr Shane.'

'Dashed women won't leave you alone, eh, Philip?' Someone's voice fell into an odd silence, as Philip read the note.

'What is it, dear chap?' asked Thomas sharply, as Philip's face whitened, sobered, and then filled with a kind of awe. He rose to his feet, charged with an electricity that communicated itself to everyone in the room.

'Gentlemen, it is from my father. He was at the Admiralty this evening. Germany mobilised against Russia at five p.m. and—'

'That still doesn't mean war for us,' Jack interrupted.

'—And Winston has mobilised the Fleet. Gentlemen, that does mean war.'

'Even then we couldn't quite believe it,' General Maitland said. 'I suppose we still thought Austria would lick Serbia into shape, and everything would settle down. Even the Kaiser was doing his utmost to hold back, though naturally we did not know that then. We knew the Cabinet was split over whether or not we should honour our obligation to France; Asquith had to exaggerate the bogey image of the wicked Kaiser – not that that was difficult – and count on his invading gallant little neutral Belgium. If he couldn't get his Cabinet to fight for France, he would most certainly get their support over Belgium.

'It was Philip with his family's Naval background who

convinced us. Mobilising the fleet for Britain was a major step. Grey had told Churchill that evening that he had undertaken to protect France's Atlantic coast if she went to war, and Churchill seized the opportunity to interpret that as the need for our Naval mobilisation. The Cabinet might not have ratified his order, but in the end one could always count on the Kaiser doing the wrong thing. News came that they had invaded after Belgium turned down their ultimatum for free passage. Twelve hours after that we were at war.'

'It will happen now. No doubt about it.' Philip's lively face was struggling with gravity and excitement. Thomas banged his fist on the table at his side.

'Is there a man here who will not fight?'

Cheers rang through the room as they all leapt to their feet, shaking hands, embracing.

'They'll take us all, of course,' cried Manders-Wright excitedly. 'We've all Oxford OTU training. We'll get our commission and I'll wager I'm first ashore in France.'

'I'll stand a drink to every man-jack of you in the first estaminet we come to,' Jack yelled.

'We'll have to be quick. It might all be over in weeks. The Navy will put the wind up the Kaiser, poor old Bill,' Philip laughed.

'It may have to. Our Army won't,' Reggie said unthinkingly.

'What do you mean, sir?' demanded Thomas.

'We have the weakest in Europe through our foolish dependence on the volunteer system. Everyone else has conscription,' Reggie was forced into pointing out.

'*The volunteer system has done us proud in the past.*'

'*The past . . .*' *Reggie sighed.* '*And what of the twentieth century?*'

Thomas looked at him, about to say something, when Anthony broke in. '*You'll take my wager, won't you, Reggie?*'

Reggie Maitland was silent, but it went unremarked in the general excitement.

'*I'll crack champagne across the bows of your ship, Philip,*' *said Jack, slapping him on the back.*

'*Don't bother with the ship's bows, old man. Try mine,*' *Philip retorted.*

'*Gentlemen, a toast,*' *shouted Thomas, and they scrambled for glasses. Josh suddenly appeared in their midst, as excited as any of them, filling glasses with claret, port, anything to hand, as gaslight glowed on young, eager faces.*

'*Gentlemen, the King.*'

'*The King, God bless him.*' *They drank.*

'*Gentlemen, the toast is England and her Empire.*' *Anthony Manders-Wright lifted his glass aloft, his handsome face serious.*

'*England and her Empire,*' *came the chorus.*

'*I've another toast,*' *cried Thomas.*

'*Give us another one do . . .*'

'*We're the Lakenham Set, aren't we?*'

'*We are,*' *shouted nineteen voices.*

'*What do we stand for?*'

'*Ladies,*' *came the roar.*

'*I'm being serious,*' *Thomas shouted indignantly.*

'*The ladies. God bless them, one and all.*'

'*We stand for artistic progress,*' *Thomas cried.* '*We light the path, the way to the future. Manders-Wright is going to look after your politics, Maitland's our chronicler, I'm an artist, Philip's going to sail the seven seas, and Jack here – Jack's our poet, our novelist, our brilliant star and . . .' He went on to detail fifteen more. 'Young Maggers here is going to be a brilliant violinist and Dukey—' he grinned – 'Noblesse oblige, eh? He'll keep the flag of England flying. He's our patron. Our Lorenzo de' Medici.'*

'What of it, Tom?' Reggie demanded, curious at the expression on his friend's face.

'We're still more or less at the beginning of a new century. Let's toast the Second Renaissance: not in Italy this time, but here. It will be spearheaded by the Lakenham Set.'

'Hear! Hear!' They drank enthusiastically, though Reggie doubted they took in half of what Thomas meant.

'When this war is over,' he muttered into his claret.

'But didn't you discuss whether or not you should volunteer? Whether the cause was right?' Gemma asked.

'No. There was no question in our minds but that it was. We had to volunteer, not just because as former OTU cadets we were expected to, but because it never entered our minds not to. We were all from old-established English families. It was expected, and their pride, that they would send their sons – and their sons would have felt dishonoured had they not gone. It was their duty. It is hard to explain it in today's terms when the word "duty" itself is questioned.'

'A duty to the past, then?'

'A duty to the future – to preserve our families, our heritage, our freedom—'

'Even if not yourselves. What waste.'

'Indeed. Most never returned.'

'It would not happen now. People think too much.'

'And you believe we did not?' the General asked quietly. 'That we just rushed blindly into war? Of course we did not. We thought, but along different lines from today. We thought not of the present but of the future. We fought not to preserve the old world, which even we could see was changing, but to ensure it progressed from the best of the past into a disciplined better future. We believed that when the Kaiser was licked, Britain would preside over a new golden age of peace and progress in her Empire, and since that was so large, it would be – ' he hesitated – 'I suppose Thomas's Second Renaissance, if you like. Was that such a bad dream?' He paused.

'Unfortunately, Gemma, I could not share it with them. I had a historian's training and knew that golden ages could be elusive. I hoped, but could not believe . . . even for Thomas.'

'A toast. You're not drinking, Reggie.'

'I'll drink to it, but I think it may be further off than you imagine.'

'Once this war's out of the way—'

'And when will that be?'

'My father said it could be Christmas,' Philip told them confidently. 'One sight of the fleet, and the Kaiser will run screaming to his nanny.'

'The day of the Navy's over,' objected Jack provocatively. 'It's the world of the air now. You'll see, it will change everything. At our next meeting after the war, we'll all—'

'All?' Reggie queried.

*There was a moment's pause. 'Some of us may die,'
Manders-Wright said forthrightly. 'Very well, but by
God we'll die well. By the end of the century, those
who are left will look back as we meet in our
bath-chairs, and cheer the Lakenham Set. We'll toast
every one of our achievements.'*

*'The claret will probably finish us off, there'll be so
many,' Thomas cried. 'By Jove, I'd like to make sure
there's something left of us.' He looked round the
room. 'Something to remember what we've said
tonight.'*

*'Steady on,' Philip protested. 'We'll be here again
after Christmas when the war's over.'*

*'Just in case,' Thomas persisted, 'something to
remind everyone that the Lakenham Set were the
bearers of the colours for the Second Renaissance,
like the Medicis in fifteenth-century Florence for the
First. Suppose the last of us left alive were to have the
duty of setting up a memorial to us – at the end of the
century when we can look back on what's been
achieved.'*

'What sort of memorial?' demanded Jack.

*'He'd have to decide. Who knows what new fields
might be conquered? Who knows what stunning
artists and writers might have come along by then?
Besides us, of course.'*

*Philip shouted with laughter. 'Idiot. By the end of
this century we'll all be gone. All by the 1970s, I'd say.
Even if young Dukey gets through to 1980, what sort
of energy would he have for building memorials?
Anyway, dashed if I want to be remembered by the
kind of stuff Dukey would set up.'*

'I say . . .' Dukey objected, hurt. He was ignored.

'*It has to be* near *the end of this century at least,*' *said Thomas worriedly, 'or it won't make sense. The crust won't be settled on the port of our achievements.*'

He was jumped on for swank by Jack, and the others gathered round cheering as they rolled round on the floor.

'*There!' Just as he was winning, Jack gave a great shriek and rolled off his prey, only to have Thomas leap on him again. 'No, dash it,' he howled. 'Get off, Tom. I've got the answer for you.*'

'*It's a trick.*'

'*No, look under that chair – my book! How did it get there?*'

'*What book?*'

'The Great Tontine, *you ass,' Jack declared, somewhere muffled underneath Lakenham's blazer. 'We'll all nominate someone who will outlive us to the end of the century. We'll make some kind of investment so the pool will grow, and when the last but one of our nominees dies, the pool will go to the heirs of whoever nominated the longest-living.*'

'*You've had too much port, Barleycorn,' declared Lakenham judiciously. 'Admit I am the winner.*'

'*No, perhaps Jack's got something,' Philip said suddenly. 'If we invest a hundred pounds each, it might make a reasonable little sum by the end of the century.*'

'*I doubt it. Even if it doubled or even tripled, we're not going to be able to build another Victoria and Albert museum, are we, to celebrate the century's glorious achievements in this Second Renaissance?*' *Manders-Wright said.*

'All right, two hundred then,' Philip agreed impatiently.

'Say three hundred pounds and I'll wrest a newborn babe from its mother's arms,' Jack laughed.

'Now that's an idea. Why don't we all find a newborn baby to nominate . . .?'

'I don't understand. What's a tontine, Grandpa?' It rang a faint bell in Gemma's mind, but she couldn't pin it down. Something to do with Agatha Christie? Hadn't she come across the word in one of her whodunnits?

'The tontine was a gamble for investors. It dropped out of favour after unfortunate shenanigans in the eighteenth century here, but it was used in New York to raise money for public buildings last century. It all began on the Continent long before that. There are several forms it can take, but the underriding principle is based on survivorship – the longest living scoops the pool. If the investors so choose they can all nominate someone else's life, whether within their own family or a stranger, it makes no odds, but the pool would still come to them or their heirs.'

'I don't think I'd want to be a nominee in a dark alley.'

'Precisely. However, respectably controlled, it undoubtedly made for an added interest in investment. For young men who saw themselves as St Georges and death as a distant figure on some far-off horizon, it was fun.'

'You participated?'

'My heart shared their beliefs, but my reason could not convince it that a new golden age was attainable with war looming. I was a historian. Golden ages may beckon, but as you follow they recede, and their path is seldom golden. My fellows, especially dear Thomas, believed they had merely to conquer the forces of darkness here on earth and the light would shine upon them for ever more.'

'Why aren't you drinking, Maitland? You're with us, aren't you . . .? That'll wash your cynicism away, old chap. You'll see . . . you'll wonder why you ever doubted us, Reggie . . .'

'We talked until the small hours. We talked of war; of our hopes and fears; of what each man saw as a fitting memorial in years to come; of what we had shared and what they were convinced we would share. We band, we happy band of brothers, marching off to war . . .' Tears ran down the General's face.

'We slept anywhere we could find that night. Josh was in despair the next morning to find carelessly discarded dinner-jackets, bottles, glasses, smoke and twenty young men sleeping off the effects of the night before. Especially *that* morning . . . at the main house the talk for the first time was of war – but we, the Lakenham Set, had something even more important to do . . .'

Two Lagondas and a Napier hurtled along the highway, in convoy, twenty laughing, excited young men packed into them. Anxiety had not yet expelled all normality from the day. To the casual observer, it was merely the Sunday of the Bank Holiday weekend. How could this casual observer know that they were knights of old about to ride into battle, and that this was their first charge?

The Darenth Valley Friendly Society Orphanage at

Sevenoaks, although warned by telephone of their visit, was somewhat surprised. It was not used to the gentry turning up in such quantity, nor to the gentry turning out to be not the ladies of the house about their bountiful business, but the young sons and heirs. However, hastily gathered gifts from the old children's nursery and the Lakenham gardens endeared them to the orphanage staff, and the promise of cheques for their funds to be despatched on the Tuesday, warmed them even further towards their visitors. Their explanation of wishing each to choose a baby to 'adopt' as it were, while they went off to war, was met by sympathetic ears.

"Tis certainly a most noble sentiment,' the sister decided, the suggestion of a tear in her eye. She had lost a brother in South Africa and a sweetheart on the Khyber Pass. From some distant room the sound of 'All Things Bright and Beautiful' *sung by scores of childish voices floated through to them.*

'Jolly.' Anthony grinned approvingly at the sister.

'Great poetry, eh, Jack?' Thomas agreed.

Jack nodded fervently. 'Tophole.'

'Now I'm not quite understanding why only babies are of interest,' mentioned the sister, somewhat hesitantly, unwilling to upset the source of such largesse.

The Lakenham twenty looked at each other. 'Ah, just pure sentiment, Sister,' Anthony assured her, looking his most earnest and reliable. 'If there's to be war, and there might well be, we want to think of a baby in some small way our very own, growing to be a child here under the English heavens. In due course, should we fall for our country, the babe, come to manhood, might spare a thought for the man who

*made his childhood a mite the richer, and we our-
selves die the happier.'*

No doubt about it, thought Reggie, Manders-
Wright was going to be a great politician.

The sister sighed, convinced. *'I'll be taking you to
the nursery then,'* she said softly.

Thirty children under the age of two crawled,
scurried or yelled peevishly from cots. The Lakenham
Set braced themselves to coo. The effort was soon too
much for them.

'Who's that little filly?'

'A little lad, in fact,' the young nurse chuckled.

'He's wearing a dress,' Jack pointed out disapprovingly.

'Babies do.' For the first time the sister looked
slightly suspicious at the resulting shout of laughter.

'That one looks in good form.' Philip pointed out
one sturdy baby, bawling lustily from the cot.

'Let's have a race for the little nippers.' Thomas
was suddenly inspired.

'You'll do no such thing, Lord Lakenham.' Sister
had reached the borders of tolerance.

Baulked, the Lakenham Set summed up quietly
amongst themselves. *'That one's got good legs.'* They
were seen kicking in the air in the cot.

'What about that chubby chap?'

*'A gelding if ever I saw one . . . I'd stake my shirt
on that one in the Derby.'*

*'Mine's the bouncing babe over there. Who's he,
Nurse?'*

*'His name's John sir he were found on the
doorstep two months ago Sister calls him Peacock
'cos he were wrapped in a blue and gold shawl,'* the

nurse delivered all in one breath, overcome by the attention paid to her by this tall, immaculate member of the gentry.

'John Peacock. Yes, he's for me. Do you hear me, John Peacock? You're not going to die before you're ninety-five.'

The baby screamed, and hastily Anthony turned away, in case he was expected to hold it or do something equally terrible.

'Who's that one, Nurse? He looks a stayer after my own heart,' declared Jack. 'Black hair, like mine, a bit of a daredevil too, I'll warrant. Mind you, don't do anything too daring, old chap.' The baby blinked as if to assure Jack there was no danger of that.

'That's our little Stanley.' Sister was pleased. 'A lovely little fellow. He was orphaned at six months.' She went over to rescue Stanley's moth-eaten teddy bear.

'I'm choosing a girl,' Philip declared. 'They live longer nowadays. That's the one for me.'

'Rather on the scrawny side,' Jack pointed out. 'Narrow hips. May have trouble doing her duty to the future of mankind.'

'Just you stay single, my lass,' Philip commanded her judiciously.

'Little Gladys Smith.' Sister swept back to them. 'Aren't you a lucky little girl, Gladys?'

Gladys paused and considered this, eyeing Philip scornfully. She turned away and fell asleep.

'I'm for that pretty little stunner there.' Victoria Ireland, her fair hair already curling into soft ringlets, cooed at Thomas.

'All that glisters is not gold,' said the sister sanctimoniously. Victoria must have understood, for she

52

pouted at her, and turned her attention back to Thomas.

And on and on, until of the twenty only Reggie had not yet chosen.

'You're not backing out, are you, Reggie?' Thomas asked in alarm.

'No fear. I've given my word. Who's left? I'll choose – ' Reggie's eyes skittered around, alighting on the puniest child in the room – 'that one. I'll have that one.'

'Oh.' Sister was disappointed. 'That's only Ted Parsons.'

'On the Tuesday morning, while the nation waited on tenterhooks, we went to the bank. We chose a small one, Howitt and Sage, which had a good reputation, but was not personally known to any of us. There we set up the trust. I fear they thought us quite mad. But we had influence, we had power – or rather our families had – and we had the money, since by then we had all reached our majority and had at last disposable funds. Much as our solicitors disapproved of our insistence on haste as the papers were drawn up, there was nothing they could do. Although two hundred and fifty pounds each, the final amount agreed, was a considerable sum in those days, it was hardly likely to bankrupt us. Manders-Wright, our spokesman, was adept at getting his own way, and he got it. Naturally it was not completed in a morning, and there were probably, the solicitors warned us, legal flaws because of the need for speed. Nevertheless, by piling on pressure it was achieved before we marched our separate ways to war.

'And to war we went, bearing our hopes, our youth,

our future as trophies before us. When we returned –
those of us who did so – we had left them all behind, in
Flanders, in Mesopotamia, Gallipoli – wherever man had
fought man.'

'And what happened to the Lakenham Set?' Gemma
asked gently.

'That summer's day in 1914 saw the end of it. Eight of
the twenty survived the war, and found they had no heart
to grapple with lost ideals. We had no spur any more to
meet as a group. When I met with one or the other as
friends, the past was never referred to, nor the bright
future of which we had dreamed. We confined ourselves
to the present.

'Some private soldiers came back from the war still
believing in a better world to come. We knew there
would be none. Our kind had died amid the poppyfields
of Flanders, and the private soldiers who hoped for a
better deal still sold matches for a pittance in the street
ten years later. For a while, in the twenties, we hoped
there might after all be a chance, yet after the Versailles
Treaty we should have known that was impossible.
Especially me, but even I did not foresee the mess the
twentieth century turned out to be.

'Jack was dead, our bright star. So was Manders-
Wright, on whom we depended for leadership through
the "golden age". Countless others who should have
been the country's future lay dead. Of the eight of us who
came back, only six still lived by 1934 – the last year we
met our orphans.'

'*Met* them – so you did follow up the tontine?'

'No. We forced ourselves to meet the orphans once a
year for the sake of our dead comrades and what they had
hoped for. We never spoke of the tontine, never enquired

into its progress. In 1934, however, when the orphans were about twenty-one and had long left the orphanage and were drifting apart, we stopped the yearly parties with great relief. There was no need to be forced to remember any more. Hitler had come to power in Germany, and put paid to any lingering hopes of that Second Renaissance. Though they never spoke of it, I felt my friends in some way blamed me, perhaps for not believing sufficiently strongly. As in *Peter Pan* one must really believe in fairies to bring a Tinkerbell back to life. When I met Thomas and Philip after that, we simply ignored the whole matter. Of course we did not realise—' he broke off.

'So why now?' Gemma asked, since he seemed unwilling to continue.

'Philip died in 1968, leaving just Thomas and myself. When Thomas died ten years later, his son Charles found out the legal position of the Folly for the first time. He had been going to convert it into flats to sell to cover death duties. You see, in addition to his own two hundred and fifty pounds, Thomas gave the Folly and its land to the trust, merely keeping an eye on it from time to time. He had not the heart to take further steps about it; he could not face it any more than I could have done. I fear the tontine was somewhat of a surprise to Charles, and he demanded full explanations from me. He then took a decision against my advice. He decided to find out what the current position was from the trustees. I could not blame him. Rationally it was the sensible thing to do, but emotionally I fear I did all I could to ignore it still.' He paused.

'Oh, Grandfather, you can't stop there,' Gemma said, agonised. 'Don't tease.'

He sighed. 'Very well. The original private bank had been taken over three times since the 1930s and is now part of a major City merchant bank. The trust was on suspense all those years since 1934; with no dividend to pay out, and only accountable once notified of nineteen orphans' deaths, there was no necessity for the trustees to take active steps to seek out investors or their heirs. The boot was on the other feet, to keep the trustees informed of our movements. But through common unspoken assent we did not.'

'And the orphans? What happened to them?'

'It took Charles and his family years to track them down. They naturally did not wish to get embroiled in huge private investigators' fees, and it was not the trustees' job to seek the orphans out. Under the terms of the tontine each investor has to notify the trustees of their nominee's decease. Naturally none has done so. After enquiries it transpired that fifteen of the twenty orphans were dead. Four were known still to be living: those nominated by Manders-Wright, Jack Holland, Philip Shane and Thomas Lakenham.'

'That's only nineteen,' Gemma said slowly. 'What of the twentieth?'

'That was my own nominee. He was not expected to live long. However, he was apparently still alive in London in the late 1940s or early 50s. Since then he cannot be traced. I chose a weakling deliberately because I had no wish to lay upon my heirs the responsibility of establishing a memorial to something I could not believe would happen – a Second Renaissance – despite my longing that it would. Although it has not come about, I now feel differently about it. What the Lakenham Set wanted has a validity of its own – ideals should be commemorated even if reality fails to live up to them. I realise it is late in the day for me to change my mind, but, Gemma, you now accept special assignments. I have one for you. I wish to employ you to find my nominee. Find Ted Parsons.'

Chapter Three

'Paul, Paul Shane. We met on Sunday.'

'Of course.' Gemma was both amused and irritated to hear a warmth in her voice not usually present in answering business calls. She banished it. A day's brooding on the Lakenham tontine was insufficient to prejudice her plan of campaign by such instinctive reactions, and the continuing stifling heat clouded judgement.

'I thought we might meet,' he continued somewhat hesitantly.

She took a deep breath before replying with the right amount of enthusiasm. 'That would be splendid. I can't manage this week, I'm afraid. Early next?'

'Oh.' A slight pause. 'Monday?' he asked with mock plaintiveness.

'That would suit very well.' Even so, by the time she replaced the receiver, she had an obscure feeling she had put a foot wrong somewhere, and was annoyed that she could not analyse where.

'Private booking?' Loretta appeared in the office doorway. 'You don't normally blush when you clock in a school run.'

'Not a blush. Not a school run. Not a booking.'

'Admirably succinct.' Loretta gave her an amiable

smile, crossed to open the window even wider, stripped off her light jacket with a sigh of relief, and sank into a chair, her long cotton-trousered legs sprawled out before her. Big-boned, big-hearted, capable Loretta, with her lion's mane of tawny hair. 'Problem?'

'Slight case of a missing person. You did one once, didn't you? Where do you start?'

'Round up the usual suspects,' Loretta quoted promptly.

'Being?'

'Last people to have seen the said MP.'

'This MP disappeared forty-odd years ago.'

Loretta whistled. 'Try Radio Two, or local radio stations with the Where-are-you-now-Joe-Bloggs? programmes. Plus of course good old registrations and BT archives for old telephone directories. Electoral rolls. A name like Marmaduke Butter-Parsnips would help of course.'

'How about Ted Parsons?'

Loretta laughed. 'Darling Gem, when you buy problems, there's always a built-in mega-attachment for free. How do you manage it?'

'This one managed me.' She gave her a brief run-down on Ted Parsons, since Loretta had been out when Gemma had told Lisa earlier. No need to ask for confidentiality. That was understood. No need to explain fully either – yet. Tontines and follies sounded ludicrous in an ordinary working environment. She was hoping time would put it in perspective, force it from the mists of storyland into the closely defined lines of a job. By Monday, surely, that would be so. And Paul Shane would be safely part of it.

'So it's a special.'

'Yes. For my grandfather.'

'If I have to drive that repulsive Jennings out to court again, I'll bring a cat-o'-nine-tails with me.' Lisa, her other assistant, came in, looking as immaculate and unflappable as ever (a sham since she could produce enough hidden worries to keep counsellors in business for many a long year). Though physical courage was something none of them lacked, their emotional strengths varied and fortunately harmonised.

'Bread and butter, Lisa,' Gemma told her smugly.

'I'll have my bread without butter then, thanks, Gem. What's next, Kirsty?' she called to the outer office. The ground floor of their old cottage premises had once been a bootmaker's, and his showroom and workroom were now respectively Kirsty's reception room and a general meeting point office. To go upstairs was a signal that one was either switching off temporarily into the 'Collapse Pad', as Loretta termed it, or that one Wished To Be Alone in the private office that, judging by the scrawls and transfers Gemma had scraped off when she first moved in, had once been the baby's bedroom.

Kirsty appeared in person, and her vacuous face suddenly lit up like a robot going into action, wheels whirling, as she indulged her speciality. 'The wrinkly from Number Ten. Over to her sister's, wait and return.'

'Another dream-packed day. Great,' Lisa said resignedly.

'Tomorrow Samarkand,' Gemma promised.

'I ain't got that booked in, miss.' There was acute alarm in Kirsty's voice.

'A joke, Kirsty.'

Kirsty looked at her own three permanent wrinklies

(aged twenty-six, Loretta; twenty-seven, Lisa and thirty-seven, Gemma) and humoured them. Her face split open in an uncertain grin.

'Could you get Arthur in to cover for a few days, Kirsty? I'm going to be tied up.'

Sixty-year-old Arthur Wallace drove part-time for them, in between odd-jobbing for the whole village. Placid, and with no hang-ups about working with a pack of females, he saw his role as one of saviour and protector. They did not disillusion him, for they liked him and they needed him. In fact, since they were all proficient in self-defence, and Loretta had a black belt in judo, it was rather more likely they'd be Arthur's protectors, but it gave him a talking point in the Green Knight, and none of them begrudged him it.

'I've got a London run and return tomorrow. I'll get started then,' Loretta offered. 'How much time do we have?'

In theory, plenty was the answer. But Gemma still feared that, now the hundredth birthday was past, her grandfather might feel no need to linger. Although Grandfather *had* good reason to live, she argued to herself. He wanted to see the aims of the Lakenham Set put into effect, to know that belatedly he had done all he could. It would be a race between his emotional strength and his physical capacity.

'Not long.' Gemma looked at them both squarely. 'I want him found before my grandfather dies.'

'I'll start in St Catherine's, and BT archives,' Loretta said briskly.

'St Catherine's?' Gemma queried unthinkingly.

'Certificates, dear,' Loretta explained kindly, as to a child. 'Marriage and death. It's quite likely he's dead, after all. You said he was born in 1914.'

Gemma was thankful for the cold light of reason, which unusually she was unable to apply herself. Even so, she trusted her grandfather's instinct: Ted Parsons was very far from dead.

'My dear Gemma, don't worry at all. I should act in precisely the same way.' Charles Lakenham's round, impassive face lit with sudden warmth. A careful man, but not a cold one, Gemma decided. If she had been born the child of Thomas Lakenham, so might she have been. The Thomas Lakenham she had known bore little resemblance to the Sir Philip Sydney-like figure her grandfather had re-created for her in the Folly; the all-round Renaissance man. That man had vanished in the First World War. All that remained to the outsider's eye was an outer shell, the noble profile, the commanding presence, the disciplined, grave man who retired from the Lancers to take his place in the House of Lords. His painting became a private interest only. If anything were left of that earlier youth, it was shared only with Philip Shane and Reginald Maitland. To have grown up in Thomas Lakenham's shadow must have been daunting for his heir Charles – yet not so daunting that he had not the initiative to acquire a beautiful Italian wife, an artist. Their family had long dispersed, and there had been no evidence of them at her grandfather's party. She vaguely remembered other children running about on the lawns of Lakenham House on that misty summer's day of her youth – probably indeed Paul himself was there, being Philip Shane's grandson.

Charles Lakenham, when she telephoned him on Tuesday evening, had readily offered to tell her all about the

trust and the financial position, but this was precisely
what she hadn't wanted.

'An impersonal atmosphere might be better,' she had
suggested tactfully. 'At the bank, perhaps.'

He obviously took up her unspoken objection – that he
was an interested party. So interested indeed that he had
politely suggested he should accompany her to the bank,
and she could hardly object. Indeed, she was grateful,
since the bank would talk more freely with his acquiescence than if she went alone, a mere investigator for
her grandfather.

The famous merchant bank of Taylor Whittam dated
back over a hundred years. It had recently moved to a
new City office block, functional and practical, all glass
and silent marble corridors. Why had she imagined an
interview with an ancient gent in a dusty vault in an even
more ancient mansion? The banker who greeted them on
emerging from the glass lift was hardly ancient. He
bounced in beaming, in striped shirt, gaudily patterned
tie and an erratic head of hair that bounced as energeti-
cally as its youngish master. About her own age, she
reckoned, perhaps a year or two younger. Felix Potter
(he would be called Felix, she thought) explained enthusiastically all over again about the four known survivors
and the fifth missing one, but she did not object. It put it
in context for her. Here she could regard it as not the
romantic last fling of a group of young men of another
age, but as something more concrete: a business arrangement, of sorts.

Apparently Mr Potter did not regard it in quite the
same light. 'I must say it's fascinating. A real throwback.
I couldn't believe my luck when I was given charge of it. I
think only the computer knew the trust was there,' he

confessed happily, 'until you, Lord Lakenham, came along fifteen years ago. Most of them here then didn't know what a tontine was, I gather. I didn't, anyway.'

Great, thought Gemma. If you don't, who does?

As if reading her thoughts, he hastened to display his erudition. 'They're not used today, of course. Far too many sinister possibilities.'

'Sinister?'

'These Little Goes, you know.'

'I don't, I'm afraid,' Gemma told him firmly.

His eyes brightened eagerly. 'Ah well. In the eighteenth century, insurance was a new sort of gamble and led to every racket under the sun. The Little Goes were all the extraordinary things people gambled on for a payout. After the South Sea bubble, things were never the same again. A lot of the Little Goes were based on the tontine principle – survivorship. As if you had a bet on whether the Prime Minister or the Foreign Secretary would pop off first. A long-term prospect, of course, and when people got tired of waiting, they might try a bit of premature dispatching. It got so bad that in the fourteenth year of George the Third – I didn't know all this, I had to look it up,' he told them ingenuously, 'they had to enact a statute outlawing gambling on lives when the person concerned didn't have an interest in the policy. That may be why, in the Lakenham case, to be on the safe side the trustees did their job thoroughly: whichever of the nominees survives longest gets a twentieth of the proceeds. The other nineteen-twentieths go to the heirs of the person who nominated him. Or, in the case of General Maitland, to him, of course.'

'You mean the money is tied up in a trust and is handed over as a trust?'

'Yes and no. It's an interesting case. The money is in a fund – that will provide a few interesting tax problems in due course – ' his eyes gleamed again ' – and whoever gets it in the end, our responsibility as trustees would be to hand over the funds to the surviving nominee and the heirs of the person who nominated him.'

'With what restrictions on the use of the money?'

'On the surviving nominee, none. On the heirs of his nominator, so few as to be of no importance. On condition,' he glanced at his papers, ' "he shall commemorate the achievements of the twentieth century and the Lakenham Set". What's a commemoration, after all? And what sort of achievement? It's so wide that he can make a token gesture and blue the lot in Majorca if he wants. Who's to protest?'

'The other heirs could ask the trustees to intervene,' Gemma pointed out, somewhat taken aback.

'No grounds. It doesn't specify how much money has to be used in this memorial. It may deliberately have been widely drawn up in order to give the heirs scope.'

'And what if Ted Parsons can't be found?' Charles asked. 'You recall I told you so far we've had no success.'

'Ah. Another little problem,' Felix Potter said with glee. 'If three of the other four green bottles drop off the wall, we institute formal searches as trustees for Mr Parsons. Until we have proof of death, we have to hold on to the money, since obviously there's the chance he'd turn up later. So it's in both your interests to do all you can to track Parsons down.'

Gemma turned to Charles. 'How far did you manage to get, Charles?'

'Not too far, since it took us long enough to track down the other nineteen, dead or alive, and we left Ted Parsons till last, as your grandfather would not be pleased if he had known we were actively seeking his nominee. He'd made it quite clear that he wanted nothing to do with the whole matter. I must say, his attitude has changed considerably. Perhaps because of you.'

'Me?' asked Gemma in surprise. 'I thought it was because his hundredth birthday brought it to a head.'

'In a way. You are his heir, after all.'

Heir? Gemma suddenly felt poleaxed. How could she have been so stupid? She had been so caught up with seeing this as a job, the obvious was beneath her nose and overlooked. She was Reginald Maitland's only close relative. Of course he'd taken her to the Folly, of course he wanted her involved. But he hadn't wanted to pin her down so precisely by telling her she must find Ted Parsons because it was in her own interests to do so (though that was questionable). Instead, it was a mission, a job, which she was bound to fulfil, but that she could – in theory – remain detached from. It was her choice. If she reported soon on Ted Parsons, alive or dead, she could detach herself; Grandfather could even change his will, if she so wished. But the mission must first be accomplished.

'Of course,' Potter was saying to Charles, 'tontines weren't always unrespectable. The Government of the day tried to launch a tontine to establish the Bank of England.'

'What happened?' Charles asked.

'No one was interested.' Potter laughed. 'It seems the irregular is often more popular than the respectable. More fun, I suppose.'

'I'm glad you think so,' Charles retorted mildly. 'Also somewhat more expensive, I might point out. Our investigations have not been cheap.'

'Another gamble in a way.' Felix was not to be reproved. 'Do all the heirs and nominees now know of the situation, Lord Lakenham?'

'They were all present, save of course Mr Parsons, last Sunday at Lakenham House. I invited them for the specific purpose of telling them. It is a relief not to be carrying the knowledge alone any longer. I assumed, wrongly, that Gemma would already have known.'

'Rivals meeting face to face. Wish I'd been there,' Potter said.

'It added a certain spice,' Charles replied calmly. 'However, better to face the tiger than have it creep up from behind.'

'In theory. The result is much the same,' Potter pointed out.

'And what's that?' Gemma asked.

'Sudden death.'

'But . . .' Gemma stopped, as she took in what he implied. 'How ridiculous,' she said indignantly.

'Not so ridiculous,' Potter rejoined. 'There's a lot at stake.'

'There's a question you haven't yet asked, Gemma,' Charles told her. 'And you should, as General Maitland's heir.'

She was about to ask what – but then she knew. 'Of course,' she said steadily. 'How much does the trust now stand at, Mr Potter?' She tried to make wild guesses in her head. Twenty times two hundred and fifty pounds, plus the value of the property and interest. The property might be the most valuable, being where it was, save that there'd be no planning permission granted there. No supermarkets for the Darenth Valley.

'Ah well, there we have it. The fund hasn't been

touched, you see, and the original trustees were given a wide power of investment. Rather by chance, I suspect, they did a good job. For some reason much of the money was invested not in building societies and bonds, but in a small firm that made sporting rifles. During the First World War it turned its hand to service armament, and thereafter kept both strands going very lucratively. In the Second World War it was taken over by the Government for armament manufacture, and when it was returned to the owners they saw the light. Sporting guns were relegated to a subsidiary and the main firm floated and expanded into armaments in a big way. You know it now as Hayward and Hawling plc. It supplies a third of the armament for every war from the Baltic to Bali-Hai. So the tontine fund has done rather well. It stands today, less the trustees' expenses, and the liability to the sole surviving nominee, at around fifteen million pounds, Miss Maitland.'

Fifteen million pounds? Potter's warning, which she had assumed pure melodrama, assumed a new significance. She even felt she should view her meeting with Paul Shane in a different light. Instead of the cottage, she asked him to come to the office. Quite why the size of the award should change her attitude so radically, she was not sure. After all, as an heir she would be in no danger, she argued logically, since her death would change nothing. The right to the tontine would simply pass to her heir, or her grandfather's second choice. If there were danger – and why should there be, for they weren't living in the eighteenth century now? – it would surely be the nominees at risk, either from the heirs or indeed from each other, since whoever lived longest

69

scooped a twentieth of the pool.

As soon as Paul arrived, she realised she'd been foreseeing dramas where there was none. He was the same easy-going, laid-back man she'd enjoyed chatting to at Lakenham House, and she could have taken him to Waynings without problem. He would have fitted in perfectly – and, after all, he was Ellen Shane's great-nephew.

'Over the shock yet?' he asked as he sat down in the chair across from her desk in the upstairs sanctum. 'That party at Lakenham House was quite something. When I spoke to you, of course, I assumed you already knew all about it. It was only afterwards that Lord Lakenham told me you were innocence itself.'

'No reason I should have known. I'm not involved,' she extended the truth protectively. 'My grandfather is still alive and very hale and hearty.'

'I gather from Potter you've been detailed to find Ted Parsons.'

She was annoyed and showed it. 'If so, it is no business of his.' Or of Paul's, she implied.

It was not lost on him. 'One of us would have had to do it,' he pointed out placatingly. 'Ted Parsons would be eighty now, and has probably gone to join his fellow fifteen. It's just a question of making sure. That's why I came to see you. On behalf of the other heirs.'

'What for?'

He laughed. 'Don't look so suspicious. We haven't got him locked in a cupboard.'

'But we are on opposite sides,' she reminded him. No harm in maintaining distance – for whatever reason.

'Of this desk, maybe. Look, it's warmer now. Why don't we go and enjoy the sunshine outside that pub of yours? Why does the sign have a large green gent with no face and a large club, incidentally? I thought green men, knights or not, were part of an old fertility cult. Jack in the Green and all that.'

'So they probably are.' She welcomed the tangent he was deliberately offering. 'But there's an old legend that Sir Gawain met his green giant here – the battlefield was supposed to have been where my cottage is. Hence its name, Waynings. More mundane people might suggest that "place of the wagons" is more likely as a derivation.'

He laughed. 'Soulless idiots. Anyway, the pub looks rather good from the outside. Like you,' he added, eyeing her hair and short-sleeve crisp blouse appreciatively.

Damn him for moving off tontine territory. 'I always look good,' she assured him blithely, 'but this dazzling exterior hides bullet-proof armour against flattery.'

He grimaced. 'Pity. Let's go nevertheless.'

The Green Knight was almost deserted, as usual on a Monday, and for this she was grateful. She didn't want the worthies of Bishopslee hearing of tontines or fifteen million pounds. Paul ordered the drinks, and they took the menus out into the small garden.

'What might you recommend?'

'Avoid the lasagne,' she advised. 'They get the word pasta mixed up with plaster here.'

'When in doubt, have a ploughman's?'

'They're usually good.'

The breeze that had been so refreshing all the morning had dropped, and oppressive heat was creeping back. She wished, like every day this week, she could watch Wimbledon, *be* at Wimbledon, anything but drive cars, make polite comments, negotiate traffic. The time she could reasonably take off to study Ted Parsons was becoming prized, if only for that reason. St Catherine's House had revealed no likely death or marriage certificates, nor had the old telephone directories yielded any obvious leads. She was hardly surprised. Charles Lakenham's private eyes must have been over this ground a dozen times, but one had to start somewhere.

'Tell me about your taxi business,' Paul said as he returned from ordering the food.

It would do as an ice-breaker, and she recited the litany objectively, while trying to decide whether and if she should cross the boundary out of strict business-land. She still liked the look of that quirky, humorous mouth.

'What were you doing before that?' he asked when she came to a halt.

'Accountant,' she said briefly.

'And why – no, don't tell me. You gave it all up for the simple, country life and independence. For the glory of being your own mistress and one of the great self-employed.'

'Something like that,' she agreed.

He glanced at her. 'I've gone wrong. Consider it unsaid.'

'It doesn't matter.' He looked so anxious she tried to reassure him. 'I changed careers after my husband died.'

'I see.'

She thought perhaps he did.

'I envy you,' he went on. 'You did what I wanted to, but never had the courage. My wife died too – cancer, when she was twenty-six.'

'That's too young,' she replied inadequately. 'I'm sorry.'

'So was I. She was one of life's stars. Like my great-aunt Ellen – the gods grew jealous.'

'Did you know my grandfather and she were in love?'

'No.' He looked at her in surprise. 'That's rather splendid. Let's have another drink to our families? Joint past.'

'No, thanks. There's a limit to my enthusiasm for tonic water.'

'What time do you come off duty? I could get you roaring drunk tonight, if you like.'

'I never go off duty,' she informed him primly.

'Your husband must have been a remarkable man,' he replied quietly.

'He was.' Was he, in fact, or just to her? It didn't matter any more. That was over. She was on her own now. *And she didn't want to talk about it.*

'We're on the *same* side, you know,' Paul told her seriously, switching diplomatically back. 'Not opposite. It's in all our interests to find out what's happened to Ted Parsons. It would delay things unnecessarily if we can't trace him. I put my faith in you. That's why I've come. To see if I can help.'

'Help?'

'Yes. Two heads and all that.'

'I've two assistants already.'

'And a business to run.'

'True. May I – ' she hesitated – 'think things over? I'd certainly like to talk to your orphan.' She laughed. 'Doesn't that sound silly? Your nominee, I mean.'

'Ah.'

'What do you mean by Ah?'

'Then you'll *need* my help.'

'I've got all their addresses.' Should she have admitted that?

'My dear Gemma. I'm a solicitor. How could I let you

nobble my horse without my being there to see fair play?'

'Why should I let you help me trace Ted Parsons? You might nobble mine,' she countered swiftly.

He sighed. 'Checkmate. I thought you'd take pity on a crabby old solicitor, who wants a real adventure in his dull life. Besides, it would be an excellent way of getting to know you.'

She stiffened.

He noticed. 'Only testing the bullet-proofing.'

'It has no holes. Particularly near the heart.'

'How about the mouth? The apple pie looks good.' He twisted round as the barmaid flashed by him with a tray.

'Apple pie sounds excellent,' she agreed. 'And I'm prepared to let you accompany me to Gladys Norman, née Smith, to prevent foul play.'

'Our Gladys lives over the café in fine traditional style. She and her lovely son Bert,' Paul told her as they dived off into the warren behind London's Liverpool Street.

'You didn't tell me there was a son. And a Mr Norman?'

'No. No mention of Dad. After all, Bert is in his mid-fifties. Dad probably popped off after an overdose of bacon butties years ago.'

It was an area of narrow streets, tall, drab, smoke-blackened Victorian terrace houses, converted into equally drab shops on the ground floor, many with 'To Let' signs up that bore signs of much weathering. Now Gemma could see how 'Gladys's Sunshine Café' would fit in here, however incongruously named for these streets where sun was fitful. This was a world away from the glitzy snack bars that served the offices of the Liverpool Street area. It was a backwater, a hidden remnant of

Victoriana which had sluggishly dribbled into the 1940s and 1950s and then stagnated.

'Here it is.' Paul stopped.

She looked up at the sign, 'Gladys's Sunshine Café' once proudly painted red and gold, now faded and chipping. As for the café itself, Gemma could almost have described it without peering through the windows. It was afternoon, and a hot one, though there was a welcome breeze now. Tired heaps of ready prepared rolls and sandwiches wilted in the window, a testament to the obligatory take-away lunchtime service. The fillings peeped cautiously out, uninspired and unappetising. No choice of avocado and chicken here, no chicken tikka, no tuna and peppers, only cheddar cheese, tomato and pickle, and anaemic beef and ham. The real business of the café must continue behind this uninspired frontage.

As they walked in, Gemma was pleased to see her theories confirmed. The old mahogany tables, adorned with plastic tablecloths, sauce bottles, cruet and dried-up mustard, couldn't have changed in fifty years at least, save for the plastic element perhaps. Nor had the menu. Egg and chips; bacon, egg and sausage – she could almost recite it without reading it. The smell of chips still stifled the café, although it was about three, and a heavy curtain shrouded the mysteries of the inner sanctum from the café itself. Gladys's Sunshine Café was a throwback to a vanished past. Three tables were still occupied, but it was another few minutes or two before a burly man emanated from the rear quarters, wiping his hands on a teacloth. He grinned amiably.

'Good afternoon, Bert,' Paul greeted him briskly.

She hadn't seen Bert at the Lakenham House party, Gemma realised. She'd have remembered him. Big, burly – and not one of the world's great thinkers. So Paul had been here before. Naturally enough, she supposed.

'Ah,' Bert grunted. 'Mum said you'd be coming, Mr Shane. She's behind.'

Ma was the brains of this outfit obviously – by a long chalk, Gemma thought as they followed Bert through the plush curtain. 'Behind' was as much a throwback as in front. Goodness knows what the food inspection people made of this smoky kitchen, with its primitive sink and décor, albeit the equipment looked reasonably modern – a concession to get past the regulations, she presumed. It looked suspiciously clean, however, and she tried to suppress the ignoble thought that the actual cooking was still done as it always had been. Another curtain – the fire door was jammed back – separated this from the living room where Gladys Norman was snoozing, far from quietly. She'd guessed right – it was the small sharp-eyed old lady she'd picked out on Sunday as looking so incongruous. Here, the cardigan and old flower-patterned dress didn't look so out of place, not in a room where the only item dating later than about 1955 was the television set.

'Gentleman from Lakenham House, Ma,' Bert bawled without compunction. 'And lady.'

Gemma hadn't talked to Gladys at the party, but close up she saw the character in the face as Gladys's eyes flew open. She was a bright-eyed sparrow of a woman, her years betrayed only by the wrinkled skin and shrivelled frame. But the face still spelled 'tough', Gemma decided. Anyone who tried to nobble her would be in for a hard job.

'This is General Maitland's granddaughter, Gladys,' Paul introduced her. 'You remember it was his hundredth birthday last week.'

"Course I remember,' she snapped. 'Think I'm off me marbles?'

'I'm sorry we didn't meet then,' Gemma said sincerely. 'I didn't know about the tontine until later.' Would Gladys know what tontine meant, she wondered?

It appeared so. 'And now you're chasing round here just like the others wanting to know about Ted Parsons, I'll be bound.'

Taken aback Gemma might be, but she wasn't going to betray the fact – especially since Paul was looking amused. 'Yes. As Mr Shane points out, it's in all our interests to find out whether he's still alive.'

'If I live long enough it will be. Mind you, I can outdo them other lot. Don't you worry about that, young man.' She cackled, in high good humour. 'Well sit down both of you. Don't stand around like a couple of tarts.'

'I really came to—' Gemma began.

'Size up my form, eh? Will the old girl last the course?'

'If you would describe Ted Parsons for me,' Gemma finished, determined not to be thrown. 'Anything, just to give me an idea of what he's like.'

'Ain't seen Ted since 1934. Neither hide nor hair.'

'Have you *heard* anything about him then?'

'Maybe,' Gladys said noncommittally.

'Can you tell me what?'

'Can't recall. Might have been someone else, now I come to think of it.'

She'd get nowhere this way. 'Then could you just describe the Ted Parsons you remember? We can't find an obvious death certificate, so it's at least possible he's still alive.'

She snorted. 'That runt? Nah.'

'Nevertheless, if you could tell me a little about him:

his likes, his dislikes, anything that singles him out – false leg, that sort of thing.'

'Strawberry birthmark?' Gladys sniggered. 'The long-lost heir to the dukedom revealed. Nothing like that about Ted. He were a loser. Sunk into the crowd, did Ted.'

'Did he wear glasses?' Gemma pressed on. 'Did he have a nickname? That's the sort of thing professional investigators like to know.'

'Professional investigators?' Gladys mocked. 'Narks, police, fuzz, bill. That's what we call 'em round 'ere when we're being polite, eh, Bert? And they *are* round 'ere, aren't they, son?'

'Yes, Ma.'

So her suspicion that the café was used for more business than the ritual exchange of bacon and eggs for money might be well founded. Although if it was, it was nothing to do with her.

'What do you say, Bert?' Gladys asked. 'Shall I help the lady?'

'Yes,' answered Paul firmly for him. 'I need to know, too.'

Gladys didn't even look at him. 'Ted Parsons were a weak baby, so the orphanage told us. That's why they called him Parsons – they had 'im there thinking old Ted was going to die on them, summoned the Rector and nothing happened. That's Ted for you. Cussed.'

So he wasn't always a loser, Gemma reflected. 'Where was he found?'

Gladys shrugged. 'How should I know? I was only three months old when Ted come. On the doorstep, most of 'em.'

'You've no idea who his natural parents were?'

'Nah. None of us did. We weren't allowed to in those days. Mind you, we didn't make all the fuss about it there is today. Reckoned if they didn't want us we could do without them. I've done all right.' Gladys looked round her domain complacently.

'What did Ted look like when you last saw him?' Paul asked.

Gladys considered. 'Small, weedy-looking,' she said at last. 'Later he shot up a touch, but he were still scrawny. And he got stronger than he looked – which was like a bleeding anemone that never got to the light, if you see what I mean. And clever, oh yes, he was clever at his books all right. What we had of 'em.'

That was said with some bitterness, Gemma noticed, and wondered why. 'What happened to him after he left the orphanage?'

'His birthday – well, what the orphanage allotted 'im – was February. But he left at the end of '27, same as me. I went into service and 'e came too, see? Up in London, in Belgravia.' She mimicked the accent. 'He were the handy boy there. I was in the kitchen. That's 'ow I learned to cook,' she told them with pride. 'You never get on if you don't take your chances.'

'How long did you stay there?' This at least was an advance.

'I were still there in '34, but 'e left a couple of years before that. Trouble,' she added succinctly.

'Did you keep in touch?'

'Nah. Saw him at the parties though, so 'e must have kept in touch with someone. But when those of us born in 1913 had our twenty-first birthday, our kind patrons stopped the entertainment. End of '34 that was. Those parties were the gentry being kind, so we thought. I might have known. Kind! They were betting on us like horses. Well, this mare's going to win the race, don't you doubt that, Mr Shane.'

'Money,' contributed Bert. He had been silent so long, Gemma jumped.

'That's right, son. A cool three-quarters of a million. So just you make sure your Mum stays alive. Now get your backside in there and make sure none of them buggers gets out without paying.'

Sullenly Bert wandered back in, though without any great signs of hurry. Gladys sighed. 'Care in the community, eh? Who's going to look after him when I've gorn? Answer. Seven hundred and fifty thousand smackers. That's who.'

'All the more reason to track down Ted, Gladys,' Paul pointed out. 'Now think. Are you sure you've heard nothing from him? Where was he working in '34?'

'Chauffeur somewhere. Posh, too. But the family got wiped out in the blitz. One of the bombs meant for us – I'd moved east by then – that accidentally dropped up West.'

'Ted too, do you think?'

She gave Gemma a withering look. 'Ted weren't that weak, I said. He'd have been called up, wouldn't 'e? Or war-work of some kind. 'E might have gone in the war, for all I know. But I don't see Ted Parsons dying for his country at Alamein somehow.'

'You hinted you might have heard of him again.'

'Nah, I didn't hear nothing. I only ever saw one of the orphanage old crowd after the war, and she got TB and died. She were sweet on Ted as a kid, and if anyone knew, she did. But she didn't say nothing. Not that I asked her,' Gladys finished triumphantly.

Gemma gritted her teeth. Normally in her work she had no problem maintaining a front with less than likeable people, but when personally involved it took considerably more effort. 'What about his likes and dislikes?'

Gladys cackled. 'Fish and chips, fat blondes and fags. That do? Not bad for over fifty years, girl.'

'Seriously, Gladys,' Paul said pleasantly.

'He were a skirt-chaser,' Gladys sullenly responded, 'right from the age of eight or nine. He were a terror. Every time you turned your back, he'd have his hand in your knickers. That do? Stick that on your missing persons' noticeboard, will you?'

'Excellent. More details like that, if you please,' Paul said appreciatively. He'd got the knack of handling Gladys better than she had, thought Gemma, reluctantly admiring.

'Anything else?' she asked.

'You never quite knew with Ted,' Gladys volunteered. 'You had to be the first one to make a move, or he'd have you. You thought you'd got the measure of 'im, and then you found you didn't.'

'Did you like him?'

The question took her by surprise. 'Like him? Who could like him? He was a right bleeder. He'd have sold his own granny for a quid.'

'So he's unlikely to have fallen victim to a woman's charms,' Paul said idly.

'More likely running a string of whores,' she informed them generously. 'Popsies *and* pansies, if he thought he could get a bob or two. Not too particular . . . 'Course,' she added fairly, 'he were only twenty when I last saw 'im, but I bet 'e ain't changed. Another thing – ' warming up – 'if he saw anything like trouble, he'd do a runner. Leave someone else to cop the lot.'

Gemma changed tack. 'What about your fellow orphans whom you met on Sunday. John Peacock, Victoria Ireland and Stanley Drew. Had they changed much?'

'That Victoria was still a stand-offish, ambitious little tart, making out she's better than the rest of us. Hoity-toity – she wants to talk with the posh folk, not swap stories of Nursie and Naughty Little Doings back at the orphanage with the rest of us. She was determined to get shot of us right back then; she came to the parties because of meeting the posh folk, not us. I've seen her on the telly credits, and mincing around like she didn't know what the word "orphanage" meant. Tell you the truth, I'd forgotten all about her. Quite a laugh I 'ad when His Lordship introduced her at the Lakenham do. She was in no hurry to remember where she came from – till she realised there might be money in it. Then she became interested all right; started sizing us up as if we were all up for "Miss World". You'd think she'd have enough dosh with being on the telly and all.'

'And Stanley?'

She snorted. 'Stanley's only Stanley, ain't he? He always was and always is. Recognise him anywhere, the great twit. Bleating on about how nice to see us and how nice it would be to have some money so as how he could go and live by the seaside in Spain with his sister. Now John Peacock, 'e's different. I liked John. Mind you, 'e were a bit slow but we got on all right. Not that I had much to do with him after we left, me being a townee then and him a countryman. He could do with a bit of money, I reckon.

'Yes,' she brooded. 'Reckon we all could do with the money. Share it out between us. Better watch out we don't all get together and fake a few deaths, eh? Conspiracy to defraud. That would fix your tontine, wouldn't it?' she leered.

'It's an idea,' Paul joked. 'Just make sure you're the one that scoops the pool, though.'

'Why don't you stay on and have dinner this evening?' Paul asked as they left.

Gemma considered. It was a long time since she had dined in London other than solitary or business dinners. Though this, too, she supposed, would be business of a kind, if more enjoyable. Wise? Well, it was a long time since she'd done something that might not be wise. 'Very well.'

'We can discuss who we see next.'

'We?'

'Sorry. I thought you'd appointed me your Watson.'

'Sometimes Sherlock works alone.'

'So he does.' He grinned ruefully. 'Take care of yourself, Gemma, won't you? Seriously.'

'Why do you say take care?' She returned to the subject later, in the Soho restaurant. Even as she spoke, million-pound signs flashed before her. 'It's in their interests to find Ted, as you pointed out,' she said slowly. 'Why should Gladys or the others want to stop me?'

'When there's money around, a lot of nasty things crawl out of woodsheds.'

'I'm not Aunt Ada of *Cold Comfort Farm*.'

'I can see that.' He put out his hand across the table and touched hers lightly. 'Just keep a wary eye open.'

Some small part of her noted with interest that she hadn't mentally shrunk away at his touch – and the part had nothing to do with business.

'What would you do with the money if Ted Parsons is alive and manages to outlive our determined Gladys and the others?' Paul asked her. 'That's if it falls to you to decide,' he added quickly.

Was it wise to be drawn into this? Her conversation with her grandfather after she had returned from London with Charles Lakenham last week was all too vivid in her mind . . .

'*Am I your heir for this trust, Grandpops?*'

'*Yes, Gemma. It will not, I realise, be easy.*'

'*What do you want me to do?*'

'*I want you to fulfil the wishes of the Lakenham Set.*'

For a moment she thought he was joking, then saw that he wasn't. '*Even though their Renaissance never took place? Despite the mess the world is in, and Britain in particular?*'

'*Because of all those things.*'

'*And suppose it is not possible?*'

'*You must find a way to interpret it so that it is possible.*'

They had clashed before; they were of the same mettle, she and her grandfather.

'*Must is not a word that generals employ,*' *she said gently.* '*They know that even strategy has to give way to the demands of tactics if need be.*'

He sighed. '*You are right. Gemma, I must leave it to your integrity to do what is best in the circumstances.*'

'I don't know,' Gemma answered Paul truthfully, 'though of course I'd look first at what the Lakenham Set had desired.'

'Not a very long look, I presume.'

'Why not?' she asked sharply.

He looked astonished. 'Half the world is starving, the other half at war – or both. What good is a new museum to the past?'

If she answered, the way ahead was slippery, but she could not ignore the challenge. 'Maybe inspiration is as essential as bread for life. What would you do?' she countered quickly, unfairly. 'Have you decided?'

'I've thought of little else. When Lord Lakenham told us about the money at that weird party, it was just as if the heavens had opened up and said, "Mind your head, Shane: here's that consignment of manna you ordered years ago." '

'For what?'

'My wife died of cancer in great pain of body and mind. It made me believe there had to be something else on offer to alleviate it, other than what there then was. What little there was, was fighting prejudice. Now the time is right. That's why the hope of that manna has been thrown to me now. If – no, I'll say *when*, Gemma, I'm sorry – I get that money, I'm going to start an integrated community care centre, somewhere where there's nothing like that yet available, for both preventive care and complementary medicine. I've already started looking, in fact.'

Gemma watched his face, far away in his own world, absorbed in turning a far-off dream into reality through sheer determination.

'Homeopathy and counselling, medical methods of other cultures, international symposiums . . .' He must have talked for fifteen minutes or so until, suddenly aware of her presence once more, he stopped, looking somewhat sheepish. 'I do get carried away. But you see why I can't pay too much attention to the Lakenham Set's idealistic ideas. What practical good would they do, for we live in a practical world?'

'But it wouldn't be *our* money to do what we liked with,' she pointed out, 'and we know what they wanted done with it.' She wanted to say it was a question of integrity, but that would not do, for Paul had his own integrity, and would stick immovably with it.

He brushed aside her point. 'I could call it the Lakenham Centre, of course. Then they'd be remembered. We'll have a library with their books in too, their pictures on the walls.'

'That's only lip-service to what they wanted.'

'The kind of lip-service I have in mind delivers medicines to the sick to soothe, calm and cure, and to help suffering.' He paused, glancing at her. 'Or,' his tone changed, 'I can think of another kind of lip-service?'

'Can you indeed,' she said, glad of his olive branch to break the tension. 'Not here.'

'I'll take a rain-check. Seriously, Gemma – ' he snatched back the branch – 'what they wanted is an anachronism today. As if Richard Branson announced Virgin were going in for stage-coaches.'

'Not necessarily,' Gemma was surprised to see her hand was shaking slightly. However pleasant this dinner was, however much she liked Paul, they were far from the only players in this game.

'*A cool three-quarters of a million . . . so just you make sure your old Mum stays alive . . .*'

Gemma was glad she'd insisted on visiting Stanley Drew on her own. Paul was clearly hankering to accompany her, but she needed to remember she was Gemma

Maitland working for her grandfather, and not working in tandem with Paul, however enjoyable it might be. Stanley was the nominee of Jack Holland, VC, whose heir was now, of course, the Sharon Stone look-alike.

The Dartford Tunnel was its usual bottleneck, and it took her fifteen minutes to negotiate the BMW between the lorries; she turned off the M25 with relief at the Brentwood exit. Typical that she should have chosen the hottest day so far in the heatwave. Drew lived in a semi, as clean and soulless as a hospital ward. He led the way with obvious pride to a sitting room, heavy with the atmosphere of long disuse. Even the photographs managed to look neglected. There was one of an elderly Stanley, receiving a package from a circle of jovial gentlemen – obviously his retirement. Another was of a younger Stanley on his wedding day. She wondered if Mrs Stanley were still around. This room suggested not. Stanley himself was in good nick, she thought, for his age, although his slightly florid face reminded her he had heart problems. He brought in a half-milk, half-water coffee from the kitchen, and a plate of biscuits.

She braced herself. 'Lovely,' she told him warmly. 'This is good of you.'

'Quite a little surprise, isn't it, all our possible nest-eggs?'

'Not mine, in fact, while my grandfather lives. I'm hoping to track down for you all what's happened to Ted Parsons.' Gemma slightly emphasised the 'all'.

'I hope you do. I do hope so,' he assured her fervently. 'Dear old Ted.'

'Mrs Norman, Gladys Smith, didn't seem to like him,' Gemma couldn't help remarking, somewhat surprised at this enthusiasm.

'She didn't know him like I did,' was his slightly peevish reply. '*None* of them knew him like I did. We had talks. He was my friend. Look!' He heaved himself up and hurried to the windowsill. He brought over a framed photograph for her inspection. Out of the deep frame grinned a group of children sitting crosslegged on the grass in front of a large Victorian building. The girls wore identical pinafore dresses and boots, the boys identical jackets, trousers and caps. 'That's Ted!' Stanley pointed out a boy almost lost between two bigger children. Lost physically, maybe, she thought, but even at this distance, and taking into account the poor focus, the photograph couldn't hide the smirk on his face. I know something you don't, it seemed to be gloating.

'And that's me in the row behind.' Stanley's finger pointed to where a young Stanley, instantly recognisable, peered out anxiously from behind round glasses.

'When did you last see Ted?'

'We lost touch when we left the orphanage,' he replied wistfully. 'He went into service, I went into an office.' Pride filled his voice. 'I was head clerk ten years later – highly valued, you see. Then I went into the bank, and never looked back. They kept my job for me while I was in the Army Pay Corps during the hostilities.' He studied the photograph, as if amazed himself at what that young Stanley had achieved. 'Ted – well, unfortunately no one understood his qualities. I only saw him at the parties, when he came – it wasn't always he did.'

'Do you remember him at the last one in 1934?'

'Yes. I remember that very well.'

'Wotcher, Stanley, me old mate.'

'Good to see you, old man,' Stanley said, trying not

to feel superior, because he'd done well.

Ted biffed his fist into Stanley's stomach. 'Done well for yourself, eh?'

'Yes, and I'm sure I could arrange a little position—'

'Not me, mate. Not me. The open road, that's what calls me. The world's my stage.'

'You'll land in prison if you're not careful.' Stanley laughed, more than a little relieved his generous offer was not to be taken up. You never knew with Ted.

'Now why do you say that, old son?'

'I don't know, Ted. I just feel you might.' He was a little boy again, anxious about his protector.

'Bet your bottom dollar I don't. Listen, Stanley mate, I'll be all right. You remember that, old son. I'll be all right,' he emphasised. 'See you next year, eh?'

'Yes, Ted. Mind your step, won't you?' Stanley watched Ted slip quietly out of the door. He had this odd thought he'd never see him again.

'I advertised for him once, in *Family Favourites*, I think it was. I pretended we were related. We were, in a way. You're too young to remember that programme of course. I never heard anything. And I did think I saw him just after the war, as I was walking along Bond Street. But it wasn't. Aren't you Ted Parsons, I said? No, he said. Well, Ted wouldn't have cut me. Not Ted. I did feel foolish, I can tell you.

'I'd like to see him again,' Stanley rambled on. 'My heart isn't strong, but if I take it easy, I can last for years, the doctors say. With all that money, I'd like to go to live near my sister. I've always liked the sea. Or live in a

home. But you need money to live in a nice one nowadays.'

'You'd have enough to do that.'

'Yes, you can do a lot if you have money.' He
ruminated on this irrefutable fact.

Victoria Ireland's elegant flat in Holland Park was a far
cry from Stanley's semi, as were her brittle movements
from his ponderous heavy stride. It was easier to believe,
though, that she was about eighty than that he was, for all
the money she obviously spent on her face, her carefully
manicured hands, superbly shod feet, and coiffured hair.

Her hands, with their long thin fingers, were never still,
gracefully fluttering to illustrate her every point. Meanly,
Gemma came to the conclusion that someone had once in
her far-off youth informed Victoria she had pretty hands,
and she had been at pains to display them ever since.
Gemma was interested to meet her close up, after her
former TV roles as an ageing comedienne. Off-screen her
age was more apparent from the wrinkles and the slightly
desperate look in her eyes. She had been married at least
once, Gemma knew from the gossip magazines, but there
was no sign of a husband here, no photos, no male
accoutrements. This was the apartment of a pampered
lady. Victoria had never been particularly famous in her
youth, but had suddenly come to fame at a time when age
was no longer perceived a barrier to women's success on
TV.

She seemed never to relax, but was always gently
moving like the leaves of an aspen tree, Gemma noticed.

'I don't see that I can help you, Miss Maitland.' The
voice, pretty enough on TV, merely sounded whining.

It was not a promising beginning. 'I just wanted your

impressions of Ted Parsons – what you remember of his appearance, his likes and dislikes, and anything at all you can tell me of his movements.'

'We are speaking of seventy years ago, my dear.' Victoria gave a light laugh. 'Can you remember details of all the children with whom you were at school?'

'Only some,' said Gemma dismissively. 'But it wasn't really seventy years, for you saw him at the parties, didn't you?'

Victoria drew on a cigarette. 'With many others present. I can't really recall Ted Parsons at the parties. Had he been present at Lakenham House last week, no doubt I should have recognised him, as I did the others. As it is, I remember the name, but can't fit a face. I'm so sorry.' She smiled graciously. If that was to indicate the interview was at an end, she was sadly mistaken. Gemma stayed put.

'I take it you've heard nothing of him since the war, then.'

'It was such a pleasure to find I had been nominated by Lord Lakenham,' Victoria replied, as though this was only natural in view of her own exalted status.

'Do you hope you will win the jackpot?' asked Gemma boldly.

'Naturally,' Victoria replied coldly – and somewhat warily, Gemma thought. 'The older one gets the more one requires money. This flat is only rented, for example. Yes, the money would certainly be nice, and I would most certainly do something for the Lakenham Set. You may tell your grandfather so. I have already discussed this with Lord Lakenham. I will certainly do my humble best to bring the Twenty to prominence again.'

Like hell she will, thought Gemma, while voicing

approval of such sentiments. If mental toughness were to be the deciding factor, Gladys would be given a run for her money.

Gemma was glad she had left John Peacock till last. He had been the nominee of Anthony Manders-Wright, whose heir was now a reclusive lecturer by the name of Frederick Wright. What had happened to the 'Manders', Gemma wondered, intrigued. Recluse he might be, but he had travelled from the Midlands to Lakenham for the party nevertheless.

The heatwave had broken now with a vengeance, and she was eager to get back home to dry out. She'd had to park a long way from Victoria Ireland's flat. Peacock lived in a cottage in Lakenham village near the railway station, now that his son had taken over his job as gardener on the Lakenham estate and the cottage that went with it. It had come as some surprise to her to discover Peacock's association with Lakenham House from Paul, since Charles had not mentioned it. Like Stanley, Peacock had the air of one well used to managing on his own, but in his case it was unconscious – and, she suspected, more efficient. She guessed he'd been a widower – or divorced – a long time. The former probably. She couldn't see anyone deciding to divorce John Peacock. He was the nearest to a human being she'd met in the job so far, apart from Paul, and she took an instant liking to him. He had the red-brown face of a man who had worked all his life in the open air, and age wasn't going to deprive him of that look.

'You could've knocked me down with a feather when His Lordship told us last week. I worked at Lakenham House for twenty years before I finally retired ten years ago, and never an inkling. Not from His old Lordship, that was, him of the Lakenham Set, nor the new, not even when they first took me on. After all, it's a gentleman called Mr Wright who's interested in me, or rather how long I live.' He laughed. 'I met him at the House that Sunday. One of them professors, at a university in the north somewhere.'

'Do you remember Ted Parsons?' Gemma asked him, after she'd explained her mission more fully than over the phone.

''Course I do. I didn't like him much, but he could make you laugh. He did impressions. He used to laugh at me because I was good at nothing. That was only then. Later I discovered I could make things grow – plants, vegetables – and here I am.'

'Did you go to the last party in 1934?'

'Yes. He laughed at me then too, for not being ambitious, like. Ted, I says back, if you stays where you are, because that's what you does best and likes doing it, that's good sense. But look at you. You don't know what you want. No, I've had no cause to complain, always had a job, good wife, though she's long gone, good boy too. He keeps an eye on me. So does her ladyship, come to that, for all she's a foreigner.'

'And Ted? You've not seen anything of him?'

'Not so much as a whisper to the bees since '34.'

Gemma left him with mixed feelings, almost wishing she'd had Paul with her to talk things over with. She seemed to have had four different people described to her.

Clever, funny, likeable, kind, adept at vanishing, ambitious, sly, cruel, a right bleeder. Will the real Ted Parsons please stand up?

And tell me where you are.

Chapter Four

'On the whole,' Lisa told Gemma forthrightly, 'strawberry birthmarks might be quicker. For sheer excitement, give me the Ashford station run every time.'

'Nothing?'

'Far from it. Plenty. Every other male was called Ted Parsons according to the electoral rolls of London for '35 to '55.'

'And every one of them got married,' Loretta chimed in blithely. 'It's hard to know where to start.'

'People didn't move round so much in those days,' Gemma said hopefully. 'I'd put my money on his staying in London. That's where he was rumoured to be seen last.' Who by, though? she suddenly thought, but the answer would not come. It was, she supposed, too much to hope for that Ted Parsons would have sprung to life through the routine searches.

'During the war they did move around,' Lisa pointed out.

'And after it,' Gemma added. 'My grandfather . . .' *Grandfather*. Of course. She'd been missing a point. Small perhaps, but at this stage everything needed following up. She grinned evilly at her lieutenants. 'Carry on the good work.'

She had always liked his Tenterden home, even on a cheerless day like this one. Its tall, red-brick frontage seemed welcoming, unlike some of its neighbours around it. Perhaps it had something to do with Mrs Plummer's presence. To have a live-in housekeeper was a luxury nowadays, and Gemma often wondered if her grandfather appreciated his good fortune. He treated her much as he had his batman, with a kindly indifference, or, on occasion, with the grudging respect due to his Chief of Staff. Fortunately, Katherine Plummer had got his measure, obviously decided that this was where she wanted to live, and was prepared to accommodate all reasonable divergences from perfection. She had lived there for twenty-two years, moving in two years before Gemma's uncomplaining grandmother had died, and shortly after Mr Plummer had vanished with the girl from his local Wimpy Bar.

It was not one of her grandfather's good days. He was sitting as usual in the library, his head sunk on his chest, and a rug over his knees. He sat there, rain or shine, and today was definitely one of the former. Even the orchids that were his passion seemed to droop in sympathy. He looked even slighter than when she had last seen him. Fortunately Tenterden was a fairly frequent destination for a taxi run, and if none materialised she assuaged her business conscience by offering cheap return shopping trips to the ladies of the village.

Her grandfather woke up with a start, lost for a moment, until comprehension came into his eyes. She dreaded a day when it might not do so.

'Gemma! How delightful.'

She sat down in the armchair opposite him, waiting until he was fully awake and the colour had come back into his cheeks.

'Ted Parsons,' she announced, smiling at him.

'You've found him?'

'Not yet. Another question, Grandpops. You told me he disappeared in the late 1940s or early 50s, but Paul Shane and I have seen his surviving orphanage companions and they only talk of him in pre-war years. How do you know he was around as long as that?'

He did not answer, instead resting his hand on his desk, staring up at his shelves of books, as if the history of warfare might provide the answer for him. She was about to rephrase her question, when he remarked inconsequentially: 'Good lad, that.'

'Who?'

'Come now,' he said mildly. 'It would be nice to see you part of the Lakenham Set, one way or another.'

'*What*?' She stiffened, following his reasoning through long experience. 'I like Paul, but it doesn't mean I can just sweep Bill under the carpet. And don't you think,' she teased him gently, 'you're just a little influenced by Ellen Shane?'

He wasn't listening, and his eyes closed once more.

Her heart sank. She wasn't going to get anything more out of him today. Probably this was just a bad day – there had been more of them recently – and not the beginning of a decline. All the same, it was a sharp reminder that time was passing. If she was to find Ted Parsons alive and present him to her grandfather, the task was urgent. Over the last few days she'd realised how much she wanted this to happen. With Ted alive, she argued, her grandfather could focus on what form he would want the Lakenham Set's memorial to take. At the back of her mind, though, was another reason, a selfish one which she stifled but which would be extinguished: if Grandfather was to pronounce his wishes, she would have something to guide her, something to lift the burden from her own conscience, should she be the eventual recipient of the tontine fund.

'Up late,' Mrs Plummer remarked cheerfully to Gemma as she brought coffee in, and nodding towards the General. 'Reading till all hours again.'

Both of them knew late hours had little to do with her grandfather's lassitude.

'General!' Mrs Plummer bawled, perpetually under the impression that the General was deaf. 'Gemma's here, and your coffee.'

Reginald Maitland opened an eye, and gave her a glare that had felled officers at twenty paces. It failed to have the same effect on Mrs Plummer, who, oblivious to her intended fate, went out into the garden.

'How did you know that Ted Parsons was in Britain after the war, Grandpops?' she tried again.

'I heard it at a regimental reunion, of course,' he told her briskly. 'Where else does one learn what goes on in the world?'

'Ted Parsons was in your regiment?'

'Naturally not.' He was impatient. 'I have already told you I have not seen him since 1934. I flatter myself that I would at least have recognised the name, even if he were not in my battalion. I seem to recall it was Beaky Dawson – yes – he was a brigade commander who was invited as a guest of honour. Essex regiment, I believe,' he added dismissively. 'It was the annual reunion of the Queen's Own Royal West Kents, as it then was.' There was some bitterness in his voice, for he had never quite accustomed himself to the amalgamation of the Buffs and the Dirty Half Hundreds in 1961. 'Discussion turned to the Great

War and the three hundred soldiers shot for cowardice –
terrible business. Veterans knew about it, those of us
who'd been junior officers at the time, but it hadn't yet
become the matter of debate it is today. From that,
conversation proceeded to the nature of cowardice.
Beaky, I recall, differentiated perceptively between the
cowardice caused through shell-shock and similar medical
conditions, and a deliberate avoidance of danger by a
man in full possession of his wits. He instanced a man
under his command in France in 1940, up before him on a
LMF charge, Lack of Moral Fibre. His name was Ted
Parsons. Naturally the name interested me, and one or
two inquiries convinced me it could well have been the
same man. Whatever the outcome of the charge, and
Beaky could not remember – save that he joked about
how the fellow had led the retreat to Dunkirk, the man
was coincidentally back under his command in the desert
in '41, and went into the bag. Beaky was quite sure it was
a deliberate surrender.'

'The bag?' Gemma teased him gently.

'Prisoner of war, my dear, as you know quite well.
Allow me some jargon of my trade. Anyway, he must
have survived the war, because Beaky was convinced
he noticed him in Bond Street, and smartly dressed
too, a few years after the war. Beaky only remarked on
it, since it was a lesson in the morality or immorality of
survivorship. An interesting question, and I believe the
reason that I am convinced Ted Parsons is still alive. If
he survived Beaky Dawson, I am quite sure a German
PoW camp would have presented few problems in
comparison.'

There were advantages in being a general's granddaughter

and one was – on occasion – the magic way that doors barred by iron to others could miraculously fly open. Even at the Ministry of Defence. Leave the enemy an honourable retreat if you required their cooperation in the peace, was another tactic of her grandfather's. Thus, a murmur of merely tracing present whereabouts, with positively no publication involved; a mention that the said man had been a PoW and that all that was required was the name of the camp, whether he died in captivity or was demobbed, brought forth a promise to 'look into it'. The look had taken place, and now she found herself marching in the wake of a messenger along long anonymous corridors, unadorned with concessions to frivolity such as prints or drawings, for the answers. Presumably such information was so hush-hush that it could not be voiced over an open telephone line, she thought, amused, since she had been asked to attend in person.

There didn't seem anything hush-hush about the lieutenant-colonel who greeted her. If he was a faceless scion of Whitehall, she was a shrinking violet.

'Edward Parsons, Private . . . Taken prisoner at Tobruk, 1941. Sent to Stalag 344 Lamsdorf PoW Camp, evacuated to Nuremberg, spring '45, liberated and repatriated by the US army. Officially demobbed 1945. No further record.'

'Can you suggest anyone that would have?'

'There's a regimental association you might try.' He glanced at the full record before him. 'I doubt if he's the sort to rush along to reunions, but it might give you some sort of lead, especially if anyone from his company or battalion went into the bag with him. I expect it has some sort of newsletter. You could advertise for him.'

'Advertise?' Her spirits sank. Months and months of waiting.

He watched her face, and said compassionately: 'If people want to disappear they will – and, looking at this, I'd say your chap was the disappearing sort.'

Back along the long corridors, this time allotted to a different messenger as escort, hopes once more dashed. Perhaps they had been unreasonable ones, but the prospect ahead seemed at the moment uncommonly like this corridor: punctuated by fire-doors, that opened a vista to yet more of a plod lined by closed doors. Even the nameplates managed to look anonymous, the clouded glass panels giving no hint of activity within. There was the occasional sound from behind these bastions – printers, raised voices on the telephone, the murmur of conversation – and— She stopped abruptly. A whistle – as out of place here as in the garden outside Waynings. No, it was her imagination, *it must be*. It wasn't even the same song. 'It's a long way to Tipperary . . .' A far cry from 'Daisy, Daisy'. You couldn't identify a whistle as you could a singer. After all, plenty of people must still whistle. Mustn't they? It was just out of fashion. She had only to open that door-handle, thrust open the door and—

And what? Ask 'Are you the same person who whistled outside my cottage two months ago?' It sounded crazy, even to her. Imagination. She was yowling at nothing, just like Launcelot. She had only to open that door and . . . For no reason, save one Launcelot would have recognised, she took the other option. She hurried towards the messenger who had realised his charge was no longer close and was marching purposefully back. Her footsteps quickened; had he not been there she would have broken into a run. As they turned the corner, it was even more stupid to imagine that the sound of 'Daisy, Daisy' was floating after her.

Twice her hand reached out for the telephone, and twice she pulled it back. She would not ring Paul. Not for the wrong reasons. Not because underneath she suddenly felt she'd like to discuss progress with Paul. That would be ridiculous for Biggles Maitland, Special Agent, as Loretta and Lisa unanimously dubbed her. She supposed it was because somewhere at the back of her mind lingered her grandfather's comments. Did he really hope she would marry Philip Shane's grandson? If she were him she might hope much the same, but that didn't make it any the more likely to happen.

She forced herself to take Bill's photograph out of its drawer in her bedroom. She didn't keep it there because it brought tears to her eyes if she did not. It was simply that she did not want to be reminded of Bill. He was in a different life. In this one she had to make a success of being alone. And it was not making a success of it alone if she reached out for a man every time she heard an odd whistle in the night. Even if it were Paul she reached for.

In the end she didn't need to reach very far. Paul turned up at Waynings the next day.

'They said at the office you were here, as naturally I went there first,' he told her virtuously, kissing her cheek. 'Are you on call or free to chat?'

'Neither, in fact.' She felt wrongfooted at having been forestalled, not the least because of her pleasure at seeing him.

'Ah. Fortunately I come bearing gifts for a wayward goddess.'

102

'Gifts?' He didn't seem to be carrying anything.

'Nothing so dull as flowers for you, Gemma. This is a special gift, in view of the fact that you haven't contacted me. I needed an excuse to find out whether you were wining and dining Ted Parsons at this very moment. Here . . .'

He pressed a piece of paper into her hands.

'Johnnie Castle,' she read. 'Not – ' a sudden excitement – 'an alias for Ted?'

'Alas, no – at least, I hadn't thought of that. All the more reason for you to catch the Paddington Cornish Riviera with me.'

'We're eloping?'

'Not yet. A clean weekend in Cornwall is all that's on offer.'

She laughed. 'You'd better come in. Unless you prefer the garden now the sun has deigned to come out.'

'Garden sounds delightful.'

'You can share the best chair with Launcelot.'

'I take it Launcelot has four legs?'

'And a lot of black hair,' she assured him.

Fortunately Launcelot was nowhere to be seen and, having provided tea and biscuits, trying to hold back curiosity, since she was sure this was exactly what he was trying to arouse, 'John Castle,' she said at last. 'I assume he has something to do with Ted Parsons. Or had. But how did you get it?' emphasising the 'you' by mistake.

'My brain doesn't stop working,' he told her reproachfully, 'when it's not with you. I told you I wanted to track down Ted Parsons as much as you do – if only to prove he's well and truly dead. We've got to this point at the same time. John Castle was in Lamsdorf with him.'

'Then you're ahead of me,' she pointed out.

'My family comes from a long line of clairvoyants.'

She managed to laugh. 'I'm sorry. I'm being unconscionably rude. I don't often get asked for a clean weekend.'

'What an interesting life you must lead.'

'You know what I mean.'

'That you'll come.'

'I'll think about it.'

'Think all you like. I'm going, I'm under no obligation to pass on to you anything John Castle tells me. He's ex-directory, so you'll have a tough time tracking him down, and by the time you do I will have convinced him not to talk to you. Your only hope is to come with me, clean or dirty.'

'Do I get the choice?'

He looked at her and took her hand in his. 'No. It's clean. Dear Gemma, you have a sturdy iron cage around your heart with a large warning notice! "Keep Off, Vulnerable Lady Within".'

John Castle tackled the moors as if he were in training for a marathon, and Gemma had to struggle to keep up with him and Paul. He looked younger than Ted Parsons would now be – hardly into his seventies, tall, and with the weatherbeaten look of the Cornish dweller. Even so, he was going some. She stumbled over a rock, but managed to keep her balance. She hadn't come too well equipped for granite rock avoidance, and felt the impact through her trainers. John Castle looked round at her stifled exclamation.

'Not too thoughtful of me to have dragged you up here. That's the penalty you have to pay for the privilege of listening to a man's memoirs. I have to tramp up here every morning or I can't breathe.'

Here, where the Cornish peninsula thinned out towards Land's End, the moors were magnificent. She could see nothing but granite rock, coarse grass, with a sea on either side only a few miles away. There was nothing to break the horizon but a wandering sheep or two, and a disused mining chimney standing stark on the skyline.

'I daresay I'd feel like you if I'd been in a PoW camp,' Paul observed.

Castle glanced at him, the tick in his eye very evident. Forty years in Cornwall hadn't managed to vanquish that. 'It isn't just the need for space, and the lack of human habitation. It's that here one lives in proportion to time, balanced, satisfied, like a Mozart concerto, or a Greek drama. You see that pile of granite up there, partly covered over with bracken? That's a group of Stone Age huts. Remains of. These hills are littered with them. Phoenicians, or Trojans if you believe the legends, settled here. Came and passed. Look at my place down there. Do you think there'll be any signs of that in another thousand years or so? Do you think it matters a damn?'

Gemma looked back at the granite cottage standing by the St Ives Road, some way from the village. From here, it was isolated, forbidding, like its owner.

'Fine enough now, eh?' Castle continued. 'But come the winter and it's bleak.'

'Will you stay here?' Paul asked bluntly.

Surprisingly Castle didn't seem to mind. 'Which way I fly is hell; myself am hell,' he quoted. 'What's the point? How could I work anywhere else? How live without work?'

'Work?' asked Gemma.

He shot a look at her. 'I'm a painter. Not without honour,' he added caustically.

She deemed it wiser to say nothing. To apologise would make it worse.

'Come in and see. Then you can ask me about Ted Parsons.'

The cottage walls were massive, keeping it cool inside, and a fire was burning in the grate, welcome on a cheerless day like today. The best light to paint the moors perhaps, judging from the profusion of oils and water-colours on the walls, but not for a holiday season weekend. Paul evidently had no qualms about studying the pictures, for he went up close to examine them. She remained in the centre of the room looking around her. They were bold, impressionistic – and she wasn't sure she liked them, for they had a stark savagery about them that suggested their painter, as well as their subject, was not always full of bonhomie. These rocks did not suggest their painter's ordered interpretation on them; on the contrary, they had a mysterious and gloomy infinity about them which suggested more his cry of despair at interpretation eluding him, a monstrous horror that lurked, biding its time to descend.

'I see why you don't want to leave here,' said Paul at last.

Castle nodded. 'Sit down,' he said more amiably. 'You can talk about Ted now – I'm ready.'

'Do you know whether he's still alive?' Gemma came straight to the point.

'No idea. He wasn't the cards at Christmas type. I haven't seen or heard from him since I was repatriated in '45. The Germans force-marched us all west as the Russians got closer.' He grimaced. 'I'd have sooner taken my chances with Ivan than do that Sunday stroll again. Ted stayed behind with the rest of the sick and wounded.'

'Sick?'

Castle snorted. 'If you're a weedy scrap like him, it's easier to get away with it. Pneumonia, so he said. Perhaps he died there – I wouldn't know.'

'We know he got back to the UK.'

Gemma's hopes sank. If this was the best lead they had, they had as much chance of finding him as Lord Lucan.

'Did you like him?' Paul asked.

Castle considered, the tic in evidence again now. 'I saw a lot of him. It wasn't a question of liking or not liking. We were there together. Like working with someone but unable to get away in the evenings and tell the wife what a bastard he is.'

'But you knew him well, at least.'

'No one knew Ted well. Now you see him, now you don't. You only knew what he wanted you to know.'

'Wasn't that difficult in a PoW camp?' Gemma asked.

'No. Not the way things worked there. The pack system. You gravitated into groups. Those that were dead set on escape, and those that decided to sit tight. We were told it was our duty to escape if we could. Outside, with hindsight, that makes sense. Cause what disruption we could was the general idea. Tie down the German troops looking for us. But in there some saw things differently. We were stuck in Upper Silesia and the odds against our getting out were pretty high. Escape plans were something to pass the time, but as for actually going, the chances were slim. A few nasty stories got back to us and the goons made sure they did. I got out once on a good scheme. Went out with the weekly wine delivery – for the goons, not us. I was back in the cooler before they had time to miss me. After two weeks in solitary I thought, that's it. Not again. I'll do my bit for the war effort some other way.

'It was then I got to know Ted. I was on a work party with him and the other chaps were commiserating with me. Not him. He said it was my own fault, I should be spending the time to better purpose. What was the point of wonderful schemes to get outside the wire if you couldn't speak a word of the lingo? I should be learning, not dashing around like a bull in a china shop. We had all sorts there. University types, businessmen, gentlemen of the night: you could learn any trade you wanted from classics to housebreaking if you'd organise yourself. He'd been there since '41 and I only got my come-uppance in '43, so he had a head start. Later in the war, the Red Cross organised it so we could take RSA exams. We had a theatre, library – everything but freedom.' His eyes moved to the moor outside. 'Ted had already learned German and Italian, so he passed them, and Spanish too, I think. And there was his speciality, of course.'

'What was that?' Gemma asked, hopefully.

'His bit for the war effort was teaching forging. They didn't have an RSA exam in that. He was a wizard at forging signatures and papers and the like. He did all the papers for the escapes – and pretty good at it too. I asked him to teach me – just for the interest.' Castle grinned. 'I became quite good at it, but I didn't have Ted's knack. That's why I've stuck to these,' he glanced at the paintings on the opposite wall, 'and not turned myself into another Tom Keating. Ted wanted something in return, naturally.'

'And what was that?'

'Drawing lessons.'

'That doesn't seem like the Ted Parsons we've heard about so far,' Gemma said.

'Perhaps not. He'd never done so much as a sketch of a tree before, but he'd always wanted to, he told me. He wasn't bad either. I taught him perspective, planes, use of line and light, anatomy, colour, all the basics.'

'I suppose,' Gemma asked diffidently, 'you didn't keep any of your sketches of the camp?'

'A few.' Castle was guarded.

'Would any of them be of Ted Parsons, or by Ted Parsons?'

'Portraits aren't my line.'

'Look,' Gemma plunged, 'all we want to do is to find Ted Parsons now. It's only the present that counts. Not what happened all those years ago. We can't explain fully, but finding Ted Parsons is a vital step in the creation of a major new artistic enterprise.'

'The Ted Parsons I knew is a long way from that world,' Castle said drily.

'Maybe. But he's essential all the same,' Gemma said, aware that Paul was saying nothing.

'Fairy-tales,' said their host dismissively. 'Nevertheless, I suppose I've no rational grounds for holding back. But I'm too old for loft excavations. You'll have to do it.' He turned to Paul. 'There's a ladder,' he added encouragingly. 'Old brown suitcase tied round with a belt of some sort. You'll find it somewhere. Bring it down, there's a good chap.'

The good chap obediently disappeared upstairs, and from the shouts and muffled voices she gathered the search was successful. Paul reappeared with the suitcase followed by Castle. 'You'll find a red-covered sketchpad in there somewhere.'

'Are all these from the camp?' Gemma stared at the hundreds of sketches loose inside the suitcase, as well as several bound pads.

'Only the pad. They didn't send Pickfords to help us when we left the camp.'

'No. Stupid of me.'

'Is this it?' Paul produced a red pad with a flourish.

John Castle barely glanced at it. 'Yes.'

Gemma went to sit by Paul on the sofa, as he opened it. The sketches were rough and unfinished, as though the artist in him revolted at his subject matter.

'Why did you do these if you hated it so much?' Paul asked.

'I was decoy. I sat sketching while folks were tunnelling, poor sods. The goons were interested, it diverted their attention, especially if I drew them.'

'Do any of these show Ted Parsons?'

Reluctantly Castle took the book and leafed through. 'There.' He tossed it down on the coffee table. The sketch showed a table and, sitting across from the artist, a thin man, hunched over what he was doing, concentrating hard as he looked downwards. Even this position could not hide the sly intelligence in the face. Gemma wondered whether John Castle had subconsciously chosen that pose because the sitter was not looking at him, perhaps representative of the sitter's personality. Always looking away, beyond.

'Some said he was a collaborator,' Castle volunteered. 'Because he spoke German and was always chatting to the guards.'

'Did you think so?'

'No. He wouldn't stick his neck out, that's for sure. Not through scruples but because safety began at home was

110

Ted's motto. He was a loner – if he chatted to guards it was because he might learn from them, not the other way round. There was one called Helmut, I remember.'

'Wasn't there anyone else he was friendly with?'

Castle considered this. 'He wasn't popular. Never knew quite where you were with him; something of the magician about him. He would direct you to think one thing, and all the time he was planning to do something quite different. He dropped me once he reckoned he'd sucked me dry on drawing lessons, and towards the end I seem to remember – you've got to realise this was nearly fifty years ago – he was friendly with a nice chap called Joseph Barnes. A Londoner – and *him* – ' Castle suddenly warmed to his theme – 'I *did* hear of. Someone told me he was running a barrow in Wandsworth somewhere. Junk, old furniture, that sort of thing. Lower end of the market. There was a crying need for that after the war, what with so many having to set up new homes one way and another. We missed all the bombing, of course.' Castle stared out of the window where the white rump of a rabbit was zig-zagging through clumps of grass. 'Ah well.'

The sun was condescending to shine fitfully above them as they sat on the grassy cliff garden of the hotel.

'I'd live here if I were a painter,' Gemma said lazily, stretching a sweeping hand towards sea and rocky cliffs.

'Moors are more infinite than the sea.'

'You can't be more infinite. It's ungrammatical.'

'Artistic licence.'

'*Are* you an artist?'

'In some things.'

He drew her to him and kissed her. It seemed quite natural and very satisfactory. *Breathless we flung us on the windy hill* . . . The Lakenham Set. Gemma Maitland, Paul Shane, Reggie Maitland and a girl called Ellen. It would be very easy . . .

'I do believe,' Paul said softly, 'I detected a glimmer of a response.'

'A slow glimmer,' she said apologetically. 'It's been a long time.'

'No one since Bill?'

'Yes, in fact,' she hesitated.

'A rebound? A mistake?'

'No, neither.' How could she explain? But then she didn't have to, she reminded herself.

'Me too,' he said after a moment. 'My then secretary.' He grimaced. 'I never thought I could be so clichéd. But it seemed a good idea at the time.'

'Comfort?'

'No such thing, as you know full well.'

Gemma felt Bill nodding approvingly and cheered up. But, being Gemma, there was something she had to pursue first. 'Why were you so unforthcoming when I was trying to persuade him our motives over Ted were of the highest?'

'You know why.'

'Because I talked of a Lakenham memorial in terms of art?'

'I couldn't go along with that, Gemma.'

'How could one take the money and use it for something different than the original donors had intended?'

'How could one waste millions on a project that will save no lives?'

'Art – inspiration – isn't quantifiable.'

'All the more reason to invest in something that is,' he said fiercely.

Her grandfather's hopes leaked away . . . How could she and Paul make a couple with such a gulf between? 'Is there no common ground?' she asked.

He looked at her, took her hand. 'There's always common ground. It's a question of how much.'

Quite what good she thought she'd do here in Wandsworth, trying to track down a barrow that had perhaps traded somewhere here forty-odd years ago, Gemma wasn't sure. She supposed it was a lead of some sort, however tenuous. After all, Ted Parsons had to have left some trace somewhere, even if he died donkey's years ago.

Paul had regretfully declared he had too many clients to accompany her. She felt sneakily glad, for she wanted a breathing space to think what she would do next – she, not *they*. The weekend had been quite pleasant – no, she was deceiving herself, very pleasant. Cornwall, even in the midst of the holiday season, had a strange magic of its own, when its atmosphere could be savoured alone, not diluted by too many people around. Not all had been pleasant though. The crying of the seagulls outside the hotel brought back memories of Bill and holidays in Skye, until she deliberately closed her mind to them. Better to concentrate on the Lakenham Set, and an ever-narrower path to Ted Parsons. Time to advertise in *The Times*, I suppose, Paul told her lightly. The advertisement had duly appeared yesterday. There had been no immediate response.

'It could take a couple of years,' Paul had blithely added in the train coming back. 'We had a client once for whom we had to advertise for a long-lost relative, since she died leaving all her money to him. When the relative heard about the advertisement a year or so later he was so excited he popped off too, leaving me with an even bigger problem.'

'And bigger fees.'

'Cynical, and not altogether true. Some jobs you just want to get shot of. Would you want to drive some old bore round and round the M25 for eight hours or so just because it would earn you a big fee?'

'No.'

She packed the Ford with some difficulty and began her tour of Wandsworth second-hand trade – still thriving, she saw. Thank heavens for the Yellow Pages. Armed with her list, she marched into the first . . . then the second . . . and the third. The words began to take on a rhythm of their own, she repeated them so often.

'I'm hunting down an old member of my family who's disappeared. He used to run a barrow somewhere after the war, selling second-hand furniture. His name was Joseph Barnes.' She tried not to wonder precisely what finding Joe might achieve. Precious little, probably. Merely another who had 'lost touch'. Then, at last, at long, long last, *Geronimo!*

'Barnes? Never heard of him, but you could try old Sam who used to run the shop before me. He goes back before the war. In an old folks' home somewhere near Putney.'

At least it wasn't Timbuctoo or Tipperary . . . *It's a long way to Tipperary* . . . She put the disconcerting memory firmly out of her head.

Sam Jenkins, fortunately, was still in command of most of the considerable wits he must have been born with, not one of the hopelessly still figures lolling in chairs, looking out of the lives they once possessed. He was sitting in an armchair, one foot extended on a stool, wearing a neck brace and studying the racing pages, which he laid aside reluctantly. It took some time and lengthy explanation to say what she was after, but Gemma got there in the end.

'Joe? 'Course I remember him. Had a barrer – and then moved up in the world. Took a shop, did some restoring for me. He were good at that. He was my runner for a time.'

'Runner?'

'When you get something good you need someone to run it round the posher shops to get the best price. Or you did. Probably done by computer now,' he added gloomily. Then he cackled at his own joke.

'Did Joe ever talk of a friend from PoW days? Ted Parsons?' A long shot, and it failed.

'Might've done for all I know. He worked with some mate.' He exclaimed, 'I tell a lie. Blow me. It weren't Joe did the running. It was the other one. Ned. Ned Williams.'

She'd struck gold and found it fool's gold. 'Is Joe still alive?'

'Nah. He went bankrupt. Broke his heart.' There was a certain relish in his tone, for all Joe was a nice chap.

'And Ned?' Why she was asking she didn't know.

'He hopped it, didn't he?'

This was getting nowhere. Fate was like that. It offered you a seat and then pulled the chair out from behind, she thought bitterly.

'Joe's son's alive,' Sam told her hopefully, seeing her crestfallen face. 'Comes to see me sometimes.'

She supposed a son was better than nothing. He might

have old address books, or have a line on Ned Williams who might know . . . Who was she kidding? With her luck? No such chance.

'Do you have the son's address?'

'No.'

She began to think as a special agent she made rather a good taxi-driver. Normally she did not get emotionally involved with her cases, of course. It was bad luck this one was different. She was acutely aware that every day that ebbed away without being nearer to Ted Parsons lessened her chances of flourishing him at her grandfather before he died.

Sam cackled. 'Cheer up, love. I've got his telephone number.'

'Barnes here.' The voice was sharp, educated, and accustomed to getting its own way. The Hampstead number surprised her, especially when she looked it up and saw the address. Either Joe's son had done very well in his career, or his father had run an exceptionally profitable barrow after his bankruptcy. Then light dawned. It was *Henry* Barnes, the well-known barrister.

Telephone, or write? She had taken a deep breath. Instinct told her telephone – it was, after all, she reasoned, a simple request.

'Who did you say you were?' the voice repeated sharply after she had explained her mission.

'Gemma Maitland. I'm the granddaughter of General Maitland of the Lakenham Set.' (It sounded good, even if he had never heard of any of them.)

'And the name of the man you are looking for?'

'A prisoner of war, friend of your father's. Ted Parsons, who—'

116

'Hardly a friend, Miss Maitland,' the dry voice cut in.

'So you know of him, at any rate. After the war?' she asked with barely controllable excitement.

A pause. 'You had better see Rosalind Chambers, Miss Maitland. I'll give you her address.'

'Who is she, please?'

'My father's companion, we'd probably call it now. His mistress. My mother died during the war.' He gave her an address in Blackheath, SE3. 'I advise you not to telephone first. You might not get a very good reception. You will find her in most of the time. And, Miss Maitland . . .' he added as, somewhat puzzled, she thanked him and prepared to ring off.

'Yes?'

'Should you find your Mr Parsons, I'd be most interested to learn his address.'

It was beginning to feel like a treasure hunt. Solve this clue and you might be provided with another to solve at the end of it. The difference was that there might or might not be a prize at the end.

Gemma put the phone down, and went out into the kitchen to sort out the question of supper. Her mind was still on Ted Parsons and it refused to be excited by the idea of whipping up a tasty little meal or one from scratch. The Green Knight? Or the freezer? The latter won, with the thought that her subconscious could go on working on the matter of Ted Parsons even while her conscious self was concentrating on the mechanics of meal organisation and microwaving. Just as the pinger went, the telephone rang again.

'It's Paul.'

'Is anything wrong?'

He sounded immensely serious. 'Depends on your point of view.'

'What's happened, Paul?' she asked sharply.

'John Peacock's dead.'

'*What*? But I only saw him a fortnight ago,' she said fatuously. 'Dead? What of?'

'Charles told me it's probably some kind of food poisoning. There was an empty tin of fish in his rubbish bin. He tried to ring you but your office said you were out all day, and he didn't want to call on a mobile. I said I'd tell you. And Frederick Wright, and he's informed Felix.'

For a moment she'd almost forgotten that the trustees had to be notified of any deaths.

'That nice old man,' she said slowly.

'Yes, I liked him too. It means the pace will quicken, Gemma.'

Gemma walked back to the kitchen. It was obvious what Paul meant. Four certainties had been reduced to three, and there was all the more need to find Ted Parsons quickly. She stared at the meal still revolving on the microwave awaiting her convenience. What had looked so appetising failed to do so now. Hunger had vanished.

She decided to drive to Blackheath the next day, and handed over her bookings to Arthur. Rosalind Chambers sounded a formidable name, and she pictured an elegant flat, maid, and distinguished owner in one of Blackheath's stately listed buildings. It turned out to be a neglected council house on the outer edges of Blackheath, verging on Lewisham. She banged on the door with no response. Then she realised it was open. Cautiously she advanced shouting, 'Anyone at home?' No answer. At the end of a passageway a door stood open.

Tentatively, she poked her head inside. There were two splashes of colour in the room. One was a bright green parrot in a cage. The other was Rosalind Chambers, almost parrot-like herself with bright eyes, she lay full length on a sofa, spindly legs stuck out in front of her, bright red lipstick, mauve eye shadow, bright green skirt, yellow blouse, and a royal blue scarf round her neck. She could have been any age between sixty and eighty, and her dress and make-up sense had overlooked the last fifty years or so.

'Are you the home help?' Even the voice was a parrot-like screech.

'I'm afraid not.'

'Get me a sandwich, luv. You'll find it all in the fridge out there.' A once beautiful small hand waved vaguely in the direction of the gas fire.

Gemma obeyed, found her way to the poorly equipped kitchen, discovered marmite, low fat spread and a stale loaf in the fridge. Plus one egg. Nothing else. Her efforts appeared to satisfy, once a Guinness had been commandeered to join the sandwich.

'That's better. Now what did you say your name was?'

'Gemma Maitland. I gather you knew Joe Barnes, Mrs Chambers.'

'Can't get your money now, dear. Joe's gone. And I ain't got nothing.' She cackled. '*And* I'm not Mrs Chambers. Rosa . . . lind,' she drew out the name as if remembering some far-off lover whispering it thus. Hard to imagine, seeing the wreck before her now.

'I came to ask if you knew the whereabouts of a man he was in the prisoner-of-war camp with.'

'Go on, dear.' The voice was neutral.

'His name was Ted Parsons.'

119

'Was it now?' Rosalind lay down the sandwich carefully. 'And what would a nice young lady like you be wanting with Ted Parsons?' she almost spat out.

'I'm sorry if I'm upsetting you.' What *was* this, Gemma wondered? 'I just want to know where he is.'

The response startled her – a loud scream of laughter, echoed by the parrot. 'She wants to know where he is. Ain't she a laugh, Napoleon? Eh? Wants to know where Ted Parsons is.'

'What's funny, please?' At least she'd got a reaction.

'Oh, so would a lot of people, dearie. So would a lot of people like to know where Ted Parsons is. Like me, for instance, the bastard. We spent twenty years trying to find out, me and Joe. Then Joe went and died, and I'm left lying here. Nothing I can do about it. All your friends melt away when you're stuck here all day. Then you march in, jaunty as a tar on pay night, and say you want to find him. Well, when you do, ducky, just you let me know, that's all I can say.'

'Can you tell me what this is about, please? I gather you don't like him.'

It was an ill-advised remark.

'Like him? No, I didn't like him, lovely. Mind you, he were a good piece of cock, but that's all.'

'I'm sorry,' Gemma said. 'I didn't mean to distress you.' Her mind was furiously racing. This woman had *known* him, slept with him. At last she was getting warmer. Or was she?

'Distress! That ain't distress. You're good news, lady. You want to find him, and I'll tell you all I know about Mr Ted Parsons – if you tell me where he is when you find him.'

Gemma thought this bargain over. 'I can't agree to

that,' she said regretfully. 'The gain is mostly on your side.'

The old lady looked at her, slightly puzzled, then the painted face crinkled up. Tears? No, laughter, thank goodness. 'You're smarter than you look,' she conceded, 'but then, so am I. All right, ducky. Ted was in PoW camp with Joe and they set up a barrow after the war. They was partners—'

'I thought that was Ned Williams,' Gemma interrupted, puzzled.

'Did you? Well, I'm telling you it was Ted Parsons. Do you want to listen or not? Joe and I let him have a spare room in the flat. Tiny, it was, but room to bounce when Master Ted had a mind for it and Joe was out. Great days, eh?'

Gemma decided no answer was called for.

'Great days,' the old woman repeated. 'And all the time, Joe and I thought we were all friends. Dumb we were.'

'You make a good pudden, I'll say that for you, Rosy.'

'Good of you, I'm sure, Ted.' Rosalind frowned. She knew what he meant all right, but to say it in front of Joe wasn't right. Ted enjoyed it, look at the way he were grinning, the sod.

'Now, listen, what d'yer reckon? You've got a bit tucked away now, ain't you, Joe? How d'yer fancy adding to it? Sure bet.'

'Don't listen to him, Joe. The barrow's doing all right,' Rosalind said sharply.

'Be quiet, Rosy. Let him talk. You know how Ted likes to talk.'

'*Not just talk this time, Joe,*' Ted came back. '*It just needs the dear little ponies. You remember that goon in the camp, the one you all thought I were whispering sweet nothings about your tunnels to?*'

'*Not me, Ted.*'

'*Perhaps not. I spoke German, we got on well and I dropped over to see him. Got a special pass to "assist investigations" . . . I helped get him off the hook. He's in the clear, but it's tough there in Germany, tougher than here, I'd say. Make money how you can. And his way is art.*'

'*Art? Like that?*' Joe jabbed a finger at three wispy-looking roses painted in watercolour.

'*The real stuff, Joe. Yer old masters and all that. Remember how we talked about getting into the restoration business?*'

'*It's a trick, Joe,*' Rosalind warned.

'*No, Miss Know-all,*' Ted laughed, giving her a look that promised well for when he could next get her alone. '*Real stuff. Floating around all over Europe, it is. This goon can get his hands on it; can't tell you exactly how, of course, but there's Italian, Czech, Rumanian nobs all selling their Rubens for a fag. All we need is capital, and we could be in on it.*'

'*Take the barrow over there, do we?*' Joe asked sarcastically.

'*Not quite, old son, not quite,*' Ted said indulgently. '*You drop the barrow. Take a shop. Go respectable, foster your contacts like, drop a quiet word of good stuff here and there on the way. I'll go over and get it.*'

'*What wiv? A bloomin' taxi?*'

'*I got me methods.*'

122

'*And what about Customs when you come strolling in with a Rembrandt under your arm, saying, oh yes, I picked this up for twenty quid, all legal, don't you worry about a thing, officer?*'

'*You leave that to me,*' Ted told him. '*Oh, wot a little beauty I got.*' He cast a lascivious eye at Rosy's legs, or rather the gap between them. She noticed and was meant to. This time she was hard put to it to restrain a giggle.

'*And what about provenance, or whatever they call it? You expect me to just wander up Bond Street saying this is a Rembrandt, just appeared out of nowhere?*'

'*You can leave that to me and all,*' Ted winked. '*Remember the camp? And from now on I'm Ned Williams, man-about-town, partner of respectable Joe Barnes, see?*'

'Fakes with forged papers?' asked Gemma, fascinated.

'No,' said Rosalind. 'Only wish it had've been. Nothing so simple for our Ted. These were the real McCoy – nothing too flashy, the odd Monet, Dutch School, Vermeer, Raphael drawings – all true gold. Sometimes the provenances had a bit of help from Ted, but the dealers didn't mind 'cos the stuff was OK. Every expert they went to said not a doubt, so they winked their eye at a little extra paperwork provided by Ted. Made things simpler. As for getting them here, he had a variety of methods. Sometimes he brought them over, frames and all, in a collection of junk. What Customs officer was going to pick out a Rubens from Aunt Fanny's oil of Uncle Joe? Sometimes he travelled with it under his arm and forged an export licence – that said it was a good copy, naturally. School of, as they say. Ted was a dab hand at signatures; sometimes he'd put a coat of varnish on the real signature, and do an obvious false one over it, aged enough to look like a period copy. He was clever enough not to use the same method too often either.'

'So what went wrong?' Gemma demanded. At least Ted was fleshing out.

'The louse was setting us up all the time. Six years in the planning. Six years laying me. When all the time . . .' Rosalind choked.

'I've done it, Joe.' Ted threw himself in an armchair and threw down his suitcase. 'I've pulled it off.'

'Not the—' Joe couldn't even speak, he was so choked. Even Rosalind was excited.

'The Lost Leonardo, my beauties.' He seized their hands. 'What about a bit of celebrating, eh? Look at this!'

'Ted!' squeaked Rosalind.

'Ned, darlin',' Ted reminded her.

'It's champagne.'

'Bet you ain't tasted that since Gladstone drank out of your slipper, eh?'

'No – where?'

'Never you mind. Now look, I ain't got it with me, mind. But look, I got these from the same place.'

'They're only drawings, mate,' Joe said, disappointed.

'Only drawings,' Ted repeated disgustedly. 'Two Michelangelos, that's all. Straight out of Austria. Been there for centuries. And as for the golden goose – there's no doubt about it. I looked it all up in a book. After the French came galloping into Milan, it

124

*turned out old Louis, the King, had a special fancy
for Leonardo, so he made him court painter. Suited
Leo down to the ground; he were getting on a bit then.
The next king, Francis, told him to up his stumps and
come to France with him; he handed him a château
and told him to get on with it. The last laugh was on
Leonardo because he came all right, but lay down his
brushes and didn't paint a stroke. Well, would you?'*

'So what?' Joe demanded suspiciously.

'Luckily the King already had a nice little collection of Leonardo's work at Fontainebleau, see. And
one of them was this one of a dame called Pomona,
Roman goddess of fruit and displaying all her
lovelies under three veils. Only it ain't there now.
Nor did the revolutionaries get their hands on it. It
disappeared.'

'How do you know it ever existed?' Rosalind asked
suspiciously.

'Because this chum of his, Lomazzo, writing
about him after his death, said it was there. Said
Leo painted it during his last stay in Milan, and
later it vanished.'

'Oh, yeah?'

'Rosy, have I ever let you down?'

'No, you ain't, Ted. Shut your mouth, Ros.' It was
so unusual for Joe to intervene, that Rosalind obeyed
through sheer surprise.

'Furthermore,' Ted continued triumphantly, 'Her
Majesty herself has a drawing of the lady's foot by
Leonardo at Windsor.'

Neither of his listeners was impressed.

'Leonardo did the drawing to help out one of his
young men called Melzi. They were knocking around

Melzi's home sometime, surrounded by the birds and the bees and all that country stuff, so I reckon Leonardo suggested Melzi give Pomona a whirl, like he'd done. Even drew her foot for him to help him out, him being a youngster. Melzi's picture's landed up in Berlin, if you still don't believe me.'

'*Proves he knew his subject, don't it?'*

'*Not to me, Ted,' Rosy said shortly.*

'*Now look, love, this Pomona dame was just the kind of subject our Leo likes. Draperies, veil, flowers, all that stuff. Nothing he liked more than a nice technical problem, so he chucked a triple veil over the lady. Fifteen hundred and seven was the date he did it, according to the provenance.'*

'*You got some?' Joe exclaimed. 'Real?'*

''*Course I have. What do you take me for? Our Miss Pomona, or I should say Mrs Pomona, owing to the fact she were a married lady, having picked up some god or other, stayed at Fontainebleau till Napoleon signed his abdication there. She'd had her nose put out of joint when the* Virgin of the Rocks *arrived, and was sulking in a back room. Well, Napoleon's missis, seeing the writing on the wall, decided to quit her loving spouse and head for her family at home in Vienna. Marie-Louise was a Hapsburg, see. And what more natural than to contribute to the housekeeping with a Leonardo tucked under her arm? Pomona stayed there till the Austrian Empire went phut at the end of the Great War.'*

'*And then?' Joe demanded.*

'*That's where my lips are sealed, old mate,' Ted said regretfully. 'Protect my sources, see. Let's say it*

126

comes straight from the walls of Schönbrunn, not the public rooms in case the French asked for it back, into the appreciative hands of my seller.'

'How do you get to hear of it?'

'That's my business. Helmut did, that's all you need to know. Look, the game's this. We got to raise a lot on Leonardo. Even a dumb Nazi knows a lost Leonardo's worth a quid or two. Right?'

'Yes.'

'And private investors only, right? All to scoop the pool when we sell it to the National, eh? Our Pomona kicking up her heels will make a nice pair with their Virgin of the Rocks. "The Lost Leonardo." Sounds good, don't it? So we leave the Michelangelos with the buyers as surety for the money. Then when I bring the Leonardo in, we do a swap. The genuine lost Leonardo . . .'

'And he did bring it in. Oh yes,' Rosalind continued viciously. 'We handed it over to the chaps moneybagging the operation, and because they trusted dear old Ned Williams who'd been producing genuine Old Masters for the last six years, they gave him back his surety straightaway. Two Michelangelo drawings. Both genuine.'

'And?'

'And nothing. The Leonardo was a fake. That was the last we saw of Master Ted Parsons. Or Ned Williams. He'd got the money for the so-called Leonardo, *and* kept the Michelangelos. It ruined Joe *and* broke his heart. He couldn't believe he'd been had for a sucker all those years by dear old Ted. The Scam of the Century.'

'It's a terrible story.' Gemma's heart sank. The chances of finding Ted Parsons vanished to rock bottom.

'So if you happen to come across him, dear, just tell him Rosy was asking for the money back, plus the big question.'

'And that is?'

'What the bastard did with the real Leonardo.'

Chapter Five

Holidaymakers swarmed everywhere at Stansted airport. Shorts, sunglasses, T-shirts, baggage – all shouted aloud that the middle of August was probably not the best of all times to be leaving on what promised to be a harassing few days in Florence. Sense had told Gemma to leave it until the holiday season was nearing its end; instinct was pushing her right ahead. This was only the first throw of the dice in the game of chance that might – or might not – lead to Ted Parsons.

And chancy it was. 'Where do you find a lost Leonardo, Paul?' she asked, after she had told him over the telephone everything that Rosalind had had to say.

He had thought for a moment. 'In the Hermitage?'

'Try again.'

'With a lot of other Leonardos.'

'Right. But why hasn't it materialised since the 1950s, if Ted Parsons walked off with it?'

Easy one to answer. 'He sold it to one of these hidden gloaters. Or maybe, just maybe, he's one himself.'

'A Mr Goldfinger, with a secret collection hidden in a bomb-proof cellar. Are you sure they really exist?'

'No idea. I don't have any as clients, that's for sure. I

129

only wish I did. The Lakenham Centre might be somewhat nearer reality than it is now.'

'The Lak— Oh.' Gemma broke off, realising what he meant. 'Your complementary medicine centre.'

'What else?'

She had felt reproved. At least here at Stansted she felt they were at last *doing* something. But the right thing? Paul had immediately said he'd take time off and come. August was a slack month, and she'd been grateful, for it gave credence to her hunch.

'I suppose we're right in starting with Florence?' he asked doubtfully.

'Florence is *the* city for art,' she told him firmly. 'I've spent enough time at galleries and libraries in the last few days to be quite sure of that. At the very least, if no one remembers Ted Parsons, there might be a few whispers of a missing Leonardo.'

'You've a hope!' Paul laughed. 'Do you really think, dear little innocent, that if there were any such whispers, they would tell strangers wandering in out of the blue?'

Gemma grimaced. 'I suppose not. But I have acquired a few names in my searchings, and so we'll have introductions of a sort. And if they get us nowhere, we can move on to Rome or wherever we think best.'

'By the time we've worked our way down from Venice to Reggio di Calabria we should know one another quite well.'

'If that's a note of sarcasm in your voice,' Gemma said mildly, 'I should point out I didn't ask you to come.'

'But you're pleased I did, aren't you?'

'Yes. You speak Italian.'

'Fainites?' He put up crossed fingers.

She laughed, then turned her attention to steering their

trolley as the checking-in queue marginally moved forward. Why did there always seem to be more trolleys than the number of people in the queue could possibly absorb? She and Paul stood out as probably the only passengers who weren't on holiday, casually dressed though they were. No, she was wrong. That old lady looked, from her sense of style, as though she lived in Florence; moreover she was wielding a trolley like a veteran. And that man's glowering dark face was too arresting, too pugnacious, not to be Italian. Anyway, he was in the business-class queue, now she looked more closely, and as out of place there amid the neatly tailored suits as the Florentine in her own. She wondered what point those suited gentlemen were making in what had to be a plane on the small side if it were to land at Florence airport, enclosed by hills as the city was. She hoped that woman with the two squalling children was sitting right behind their immaculate backs.

By the time they had percolated into the departure lounge, anonymity had enveloped their fellow passengers. She easily resisted any temptation to follow Paul into the swarming duty-free shops, and sat down in the only available space.

'I wonder if Ted Parsons travelled like this,' she asked plaintively when Paul fought his way back to her.

'Third class all the way by train, I should think, or banana boat to Genoa. Lucky chap either way.'

It was a relief when at last they could board the satellite train.

'Abandoning no man's land for cloud-cuckoo land,' Paul remarked cheerfully as they finally settled themselves in the packed aircraft. 'Didn't you say you were told the chances of a real Leonardo turning up after all this time would be roughly equivalent to its painter reappearing in a vision with a golden harp?'

'But the facts check out,' Gemma retorted obstinately. 'It *could* have happened, just as Ted told the story to Rosalind.'

'Or it could be a complete fiction on her part.'

'Unlikely. They all seem obsessed by it, and have been for forty years. Why bother to make up the story for little old me?'

'In that case, don't you think Ted would have gone to the States first, not Italy? The Italians had not long ceased to be the enemy, and the money was in Uncle Sam's hands.'

'But Italy was still the art market centre of Europe then, even if it wasn't the Italians buying. Everything was in such a shambles after the war that apparently anybody with questionable deals over stolen art in mind would make their way there, even reputable American buyers.'

'But our Leonardo, if I can so term it, hasn't turned up anywhere, as you point out.'

'There are nearly twenty lost or missing Leonardo paintings alone, and that's a fair proportion of his output. There *must* be some kind of odds on one or two turning up.'

'*If* they existed. They might merely be confusions with the work of his pupils.'

'That's the solicitor in you talking. Look at the facts first. The chief source for the existence of the Pomona is Lomazzo, who had been a pupil of Leonardo's, but went blind and turned to writing about art. Now I gather he isn't always reliable, but he left a treatise on art with quite a few details about Leonardo. He can't just have been making a Pomona story up; he might possibly have been

confusing it with something, but there's no earthly reason
he would get a Leonardo picture at Fontainebleau confused with one by another of Leonardo's pupils – the
painting that landed up in Berlin by Melzi.'

'Not convinced. Solicitors don't like the words "isn't
always reliable".'

'Look, before Leonardo went to France, where he
died, he rented a house from the Melzis for a time on
their country estate, and their son Francesco became his
pupil, companion, whatever. What more natural than
that, as Ted told Rosalind, Leonardo suggested the
subject to Melzi because he'd already executed one
himself, and then helped him out with the difficult bits
like the foot. Artists didn't have the same outlook as we
have today. At that time they still tended to use the same
subjects, and there was no professional secrecy or jeal-
ousy as there came to be later.'

'You paint a pretty picture yourself. I'll say that for
your theory. Leonardo and his fancy boy sitting side by
side in the garden painting Pomona's foot. The only flaw
is that we'll never know.'

'We will when we find Ted Parsons.' Even as she said
it, it seemed a forlorn hope.

Heat and noise blasted them together as they emerged
from the taxi outside the hotel. Dust, blazing sun,
motor-scooters, hooting, shouting voices, and car-
horns blaring as their taxi-driver unconcernedly flicked
out lira notes in change. It was evidently a common-
place in this side street, which was incredibly narrow by
British standards, even though it was so close to the
city centre.

The hotel provided a welcome, cool refuge, with its

willowy art-deco ladies on their painted glass panels, comfortable old-fashioned armchairs, and a tray of inviting-looking long drinks zipping by on the confident arm of a young waiter.

Once upon a time she had spent two days in Florence with Bill before they were married. Time had obliterated all but fleeting memories of the city, and one obstinately enduring memory of Bill standing lopsidedly and laughing at the side of the Neptune Fountain in the Piazza della Signoria, the main square. He was laughing because a pigeon had been diving straight at her, and seemed to be lopsided because she had ducked to avoid it. Why that, of so many loving private moments? Odd it might be, but beside it everything else suddenly seemed rather pointless. Even Paul's undemanding presence as they strolled out in the late afternoon sun.

She could hardly avoid going to the Piazza since it was the tourist centre and the natural point from which to get their bearings. Better to get it over with, she supposed, as they entered the square dominated by the Palazzo Vecchio, with its copy of Michelangelo's David flanking its entrance. Then she wondered why she had worried. Bill wasn't here. How could he be, amid this soulless hubbub packing the square, of large groups, small groups, or aimlessly wandering individuals, all uniformed in the anonymous garb of the holidaying public the world over. Garb she was sharing, she acknowledged, in her bright cotton trousers and T-shirt.

'Drink?' Paul asked hopefully.

'We've just had one.'

'I need another.'

'There isn't a seat to be had.'

Somehow there was though. It began to dawn on her

that, for all his pleasant, unaggressive appearance, Paul had the determination of a rottweiler. In moments she found herself miraculously seated at a table, with a granita ice and a coffee rapidly appearing before her.

'Where first? Our chum isn't in the telephone directory, by the way,' Paul informed her. 'I checked it in London.'

'Too much to hope for. I suppose you checked both names?'

'Yes. If he's here he's using some other name now.'

'Wouldn't you, in the circumstances?'

'The consul then.'

'Yes. Then we can start on the art dealers and restorers.'

'Is that a polite word for forgers?'

'Not in Florence. Anyway, we don't know Ted was the faker of the Leonardo. Or of any paintings come to that. He forged documents.'

'True.'

'There are going to be a lot of restorers. We'd better start on the names you've been given.'

'Now?' In this heat, the excitement for the task ahead that had filled her in London had deserted her.

'Tomorrow?'

They looked at each other, well pleased.

'The Uffizi? Part of it's reopened after the bomb.'

'Let's go.'

'I'm not sure this indigestion through overdose of art is a good plan before dinner,' Paul commented, coming up behind her in the packed gallery an hour later. 'I suppose if we were subtle we'd just pick one room and be satisfied with that, instead of trying to bolt through the lot. What's riveted you suddenly? You've got that glazed look.' He glanced at the portrait. 'Lorenzo the Magnificent himself, eh? Ugly brute, isn't he?'

'In a way. Striking though. He reminds me of someone.' The resemblance proved elusive and, dissatisfied, she turned away.

'Do you still feel the Lakenham Set's fanciful idea of a Second Renaissance in Britain this century was justified, after seeing this lot?' Paul swept his arm grandly round, encompassing Botticellis, Titians, Bronzinos, Fra Filippo Lippis, as far as the eye could see, through one room after another.

'There were wars, politics, assassinations and intrigues going on in the fifteenth century, just as there are now. That didn't and doesn't mean great changes can't be taking place in other fields – perhaps even because of them.'

'Precisely. As in medicine today. *That's* the real Renaissance.'

Some of the waiters seemed resentful of the tourist mouths that fed them, others were so falsely jolly and Italian that Gemma wanted to laugh. She compromised by catching Paul's eye and grinning as they squeezed into chairs at the small table in the busy trattoria.

'Medicine and health care,' Paul repeated, thirty minutes later, halfway through a beefsteak fiorentina. 'You can't deny that's what Britain needs. No sane person could.'

'I don't deny it.' Gemma drank some more of the strong red wine. How could she deny it? What he said was true, but somewhere deep inside her a small voice still pleaded fervently the case for the Lakenham Set. Rationally she could not defend their ideals, but then the masterpieces they had seen that afternoon had been produced by more than reason.

'Why have you put your remote look on then?'

'Have I?'

'You know you have.'

'I suppose it's the principle I'm fighting, not the end objective.'

'We're poles apart. How about more red wine? It might bring our poles closer.'

'Yes,' she agreed generously, '*and* I'll have a dessert.'

He took her hand as they walked back towards the hotel along the bank of the Arno river. It felt good. Then he kissed her, and that too felt good.

'Shall I come in?' he inquired casually, as they reached the door of her room.

Dizzy with tiredness, with wine, heat and travel, it would, she realised with some surprise, be astonishingly easy to say yes. 'No' seemed an altogether more difficult word to pronounce. Yet from somewhere that word had to be found. And so did some sort of explanation, she supposed. That was even more difficult, for she could not explain it to herself, let alone to him. She compromised, as she half stumbled inside the room. 'No – please.' There were ways of rejection that didn't reject, but at the moment she felt too tired to care. 'I'm sorry,' she added.

'So, dearest Gemma, am I. Business first still, then?'

'Yes.' She clutched gratefully at this olive branch. Business? Or was it still Bill first?

This, she told herself as she fell into bed, was getting complicated. Moreover there was something bothering her which she could not pin down. Sooner or later her body would have to be consulted over its wishes – but not tonight. As she was drifting into sleep her mind crystallised briefly on what was troubling her. He hadn't seemed to mind being rejected very much. It was perhaps irritating, but was it good or bad? She fell asleep before she found an answer.

The problem with Florence, Gemma decided ruefully the next morning, was that there were far too many distractions for the serious investigator. Every iron gate, every half-open doorway offered promise: a carving, the glimpse of a time-weathered fresco, a stone angel promising peace to those that entered. Behind any one of these huge gateways might lie the secret of Ted Parsons, but which way to turn? They had decided to divide their labours. Paul elected to visit the Consul, she would track down the restorers on her list, one by one. These, coming from the reputable source they did, would no doubt represent the upper side of the market; below it might be a whole underworld which could be more difficult to penetrate. Of the two, she suspected, the lower would be the more likely to hold the clue, if any were to be found, to their quarry's present whereabouts.

She was out of the main tourist centre; now putting duty first, she had ignored the pull of the cathedral and the fairy-tale Giotto bell-tower at its side, and was walking northwards to find the first name on her list. Most of the 'restauro antico' shops she had passed looked in great need of restoration themselves, but this one was as smart as a gallery of Old Masters in Bond Street. At least, she looked on the bright side, they might speak English or French well here.

She neatly sidestepped to avoid a determined group of Japanese tourists heading en masse for San Marco, only to be hooted at by a resigned motor-scooter, swerving to avoid her instinctive step into the roadway. What would have bought an attack of V-signs in dear old Britain brought no reaction here. It was simply the way of life. She pushed open the door and went in. A stately grey-haired man greeted her, with the courteous air of one whose day was now made complete by her presence.

'I'm here on my grandfather's account,' she explained. 'Generalissimo Maitland.' No harm in trying the name-dropping approach occasionally. 'I'm looking for an Englishman who might have come to Florence in the 1950s.'

'Might?' A quizzical elegant eyebrow.

'I realise it's unlikely you would know him, but it is just possible. He would be about eighty now. His name was Ted Parsons, or Ned Williams, or even something else.' Her quest began to sound hopeless even to her, but she produced her photograph which he studied carefully.

'No.' An emphatic shake of the head.

'You're sure?' She had hardly expected to strike lucky at once, but nevertheless disappointment hit her hard.

'The art world in Florence is not small, signora, but it is not so large that we do not know our own. The photo-graph is not good.' There he was right. It had been blown up from a snapshot loaned to her by Rosalind. 'However, I would know if anyone resembling this was still here. He is not.'

He sounded so sure, it made her doubtful. 'He might be using any name now.'

'If he is still alive, I would know him. And I do not.'

He seemed genuinely sorry as he bowed her out, and it was a scene that was to be repeated many times before she met Paul for lunch to report on progress.

'How did you get on?'

'The Consulate has promised to look into it,' Paul told her.

'Did they say how long they generally took to look into things?'

He shrugged. 'They did not. The man I saw became quite interested though, when I explained what we were after. I'm sure they'll follow it up. How about you?'

'Zilch. I feel as if I'm in a dusty gold frame myself, I've been into so many shops. I've exhausted most of the list.'

'And yourself, apparently. Do you think spaghetti would revive you?'

'Plus iced tamarind juice, I'd say there was every chance.'

'Would you like the afternoon off? We could got to the Boboli gardens or Fiesole. Somewhere cool.'

'Inside art restoration shops it can be remarkably cool.'

'I see why your business is successful,' he informed her in heartfelt tones. 'Stern daughter of the voice of God.'

'What?'

'Wordsworth, writing of duty.'

'It's not just duty, it's fear,' she said unguardedly, immediately regretting it.

'Of what?' he asked curiously.

Too far to draw back now. 'Of being left with the Lakenham problem in my lap,' she explained frankly. 'John Peacock's death has rather brought it home to me.'

'If your grandfather dies too, you mean? Why? You seem to be a lady of firm ideas and ideals.'

'That's not the same as having to decide what they are.'

'And that's what you're afraid of?'

'Not just that.'

'What then?'

'Would you laugh if I said this sunshine?'

'I wouldn't laugh. I wouldn't understand what you meant, though.'

'The sun seems merciless, particularly in this city. It traps you, you can't escape. You can't see what it hides. It shines down without any gradations so that everything looks the same, it's as deceiving as the dark. I'm not explaining this very well, am I?' she broke off.

'No.'

'I can't put it any better. But I do feel there's some kind of threat hanging over us. And it's to do with Ted Parsons.'

'You need lunch,' he told her practically, thrusting the menu at her. 'Spaghetti, spaghetti, spaghetti, or lash out on a daring lasagne?'

She gave up, and laughed. 'Spaghetti would be wonderful.'

Perhaps he was right. Perhaps there was nothing more threatening here than the prospect of a long, ultimately disappointing search.

Perhaps.

Linger as they did in the restaurant, they were still out before the siesta period was over. 'Let's strike west,' Paul suggested. 'I passed a few *restauro anticos* on my way back from the Consulate.'

'Why not?' she agreed.

Once away from the river and the tourist centre, the city changed its nature. Here the streets were more anonymous, the shops mostly serviced everyday living rather than sprouted credit card symbols. Away from the huge palazzi, the old fortresses of the centre, there were grey exteriors, obviously apartments and houses, with here and there an interesting byway or gate that promised riches which could not be seen. Here too they struck unlucky with what restoration shops there were. Only one produced any sign of hope.

At first the familiar answer, once they had put their question and flourished the photograph – 'No.' Not that this man would have known him in the fifties, thought Gemma. He would hardly have been born. Then perhaps the sight of Gemma's crestfallen face softened his heart. A torrent of Italian poured forth, to which Paul listened intently.

'He says his father may remember him, if we care to wait till after Papa has finished his siesta.'

She supposed it was progress of a sort.

Thanking him as fervently as if he had produced Ted Parsons out of a Renaissance chest, they left to await Papa's convenience, wandering down to the river.

'Even the churches have siestas,' she complained, faced with a closed door.

'This cloister doesn't seem to be.' Paul peered in, seeing a welcome 'Open' sign. The cloister was small, with faded frescos on its walls.

'Remarkable the way they've survived at all,' said Paul idly.

'It's the weather. So dry,' Gemma explained. He looked at her. 'I read my guidebook diligently,' she added, grinning.

'Then you'll be able to tell me what hidden treasures lie in here.' Paul flicked in a coin for the light inside a room leading just off the cloister.

'I've no idea – but does it matter *what* it is?' she replied a few moments later, as she stood before the huge fresco that dominated the room. 'It's breathtaking.'

'*The Last Supper*,' Paul observed unnecessarily, for who could mistake the grouped, tense figures, and the single one seated apart?

'This is what makes Florence what it is,' she said at last. 'Behind every door there's a story, and usually a masterpiece. Who was the artist?'

'Whoever he was, he was a dab hand at frescos anyway.'

'It makes me regret those wasted years at school, learning and not learning.'

'You'll have to catch up if you're aiming to carry out the Lakenham Set's weird ideas.'

It was a careless answer, somehow out of place before this delicate fresco with its harmony of form and colour. Here everything was timeless, and irrefutable. Paul's comment brought her back with a jerk to a world where there were no answers, to a problem which was as yet unsolved, and even if solved would bring uncertainty, argument and bitterness to the fore. *I don't think I'd want to be a nominee in a dark alley*. She shivered.

They were greeted on their re-entry into the small restoration shop with cries of delight, as if they were old and valued customers, and conducted with ceremony through to the inner regions, and up the curtained-off stairs to the second floor. Here Papa reclined in an armchair, surrounded by today's ephemera and yesterday's art. He struggled somewhat indignantly from his chair, but Italian charm came to his aid. 'Signora,' he murmured lovingly over her hand, so gracefully it struck no wrong chord.

'They seek an Englishman, Papa, who came to Florence in the 1950s. He was an art dealer. Signor Ted Parsons or

143

Signor Ned Williams,' the son explained in Italian.

For a moment she thought she saw a reaction as she showed him the photograph. He studied it carefully.

'*No*,' he said at last, politely handing it back. He seemed regretful.

'Are you sure? It seemed so likely he would have come to Florence.' Paul's disappointment showed as clearly as Gemma's own must do.

A shrug as if to say: who would not wish to come to Florence? 'If he was working in Florence, I would have known him,' the son translated for him. He handed back the photograph. 'The Orvino family knows everyone.'

With another charming smile from Papa, and genuine regret from the son, they were clearly dismissed. The sunshine seemed to mock them as they emerged from the shop on to the narrow pavement.

'Well, Florence was a chance shot, Gemma.'

'Chance shots sometimes hit targets,' she said shortly, disappointed and deflated.

As they walked away, they could hear the sound of raised voices from the upper windows. Angry voices. It could surely have nothing to do with Ted Parsons, but for some reason it stiffened her resolve. Surely it must have been Florence he came to, even if he left again; somewhere there must be a trace, even if only the faintest trace, left. But where?

'Newspapers,' she said suddenly. 'We'll go to the central library, look up newspapers, old telephone directories, city records, track down the British community. How about Sir Harold Acton? He lives near here, doesn't he? If anyone knows, he does surely. Anyone, even if disreputable, to do with art would come to his ears.'

Paul groaned. 'You believe in starting at the top, don't

you? Ducky, how about Venice? Or Rome first? Or Brussels or Paris? All big art centres.'

'No. I just feel – Paul, I *know* the clues are here.' She gazed frustratedly around. Somewhere in this large hot city was Ted Parsons, or the path to him.

The path to him was going to be even more tedious than Gemma had thought. She pushed her hair back over her face, conscious of sweat gathering in the heat as she sat back after examining a hundred or so 1950s English newspapers. She had a list of current prominent British residents and businesses she might approach, and this list looked even more daunting than yesterday's assignment. Impatiently she flipped the microfilm on. Weddings, funerals, parties, balls – no, Ted Parsons would not appear at any soirées, would he? Unless, of course, he'd sold the Leonardo.

She glanced at the next issue. Nothing, of course. No Mr Edward Williams. No Mr Edward Parsons. Then she saw it. That lucky chance that brings manna to the researcher. In the small print of a wedding announcement she saw: 'Also present were . . .' It leapt out at her. It shouted at her in triumph. It cried out in victory. A Mr T. Parsons was among the guests at a wedding. Not N. Williams, since that name was a red rag to a bull in Bond Street, but for some reason he had risked using his real name – presumably thinking neither Joe nor Rosalind would pursue him to Florence or split on him. Nor, she noted with glee, was it any old wedding. It was a wedding that had included as best man a Signor Orvino . . .

It might mean nothing. How could one remember who had been present at a wedding party years in the past? But it might, it just might mean something . . .

145

'I've found him!' She almost threw herself into the trattoria where Paul was waiting for her.

'Who?'

'Who do you think? Our Ted. Ted Parsons, of course.'

'*What*?'

'I thought you'd be surprised.' Complacency entered her voice.

'I'm very surprised,' he said slowly. 'Come and sit down and have a drink.'

'I deserve one. We'll drink to victory – why are you looking at me so oddly?' she asked, realising he was looking worried, not relieved.

'Tell me what you've found.'

'I've found a mention of him in a 1956 Florence newspaper. He was here. And what's more—'

He interrupted. 'I thought you meant you'd found him.'

'Almost as good as.'

'Not quite, Gemma. I'm sorry – I've bad news.'

'Bad – *Grandfather*?'

'No, *no*,' he reassured her. 'About Ted Parsons.'

Relief gave way to puzzlement. 'What kind of bad news?'

'The Consulate rang. They'd managed to trace Ted after all. Gemma, I'm afraid he's dead.'

'Dead?'

'Yes. He died early in 1957. His death hadn't been registered with the Consul – not all of them are – and so wouldn't have shown up in the St Catherine's House records.'

'But – ' She stopped for what she was going to say had been childish, born out of let-down, disbelief and shock. *He can't be dead*. But dismally she realised there was no earthly reason he couldn't be.

Paul went on quietly to explain about death certificates and so forth. 'We'll need them for our Mr Potter.'

'Who?' Despondently she remembered. The tontine. The trustees had to be notified. She felt as if she'd somehow failed her grandfather, by having to tell him the quest was at an end. She looked at Paul, read compassion in his face, and tried to remember she was a professional.

'Paul,' she said steadily, 'I still have to report to Grandfather. I know I'll have the death certificate, but would you think me odd if I asked to see the grave?'

He hesitated. 'No. I suppose I'd want to do the same in your shoes. Here am I, still in the tontine, telling you your fellow's dead and so you're out. You're right to want to check it out for yourself.'

'I didn't mean . . .' she cried. But she supposed that's just what she did mean. And there wasn't a damn thing she could do about it.

The plain gravestone told her nothing save that Ted Parsons had not been rich. It lacked the florid ornamentation of most Latin-built grave monuments. The hot, dusty taxi-ride northwards through the city had taken them past gardens and green spaces on the outskirts that had distanced her from the sharp sense of failure that had haunted her in the city centre. There Ted Parsons had seemed within her grasp; here he was elusive even in death, reduced to the anonymity of words. The end of the trail.

'Seen enough?' Paul asked at last. She had been staring at it long enough.

'Edward Parsons, born England, February 1914, died Florence, March 1957. *Requiescat in pace*.' Paul squatted

down. 'These flowers are quite fresh, you know. Someone still knows of him. What's the matter?' he asked
sharply.

'Nothing.'

'You've gone white. Shock?'

'Of a sort. I thought I saw someone I recognised, that's
all.'

He had been there, by those cypress bushes. Perhaps
he still was, but she could hardly rush over to find out.
After all, it was nothing important, merely that she had
remembered whom that portrait of Lorenzo de' Medici
reminded her of. It was that man in the business class
check-in queue at Stansted. The man who she could have
sworn had been watching them from the shade of the
cypresses. There was nothing there now, nothing but heat
and shadows, and the cicadas singing their endless song of
the sun.

'See the conquering heroine comes,' carolled Loretta as
Gemma came into the office.

'On the contrary.'

Loretta shot a glance at Gemma's gloomy face. 'Tell
you what, you can take old Ma Jessell to the hospital for
me. That'll cheer you up. Nothing like a nice varicose
vein for a spot of cheerful conversation.'

'Thanks, Loretta. I appreciate the thought.'

Loretta laughed. 'Cup of coffee instead?'

'Better.' Then, as Loretta busied herself with mugs and
spoons, 'He's dead.'

'I take it you mean our Ted?'

'I do.'

'And how do you feel about it?'

The kettle steamed, the pictures offered their familiar

focal points, the job lists lay awaiting her on the table. An endless parade of Mrs Jessells yawned before her. Once she would have relaxed in this scenario. Now frustration forbade it.

'Othello's occupation gone?' pressed Loretta.

'More than that. It's hard to explain. It just seems the wrong *end* for the job.'

'Life often provides the wrong ending.' It was a mistake; Loretta realised it and swore. 'Sorry.'

'Don't be. It's eight years ago. I'm a big girl now.'

'Maybe.'

Gemma decided to let this pass. 'I suppose I'm just irritated at the anti-climax. And how am I going to tell my grandfather?'

'Right away and straight out. After all, you might find he's forgotten all about it, that it was the whim of a moment to hire you. He might be pleased to know he doesn't have to worry about it any more.'

'I don't see Grandfather turning round in the middle of a charge, or forgetting he was on the battlefield, do you?' It was a rhetorical question, since both of them knew there was no such chance.

'No, I suppose that wouldn't impress the troops – though he's only got one trooper, and that's you.'

'Unfortunately I'm not just a trooper; I'm second in command.'

'No longer.'

'No.' Gemma considered this. The Lakenham tontine and its eventual resolution was now out of her field of play, and over to Paul or Charles Lakenham, or that blonde girl. One of them would have fifteen million to decide what to do with. What kind of memorial would young Blondie put up, she wondered, fighting back her sudden fury. Paul must have it, or Charles. Which? Which horse would she back? Not that she had a role any longer. Not in that – nor in the Leonardo. Poor Pomona would remain as lost as the story of Ted Parsons himself.

'I suppose I'd better break the news to Rosalind Chambers,' she said without enthusiasm.

'Leave it to your famous Paul,' Loretta watched her in some amusement. 'I suppose it *is* Ted Parsons you regret losing, not your little playmate Paul?'

'Don't be ridiculous.'

Loretta laughed.

'Are you sure he is dead?' the General asked briskly.

'As sure as a death certificate.'

'Ah.'

Gemma decided to come the very next day to break the news. She had notified Felix Potter and she didn't want him in contact with her grandfather before she had had the chance to break the news herself. It was cloudy, wet and depressing, and she had to work hard to throw off her dejection before seeing her grandfather. Not that he would be deceived.

'Do you mind?' she asked her grandfather bluntly. He was so long in answering she feared his answer.

'Mind?' he replied at last. 'Do you know, Gemma, rather to my surprise, I fear I do.'

'Why aren't you drinking, Maitland? You're with us, aren't you?'

With them, but when the chips were down, not of them. Time had proved him right, and that made it all the harder. Ted Parsons had been his means to win his passage back, and now it had been taken from him.

'Tell me, Grandpops, had you had the opportunity to

create the memorial, what would you have done?' She held her breath. Was she doing the right thing, by forcing him to think of this now when the chance was lost? For a moment he looked bleak, and she cursed herself for mentioning it.

'I'm not of today's world, Gemma. How could I bridge the gap between the generations? It needs someone younger than me, I fear. I represent what has passed. It needs someone else to extract its essence and combine it with the new. What do you see as the new?'

'Awareness of the individual, I suppose,' Gemma replied after consideration. Perhaps, after all, she had not been wrong to raise the issue. 'And that has been born of wars that you fought. Awareness of private pain and suffering, and the need for the struggle to overcome them.'

'So you would go along with Mr Shane's medical centre as a fitting memorial?'

'You know about that?'

'Indeed I do. There is a man with admirable determination, and it is in a good cause. It would be one way to a memorial.'

'But not what the Lakenham Set's choice would have been. Your choice.'

'I am more interested in what yours might have been, Gemma.'

'How can I know *now*?' she answered vehemently. 'All I know is that the Second Renaissance has not happened. There has been no explosion of creative vigour, so where lies the way to fulfil what they wanted?'

'In some directions it has, would you not agree? Strides in science, education, medicine—'

'Achieved on the foundations of what the Victorians

began. They had the vision and ideals. We merely built on them.'

'As the Renaissance artists did on Giotto. It could not spring fully matured from nothing, but that did not invalidate its strength.'

'That's true. If I'd had the chance, I suppose I would have wanted to mark the material achievements with the new values we've established. No longer the rich man in his castle, the poor man at his gate, but an awareness that both the rich man and the poor man are the same in human terms. There's still so far to go that any step towards ramming it home would be worth while. After all, the Renaissance reflected not an ideal, but what was actually going on at that time: the spiritual values, the material, the very confidence of Florence under the Medicis. A medical centre could not achieve that.

'On the other hand, would that have given me the right *not* to provide it in an age which is so utterly different from that of 1914? Paul wants to—' She broke off, realising she was talking to herself. Her grandfather's eyes had closed, and she was annoyed with herself for tiring him. It wasn't his problem, and thank goodness, it wasn't hers any longer. The fence she sat on was uncomfortable enough, but with the weight of responsibility on her shoulders it would have been unbearable. It might yet be Paul's – only he didn't view it as a problem. She envied him his single-mindedness.

Paul had not rung. She told herself she didn't mind. After all, he must be catching up after his absence, and they'd only been back three days. She debated whether to call him and decided against. She unlocked Waynings' front door, and then remembered with some annoyance that she was on call this evening. Perhaps no one would want to go anywhere. Some chance, on a hot summer's evening like this. Night-clubs, pubs, restaurants, late trains – oh, joy. There were some benefits to being an accountant.

Launcelot was prepared to be tolerant after a week's sojourn in kennels, and his cry was muted as he meekly followed her in. Home smelt wonderful; all it needed was a warm pie baking in the oven and security would be hers. She debated about going to the pub, and settled for a microwaved meal. In honour of Italy, chicken cacciatore seemed a good idea. So did a whisky – until she remembered she was on call.

There was a small pile of mail on the mat from the morning post, which she gradually worked her way through. One appeal, one acknowledgement, two 'you may already have wons' (it was Friday the thirteenth – they had to be joking), an electricity bill, a letter from a friend in New Zealand, one from Dundee (old friends of hers and Bill's), and one in an unknown hand. She began with this. The address was familiar, even if the writing wasn't. It proved to be Victoria Ireland's. Intrigued, she sat down to read it.

It was a request, almost a demand, for Gemma to visit. Her first impulse was to say no, but curiosity got the better of her. She would tell her of Ted's death, and see what reaction that brought forth.

Victoria Ireland already knew, it transpired when she telephoned her. 'Mr Drew told me,' the remote, tinkling voice informed her. 'He heard from Mrs Norman.'

And Mrs Norman must have heard from Mr Shane, thought Gemma crossly. Who hadn't bothered to ring Gemma.

'I'm sorry,' she told her sincerely.

A short silence. 'I would still like to see you, Miss Maitland.' It was a tone of voice Gemma was well used to from her grandfather. They-who-must-be-obeyed.

'You realise I have no standing in this now,' she told Victoria.

'Please come, Miss Maitland.'

Victoria Ireland looked ill, frailer than when Gemma had last seen her, and far shakier. Her face was pale, and shadows on it suggested pain; she walked with great care, stick in hand. 'No doubt you would like some tea.'

This was a ploy Gemma knew well, and she knew her cue. 'Let me get it, Miss Ireland.'

'Earl Grey, if you please.' Victoria coughed, and gave a disarmingly girlish grin. 'The doctor says I shouldn't smoke, but why not? It won't make any difference now. A year at the most, he thinks.'

'I'm very sorry, I had no idea.'

'Nor I,' Victoria said surprisingly, matter-of-factly. 'That's why I wanted to see you, however. It concentrates the mind wonderfully. Don't let this prevent you getting the tea,' she added.

Gemma jumped. She'd forgotten it in the enormity of Victoria's news. She returned shortly with a tray laid for tea, and when she returned with the teapot, Victoria was carefully rearranging the porcelain cups. Something in her arrangement had clearly displeased her hostess. 'Dear Noel liked them set just so,' she explained. 'It became a habit with me.'

'Noel?'

'Coward.' A note of asperity at Gemma's foolishness entered her voice.

'You do realise I have nothing to do with the tontine

now, save for an outsider's interest?'

'And Mr Shane.' Victoria lit a cigarette and puffed only slightly to the right of Gemma's face.

'Not even that.' She made her reply as pleasant as she could.

'Aren't you interested in Ted Parsons?'

'Not now he's dead.'

Victoria leaned over to stub out ash. 'What impression did you gain of Mr Parsons during your investigations?'

'I'm sorry, but does it really matter? I was working for my grandfather.'

'It matters very much, Miss Maitland. As dear Larry used to say, everything matters. It's a question of degree. Please humour me.'

It struck Gemma that life had perhaps humoured Miss Ireland rather too much. She doubted dear Larry had said anything of the sort. Certainly one of the many photographs prominently displayed showed a sylph-like Victoria with a steel-like arm clasping those of Laurence and Vivien Olivier possessively. Others, some wedding photographs – two of them hers apparently – displayed a smiling, beautiful Victoria, with the same bony, though younger arm, now thrust through that of a nervous-looking bridegroom. All other photos were professional career photos. Nothing from her early life. Understandably, Gemma supposed; Victoria might well wish to forget her orphanage upbringing. Today it could be a publicity bonus, but in the era that Victoria belonged to, it would hardly have been that.

'You have talked to all of us, and to others who knew him,' Victoria persisted. 'What impression do you have?'

'A clever man, out for himself. No feelings for others, save when his own interests weren't involved. Streetwise,

I suppose you could call him. How would *you* describe him, Miss Ireland?' Two could play at this game.

Victoria made play with the sugar-tongs before replying. 'I regret I misled you on your earlier visit, for reasons I will not go into. I'm prepared now to talk about him. I do recall him very well. I *liked* Ted.' There was a note of defiance in her voice, as if she expected Gemma to contradict her. 'He was funny, amusing, quicksilver, like me.' Complacency entered her voice. 'I liked him very much.'

'Then I'm sorry.' Gemma restrained herself from showing the annoyance she felt.

'What about?'

'That you've had the news he's died.'

'It might not be entirely bad news,' Victoria pointed out practically. 'It brings me nearer three-quarters of a million pounds – though I doubt if I shall live to see it,' she added. 'And after all, I haven't seen Ted for decades. There was no *amitié amoureuse*.'

'Nevertheless, his death—'

'Are you so sure of that?' Victoria nervously interrupted her.

'But the death certificate is quite clear.' Gemma was nonplussed.

'Now I want you to promise, Miss Maitland, that you won't talk to *anyone* about this.'

'Very well,' Gemma said soothingly, seeing her agitated face.

'I don't think he *is* dead!' Victoria glanced at Gemma to see how she was taking this startling statement. 'He *was* streetwise. It would be just like Ted to fake his own death if he wanted to escape something or someone.'

Something or someone? Because of the lost Leonardo?

But it was ridiculous, wasn't it? How could he have faked a death certificate? Yet somewhere deep inside her a voice was calmly saying, 'Of course he could.' So it might not be the end. A rush of emotions, a certain excitement, a fear, leapt and clawed at her stomach, but then slipped back into cautious curiosity as reason reasserted itself.

'You've no other cause to think he could still be alive, Miss Ireland, than that you don't think Ted was the type to die. Is that it?'

Victoria stared coolly at her. 'Yes.'

'That's not enough.'

'And something he once said to me,' Victoria added quickly. 'I met him after the war. I was in a second-hand shop in Chelsea when he came in. We had a drink together afterwards. He was dressed like a spiv,' she said distastefully, 'but boasted he was doing well for himself. I told him to be careful if he was up to anything crooked. He said, "Even if you hear I'm in the last box, Vicky, don't believe a word of it. It'll take the archangel Gabriel to come down in person to drag me up there, and that won't be till the last trump." '

'All talk,' said Gemma.

'Perhaps. When did he die, Miss Maitland, according to this certificate?'

'Nineteen-fifty-seven.'

'Was he in trouble?'

'Perhaps,' Gemma admitted.

'Well then.' Victoria sat back in triumph.

'You have no clue to his whereabouts if you think he's alive?'

'That's your task, not mine.'

'Why are you telling me this, Miss Ireland?'

'Because I liked Ted,' she repeated petulantly.

There was an airiness about this that Gemma did not like. 'There's some other reason, isn't there?'

'I want you to go on looking for him,' was Victoria's oblique answer.

'I can't do that, unfortunately.'

'*Can't*? You say you can't to a woman like *me*?' Victoria was all enraged diva. 'Here am I, eighty, still working, twelve months to live if the doctor is correct, three husbands, survivor of blitzes, wars, bombs, carver of a brilliant career from nothing . . . Ours was the generation of *can*, Miss Maitland. Yours is apparently that of *can't*.'

Gemma held her own. 'Tell me why you really want to find him and I'll consider it. After all, with Ted Parsons dead you stand to gain money much more quickly.'

'With him dead, Miss Maitland, I may be closer to money, but if he is alive, my life, such as it is, would be safer.' Her voice dropped to a whisper, and there was undoubtedly fear in it. 'I may have a year, I may have longer, but I prefer to live it.'

'What on earth do you mean?'

'There are three nominees left, Miss Maitland. Myself, Mrs Norman, Mr Drew.'

'And?'

'We only knew about this money a few weeks ago. There were four of us then. Now John Peacock's dead, isn't he?'

Chapter Six

John Peacock's dead . . . The words echoed round and round in Gemma's head as she returned home to Bishopslee. His death had to be coincidence, didn't it? He was eighty, after all. Paul had said the inquest recorded it as accidental, and Charles Lakenham, for one, would have smelled a rat if there were the slightest whiff of anything odd. She would ask him. She'd pander to Victoria thus far at any rate.

Then the unpleasant thought struck her that John Peacock was a rival nominee, so far as Charles was concerned. If anyone raised suspicions, it ought to be John Peacock's own sponsor, not Victoria Ireland's. Yes, but John Peacock was a former employee of Charles's and his son still was. Purely humanitarian grounds should drive Charles, conscientious as he was, to investigate any suspicious circumstances. Even so, Felix Potter pranced into her mind with breezy smile and gaudy tie. 'Around fifteen million, Miss Maitland . . .'

Impatient with herself, she slid into her car at Charing to drive the few miles to Waynings. But the million-pound signs had not vanished by the time she had locked the car in the garage. 'Or in the night, imagining some fear,/How easy is a bush supposed a bear!' All around her were many bushes and, try as she might to resist, her footsteps quickened as she passed them. Inside she relaxed as the familiar and the rational greeted her. Charles Lakenham – even supposing for one moment that that laid-back exterior hid a murderous disposition – would logically be the last person to have had evil intent towards Peacock now. Charles had known about the tontine for fifteen years or so. He had had all the time in the world to nobble the opposition quietly. After all, it was the Lakenhams who had brought John Peacock into their employ in the first place. They must have known who he was.

Why bring him? Because he was a rival nominee, was the instant reply thrown out by her brain. Nonsense. Much better to guard their own candidate. Finally she laughed. 'You are ridiculous,' she told Launcelot firmly. 'Quite ridiculous.' Launcelot yowled crossly in protest – or perhaps because he was hungry.

Nevertheless she would ring Paul and ask him more about John Peacock's death. No, that was an escape route. She'd settle it herself. Gemma glanced at the answering machine, with its bland figure '1' displayed, and resisted the temptation to play it back right away. Tomorrow would do, even if Paul had called. Tonight she had other matters to think over – primarily Ted Parsons. Tomorrow the very idea of returning to Florence would seem crazy, she tried to tell herself, and yet that was where this restlessness inside her was ordering her to go. Wasn't she mad even to consider it, she asked herself, merely on the strength of an elderly woman's hunch, a sick woman with a bee in her elegant bonnet?

Look at the facts before you settle strategy, she told herself, *then* consult instinct. It was as good a method as

160

any, and she settled herself down with a glass of wine to study those facts. Number one: there was a death certificate stating that one Ted Parsons of unknown parentage had died of lung cancer in 1957. Two: Ted Parsons had been variously described to her as streetwise and a weedy scrap. He'd had several years in a PoW camp and several more years rushing round Europe and London in a somewhat murky underworld. Neither would have done his constitution much good. Three: she had seen the grave. Number two was circumstantial, one and three were not. Against these could be set only one fact: Ted Parsons was a forger. But add to that her grandfather's instinct, seldom wrong, and Victoria's conviction – and Gemma's own obstinacy.

It was the last factor tilted the balance. If she didn't follow this up, somehow she might always feel she'd let her grandfather down, that just perhaps there was a factor she'd overlooked – and, worst of all, that her own unwillingness to take responsibility for the Lakenham Memorial was the reason. Moreover, somewhere an elusive Ted Parsons might have got the better of her; a grinning face already seemed to mock her. Return to Florence? Why not telephone, write, make inquiries here? Gemma knew the answer to that one. She would get nowhere save by seizing the bull by the horns, and the bull was called Papa Orvino.

Only two questions left to ask herself now. Should she tell her grandfather what was happening – and should she tell Paul? The first was the simpler to answer. No. She was following a whim that would most probably end in a second disappointment, so great were the odds against success. Better to wait until there was a definite sign that he might be alive. That meant she had to go quickly. As for the second – in Paul's place, she would be furious at being left out. Paul had consulted her at all points. On the other hand, she had promised Victoria Ireland to say nothing to anyone, and though she could avoid raising her grandfather's suspicions, Paul was a different matter. She reminded her pricking conscience that he hadn't rung her – unless he were recorded on the answering machine. Suppose she just left it on until she returned?

Fifteen minutes later the telephone rang in the middle of cooking her omelette. She fought the instinct to answer it. She let it ring, until modern technology settled it for her. The prompt click told her no message had been left. The omelette tasted like stolen nectar.

Gemma arrived in Florence, hot, cross and convinced she had made a vast mistake. There had been no room on the direct flights to Florence, and she had been forced to take a scheduled flight to Pisa entailing a hot train journey; only the fact that she had been able to book into the same hotel comforted her. She sat in the taxi, quite sure, faced with the reality of the same hot, crowded city, that she was on a wild-goose chase, and glad at not having confided in Paul. She had a notion that Paul rarely followed hunches, and might think the less of anyone who did. He had left a message on the answering machine – to apologise for his silence, on account of pressure of work, and to say he'd be in touch. Big deal, she'd thought, rather sourly.

'*Scusi, signora.*'

An admiring glance from an Italian who swerved to avoid her as she got out of the taxi did her no harm at all. Nor did a change of clothes and a cold beer. She emerged into the city refreshed and heartened. The air at home already held a hint of autumn in it, and it was satisfying to find that late August in Florence was still high summer.

It had its effect on her. Her pleasant refusal to be deterred eventually won from the son a grudging agreement to her seeing Papa once more, on the following morning, though he certainly regretted ever having been helpful in the first place. True, she had resorted to what might be termed extreme methods. She was in no hurry, she had intimated. She would wait until Papa's siesta, dinner, visit to Aunt Elisabetta, etc, were concluded. She banked on the fact that (a) no Italian could resist a pleading woman for very long and (b) any Italian would assume he would be able to get rid of the said woman without trouble. She had declared she could return at a specific time of their choosing, or she would be only too pleased to wait right now.

The murmur of voices had told her what she wanted to know. The discussion was going on far too long for there to be nothing worthy of discussion. She had the happiest feeling that her foot had hit the right path at last. It might be a dead end, but at least it was going somewhere.

'*Buongiorno, signore*,' she greeted him, as she was shown up to Papa's rooms on the Tuesday morning.

'Signora.' He took an unusually long time bowing over her hand. Playing for time, while summing up the opposition, she thought, amused in her excitement.

'Forgive my returning, but it occurred to me that—'

He interrupted her, shrugging apologetically. '*Mi scusi*, more slow, signora. I no understand English well.'

'French?'

'No.'

He didn't seem to have quite so much difficulty last time, she noted, although it was true she'd had Paul's services as translator on that occasion. She began again slowly.

'*Signor e Signora Lorcino, amici?*'

'*Sì.*' A discernible wariness, as though she had taken him by surprise.

'*Nozze* – you were *testimone*, best man?'

'*Sì.*' Surprise now.

'The man I seek, Ted Parsons, was also there. Do you not remember him?'

'No.' The shutter had come down in his face as over a camera lens at the name. Yet she was sure she was getting somewhere. How to get further was the problem. One last hope.

'It is in Signor Parsons' interests that I seek him. *Per il suo profitto.*' Her dictionary had rendered sterling value.

'No.'

Not enough, it seemed. '*Io non nemico.*' She wasn't an enemy, she tried to convey. '*Amico.*' She struck her chest, feeling as if she was taking part in grand opera. Her effort brought forth a flow of Italian directed at son Mario as much as her, from which she gathered the implication that that was roughly what the Mafia would say too.

'He do not know, signora.' Mario stood behind, protectively, almost aggressively now, she thought. They waited, watching her for her next move. Frustrated she remained sitting, and somehow must have conveyed they would have to throw her out bodily. Papa spoke again to his son, rapidly and at length. Mario eventually nodded. '*Domani,*' he said to her on Papa's behalf. '*Domani sera, signora.* My father will have interpreter. He wishes to know more.'

A way of getting her out of the house, a hope of

steering *profitto* in the direction of *numero uno*, or a tiny light at the end of the tunnel? Only at the very back of her mind was the warning that the path to Ted Parsons – if there was one – might lie through dangerous country. And she ignored it.

By the following evening she had art coming out of one ear and pasta out of the other. Both left her reeling with overdose, both were impossible to avoid in Florence. Determined to fill every moment, and not dwell on Ted Parsons, she had unwisely taken on a visit both to the Pitti Palace and the Palazzo Vecchio, not to mention two of the churches on the south side of the Arno. From the surfeit of riches thrust upon her during the day, two images stood out: one of Michelangelo, both in sculpture and paint, towering over his contemporaries in vigour, boldness and perspective, inside the very soul of man; the other another portrait of the man who made it possible, the patron, Lorenzo de' Medici. How could a man so ugly manage to look so magnetic? What was it within him that drove him on to represent so consummately both aspects of the age: unstoppable, ruthless ambition, which expressed itself in pitting man against man, country against country in war; and side by side with that the superlative glory of man's ultimate achievement expressed in art? And *that* brought her back to the Lakenham Set memorial. Which promptly returned her to the disagreeable thought of Ted Parsons.

She was glad she was alone, without Paul. She was best alone. Once she had been best with Bill, but that was another life. If there was to be a best with Paul, she still had to find the way, for Paul was indivisible from the Lakenham tontine in her mind – and the Lakenham Memorial. If Ted Parsons were still alive, the problem could well be dumped right back at her door.

What would Bill have chosen to do about the memorial? She sat for a moment and tried to think, but she had denied his memory too long. Painfully she forced herself to acknowledge the truth that she did not know what route he would have chosen. She was alone, by her own choice, yet more desolate than at any time in the last eight long years.

Papa had just finished his supper. Antonia, Mario's wife, was clearing his dishes away as Mario ushered Gemma in. Somewhat to her surprise, both of them were in jovial mood, which might owe something to the bottles of full-bodied red Montalbano lined up on the dresser. Mario made great ceremony of ushering her to a seat, underneath the reproduction of Leonardo's *Annunciation* – fittingly enough. In Florence art was everywhere, whether it was original or reproduction mattered not to the average Florentine. It was part of their daily life, not a heritage from the past to be locked away unloved. It was a way of life that her image of Ted Parsons as a cheap crook did not fit.

'*Buonasera*, Roberto.'

Gemma jumped at the unexpected, deep voice from behind her, and turned round as Antonia ushered in the newcomer. She supposed she should have known. It was inevitable they should meet. It was the man in the business-class queue at Stansted, Lorenzo de' Medici's look-alike, the 'ugly brute' of Paul's casual comment. It was the man who had stood in the shade of the cypress tree. He was a large man, perhaps in his mid-thirties, filling the doorway, evaporating the mood of bonhomie and replacing it with chill. Or was that her imagination?

Perhaps it was, for her hosts were greeting him cordially. As for her, she could only stare at him as if hypnotised. He glanced at her; an eyebrow raised itself slightly. There was no smile on his face of polite welcome, merely a nod acknowledging a stranger's presence before he greeted Papa and Mario. Then at last he turned to her.

'I'm John Piacenta, signora.' For all the Italian name he was undoubtedly British. 'Signor Orvino's interpreter. And you are—'

'Gemma Maitland.'

His handshake was firm, uncompromising. She had the instant impression he liked her little more than she did him. No, *liking* wasn't at stake. He was remote – he was *judging* her, she realised. But on what? And why? She countered that by plunging in: 'Have we met before?'

'I don't think so.' At least she was spared any guff like, 'I would have remembered . . .'

'You live in Florence?' she asked.

'I come here frequently. I have a flat near the Pitti Palace.'

'You're fortunate.'

He did not bother to answer her platitude, to her indignation. If she was making an effort, why should not he? It occurred to her only afterwards that there was no reason that any effort should have been involved.

'Ugly brute', Paul had said, yet in this man's case that was only part of it. His face was arresting, and attractive by some standards, and she guessed women might well flock round him. He wasn't her type, but close up the resemblance to Lorenzo still remained valid. It commanded attention without conscious effort to dominate. A man to be wary of.

'Begin, Miss Maitland.' He sat down as casually as

though he, not Orvino, was giving the audience.

'About what?'

'I've no idea,' he pointed out mildly.

Gemma kept her voice calm. Losing control of her temper would achieve nothing. 'I've tried to explain to Signor Orvino that I'm searching for a man called Ted Parsons who disappeared in the early 1950s from London. I believe he came to Florence.'

Piacenta seemed about to say something, then, as if recalling he was not a principal in this affair, related what she had said to Papa. Papa replied, and Piacenta turned back to her. 'Why did you think that?'

'I've been told he was involved in a fraud. A big one.'

'What sort of fraud?'

'Concerning works of art after the Second World War, but I can't tell you any more. I don't even know if that information is correct.'

'Why do you believe he came to Florence?'

'Where else to profit by the fraud?'

'How can Signor Orvino help? He does not know the man.'

Now she had him. He would not have invited her back if that were the case. Everything depended on how she played the next card. 'I *know* he has at least met him, even if he does not remember him.'

A pause this time. Then: 'Tell him what the fraud is.'

'I can't,' she repeated. 'There are people still around in London who want to know where he is.'

'Is it likely that your Mr Parsons would want them to know?'

'Naturally not. But *I* am not one of them.'

He looked at her pityingly, it seemed to her, enraging her. 'How can Signor Orvino know that?'

'Why should it matter if he does not know him?' she countered sweetly.

A long conversation this time between them, and finally Gemma grew impatient. 'What are you talking of, please?'

'It is possible that Signor Orvino might be able to find out more about this man, though if it is the man he is thinking of, he is dead.'

'I do not believe that. I believe Ted Parsons is alive.'

Another silence, then Piacenta said: 'May I speak with my own voice, Miss Maitland?'

Gemma nodded.

'You and Signor Orvino seemed to be engaged in some kind of chess, prowling round the board, looking for an opening. One of you must make a move. I think if you examine the facts it has to be you.'

'How can I trust—'

'Avoid the word trust, Miss Maitland. It is not relevant. Moving the game forward is.'

'Then explain your role. Are you pawn, knight or umpire?'

'Umpire.'

'How chosen?'

This annoyed him. 'I am a friend of Signor Orvino's. What else?'

'Then why were you at the cemetery, watching me at Ted Parsons' grave?'

'You're speaking in riddles, Miss Maitland. If you agree Ted Parsons is dead, why are you wasting our time?'

He had made a mistake using emotional words like 'wasting our time'. She had a hunch this meant she still had a hold on the situation – tenuous, but there.

'Because I don't believe my Ted Parsons is in that grave.'

'You take a lot of convincing.'

'Why were you there?' she demanded again.

'Are you sure it was me?'

'You were in Florence at the time. I saw you at Stansted airport.'

Now it was she putting a foot wrong, and she was aware of it as soon as she had spoken. So was he.

'There's no rule against that.' The subtone of his voice said: I seem to have made an impression on you. Control had been handed back to him and he seized it. 'Let me explain myself, Miss Maitland, if you are hesitating to say more simply because of me for some inexplicable reason. My private interests involve military art; there are splendid examples in Florence. Signor Orvino has become a friend of mine through that interest. He is an expert on Vasari, whose splendid battle scenes you have no doubt admired as a tourist in the Hall of the Five Hundred. That is all there is to the deep mystery of myself. I'm not old enough to be one of your potential assassins from the fifties, nor young enough to be their hit-man. I am far too concerned for my own skin. Your Mr Ted Parsons may rest at ease in his grave.'

'I believe it to be an empty one,' Gemma replied obstinately, realising she was fast losing this battle. He was a dab hand at military tactics himself. 'Strange things have been happening, and when money is involved they tend to be murky.'

'I suggest you move on to the board, Miss Maitland?' Or leave, added Piacenta's subtone.

She had nothing to lose. This, after all, was fact. She'd move out into the open. 'I've nothing to do with the art

170

world. My grandfather, Signor Orvino, is General Reginald Maitland, who won a Victoria Cross in the First World War. He is still alive, and I'm carrying out a job for him in looking for Mr Parsons. A merchant bank in London wants to know where Mr Parsons is, since he might come into some money.'

'Might?' queried Piacenta.

'If Ted Parsons survives longer than three other people. But the money has to go to *him* and not his heirs. So it is essential to find him alive.'

This was relayed (so far as she could tell) to Papa, then Piacenta turned to her again. 'Signor Orvino regrets to tell you Mr Parsons is indeed dead. He did know him. He was a crook, but Signor Orvino liked him and did not wish to give information away unnecessarily to strangers.'

'Please tell him I still do not believe he is dead. I believe, of course, Signor Orvino may think so.' Like hell she did, but if that doesn't checkmate them, nothing will, she thought with some satisfaction.

Another discussion between the two men.

'Signor Orvino asks which bank in London?'

'Taylor Whittam.' So the checkmate was working. She continued as offhandedly as she could. 'The trustee is Mr Felix Potter, and the reference is the Lakenham tontine.'

The waiting was agonising, the answer when it came deflating.

'Mr Parsons is dead. Signor Orvino regrets he cannot help you, but invites you to a glass of an excellent Chianti Classico.'

The compensation – or the booby prize?

When at last Gemma left, she was dazed with the combined effects of concentration, disappointment and red wine. Three glasses had been the least she could get away with, while the men talked mostly in Italian with a polite minimum in English. She couldn't fault Piacenta's manners, but why did she feel so strongly that the dominant role in the evening had been his, not Papa's?

'Where are you staying?' She found Piacenta suddenly at her side, having come up behind her. 'I'll see you back.'

'I'm perfectly all right, thank you.'

'I'll see you back,' he repeated.

She sighed. 'I appreciate your offer, Mr Piacenta, but I'm a taxi-driver. If I can handle drunks at late-night clubs, I can handle Italian muggers.'

'I'll see you safely back to your hotel.' Once again he'd turned the tables, damn him – and of course he was right.

She calmed down. 'I apologise. I didn't mean to go butch on you.'

A shrug, that might have been amusement or indifference. Perhaps to make a point, perhaps to rile her, he took her arm as they crossed the street. 'Where are you staying?'

'In the Via Porta Rossa.' She wondered if this were a ploy to ask her out for a drink or invite himself in. She dismissed the thought. Not this man. He talked casually of the glories of Florence, asked her reactions and interests, nothing personal. She couldn't fault him. No ploy this. By the time she had passed through the glass doors of the hotel and turned to bid him goodnight, he had already left.

Or so she thought.

Gemma collapsed on her bed and tried to sum up the evening's achievements. It was simply done. Nothing. And yet there had been something there, she could

172

swear. All that trouble to answer a stranger's simple question? Her thoughts were interrupted by a knock on the door. Hotel staff? John Piacenta? Surely he wouldn't have the nerve to come back and up here?

She opened the door a crack, ready to slam it shut. But she didn't have to. 'Paul!'

She froze with horror, combined with shock. This was a Paul she'd never seen before. Furious wasn't in it. 'Can I come in,' he demanded grimly, 'or do you want to fight downstairs?'

She opened the door wider, taken aback. He came down, sat down in an armchair, and she warily perched herself on the bed.

'What,' she asked carefully, 'are you doing here?'

'My very question to you. Only it wasn't going to be so politely worded. How the hell do you think I felt when I rang your office only to be fobbed off by some dame called Loretta that you were out on a job, away on a job, and finally, *finally*, discovered the job in question was in Florence. Just what the blazes is going on, Gemma? Don't you think I have a right to know? If it's to do with the tontine, we had a pact, remember? And if it's not, common courtesy should have made you ring me to tell me you were coming back here.'

'I needed to follow this up alone,' she told him coldly. 'And we didn't have a pact. We carried out some investigations together, that's all.'

'And we'll go on doing them together too – whatever they are.'

'Will we indeed?' she asked dangerously.

'We will. Gemma, you don't know what you could be getting into.'

'And you do? How? What?'

'I don't know,' he replied calmly. 'All I suggest is that where large sums of money are involved, all one's antennae should be up and working. You seem to have folded yours down out of action.'

'Very cryptic.'

'Gemma.' He came and sat next to her, conciliatorily. 'I was worried sick when I arrived at the hotel and they said you'd booked in but were out. I've toured every trattoria in town. I thought something had happened to you, and that I wouldn't like. One little bit.'

'I'm all right, Paul. Why does everyone think I'm a fragile little woman suddenly? I'm thirty-seven, an experienced traveller and my antennae, as you term them, are in perfect working order. I'm hardly a damsel in distress, and quite what danger you have in mind, I haven't the slightest idea.' She knew she was being unreasonable and that it was guilt at her own behaviour caused it. But it was out now, and the zones of darkness that lay still uninvestigated in this case were going to remain her secret.

'Tell me why you came back, Gemma,' Paul demanded quietly.

'I can't.'

'You don't trust me, is that it?'

Trust? She thought of John Piacenta's words. Moving the game forward was important, and only she could do that at the moment. 'It isn't a question of trust, but of a promise to someone else.'

'Eliminating any desire to have a holiday in the art galleries, the only reason you might have come back is that you've got a clue as to where the Leonardo is.'

'The Leonardo?' Gemma, completely taken aback, was almost inclined to laugh. 'You must think me very mercenary,' she finally answered lightly.

'Not at all. If that's it, I assume you have plans to track it down, flog it and set up your blessed Lakenham Memorial, now that Parsons is dead.'

She had misjudged him. 'Something like that.'

'Armistice?'

'Yes. No unconditional surrender, though. And certainly not that sort,' she added quickly, as he put his arm round her.

'You forever misjudge me,' he said in mock hurt. 'We'll both know when it's the right time – and I see from your face it isn't now. You're probably right. We're both far too prickly, more's the pity. So when do you intend to tell me what's up, and how long we're going to stay here?'

She overlooked the 'we' in the spirit of armistice. 'A couple of days perhaps. I don't know yet. I'm in limbo, thinking my way through.'

'In that case we'd better spend tomorrow with heaven and hell in the form of Church art, don't you agree? Or do you have other plans?'

She hesitated, then gave in. What more could she do, after all? She could try to track down the couple whose wedding Ted Parsons had attended all those years ago, but was there any point? Orvino had been their best man – he would be in touch with them long before she if there was a secret attached to Ted Parsons' death.

'Agreed.'

It happened in the huge basilica of San Lorenzo. She was absorbed in the magnificent Bronzino fresco of the *Martyrdom of St Laurence*, when she realised the man in the grubby raincoat like a down-at-heel Columbo was standing remarkably close to her. As she moved away towards the columns of the awe-inspiring nave, he followed her. Only his mournful, anxious expression made her realise this was not the normal attempted pick-up.

'*Scusi.*' At that automatically she began looking for spare change.

He waved it aside, to her surprise. 'Signora, come please.'

'Where?' she asked sharply.

'Signor Parsons.'

'*What*?'

'Come.' Nervously he plucked at her sleeve, glancing round him as though assassins lurked behind every Michelangelo pillar. Further up the aisle she could see Paul disappearing towards the sacristy. Should she rush after him?

'Only you,' Columbo ordered, as if following her thoughts. So he must have been following them from the hotel, waiting to catch her alone. And that meant John Piacenta's intentions were rather more than chivalrous in accompanying her home last night.

Should she go with this unprepossessing man? How could she exclude Paul again? How could she *not*? She knew she had no choice: Paul or no Paul, danger or no danger, trap or no trap, any clue to Ted Parsons had to be followed up immediately. This was too close in time to her visit to Orvino not to have some connection. Her mind made up, she followed the man as he quickly hurried through the main entrance, out into the burning sunshine of midday Florence.

All around her was the normal Florence scene, the stalls of the leather market, tourists everywhere, beggars, shops open for business. Perfectly normal. Yet the man seemed frightened; or was it the air of one who lived in fear, rather than fearful of some imminent danger?

'Where are we going?' It was an inane question, meant more to keep in contact than as a serious request. 'You are Ted Parsons?' she asked suddenly when he did not reply.

No, how could he be? He was far too young, fifty, sixty maybe, not eighty, that was for sure. He was walking too nimbly for a start. Was she being foolhardy in following this stranger? Maybe, but the opportunity had to be seized. He pushed his way through the crowds of the leather market, and a mob of tourists surging towards the Medici chapel. The smell of leather assailed her nostrils, the noise of shouting stallholders and tourists screaming over the hubbub did the same to her ears, and she was glad when he turned down a side street. He didn't look at her, scurried along, eyes on ground, as if to dissuade her from talking.

At last he stopped at a door so anonymous-looking she would not have noticed it; old, and with faded, peeling paint, it was securely locked. Suppressing a slight qualm, she followed him in, and found herself in a high covered passageway between two houses, dark since its far end was blocked by a wall two storeys high. They seemed to be marching straight for it, but almost at the end, he unlocked a door on the right, and disappeared inside.

Did Ted Parsons live here? A sudden leap of excitement surged through her, but as soon as she entered she realised this floor at least was uninhabited, save by mice. A clutter of old frames suggested it might once have been a shop, a cobwebbed broken armchair and an ancient stove that it might have been a home. Puzzled, it occurred to her Ted might live upstairs, but her guide went straight through to a door at the rear. Unhesitating

now, she followed. He was obviously heading somewhere, and if she was going to get biffed on the head or
jumped on, now was the time; she braced herself to react
quickly. Nothing happened. The man looked nervously
behind him every so often, either to ensure she was still
with him, or in fear of the hounds of hell at his heels. At
the back entrance there was a lengthy procedure to deal
with double locks and padlock and chain, while she
waited impatiently, until the door swung open – inwards.
Eagerly she went through and immediately was pulled up
short. What had she expected? Whatever it was, it wasn't
this.

There was nothing but an apparently impregnable high
brick wall, a foot away from the door. No wonder the
shop was so dark. There was no entrance in the walls,
nothing, only the glimpse of a tree peeping above the
walls that surrounded this secret garden.

This is ridiculous, she thought wildly, as, urged on by
her guide, she found herself squeezing, half sideways,
along a gap perhaps a foot wide to the far end of the wall,
and up the next side, which looked equally devoid of
entrance. Or was it? He stopped at what looked like part
of the wall, but proved to be a door so cunningly painted
it seemed part of the brickwork. There was not even an
obvious keyhole, but such a fortress as this undoubtedly
had a means of making itself secure. The door swung
open, and impatiently he beckoned her in, glancing to left
and right along the path as though even now they were
under scrutiny.

She found herself in a small garden, boasting nothing
much to the English eye, accustomed to riots of flowers,
even in September. But this garden was carefully tended,
with a small cypress, a large orange tree, and neat

pathways. In one corner there were growing plants – basil? In contrast, at the far end of the garden, a sprawling vine grew as and where it wished, bunches of ripening grapes hanging in profusion. But no door was visible. High above her to one side she could see the vast domes of San Lorenzo, and wondered just where they were, half annoyed, half intrigued at finding herself locked in.

Her guide, with no thoughts of imminent assault in mind, hurried to the vine. As he swept the tendrils aside, she saw that the wall it covered was in fact the wall of a house with a portico of pillars with peeling paint. It was shabby indeed, a contrast to the neat, cultivated garden. Inside the front door, as he pushed it open, lay nothing but darkness and decay, and her nostrils recoiled from the smell of deserted house.

No hope of finding Ted Parsons ensconced in a leather armchair perusing *The Times*. Here she saw nothing but a crumbling house, as they entered one deserted room after another, with peeling paint and bare, rotten floorboards. To one side a staircase went up, which looked rickety and rotten beyond belief. This for the first time frightened her. Where the hell was she? Was Orvino planning to murder her in this hidden ruin? Had she gone one step too far with him? Her body might never be found. Suddenly gripped by sheer terror, she turned to rush out of this house, but the man, grasping her intention and moving quickly to her, grasped her arm firmly.

'Follow, *per favore*.' His intention was clear enough. *She had to go up that staircase after him*. Every step was taking her further into the unknown. Where was Paul? What was the use of worrying about that now? She took hold of herself. This man might be armed. If so, she didn't stand a chance of escape whether she stayed or tried to make a run for it. If he wasn't armed, she stood a fair chance of holding her own either way – whatever lay up there. Gingerly she began to follow him up the stairs. To her surprise, it was not as rickety as it appeared. Only the balustrade gave to her touch. The steps looked in bad repair but were solid. Intrigued, she saw they were not of wood at all, but marble once painted to look like wood, though the paint was chipped and cracked giving a false impression. The curved flight led to a landing which led back along the length of the entrance hall with rooms opening off. There the landing was genuinely crumbling, some floorboards had even given way. But she was not being asked to negotiate this. Instead her guide unlocked a narrow door on the left at the top of the stairs, so dark, so unobtrusive, she had not seen its presence.

She stepped in after him, and found herself in what seemed to be another entrance hall, still shabby, but not in such bad repair. Wood floors, shabby ancient furniture and pictures, and an old tapestry on the far wall. In its way it might still be a home, even lived in after a fashion, judging by the ticking longcase clock. From its high ceiling and the massive outside wall, this could have been part of one of the old Florentine *palazzi* built by the rich nobles of medieval Florence to suggest to their enemies that keeping out might be a good plan. But who would build such a fortress here and, more to the point, who lived in it now tucked away from the outside world? Hope surged up once more.

Her guide led the way through to another room, then another, unlocking doors as he went. Each was equally palatial in space and equally poorly furnished, barren of atmosphere. In the fourth, larger than the others, he stopped, and took off his raincoat to reveal a suit that had long seen better days. What now, she thought warily?

He threw out his chest and prepared to speak. '*Io* Ted Parsons.' He pointed proudly at his chest.

He had to be joking. 'You? You are too young,' she told him firmly. 'I don't believe you. Where *is* he?' For he must know, he *must*.

'I *am* old. *Io* Ted Parsons. What you want with me?'

Fear fled and anger replaced it. This was some trick of Signor Orvino's. No, that wasn't right. This was some trick of Ted Parsons, the serving maid dressed in the mistress's garb. At last she was near, and desperation made her bold. 'Where *is* he?' she shouted.

There was fear everywhere here, except in her. The place smelled of it, it came from him, it came from the house itself, and it must come from Ted Parsons.

'*Io* Ted Parsons,' he screamed out.

She ignored him, thinking furiously. There was no exit from the room save the one they had entered by. Her eyes ran quickly round. Or was there? Had he used the same trick as outside? All these rooms were on a line. Suppose there were another beyond this. Upstairs – another floor? They had passed a staircase – should she go back and make a dash for that? Or risk her hunch, that hidden behind the tapestry in that far wall was a door through?

She began to speak to him normally, as though accepting he was indeed Ted Parsons, strolled to the window, then, as he came towards her, tripped him up heavily and sprinted for the far wall, ignoring shrieks of pain and fury. Fingers scrabbling at tapestry, panelling, paintwork, desperately seeking – and at last finding. With retribution now hurtling towards her, the fear of what might lie ahead was forgotten, as the door swung open and she catapulted into – nothing. Yet another empty chamber. Empty of human life, that is, but not of everything. There were old tapestries on all the walls, ancient armchairs huddled companiably together, a large oak table, and dining chairs.

She tried to lean against the door to stop her pursuer, but his fear lent him strength and she was being pushed forward. Into what? She pushed hard back against the door, then sprang away from it, so hard that it gave suddenly, sending him stumbling in off-balance.

Seconds to act. Where? How? Forward surely. On to the chessboard. This time there *was* a door, innocent and gleaming white beside the tapestry next to it on the shabby wall opposite. What lay beyond? The door lured her. She would open it, her Pandora's box. But inside? The man regained his feet, screaming at her, fear in his face. Fear? Why? Of her? Nonsense. What then? *Of what lay behind that door?* She rushed at it, turned that gleaming gilt handle, pushed the door violently and stumbled inside.

Blazing colour, light, and painted figures everywhere, walls alive with colour and people. A church? A Sistine chapel? A rounded dome in painted ceilings? Something screamed in her head 'mine eyes dazzle'. Impressions were all she had time for, for her pursuer was clutching at her now. And then she saw, even while she fought him off. There was a throne, and on it sat a man. A man? No, a person, a thing, who screamed out in terror even as his servant fell into silence. Cried out: '*What do you want with me?*'

It was a peacock, a doll, a clown, dressed in white satin, face painted white in a grotesque mask – his painted lips screamed out again as his hands with the long, long fingernails clutched terrified at the arms of his throne.

'*What do you want?*'

No choice now. Repelled, fascinated, terrified – she had no time even to register these emotions as, throwing off her pursuer, she rushed up to him. To it. Now she knew. Oh yes, she knew all right. 'You are Ted Parsons.'

He screamed out in fear, cowering away from her. 'Get away from me. Take her away, Giovanni.' He leapt from his throne, crouching behind it, trapped in the space between the throne and the painted wall behind him.

Giovanni was quiet now, poised, waiting for her to move. She advanced to her prey, standing above him, forcing herself to look down on him. He was like an animal shivering with fear. She had found Ted Parsons at last – and he was a madman.

'You are Ted Parsons,' she hurled at him again.

'I am *not*.' For a moment those eyes were rational, before he screeched out suddenly, holding up his arms before his face. 'Giovanni, *aiuto! Per favore.*'

She backed away, and he gained courage. Cautiously he stood up, walked round to his throne, touching it for reassurance. Then he threw his arms wide, encompassing all the proud glories of his own private Renaissance. 'I – ' He glared at her with glittering eyes of hatred – 'I am *Tositi*!'

Gemma walked away as if in disgust at his absurd claim. Giovanni – his servant? – pulled her away even further. '*Io* Ted Parsons,' he gabbled. 'Tell me, tell me, what you have come for.'

Tositi sat down on his throne again, a certain complacency now all seemed settled, picking dirt from the white satin. He did not speak, but smiled happily to himself.

Gemma firmly addressed the white mask again, ignoring the servant. 'I need to talk to Ted Parsons.'

But he had regained his confidence. 'I am Lorenzo Tositi. *Finito*.' He waved a hand, the audience was at an end.

Giovanni was only too anxious to carry out his master's orders, grasping her arm none too gently. Within seconds, he was lying on his back on the ground. She wasn't going to be stopped now.

A howl of pain, not from him, but from Tositi, who leapt up as she came purposefully towards him. She had nothing to lose by boldness, everything to gain. From nowhere a sword appeared in his hand – hidden in the throne? It was old, and short.

'Keep away!' high voice almost shrieking. '*Finito*.'

'Mr Tositi, you have nothing to fear from me.'

'*Basta, basta!*'

'I'm not interested in the Leonardo.'

An infinitesimal pause. 'Leonardo?'

'Signor Tositi, let's just pretend for a moment that you are Ted Parsons and I will explain what I want.'

'You're here to kill me.'

'I want to talk to you, that's all.'

'Kill, kill,' he yelled, looking to Giovanni for help. This time he got none.

Then he was slavering again, almost crying in fear, dropping the sword.

'Sit down, please. I don't mean you any harm,' she said soothingly. As she came close to him, realising the battle was all but won, she saw with distaste that the white satin was grubby, the fingernails dirty, and behind the white mask his grey hair was greasy and unkempt.

'Go away, I don't like people.' The voice was shrill, pettish, heavily accented.

She could sympathise with that at the moment. 'Let me tell you about Ted Parsons. I'm sure you will be interested, and I'm sure you are British, for all your accent and name, Mr Tositi.'

He started to say something, but she simply said, 'Listen,' and he stopped.

'Ted Parsons was born in an orphanage, and he, along with nineteen of his contemporaries, met every year for a party up to 1934. Usually Ted attended, sometimes he did not. He went into service for a time and, during the Second World War, he ended up in a PoW camp. It doesn't *matter* what happened afterwards, save that he needed to get away from London and start a new life. What is important is whether he's alive or not.'

A flicker of what might have been interest showed even through the white mask.

'If he is alive, and if he outlives three of his contemporaries from the orphanage, he stands to gain three-quarters of a million pounds, that's well over eighteen hundred million lire.'

No doubt about there being signs of real interest now. He was listening closely, though saying nothing, his Grand Guignol figure poised elegantly on his majestic gilt throne. Then he decided to enter the conversation.

'They'd try to kill Ted.'

'Who?'

'Those people from the orphanage.'

'They are old friends. Why would they want to kill him?' John Peacock's dead, isn't he, came into her mind.

'Who are *you*?'

He sounded so like the caterpillar in *Alice in Wonderland*

185

that for some odd reason it made her feel surer of her ground.

'There are four sponsors who stand to gain too,' she told him. She wasn't going to alarm him by telling him how much. 'My grandfather is one of them. Ted Parsons might remember him. General Maitland.'

She was almost sure she heard him mutter, 'The Captain.' Had she struck the right chord at last? Apparently not.

'Ted's dead,' he told her flatly.

'I think not.'

'He is, *he is.*'

'No.'

His eyes fell away. 'Who are they, these orphanage people?'

'Victoria Ireland, Stanley Drew, Gladys Smith.'

A long wail, and he covered his face with his hands. He was crying, she realised with some horror. She forced herself to touch his shoulder, trying not to shudder.

'Mr Tositi,' she said gently.

He looked up. Tears had run rivulets in the white paint and blurred the painted eyebrows. 'He's dead,' said the clown's mask pitifully.

'No.'

'Captain Maitland?'

'Yes.'

'Ted will be safe?'

'Yes. I'll look after him.'

'How much money?'

She told him again. There was a long pause. On tenterhooks she waited. Finally he lifted his pitiful face to hers. The mask looked quite blank as he said:

'Ted can outlive all them bleeders.'

★ ★ ★

What the hell was she going to tell Paul?

Exhaustion as she tramped back through the heat took away from her exhilaration. After all, he would scarcely share her triumph at finding Ted Parsons, she remembered. Ted Parsons registered dead increased his chances of scooping the tontine fund; Ted Parsons claiming still to be alive was another matter. Then there was her own behaviour. Trust, as he pointed out, came into it. She had left him literally 'waiting at the church'. How on earth was she to explain why she had done so? She decided her best plan was to go back to the hotel and wait for him. In the event there was no waiting necessary.

As she walked through the door into the lobby he was waiting for her, his face serious. He took her by the arm, drew her to a chair. Now for it. She opened her mouth to explain, but he stopped her. 'It doesn't matter, Gemma. There's been a telephone call. I took the liberty of answering it for you. It was from England. Gemma, darling, I'm sorry, it's bad news. This time it is your grandfather.'

She said nothing, waited, licked dry lips, and felt the chill spreading through her body.

'He died early this morning.'

Chapter Seven

It seemed to Gemma she was on a high clifftop looking down on what was happening beneath her; down there, in the everyday world, she had moved into her grandfather's house in Tenterden, where the phone rang all day long, with arrangements for the funeral and discussions about the memorial service. There was Mrs Plummer too to consider; her grandfather had provided for her financially in his will, but there were some matters wills could not look after, and Mrs Plummer's feelings were one of them. Setting her to superintend catering arrangements was an immediate palliative, while Gemma herself attended to business. All the while the other Gemma, high upon her clifftop, was unable to believe that at last it had happened, or perhaps she was just not wanting to believe. She couldn't remember how she felt after her father's death, but she was only a child then anyway. And Bill's – no, that she would not even contemplate again lest she have to relive it. There was, after all, one major difference between then and now. Then there had been her grandfather. Now there was not.

She had not even had time to tell him that Ted Parsons was found: now she had only half-remembered conversations about his wishes to recall. Now the responsibility for following them or not was a sword of Damocles that might or might not fall upon her. Why did one always think there would be a tomorrow? She had blithely assumed so, only to find Grandfather gone, leaving a tearing loss for the love that had accompanied her through her life, that had sent her into battle like the Romans to return with her shield or on it. This she had done, only to come back very much on it, so far as she could see: one husband, lost; no children, her own fault; one career abandoned, another one functioning very well without her. Oh yes, Gemma Maitland was waging the battle of life very successfully.

At least she had an excellent chief of staff in Paul, she thought wryly, but gratefully. He hadn't questioned her at all about her movements in Florence; he had let her talk, endlessly, repetitiously, inconsequentially as thoughts crowded into her head. She talked of her grandfather, of her job, about herself – only on Bill did she still hold back, and the Lakenham Folly, as Paul had dubbed the tontine. Paul couldn't be with her every day, naturally, especially since he'd already taken enough time off, he explained ruefully. Whenever he could, he was at her side, however, and that was the important thing. He stayed with her in Tenterden, even remaining alone one night when she had to return to Bishopslee for something. He stayed over the Bank Holiday weekend and didn't seem to mind talking to her through much of the night, driving up to London early on the Tuesday. Did they eat? She supposed they must have done somehow, though she seemed to have little memory of it. Odd. Snatched meals in pubs, meals put before them by Mrs Plummer, grateful for a role in life while she adjusted to the future. She remembered chiefly these past days as endless rifling through papers, through the address books for telephone numbers, through all the paraphernalia of a life. She had one vivid memory of Paul's lips against her hair, one evening, his arms round her body, caressing her breasts gently, comfortingly, then moving over her, conveying warmth and sympathy more than words could do. Yes, the body had to be consulted soon, for suddenly the other Gemma on a clifftop had leapt down to join her twin in the real world, as she felt herself responding. Startled she had opened her eyes, to find him looking at her questioningly.

'Soon,' she said, 'so soon now.'

'If it be not now, it will be to come,' he quoted, moving away quietly.

She had to explain, but how? 'It's not the going to bed,' she tried to repair the damage. 'It's the waking up. When you're twenty, you don't think of that, and perhaps that's right. At our age, though, the waking up has to be considered.'

'You mean Mrs P. might be shocked to find us tucked up together when she lurches in with a cuppa?'

She laughed. The tension was broken as she realised he had intended. 'I don't mean that, and you know it. Would you marry again, Paul?' she asked suddenly, at a tangent, now that the danger point was passed.

'Probably. Like you, I'd take the waking-up side of the affair rather more seriously this time.'

'A helpmeet for your centre? Horses for courses.'

'Yes. Of course, life being unpredictable, I might fall for an exotic adventuress.'

'Like me?'

'Exactly like you,' he agreed fervently. 'So let me ask you, this time. Would you marry again?'

'No.' Where had that vehemence come from, Gemma wondered?

'Because of Bill?'

'He's half of it.'

'What's the other half?'

'The sharing,' she offered after a moment's thought.

'Isn't that a strength?'

'Not always.' The other Gemma, unbidden, retreated to her clifftop. Even as she did so, however, she thought of her grandfather's words: 'Good lad, that.'

What she had intended had been a private funeral service for friends and family followed by cremation, and that there should be a public memorial service later. It seemed in the case of Reginald Maitland, however, that public and private lives came to much the same thing on a question of friends. The large church of St Michael was packed, and suddenly from wishing it was as unobtrusive and quick an affair as possible, Gemma was moved by the many mourners and glad of their presence. After all, they had shared in her grandfather's wonderful life, whether they were family, ex-servicemen, or plumbers and electricians who had worked for him. Their experiences made the man: the soldier, the family man, and the last of the Lakenham Set.

Involuntarily she retreated again, looking down on Gemma shaking endless hands, following the coffin, singing hymns, standing at Paul's side outside the church, surrounded by people, wondering inconsequentially whether Mrs Plummer would have provided enough food at the Tenterden house.

'Gemma, I'm so sorry, my dear.' Charles Lakenham was before her outside the church. It was chilly and

overcast, and she shivered. Charles's round face bore
genuine concern, and so did his wife Maria's. She had a
vague memory of seeing her at the 100th birthday party,
though she hadn't talked to her there. Many of these
people had been at that party such a short time ago. She
had been right in fearing the watershed might be too
much for her grandfather. Or had it been the tontine and
worry over that? Or having assumed the opportunity to
make amends to his comrades now lost, had he felt his
time in the world was over? The shadow fell on her once
again. As it did so, she looked round, just as Charles
Lakenham and his wife moved away. A group some
distance away split up, and before the gap filled itself
again, she had a distinct glimpse of the yew trees lining
the path and of a man standing by one of them.

'Gemma, you look pale. Are you all right?' Paul had
come up to her in concern. 'You look as if you're going to
faint.'

'No. I'm all right.' She made a valiant attempt to be
just that. 'I'm seeing things, that's all. For a moment . . .'
She broke off uncertainly. 'I thought I saw the same man
as I saw in the cemetery in Florence. A time-slip. Silly,
isn't it?' How after all could John Piacenta be here?

'Where? What's this invisible man look like?'

She pointed. She couldn't very well answer: like
Lorenzo de' Medici. 'Tall, quite sturdy, and very dark.'

'Black?'

'No,' she managed to say. 'His *hair*.' What on earth
was the matter with her. She must surely be hallucinating?

'There's no one there now,' Paul said curiously.

Surely she wasn't mistaken. He *had* been there, and
yes, there he still was. She could see that unmistakably it

was indeed John Piacenta. No time-slip, no hallucination. Something snapped inside her. She rushed over to him and grabbed at his arm.

'What is it with you?' she demanded furiously. 'You're following me. Or do you make a hobby of cemeteries as well as military art, Mr Piacenta? If not, who the hell do you think you are? Some kind of self-appointed nemesis?'

The words poured out of her irrationally as Paul came up beside her.

'Paul,' Gemma turned and said shakily, 'this is the man I was telling you about, John Piacenta.' Too late she realised she would have some explaining to do to Paul, for she had not told him yet of her visit to Papa Orvino, merely that she had seen him again and asked who he was.

Paul glanced at the man. Gemma's hand was still clamped on Piacenta's arm and he made no effort to free himself.

'I don't know what tale he's been spinning you, Gemma,' Paul told her coolly, 'but allow me to introduce you. This is the Honourable Jonathan Vale, Charles Lakenham's son and heir. His chief investigator, incidentally, over the tontine affair.'

Sometimes a bush did turn out to be a bear, after all. Not today please, not today of all days, something inside Gemma was crying out. Not the tontine, not Lorenzo Tositi, *please*. But perhaps the bear was not too large after all, for Jonathan Vale did not look particularly disturbed.

'Is this true?' Gemma asked him fatuously. Why did one always speak in clichés at times like this? Because the brain could not cope with anything else, she supposed. Certainly hers had no time for subtlety. 'Why did you lie?' she hurled at him. 'Why are you here?' She could hear her voice rising and tried to control it.

'From respect for your grandfather,' Jonathan replied gravely. 'I knew him well, admired him, and shall miss him greatly. He was a fine man as well as a fine soldier. I can imagine you must feel bereft and my sympathy to you.'

If he was waiting for her reply, however clichéd, to his platitude, he would be disappointed. She said nothing.

'As for lying,' he continued, 'I told you nothing that was not true, save for one small and irrelevant detail. I am known as Piacenta in Florence. It's my mother's family name, that's all, and as her family is well known there, it enables me to move more freely around the art world. Does that explain matters sufficiently? I'm sorrier than I can say that you've been upset today. There is no secret to be revealed.' He glanced at Paul. 'And I certainly have no wish to add to your distress.'

She nodded, unable to speak, in acknowledgement of this curiously stilted speech.

'Incidentally,' he went on, 'Mr Shane is correct in saying I acted as a part-time investigation agent for tracking down those concerned in the Lakenham tontine. Including, of course, Ted Parsons, who is dead.'

'He's not, as you well know,' she wanted to yell at him. Did he really think she would have given up after that conversation with Orvino? His presence there had clearly been a put-up job, and it followed he must know the truth about Ted Parsons; must, indeed, have been instrumental in sending Giovanni in pursuit of her. But she wasn't going to pursue it in front of Paul, and not here, not *here*. Turning her back, muttering something that barely reached minimum courtesy, she walked away, to remember the grandfather she had loved, and forget the tontine that had shadowed his last days.

'I ought to be going, Gemma. Will you be all right? I mean, with the will and so on?'

'That's just business. It has a beginning, a middle and eventually an end. It's dealable with, thank you, Paul.' It's the rest that isn't, was her silent corollary. She'd been hoping he'd stay. Of course she had foreseen the anti-climax that would come as the last guest left the house, and leaving her and Mrs Plummer alone with their futures. The physical clearing-up after the gathering was agonising, but possible. The mental clearing-up was going to take longer.

Paul looked concerned. 'I'm just a little worried—'

'About what?' Lacklustre feminist hackles raised themselves.

'Now I know Jonathan Vale is still very much in the picture, I can't help worrying about what he's doing in Florence – and, come to that, what *you* were. He's an odd fish, Gemma. If Ted Parsons were still alive, I'd be quietly old fashioned and warn him off you.'

'What's so odd about him?'

'He uses people. Women in particular.'

'As sex slaves?' she asked lightly.

'I wouldn't know about that, although Annie Masters – you remember her, Stanley Drew's sponsor in the tontine – he was chatting her up.'

'Not unnatural. She's very attractive from what I remember.'

He sighed. 'I'd better come back in and explain the facts of life to you. Or rather the facts of money.'

'What on earth do you mean?' she asked wearily,

leading the way back into the conservatory. She was glad enough not to be alone, but to discuss anything to do with the tontine was the last thing she needed. She could hardly tell Paul that, though, since he'd been such a help this week.

'Money has a lure all of its own, sweetheart. You get to know that rather well when you are a solicitor. Money and marriage go together.'

'What . . .' she began, then realised what he meant. 'You mean marriage is often the way to increase money.'

'Precisely. Now do you see why it was advantageous for our Mr Vale to chat up Annie? He could be doubling his chances.'

'Doubtful,' she said, trying to be fair. 'It would be crazy of him to marry her, only to find Stanley Drew drops dead before the other nominees.'

'True, but there's such a thing as fertilising the soil beforehand. Now do you see why the thought of Mr Vale lingering round you, watching you, disturbs me – or it would have done if Parsons weren't dead. I suppose now he knows he is, he thought he would turn up at the funeral. Nothing to be lost any more, so he could come out and gloat.'

'Ted Parsons isn't dead, Paul.'

'*What*?' His face went pale, then grim. 'I know you've been through a rough day, Gemma, but you must admit this is too important not to ask you to explain it. I'll try and take it gently. Is this what you were playing around with in Florence?'

So far it didn't sound very gentle to her. 'Yes.'

'Tell me.' Tight-lipped, he interrupted her story only once. 'Vale was there, pretending to be an interpreter? I don't like the sound of *that*.'

'Why not?' she asked impatiently. 'Parsons is either alive or not alive. Either way, in order for the tontine to be wound up, the truth has to come out.'

'True, but there's a little factor you're not taking into account.'

'What?'

'Ted Parsons, status unknown, is one thing. Dead is best, from Vale's point of view, but a hint he's possibly alive opens up a can of worms. John Peacock, I might remind you, is dead.'

She sighed. 'If the Lakenhams had evil intent towards that nice old man, they had years in which to bump him off.'

'Ah-ha. So you see my point.'

'It's obvious enough.'

'And my reply is that we are getting nearer the end of the chase, and so the timescale becomes more relevant. Keep an open mind, Gemma, and a wary eye, that's all I beg. Now go on telling me about Florence.'

She did, and as the story continued found herself reliving it in some excitement. Paul did not share it, overtly at least.

'Are these genuine memory lapses, or ones of convenience, do you think? Is it a case of Alzheimer's or a past life, which he prefers to be safely forgotten? And this shabby mansion, what's the story behind it? I know you feel you can't reveal its whereabouts, but you'll have to if he is Ted Parsons. Which brings me to the vital point. How do you *know* he's Ted Parsons, apart from the fact that a crazy old man claimed to be, after being prompted by you?'

'I do, that's all,' she replied shortly.

'As in the Tichborne Claimant case, when a huge

butcher persuaded the tenth baronet's widow that he was her missing, slim, aristocratic son. As the—'

'I take your point. Are you saying my eagerness that he should be Ted Parsons overrode my judgement?'

He looked at her. 'It's getting late, Gemma, but I have to say it's a possibility. I'd have to come with you as an independent observe—'

'I can't. I promised. And you're not independent.'

'Very well,' he said stiffly. 'I understand. Then we have to take this to Potter. And probably then we'll have to go back to Florence and get your proof that Ted Parsons isn't dead but is very much alive, in the shape of a crazy lunatic who calls himself Lorenzo Tositi. Gemma,' his voice changed, 'you know this is the solicitor in me talking, don't you?'

'What does the man say?'

'The man says . . .' he began, but then broke off. 'The man doesn't say. The man feels, Gemma. He feels horrified you went into that madhouse. He feels the shadows are drawing in closer around you and he feels he wants to get you out of it.'

The stress of the day caught up and overwhelmed her. She went to him, and his arms enclosed her, as he muttered words of endearment. Finally, somewhere out of the darkness she heard Paul, the man, say: 'I can't wait any more, Gemma. To hell with the waking up.'

This time she didn't bother to consult her body. It reacted automatically as she lay on the sofa wrapped in his arms, feeling him hard against her through the thin black of her skirt. Old familiar feelings, old familiar need, but no Bill. Not yet.

'Don't, please don't say no, Gemma, not this time.'

'I couldn't. Not tonight,' she whispered truthfully.

* ★ *

'Good lad, that.'

'Who is?'

'You are, according to my grandfather.'

'And according to you?'

'Even better.'

'So, the waking up?'

'Looking best.'

She watched him drive away after the breakfast she prepared. No sign of Mrs Plummer, obviously keeping a discreet silence in her own rooms, as she had done all the week, slightly to Gemma's amusement. Paul had said he'd come down next weekend. Eight days that stretched ahead, filled with the prospects of solicitors, house-clearing and work. It was something to look forward to, anyway. More than just any old something. Something at last that gave a flicker of hope for the Gemma she'd thought had vanished for ever. Paul was a good lover, considerate, gentle, comforting. At the moment she could feel no more, but gradually as she readjusted after her grandfather's death, excitement and passion would return. The gratitude she felt to Paul for this raft to cling to was overwhelming. She had been celibate for too long; she'd forgotten what to expect. When you were young, love transformed every aspect of life, physical or emotional. Later on, you realised that afterwards you were still faced with yourself, welcome though a helping hand might be. Moreover, she suddenly realised, in some depression, her period was due that weekend. The body ticked on regardless of her emotional appointment book.

'Who was that hunk I saw at the funeral?'

'Paul?'

'Paul's a man. This was definitely a hunk,' Loretta judged.

'If it's the hunk I think you mean, I'll introduce you,' Gemma promised, remembering she'd noticed Loretta eyeing Jonathan Vale. 'I'll be only too glad if you'd take him off my hands, in fact.'

'Sounds interesting.'

'I didn't mean it like that. I wouldn't recommend him. He's Charles Lakenham's son.'

'Is he indeed? A future coronet is recommendation enough. Is there a Mrs Hunk?'

'I've no idea.' Gemma wondered if there was, but decided there probably wasn't. No woman would let that look of remote self-sufficiency hang long around a marital home. Or bed. She'd back Loretta to chase it away in a matter of hours.

With some dismay, Gemma saw that she and Paul were not to be the only interested parties present in Felix Potter's office. Charles Lakenham was already there; so was the blonde bombshell, Annie. Felix Potter interpreted her look correctly.

'I felt since this is a serious charge you are making, Miss Maitland, all the sponsors should be present. It's really hotting up,' he added in irrepressible glee, whether at the thrill of the chase or in the expectation that such hotting-up would enable the trustees to take a more active part – and a more active cheque – in the proceedings. 'It's the first time I've ever known a smashed green bottle repair itself and jump right back on the wall,' he went on in ingenuous explanation. Perhaps she had misjudged him over the money, Gemma decided. 'If it has, that is,' he finished, flashing a smile at Gemma as a signal that the floor was open for discussion.

'I gather from Potter there's a chance Ted Parsons may still be alive after all. Is there proof?' Charles asked. 'After all, Gemma, a death certificate is normally proof enough, especially when details seem to tally. Parents unknown, and age more or less correct, and you believe he went to Italy in the fifties. The death, I gather, was registered by a friend Helmut Muller, with whom he was living, judging by the addresses given.'

'Helmut?' repeated Paul sharply.

'You know of him?' Charles turned to Paul.

'There was a Helmut who was a guard at the PoW camp that Parsons was in. Probably they joined forces when he went to live on the continent.'

Thanks, Paul, Gemma thought resignedly.

'Wouldn't catch me moving in with the screws. Gay, was he?' Annie broke in before Gemma had a chance to speak.

'I've no idea,' she replied. She supposed she had it so fixed in her mind from her meetings with his fellow orphans and with Rosalind that he was very much hetero-sexual, that this had never occurred to her. Yet people change, and their tastes change – or are acknowledged more openly. Certainly his relationship with Giovanni was odd enough to suggest more than a straight employer–servant relationship, especially as there seemed precious little money around for wages. The long fingernails, the white satin could be an indication of sexual preference – or of mere eccentricity.

'I don't think,' she continued, 'that this death certifi-cate is of another Ted Parsons. I think it's a deliberate fraud on his part.'

'Did he give you any *proof* of his identity?' Charles demanded again.

'In a kind of way. He showed me documentary proof intended to show he *wasn't* – in other words, his name change by deed-poll to Edward Williams in 1946. He claimed that meant it must be another Ted Parsons registered and that the death certificate was coincidence. Yet the way I see it is that if he faked the death somehow, what better reason to use the name Ted Parsons? His pursuers would have cottoned on he'd be unlikely to use Ned Williams while living in Florence after what he'd done.'

'Pursuers?' repeated Charles Lakenham quietly. 'What pursuers, Gemma?'

She had gone too far. Damn. Felix Potter was looking remarkably interested. Then she remembered that Charles at least would undoubtedly hear about it from his son.

'He left England, he told me – ' white lie – 'because he was in trouble. He had run foul of some unpleasant people and needed to escape for good. I suppose he might actually have sought Helmut out.'

'So you've established some connection, but no proof,' Potter summed up.

'I suppose that's so.'

'What next?' Paul asked.

'I'm afraid proof is where it begins and ends for the trustees.'

'What kind?' Gemma asked.

'Strong, in view of this certificate, frankly. Photographic evidence, handwriting, fingerprints, signed statements from those that knew Ted Parsons, here and in Florence.'

'Any need to go into the faked death?' asked Paul. 'If there was one.'

He frowned. 'I reserve judgement on that. You're a solicitor, Mr Shane. Produce me what I need.'

'Why?' asked Annie Masters sharply.

'Why what?' Potter looked startled.

'Why do *we* have to produce evidence when it is only in Miss Maitland's interests to do so? No offence, Gemma,' she added, grinning.

'It's a fair point,' Gemma conceded.

'Not entirely valid, in my view,' Paul commented, as Gemma silently blessed him. 'In principle, yes, but I know Gemma well enough to think there's something in her story. I think you, Potter, might agree with me that unless we follow it up to the end, there would be an unexploded bomb lying around. One with a timer and due to explode as soon as the penultimate nominee dies, leaving one apparent survivor.'

'Yes.' Potter's curls agreed vigorously.

'So,' Paul went on, 'it's in *all* our interests to sort this out. We need proof, so Gemma needs to return to get what documentary proof she can, but first and foremost to persuade the lunatic to confess he's Ted Parsons – if he is. Not easy. But I think it better she goes at this stage rather than that we appoint an inquiry agent at this point, or that you go, Felix.'

'Isn't it rather more than documents?' Charles pressed. 'If, for the sake of argument, this old man is in fact Ted Parsons' chum Helmut, he'd have ready access to all documents.'

'Identification.' Paul followed his thoughts.

'Precisely. We have three people who knew Parsons for the first twenty-odd years of his life. They are the ones to interrogate him, surely.'

'A wrinklies' get-together in the Ritz,' Annie suggested.

'He'd never come,' Gemma declared. 'He's not in good enough shape. It would kill him.' A somewhat silly thing to say, it belatedly occurred to her, since she was sitting in the same room as three people in whose interests that event would most certainly be.

'Just a minute.' Annie had been thinking. 'Why should it be in the nominees' interests to identify him? If they do, they add another life between themselves and their inheritance.'

'I'd agree, Annie,' Paul picked up the point, 'if they were all acting in their joint interests. But people don't. They generally act in their own, which may or may not be the group interest. Group interest wouldn't want to add another life, and there partly would their sole interests lie as well. But Stanley and Victoria liked Ted Parsons, and dislike poor old Gladys. Neither of them is in good health, and might well welcome the chance of seeing Gladys done down. Moreover, Ted – if it's he – doesn't exactly sound as if he's going to make the next Olympics himself; something Gladys will quickly realise. It might well amuse her to spite the others, as she would see it.'

'Seems risky to me,' Annie muttered defiantly.

'On the whole I think Mr Shane's right, Miss Maitland, even though he's hardly taking a legal view. But when you can spare the time, I suggest you revisit your friend, Mr Ted Parsons or A. N. Other, and if you are still certain he is our man, we will arrange for our little orphans to visit him in Florence, if they can be persuaded to go. I must say, I'd love to be there,' he said wistfully, then brightened up. 'In fact, I see no reason I shouldn't be. Indeed, I'd say it was essential.' He beamed.

Gemma had an insane desire to laugh. Arrange a visit? *There?* A happy reunion of childhood friends in the palazzo with a clown in white satin. It was hopeless, but it had to be attempted for her grandfather's sake. She could not let him down again. She would go, and go quickly. No putting it off, especially now so many people knew Ted Parsons might be alive and in Florence. Suppose Rosalind got to hear? Or Barnes? Moreover, still nagging somewhere was the thought: *John Peacock's dead*.

Paul hadn't expected to arrive before the evening on Saturday. He'd be tied up with visitors from abroad during the day, he told her. At eight o'clock she was waiting impatiently. The dinner table was set, the cottage looking its cosy best. She wasn't sure why she had gone to quite so much trouble; she supposed because it was a distraction from the part of her life which had suddenly become a quicksand.

At last the doorbell rang. She switched the television off and ran to answer it, glad to be rid of her own company. It was long since dark outside, and as she pulled open the door, her welcome dying on her lips, only the one solitary light showed her that it was not Paul who stood there.

It was Loretta's hunk. It was Jonathan Vale.

She stared at him, taken aback, wondering whether she could just slam the door in his face, and deciding she couldn't.

'May I come in?' He saw her hesitation. 'We can go to the pub, if you prefer. I'd like to talk to you.'

'I'm expecting somebody.'

'It won't take long.' He took this for an invitation, as he stepped forward, bringing the aura of night into the cottage with him. How could she now say, let's go to the pub. It would be admitting weakness, and that she would not do. He took in the dinner table set for two, the wood fire crackling in the hearth, the dim lighting, but made no comment.

'Do please sit down. Would you like a drink?' She intended to keep this as formal as possible.

So did he, apparently. 'Thank you, but no. It'll delay matters.'

So much for her efforts at politeness. 'Then tell me why you're here.' She sat down, indicating he might sit where he wished. He chose not to sit at all.

'My father told me what happened at Felix Potter's meeting. As you know, I carried out most of the investigations for my father over this tontine. I gather you're going to Florence to see the man you claim is Ted Parsons. I'd like to come with you.'

'You're joking,' she exploded. Go with *him*? Come into my parlour, said the . . .

'I am not.'

She drew a sharp breath. 'Then my answer is no.'

'Might I ask why? Is Paul Shane going with you?'

'As it happens,' she retorted coldly, 'no, he is not. Do I look as if I need to trail masculine company wherever I go, Mr Vale?'

'No.'

'Then please bear in mind that Ted Parsons is my nominee now.' She'd verified that with her grandfather's solicitors. 'I have the responsibility.'

He picked up on that instantly. 'For what?'

'Proving his identity and—' she broke off.

'What else?'

'Responsibility for his life, Mr Vale.' She threw the gauntlet down.

He did not appear to see it as one. 'I'm glad you realise

that,' he answered. 'You may need to.'

'Is that a threat?'

'Of a kind. More a warning.'

She couldn't believe this was happening to her in her own home, but it was real enough. Very solidly real. Before her, Jonathan Vale, dark, Italianate, determined. 'I hear you, Mr Vale. Now would you kindly explain just what the hell you were doing at Signor Orvino's flat without declaring your interest in the matter? Just what was going on between you and Signor Orvino that I could not understand? Did you pass on his words or invent a few of your own?'

He deliberated. It seemed to her he was consciously keeping her waiting, infuriating her. 'There's no reason I shouldn't tell you, Miss Maitland.' His eye fell on her wedding ring. He must know perfectly well that she had been married. Or did he? After all, she'd heard nothing of Charles's children's doings while she was busy with her own life. She felt no fonder towards him for her concession.

'I wasn't making much progress towards hunting down Ted Parsons. I had discovered he was mixed up in the art world, however, and as I had connections in Florence, decided while I was there I'd make a few inquiries. They came to nothing.'

She stared at him. 'Go on.' Was he testing her? Did he know about the Leonardo? Was it relevant if he did?

'I had been friendly with Roberto Orvino for some while, and he had consistently denied any knowledge of Ted Parsons. However, as I have the benefit of speaking Italian, and the status of friend, I had been able to question him more closely than you and Mr Shane. He made a slight slip which gave me the strong suspicion that he had known him and moreover still did. He used the present tense once too often, but still refused to give ground. When my father told me you were now involved and going to Florence, I naturally thought I'd keep an eye on you. Lo and behold, I'm told by my good friend, very casually, that someone has been inquiring after Ted Parsons. The cemetery seemed to settle the problem, and I decided I must have been wrong. Then I heard you had gone back to Florence alone . . .' (His eye went to the table.) 'Can you blame me for wanting to be present that evening, or blame Roberto for asking me? Everything was translated accurately, I assure you.'

'Perhaps you imagined I'd come to kill my grand-father's nominee?' she inquired sarcastically.

'It does no harm to keep a watchful eye where money's concerned.'

'I'm sure it doesn't. However, grateful as I am, your eye, watchful or otherwise, will not be required when I return to Florence.'

'When will that be?'

'I have not decided.' It would be soon, and now the sooner the better. 'But I wouldn't want anything to happen to Ted Parsons before I get there.' Two could drop threats.

'I take your point,' he said smoothly. 'So wise. I shall look forward to seeing you at the reunion.'

'You will?'

'My father is sending me as his representative.'

'I don't recall Potter suggesting we sponsors attend.'

'I wouldn't miss it for the world. Nor would Annie.'

She stiffened, remembering Paul's comments about that young lady. 'That will be delightful,' she assured him. 'Mr Shane will also want to attend, if he can get away.'

'I'm sure he will manage.'

'I take it you don't have to bother about the demands of work.' It was a cheap sneer, born of frustrated anger.

'Fortunately, as a military historian, specialising in military architecture, Italy and work combine excellently. Have you studied the fortifications of San Giorgio or San Miniato?'

'No.'

'I'll explain them to you – if I should bump into you by chance in Florence.'

'Not on my account, please.' How the hell had she let him get the whiphand in this fencing match?

'A pity. Defence, even in medieval times, was a game of infinite subtlety. Take care, Miss Maitland.' He looked meaningfully at the table. 'I don't think he's coming.'

So he was up to that game. Undermine the enemy's foundations.

'No doubt Annie Masters is saying much the same.' Attack, throw out loose punches, anything but accept the defensive position.

He stopped abruptly on his way to the door. 'So you know.'

'Of course, Paul told me.'

'My apologies.'

'Not accepted, Mr Vale.' She slammed the door behind him, and leant back against it, weak with relief that he had gone. Now she could relax. He hadn't overtly threatened her, but implied threats were almost worse to deal with. She felt as if she'd been physically shaken by him, though he hadn't as much as touched her hand.

Where *was* Paul? The phone rang even as doubt entered her mind.

'Darling, I'm sorry I can't make it. The ruddy meeting's going on and on, and then I'll have to take them to dinner. I'll get down tomorrow. I'm sorry – and sorrier still for myself.'

'It doesn't matter,' she told him bleakly, as she put the phone down and stared around the empty room – and thought of the even emptier bed upstairs.

Giovanni greeted her sullenly, but she was grateful to see him at all. At the Palazzo Tositi, as she had mentally dubbed it, there was no phone, no arrangements for letters, no electricity – nothing. Signor Orvino was the only link, and goodness knows how he got in touch. Semaphore? It had taken a week for a reply to come that an audience would graciously be granted to Miss Maitland. As before, Giovanni met her in San Lorenzo, but the route to the palazzo was different.

He led her not out but further into the huge basilica, purposefully marching through, paying scant regard to tourists, prayers and burning candles. On the left was the door that led to the Brunelleschi-designed cloisters; and the Michelangelo Laurentian Library. A dim memory came to mind of visiting this with Bill, but she had no time to clarify it. Giovanni almost ran through the cloister, looking neither to left at the elegant loggia and garden, nor right to the library entrance, and pushing past groups of tourists impatiently. He went straight on down a short corridor lined with doors – perhaps where dignitaries of the church lived, she guessed – and into another much smaller cloister, empty of tourists. This one was different. For a moment she thought she was already at the palazzo, for the high walled garden with only a tree visible reminded her of her earlier visit. But this was not it. A cat lazily stretched itself in the sunshine, spared one glance at her, and scornfully passed on its way.

Giovanni hurried quickly through, every few moments looking at her as though he suspected she might have somebody else secreted under her coat. She wondered of whom or what this fear was, or had the master's fear simply transposed itself to Giovanni? And was it a real fear, or a paranoic one? After all, Rosalind and Barnes gave no indication they were setting such hounds of hell actively upon Ted Parsons' trail. Giovanni turned through a door on the far side, looking like all the others. To her surprise, however, it led not into a dwelling but another corridor, barren of ornament or atmosphere, and at its end – another door.

She shivered. She had a phobia about series of doors or arches, the infinity, the hidden horror that might lie in wait, the endless question-mark over limitless tunnelled vision. Where did it end? How many arches? How many doors? They were the crystallisation of all your childish nightmares. Would it be one arch too far, one door too many? She subdued the rising panic as Giovanni pushed at the far door. She *knew* where she was going, she reminded herself. Or did she? The dark corridor stretched ahead into dark infinity.

She hesitated and Giovanni paused. The first glimpse of humanity she'd seen from him crossed his face. He made a gesture that might or might not have been 'nothing to worry about' and pushed ahead into the darkness. Only the light from behind her lit the corridor, and once he pushed the door shut behind her there was nothing, just the sound of his breathing and her own, hard and loud. After interminable seconds he put on a torch and they flickered their way onward. The shabby corridor ended abruptly, and Giovanni turned sharply down a flight of steps with a door at the foot. This, heavy and stiff, ancient hinges squealing in the dark, swung towards them, revealing another corridor. This one at least had some dim light, provided by an arch that led into what appeared to be from her hurried glance a covered, enclosed courtyard. The occasional slit window on the outer side provided welcome air. Not for long. After a few yards, another heavy door led into a further stretch of dank, dark corridor, this time with only one slit as relief from the overpowering atmosphere.

'Are these the dungeons?' She tried to make her voice light, and failed. Was he going to push her in a well, or just abandon her here? It was the one way to ensure Ted Parsons remained dead. Even as the terror struck her, he was pushing at another door, and some light, blessed light, flooded in. Up winding stone steps that led to sanity.

They must have climbed thirty feet before the staircase emerged into a small room. Empty. It led into another and another – all empty, until they reached one that was obviously still in use as a kitchen. The equipment was primitive, but half a hung ham, a string of garlic, a pile of chipped plates and an ancient stove that had not heard of gas or electricity were indication enough. Another staircase took them down a floor, though somewhere presumably there must be bedrooms, for she was in no doubt now that she was in Tositi's impregnable palazzo. His method of fortification was not through thick walls and drawbridge, she realised, but through invisibility. From all sides it would appear simply part of the monastic buildings of San Lorenzo. Let Mr Vale, military architect, write a thesis on *that*, she thought.

At the foot of this second staircase she found she was in one of the rooms she recalled from her first visit, and she picked up a familiar trail behind Giovanni. She was wondering whether His Majesty would have changed the white satin outfit when she was finally granted audience.

Giovanni halted in the same room as before, with the tapestry-covered walls. '*Ecco* Signor Tositi,' he announced with triumph and relief. Bringing visitors in from the outside world was clearly a miraculous journey.

'*Buongiorno*, Signor Tositi.' Tact and courtesy needed here, she realised. There was no throne in this room. No white satin either. Instead, an old man sat by the window. The clown had vanished. In his place was an eighty-year-old Teddy Boy bursting out of his trousers and shirt. The grey hair was sleeked back (with olive oil, judging from the smell), the face was pale but unpainted with some attempt at shaving. Tight jacket covered tighter trousers, and the shirt hung outside the trousers, perhaps for modesty's sake since it was most unlikely that that flabby waist could squeeze itself into that waistband. The shoes too must have come with him from London.

She surveyed this vision for a moment, desperately sorting out some reaction to voice. He spoke before she did.

'What d'yer think?'

'Splendid. Mr Parsons, I presume?' she ventured cautiously.

'Nah.'

Checkmate.

'If you're not, why indicate you were when you spoke from your throne?'

'Throne?' A sudden flood of Italian between the two men.

'Signor Tositi,' Giovanni announced, 'says there is no throne. You are thinking of some other palazzo.'

Gemma laughed. 'Come off it. I mean the room with the domed painted ceiling, and all the frescos on the walls. There! The next room.' She pointed, even as she saw their blank faces.

'Here,' she said firmly, moving over to the doorway through which she had unceremoniously rushed last time. It wasn't locked, and she thrust it open and looked through the archway. There was nothing. Certainty gave way to bewilderment. No domed ceiling, no frescos. Merely plain, shabby walls. The threadbare carpets were the only sign that this room had ever been inhabited. A graceful enough room with its four pillars, each with its own gently curved beam from roof to wall, but not what she had expected. Shock made her speechless, until Tositi spoke for her.

'Are you satisfied, signora?' Tositi asked.

'No. I must have miscounted. It must be the next . . .' No, that wasn't possible, for small windows in the far wall showed this was the last room. The end building of the palazzo. She walked over, disbelieving her own eyes. She could see only a small courtyard, and beyond that the thick wall of the monastic complex through which she had come.

She returned to the tapestry chamber defeated, hardly believing what she had seen. Tositi looked puzzled, Giovanni was smirking – or was that her imagination? Either she was mistaken, or the frescos had mysteriously been spirited away – though how could they be since the whole point of frescos was that they *stayed* – or, more probably, it was a trick. *This* was not the tapestry chamber she'd been in before, and therefore was not the one next to the fresco room. Another storey? Somehow, some time, she would find out.

Meanwhile she still had to establish a basis of confidence. She was sidetracked yet again as she sat down by noticing that the inadequate trousers had opened yet further, and that either he had donned them over the white satin, or he wore very strange underpants. This was getting more Grand Guignol by the minute, the macabre was putting her off what she had come for – and perhaps, it occurred to her, was intended to do so. She must ignore it.

'This place was part of the old monastery.' Tositi examined his fingernails, which no Teddy Boy would have boasted.

'With these naked ladies disporting themselves?' Gemma glanced quizzically at the tapestries, which hardly suggested sacred art.

Tositi sniggered. 'Maybe.'

'Look,' said Gemma firmly, 'I'm here to find out about Ted Parsons, *not* Lorenzo Tositi. Are you or are you not Parsons? If so, tell me and I'll do my best to protect your secrecy, but I must know. *Now.*'

'*Sì, sì.*' Giovanni had decided to enter the lists. 'Tell her, Lorenzo. He want money, signora. *Io*, Giovanni, want money.'

Tositi sulked. There was no other word for it, she decided, watching him. He smoothed down his oily hair, looked at his hand in disgust, and wiped it on his trousers, all with great care.

'I might have been Ted Parsons,' he eventually said cunningly. 'That don't mean I am now.'

They were getting somewhere at last. 'If you *were* Ted Parsons, you're supposed to be dead, remember? Or is it

Helmut who's dead? He was living with you, wasn't he?
Did you switch identities? Forge papers? I heard what
you learned in the PoW camp.'

He looked furious. 'Well then, you'd best forget it,
hadn't you? Don't fill your pretty little head with it . . .'
He got up and came up close to her, stood over her chair,
looking down on her from the side. It was all she could do
not to get up and move away. It was more than the smell
of not washing affected her. Much more. Slowly his hand
came down to her shoulder. No, not her shoulder, it was
further now. He hadn't seen a woman for how long? She
thought wildly. His tastes *had* run very much in that
direction, even if not now. The hand touched her,
caressed her breast through the thin material. She wanted
to scream, the hairs on her neck seemed to be standing
upright in protest, but she managed to control herself –
perhaps the look on Giovanni's smirking face. He wasn't
going to intervene, no matter how far Tositi might go.

'Don't do that, Mr Parsons,' she said clearly.

Slowly he took his hand away, and relief flooded
through her; she gulped as if to get rid of her distaste.

He giggled like a naughty child, shuffling back to his
chair. 'Very Botticelli, my dear. Pretty.'

'The money,' she said firmly. 'That's all I'm interested
in. Why you left London is not my concern. You could
have a dozen Leonardos tucked away and I wouldn't
care.'

His eyes bulged. 'Get out, get out,' he screeched.

She knew she had hit the bull's-eye by the look on his
face.

'You've got Pomona hidden here, haven't you?'

'Pomona?' His mood changed yet again. He shrieked
with laughter, slapping his thigh, doubled up with mirth.

217

He pulled himself to his feet, posed with one arm behind his head, chest thrust forward, mincing on his toes. 'Oh dearie me, Pomona. Pomona!'

'Stop this, Ted,' she commanded. 'I don't care what you've got stashed away. All I want to know is: are you prepared to meet Stanley, Victoria and Gladys again?' She summoned up all the force of will she could. 'If we can't get identification, no money.'

He glared at her. 'Yes! Now will you get out?' he said sulkily.

'Only when you admit you're Ted Parsons and the death certificate was forged.'

'Nah. That's some other chap.'

'With a friend of yours to sign the certificate?' False move.

He shrank back. 'I don't want to talk any more,' he cried, relapsing into old age, feigned or not. 'I *was* Ted Parsons. But not now.'

'You are still Ted Parsons.'

'Are you sure?'

Was this for real? Was this genuine old age or playing for time? Tread gingerly, Gemma, very carefully, she told herself.

'I have papers,' he backtracked. 'I told you.' So his memory was pretty good when he wanted it to be if he could remember this last conversation so clearly.

'That isn't enough. We need photos, fingerprints—'

'Not on your bloody life!' he cried, startled into his youth.

'Were your fingerprints ever on file?'

'Nah. What yer think I am, a crook?' His voice rose.

Yes, well, she'd steer clear of answering that. 'I don't know – I'm not concerned with that. I'm concerned with your staying alive long enough for me to fulfil Captain Maitland's wishes *and* get you your money.'

He stared at her blankly. 'Did I tell you it belonged to old Lorenzo de' Medici?'

'What did?'

'Me house.'

'Tell me another.'

He giggled, bluff called.

'As you can't give us documentary evidence of who you are, Mr Parsons, you must have people to identify you. Would you be prepared to come to London?'

Ridiculous question. The old man looked totally aghast, fear flooding over his face.

'Giovanni,' he cried in a theatrically broken voice, stretching out a hand for help or comfort.

'*Lorenzo!*' Giovanni rushed to him, glared at Gemma, and put his arm protectively round him. 'Signor Tositi no leave palazzo *trent'anni* – thirty years.'

Her heart sank. He'd obviously retired here after his 'death'. There wasn't a hope of getting him into the street, let alone to London. 'Very well, I understand. Then they must come here to identify you.'

A screech of terror. '*No! Basta basta!* Go away.' He flapped his hands as though shooing geese. Perhaps he thought she would disappear in a puff of dust.

Then she realised that he might have seen this as a threat. 'Joe is dead,' she told him. 'Rosalind would not travel, *no one* connected with the art world would come. Only those connected with the tontine. The bank's trustee would come, myself, and my fellow sponsors, and your old comrades Gladys, Victoria and Stanley Drew – we all need to know for sure you are still alive.'

219

He gazed at her like a rabbit hypnotised by headlights. 'No, no!'

'Then you will have no money.'

'They will kill me.'

'Nonsense.' It was like reassuring a child. 'Your friends will be looking forward to seeing you. Wouldn't you like to see them again after all this time?'

Suddenly he began to shake with mirth, much to Giovanni's amazement. 'Rightio, it'll be a laugh, won't it?'

It looked a bizarre enough group to be completely at home in Palazzo Tositi, thought Gemma, as they gathered in the foyer of the hotel Felix had booked them all into in the area stretching north of San Lorenzo: the small pugnacious Gladys; a beefy Bert whom she had insisted on bringing; languid pretentious Victoria; stolid Stanley; sexy Annie; broad-shouldered Jonathan, hovering like a huge bird of prey; ebullient Felix Potter – and, thank goodness, Paul. Was there coincidence or significance in the way they had grouped themselves round tables: the 'orphans' sitting at one table; Jonathan Vale, Felix and the other sponsors at the other?

'Cappacheenoh,' pronounced Gladys in tones of disgust.

'It's modern, Ma,' muttered Bert, out of his depth and stealing glances to see if she had offended.

'It ain't coffee, that's all I can say. More like a milkshake, if you ask me.'

'I don't recall anyone did, Gladys,' Victoria remarked with a light laugh.

'Oh me, oh my, sorry to be alive, I'm sure.'

'Now, now, Mrs Norman.' Stanley was all anxious tact,

a falsely jovial smile lit his face. As English as they come, he looked as out of place as Gladys. Only Victoria looked at home, though she was the one who had finally taken most persuasion to attend. Her illness must be catching up with her, for she moved more slowly, Gemma noticed, and her face showed signs of the strain. Jonathan was watching her in some concern. No doubt he was thinking his nest-egg might soon disappear. She was instantly ashamed. Was it catching up with her too? These were people, and people were not to be thought of in terms of nest-eggs. But all the same she'd had three warnings now that that might be precisely how they were viewed when the chips were down.

When Giovanni arrived, he seemed even more nervous, but proceeded in a businesslike manner. In his hand was the list she had sent to Tositi of those who were coming, which he insisted on checking over before they departed. He'd missed a fantastic job opportunity as security guard to royalty, she decided. At last he was satisfied. 'Signora Maitland, please to take a group of three.'

'What *is* this?' muttered Paul in her ear. 'Father Christmas?'

'Something like it. There's a rattling good prize at the end, anyway,' she rejoined. She wondered whether the clown or the spiv would meet them today. Maybe it would be Father Christmas. She wouldn't put it past Tositi.

It was the side-street entrance again for her; in the second group, and with Victoria in it, it took some time to arrive in the room Giovanni had decreed. An empty room. Victoria looked even more strained, and sat down thankfully on one of the rickety chairs provided. It took half an hour before all three groups were assembled.

'Er, is this a joke?' Stanley looked round nervously at

the bare walls and uncovered floorboards. Perhaps he thought this was some bizarre Continental custom, Gemma wondered.

'The old bastard's done a runner,' Gladys roundly declared.

'No. That's the last thing that will happen.' That Gemma could say with confidence.

'Then why are we still waiting?' inquired Jonathan.

'It's Ted's way.'

For a moment she thought she saw the Vale mouth twitch as if actually amused.

'Parsons' Pleasure,' said Felix, laughing.

'What's the joke?' Annie asked disdainfully.

'It's where Oxford students used to bathe naked,' he told her.

'Sounds good to me. What are you staring at?' she asked, seeing Stanley's look of disapproval.

'When I was young—'

'Adam was a soprano—'

'Annie!' Paul's hand rested on her arm lightly to restrain her. She gave him a warm smile, with a sidelong look at Gemma to make sure she'd noticed.

'Is ready.' Giovanni reappeared, actually creasing his face into a smile, and they traipsed behind him into the tapestry room. To her surprise attempts had been made to suggest a party. Tapestried walls sported bunches of flowers; plates of appetisers (which, Italian or not, looked fairly unappetising) adorned the table, along with bottles of what looked like white wine.

Giovanni looked at his achievement proudly, clearly expecting the praise that Gemma valiantly gave. She earned a scornful look from Annie for her pains.

'Never mind the grub, where the hell is he?' Gladys

looked round fiercely. 'This young gent – ' pointing at Jonathan – 'says he was something to do with art. So far I ain't impressed.'

She saw Paul looking round too, and felt a momentary sense of shame that she had not fully described the palazzo to him – especially the fact that there must be another floor containing rooms with art treasures. Frescos certainly, and possibly – probably? – Pomona herself.

Gladys impatiently stalked to the door that Gemma had previously tried, expecting to find frescos within.

'Ted, come out, you old bugger,' yelled Gladys, ignoring Giovanni's wail, 'No shout, no shout.'

Gemma peered over her shoulder in curiosity, but it was still the plain shabby room which she had seen last week.

Stanley sat apart from the others, as if trying to establish he was not part of this riff-raff. Annie went to sit by Jonathan Vale. Paul prowled round, looking at the tapestries.

A trumpet-blast came ear-splittingly from the doorway through which they'd entered, making Victoria scream. Giovanni stood there like Childe Roland, slughorn to his lips, as Ted Parsons entered his audience chamber.

There was a stunned silence, broken eventually by Gladys.

'Blimey, it's the Queen of Sheba.'

'Superman,' Annie snorted.

Stanley gave a faint cry. Even Gemma had not quite expected this vision. Red, brilliant red, and satin again. Trousers, overshirt, emblazed with gold coat-of-arms, and a cape of the same material round his shoulders. No paint on his face at least. From the neck up at least, he was pure fifties. Save for the reek of olive oil.

'Wotcher.' He advanced theatrically with outstretched arms and wavering feet.

'And wotcher to you too, Mr Tositi Parsons,' Felix said warmly, revelling in every moment as he went forward to greet him, adopting the role of leader of the group.

Gladys, Stanley and Victoria, whether by accident or design, stood together, advanced together. At first, Gemma feared Tositi – for she found it hard to think of him as Parsons in these surroundings – would retreat, but he caught her eye and stood his ground.

Felix, bright-eyed, stood to one side, to gather first impressions.

'Ted,' Stanley said brokenly, clasping Tositi's bony hand in his two podgy ones. 'I'd know you anywhere.'

'That's not evidence,' whispered Felix warningly to her. 'He would be predisposed to identify him. Old chums.'

'Yeah, Stanley, ain't it? Follow my advice, did you?'

'I did, Ted, I did.'

'That's my fellow.' Tositi clapped him on the shoulder, a manly gesture somewhat ruined by the red satin image.

Gladys took her time, walking round him twice. 'Yes, that's him,' she remarked at last, leering into his face. 'How could I forget you, me old darling?'

'Ted!' Victoria shrieked aloud, pushing Gladys out of the way. 'Darling.' She threw her arms round his neck, and he removed them, not entirely to her displeasure, Gemma guessed, if the red satin were as grubby as the white.

'Little Victoria, eh? Well, well,' he said, staring hard at her. 'Fifty, sixty years, is it, darling?'

'It's good to see you before I die, Ted.' The quaver in her voice sounded genuine enough.

'You're counting on going first then, are you, Vicky? Good for you.' Ted looked at them and giggled. 'Here I am then. What more do you want, Mr Banker Trustee? They think I'm Ted. So I am.'

'Such documents as you have, if you please, Mr Parsons,' Potter told him briskly, 'and an explanation, at least, of who the man is in the grave, as it isn't you, so to speak.'

'No idea, Mr Potter. Such a pity. Quite a shock it was to hear I'm dead – in a way. Very upsetting.' Gemma's heart sank. 'When Miss Maitland here told me that fellow's name was Ted Parsons, I came over all queer. I was Ned Williams when I came here. 'Course, I got proof of a change of name.' Innocence shone from his old eyes.

'Why did you change it?' Felix asked.

Ted smiled seraphically. 'I'd bin a prisoner of war, see. It – it does things to a man.' A magnificent catch in the voice.

Not half as much as she'd like to do to the old fraud, Gemma thought crossly.

'I wanted a new life, if you get my meaning. Somehow I didn't fit into the old one any more.'

'You never did,' snorted Gladys. 'Bert, come and meet our Ted.'

Bert lumbered over and immediately began chatting, so far as Gemma could gather, about salami sandwiches.

Felix speedily replaced him. 'So you're nothing to do with the man in the grave born in 1914 whose certificate I've seen.'

'Not me, mate. Ned Williams. That's me name. Or Ted Parsons. Or Tositi. All depends.'

'There are going to be some fine solicitors' bills here,' Felix remarked cheerfully to Paul.

'Have you ever lived at Fourteen, Via Elisabetta?' Paul quoted the address on the certificate.

'Not me, me old fruit. Comical, eh, two Ted Parsons living in Florence?'

'Very,' said Paul, grinning.

'I got me passport here,' he offered virtuously. 'And deed of poll and all that. And papers from the old orphanage. No birth certificate or adoption papers, of course. Never had them when I was born.'

'And when was that?'

'You tell 'em, Stanley.'

'No, let him tell us,' Jonathan intervened.

'I don't know, do I?' he retorted. 'I was an orphan, wasn't I? The day I was *given* – ' he glanced round triumphantly – 'was 22 February 1914.'

'That's right,' Felix looked at his list. 'That's what you told me, Mrs Norman.'

'Trying to catch me out, eh, Little Lord Fauntleroy?'

'Certainly,' Felix told him briskly, 'that's my job. And the going's going to get tougher.'

'*If* Signor Tositi is Helmut or someone else who knew Ted well, they'd know his birthday,' Gemma pointed out.

'Whose side are you on, Miss Botticelli?' leered Tositi, perfectly composed.

'My own,' Gemma said bluntly. 'And yours, if you are Ted Parsons.'

Jonathan Vale was keeping very quiet, Gemma noticed. So was Paul. Fair enough, she supposed. Tositi was her nominee. By unspoken agreement she and Paul had kept apart from each other both physically and emotionally since that first day. It was almost as if a sign had gone up: Business First. Otherwise, did they not risk being driven apart by this affair? She longed to know, all the same, what he made of Tositi.

'I suggest,' said Felix brightly, 'that you four must have a lot to talk over about the old days.'

'Fifth degree, eh? Had enough of that in PoW camp.'

'What *you* did in PoW camp, I understand, had little to do with the Fifth Degree,' Gemma told him meaningfully.

'Orl right, orl right, let's be having you, me old mates. Let's see if little Victoria remembers pulling her knickers down for me behind the rabbit-hutch.'

'Did yer?' Gladys's eyes travelled to Victoria who had gone bright red. 'I never thought she had anything in there worth a second look meself.'

'Better than having it on display for a halfpenny a go, ducky,' Ted told her sweetly.

'Ladies,' moaned Stanley. 'Gentlemen. Let us remember we are old friends.'

'We grew up together,' Gladys amended. 'There's a big difference, mate.'

'You are *my* friends,' Stanley declared. There were tears in his eyes.

'Thanks a bunch,' Gladys retorted. 'Still, I don't mind being friendly, Ted.' Her eyes glinted. 'After all, unless we sort you out sharpish, we don't any of us have a hope in hell of getting our hands on the money. Nor *you*, dearie.' She glanced round from the small circle of chairs Felix had placed round Tositi, eyes bright with malice as they fixed on Gemma.

'I think I'd better join you, if you don't mind, Mrs Norman.' Felix pulled up a chair. 'I won't intervene.'

'Suits me. You kick off, Stanley. All boys together, eh? But you keep away.'

Stanley looked alternately proud and nervous of the honour done him. 'Er – what was the name of the nurse with the blonde hair who read us fairy-stories?'

'With the big tits?' Ted asked with interest. 'I dunno. Who was it, Vicky? Brown, was it?'

'You're supposed to be answering the questions, not asking them,' Victoria retorted sharply.

'Jenkins,' Ted said at last, grinning triumphantly.

'That's right.' Stanley was delighted. 'Your turn, Miss Ireland.'

'I'll go next,' Gladys said. 'Ted, *dahling*, who did you sit next to in class?'

Uncommonly decorous for Gladys, Gemma noted.

'Victoria,' Tositi replied.

'No, you didn't,' Stanley said indignantly. 'It was me.'

'Memory ain't perfect. I remember Victoria. Gladys?'

'John Peacock,' she said. 'He put a slug up your trousers one day.'

'I never did like that boy. What happened to him?'

'He's dead,' Jonathan Vale put in.

'Gone to the Great Garden in the Sky, eh?' There was some complacency in Ted's reply, and for the first time Gemma began to feel he was the survivor among this lot, not Gladys.

She'd missed something as she was considering her reaction to this – Victoria's question. Whatever it was, Ted was answering it readily enough. 'You broke your little leg, my love.'

'Right.'

Four old people, thrown back to a world that passed seventy years ago. A shared past. A past that had ended nearly sixty years ago at the last party.

'It was at the party in 1930,' Gladys said stridently.

'Young Dukey – I remember him,' said Ted suddenly. 'And Captain Maitland. A lot of toffs there that year.'

He could remember Grandfather as a man of thirty, Gemma realised, suddenly moved.

'You were sixteen, Vicky. Fat, pink, and lovely. I fancied you rotten.'

'You *were* pretty,' Stanley added shyly.

'Thank you, Mr Drew.' Victoria scented an ally and smiled sweetly.

'Never made her, did you, Stanley?' He flushed.

'Never got it together with Dukey, either, did you, Vicky?' Gladys jeered.

'My fault,' Ted informed her. 'I went into the summerhouse and interrupted you right in the middle of poor old Dukey, so to speak. Bet he never got it up again.'

Victoria stood up, trembling. 'I've heard quite enough, you dirty old man. If I needed convincing you're Ted Parsons, that alone would do it.'

What was there between these four, Gemma wondered? Something more than was being said, that was for sure.

Ted Parsons stood up, red satin cape falling gracefully into folds around him.

'Satisfied, then?'

'To be formal,' Felix interposed, 'do you identify him, Mrs Norman?'

Gladys looked at the red satin monster. ''Course I do,' she said lovingly. 'No one could forget Ted in a hurry.'

'Miss Ireland?'

'Yes.'

'Mr Drew?'

'Yes, but you're not the kind-hearted Ted I'd thought you were,' Stanley said plaintively.

'I wouldn't want to be, old chap.'

'There now,' Gladys said, pleased. 'Now we're all friends again. Ain't that nice. How about that drink,

229

Ted? Mind you, it looks bloody awful.'

Giovanni dispensed cheap wine like nectar to the gods. Lorenzo shuffled round his guests, handing out glasses, his none-too-clean long fingernails almost interlocking. Gemma saw Victoria repress a shudder as she took hers and, amused, she winked at Paul. It was Jonathan Vale who interrupted the signal, with a slight acknowledgement of the head.

'Here's to long life,' said Felix cheerily.

'Cheerio!' Gladys took a gulp from her glass and made a face. 'You need the money, Ted. I almost find it in my heart to drop dead for you. Eh, Bert?'

'I wouldn't like that, Ma.' He set his glass carefully down.

'Long life,' repeated Victoria, staring down into her drink.

'And a happy one.' Paul lifted his glass to Gemma.

Happy? While this horror hung over them? Or her, rather. Paul had his path set clear, and she envied him that. It was yea or nay for his centre. No painful struggle for money, no internal turmoil over the right thing to do. No Jonathan Vale dogging his footsteps as he did hers, like a bailiff with a summons whose nature she could not determine.

Chapter Eight

It had all gone a mite too well. That must be why she was definitely feeling a sense of anti-climax this morning. Gemma wrestled with a particularly stale piece of bread in the hotel restaurant (surely there must be some compromise between unhealthy English breakfast and stale bread even in Latin countries?). Yesterday had been all she could have wished, she told herself, a pleasantish reunion with nothing too terrible happening and Ted Parsons, alias Lorenzo Tositi, on reasonably good behaviour – for him. Today the party was leaving. Felix was now satisfied that he had enough to go on and, after he had seen the Consul this morning, was to collect his flock for the afternoon flight. She was leaving with them, for her job too was ended. There was no reason to stay, yet she still felt a sense of frustration. Something – or someone – still eluded her.

There was no sign of Paul yet. They had been observing the formalities and sleeping apart, rather to her relief. It made it easier to distance business from her private life. And this visit, bizarre as it was with Felix as sheepdog courier and its odd mixture of sheep, was very much business.

Stanley arrived in the breakfast room first, looking

somewhat lost. He brightened as he saw her, clinging to her as an oasis in the desert of foreigners.

'Come and sit here,' Gemma called, to his evident relief. He bustled over, a man with a place in life once more. Foreign hotels had foreign ways, i.e. wrong ways, his expression implied. Somehow with Stanley sitting opposite her, with his round anxious face and heavy glasses, she felt better herself. Normality established itself with the sight of the handkerchief poking from his blazer breast-pocket, none too well folded and ironed, but a small flag to his years of service in the cause of British banking. The bizarreness of the Palazzo Tositi was put smartly in its place, as a foreign eccentricity of no account.

'What will you be doing today, Stanley? Are you going with Gladys to the Accademia to see the David?' Yesterday, Bert had contemplated the statue guarding the entrance to the Palazzo Vecchio from his seat at a café table for a long time. Then he had announced that it was good. On being told by Victoria it was merely a copy, nothing would satisfy him but that he saw the original of Michelangelo's masterpiece as speedily as possible. For once Gladys had been totally bemused.

'No.' Stanley flushed with pride. 'I'm going back to see Ted,' he told her as offhandedly as he could manage. 'He wanted to – ' he stirred his coffee carefully – 'to see me alone for a chat before we left. We are old friends, you know. It means a great deal to me to see him again. I'd like him to come back with me to Brentwood. I'd look after him. I'm very good at looking after people.'

Gemma replied as gravely as she could manage, as a vision of Ted in grubby white satin prancing round Brentwood danced before her eyes. 'That's very good of you, Stanley. I'm sure he'd appreciate being asked at least.'

'Do you think so?' Stanley looked pleased at her approval. 'I *will* ask him then.'

'Morning, Gemma.' Paul drew up another chair. 'Are we select band the first or the last?'

'Good morning, Mr Shane.' Stanley beamed.

It was all too easy, Gemma thought, or was she simply expecting the extraordinary, where the ordinary was in fact the reality?

'Morning, Paul – Gemma,' Annie added as an after-thought, hurrying to catch up with Paul; she sank grace-fully into the chair Paul had brought up for himself. Catching Gemma's sardonic eye, he grinned and brought another one. Stanley was eyeing her expectantly, Gemma noticed. If he thought he had a special standing with that young lady, being her nominee, he was doomed to disappointment, she suspected. Provided Stanley were alive, that was all Annie needed of him, Gemma thought. Or was she just being bitchy, taking exception to Annie's closeness to Paul? Surely she wasn't as petty-minded as that?

'I'm going to see Ted Parsons this morning, Miss Masters,' Stanley told her loudly.

'Good on yer, sport,' she drawled. 'Geriatrics' coffee morning, eh? Take care, Stan, you're all I've got in the world.'

'I shall be quite safe, thank you, Miss Masters,' Stanley retorted primly, hurt. 'Perhaps you could care to accom-pany me as far as San Lorenzo, if you are so concerned for my safety.'

'Not on your life.' She flashed him a smile, which she obviously deemed sufficient recompense for rudeness, and concentrated on Paul once more. Gemma watched, fascinated. 'Where shall we go this morning, Paul? I'd like to go back to that market we saw yesterday.'

'Gemma and I had plans for the Bargello and—'

'OK, that will do. I don't mind a department store, if you're set on it.'

'It's the sculpture museum.'

To hell with tact, Gemma thought.

'We'll have a trip round that, then go to the market.'

'No, Annie. Can't guarantee the market.' Paul decided to take a stand. 'Why don't you call Jonathan Vale?'

Annie considered. 'Not a bad idea. I might just do that.'

Jonathan Vale was the focus of Gemma's persistent sense of unfinished business. He wasn't coming back with them, but remaining here in his flat for another day. Why? Reason told her that he could have a thousand and one tasks here that had nothing to do with tontines; the part of her brain that rejected reason wasn't satisfied. But she could hardly stay here to look after Ted's safety. She had fulfilled her mission for her grandfather and that was that. There was nothing she or the others could do but wait to see what transpired over the tontine. Whether she and Paul remained together privately was a different matter, and one far better explored in Britain, where a relationship, if it was going to work, could be taken steadily, inching little by little towards a conclusion of yes or no, not precipitated by outside influences – like the headiness of Florence.

Headiness was the right word. So much to see, so little time to see it. And seeing it, did one really *see*? Of all the magnificence in the Bargello this morning, what would she remember: the Michelangelos, Donatellos, Cellini?

Now they were a blur, but soon something would emerge from the mist and clarify into an image. The Michelangelo bust of Brutus, perhaps; blind ambition. Ambition? Or determination? Perhaps the latter.

'That's the lot.' Paul came to join her at the restaurant table, having supervised the bringing down of their luggage. Annie was already here, looking sullen, with no sign of Jonathan Vale, Gemma noted with some pleasure. Victoria was talking to her. Gladys and Bert were back from their brush with culture, sporting conspicuously brand new belts and looking as at home here as in EC2. There was no sign of Felix yet, nor, Gemma realised with some disquiet, of Stanley. Perhaps Ted had persuaded him to remain in the Palazzo Tositi in preference to his emerging from seclusion and braving the wilds of Brentwood. They would be as unlikely a set of housemates as she'd ever seen. Not to mention the gruesome Giovanni, to make the triumvirate.

Bert finished attacking his plate of salami with relish. 'We could do this in sandwiches,' he ventured to his mother in a spirit of commercial enterprise.

Gladys snorted. 'They have salami, we've got corn beef, ain't we? No difference, son. Only a name.'

Crushed, Bert relapsed into silence, and delicately removed a piece of salami skin from his mouth.

'Where's old Stanley?' Gladys asked, looking round and noticing his absence.

'Here he is now.' Paul was looking through the restaurant window across the street.

'Good,' Annie drawled. 'Hasn't been knocked on the head, then.'

'And with him,' Paul continued grimly, disregarding

her pleasantry, 'is Jonathan Vale. *And* Giovanni. Quite a little party.'

'Did you have a good morning, Stan old son?' Gladys asked him as soon as he came up to the table. 'How's Superman today?'

'What did you talk about, Stanley?' Victoria asked eagerly. 'The old days?'

Stanley did not look as if he had had a good morning, Gemma thought, noting that Jonathan Vale remained apart. He pulled a chair up close to the table, but not at it, as if he were umpiring some sort of game.

'Very, thank you.' Stanley's voice trembled slightly. 'Is Mr Potter here?'

'Not yet. Why? Lost your tickets?'

'No. I just want to see him about something.'

'Have a pizza while you're waiting,' Paul said.

'Thank you. No. I took lunch with Mr Vale and Giovanni.'

'Why?' Annie asked sharply, casting a none-too-friendly look at Jonathan.

He did not seem perturbed. 'I thought Stanley might enjoy the sole alla fiorentina – and so he did.'

'It was very nice,' Stanley said gallantly to his host, with more politeness than conviction, Gemma thought. 'With my heart, I have to take care.' He looked out of the window agitatedly. 'Mr Potter should be here,' he continued. 'We are leaving shortly, aren't we?'

'He's probably arranging taxis,' Gemma said soothingly. 'Are you all packed and ready, Stanley?'

'Oh yes. My bag is the plaid one.' His eyes flickered briefly to the heap of luggage, before he resumed his vigil by the window. 'Ted's thinking of coming to Brentwood,' he offered.

The disbelief in the faces surrounding him was patently clear. Giovanni looked as if he were about to cry. '*No, no,*' he muttered.

'Felix! There's Felix now, with three taxis.' Victoria immediately rose to her feet, fussing about looking for gloves and handbag, setting off a trail of similar activity and confusion around the table. As Felix came in the main door to the hotel, he was greeted by porters bearing luggage and all his charges struggling towards the door at the same time. Once outside, the paraphernalia of travel spilled everywhere, as the taxis prepared to move in from the far side of the road.

'Sorry,' gasped Gemma, grinning apologetically as Bert cannoned her through the door straight into Felix's arms.

'I'll never make Thomas Cook,' he said ruefully.

'But a very good sheepdog,' Gemma encouraged him from their position behind most of the herd.

How did it happen? One minute she was joking with Felix, the next she was pushed into a screaming group of people, some she recognised, others strangers. She looked up in time to see what she took to be a bundle of clothes falling into the roadway as a bus screeched to a halt with screaming brakes, a moment's dead silence, and then the screaming started again. In the street Annie Masters was running to the bundle. Only it wasn't a bundle; Gemma had seen the glasses fall from it. It was the body of Stanley Drew.

All her apprehensions crystallised inside her; sickness welled up, threatening to vomit from her mouth, as she realised what had happened. Detachedly she noticed Gladys's hat – a pre-war relic – had been knocked askew, as their party came to life, some pressing forwards, others away from the horror.

Someone's hand was clamped on her wrist, Gemma realised. Paul's – she glanced at him gratefully, and saw Jonathan Vale staring at her. Why? Or was she mistaken, for already he was bending over the body, trying to move Annie away, as Felix organised passing traffic around it.

'Is he dead, ma?' Bert's plaintive voice rose above the high noise-level around them.

'Come back inside, Gemma,' Paul urged her.

'No. There's Annie to look after.' She forced herself to go after the screaming girl, but Jonathan Vale had forestalled her, almost having to sweep Annie off her feet to get her away from the huddle of people round the body, one or two of whom were obviously first-aiders.

They managed to get her back into the hotel, and into a chair. 'Brandy?' said Paul helplessly.

'Weak tea, I think,' Victoria said solicitously.

'Not here, Victoria,' Gemma said gently.

Jonathan Vale brought over coffee, but Annie pushed it away. 'Is he dead?' she asked flatly.

'I'll go back. I can hear what might be the ambulance.' Jonathan disappeared outside again.

Paul glanced at Gemma's white face, went up to the bar and got her some water. 'This better than coffee?'

'Yes.'

Inane words and actions to fill the pit of horror, to cling to a normal world. The harsh sound of ambulance sirens closer now, and shortly a shaken Felix at last returned to them. They were all there now, silent, waiting for what he had to say.

'I'm afraid he's dead,' he told them.

Annie was grey, saying nothing now. Gladys did it for her. 'Poor old bugger. First time abroad and he falls under a bus. He said they didn't ought to go the wrong way. He never did get the hang of it.'

'Darling Stanley.' Victoria dabbed at her eyes. 'He was so looking forward to his little inheritance – if he got it, that is,' she added. 'It gave him an *interest*.'

'It gives us all one, dearie,' Gladys said matter-of-factly.

Bert shifted restlessly on his cane chair, inadequate for his bulk. 'When will we get home, Ma?'

Felix looked startled at this down-to-earth reaction. 'I'd better ring the airport and try to change the flights. We'll have to stay a day or two more for formalities, I suppose.'

'I'll help,' said Paul.

His offer was accepted like a hand to a drowning man. This calamity didn't normally fall within a trustee's duties, Felix's unhappy face proclaimed.

Gemma caught Jonathan Vale's expressionless eye. Uneasily, she remembered his offer to accompany her to Florence, so offhandedly refused. Had he feared something like this might happen? No, no one could have foreseen this tragedy. Even as she thought it, Annie put voice to the fear Gemma was trying to suppress.

'You're all hypocrites,' she burst out suddenly. 'You're pretending to be sorry, but you're all bloody glad that there's one less in the race, aren't you? *Aren't you?* Well, come on then, own up. Which of you helped Stan on his way? Which of you pushed him under that bus?'

Felix put his hand over hers in horror. 'Miss Masters, that's a serious accusation.'

'Too damn right it is,' she answered viciously. 'I *feel* serious about it. Thanks to one of you lot I've lost my stake in fifteen million quid, and you've all got one step nearer yours. Accident? Like hell it was.'

'Stanley hadn't got the hang of the traffic,' Paul said seriously. 'We all knew that. The buses just tear along, and if you make a mistake, that's that. It could have happened to any of us.'

'But it happened to him, didn't it? *With* a bit of help. I'm seeing the Bill about this, or whatever they call them round here. You're not getting away with it.'

'They will require evidence, Miss Masters, not just your suspicions,' Felix pointed out, looking ten years older without his usual look of hopeful joviality.

Annie looked round ironically. 'Any of you going to squeal? After all, if you do, you might increase the stakes even more in your favour. There must be something about not being allowed to profit by murder, isn't there? So if any of you think you saw a little tiny nudge, don't be frightened about telling me.'

'I wasn't near him—' Gemma began.

'I'm sure none of you were,' Annie jeered. 'Especially you, Gemma. And it was you got us all here in the first place too. Of course you weren't near him.'

'If I had any such stupid intention,' Gemma declared warmly, 'why gather you all round me in Florence, when I could have bumped him off in Brentwood High Street?'

'That goes for all of us,' Victoria said sweetly. 'I seem to recall the *baggagistes* were closest to him.'

'Oh, swipe me, the *baggagistes*,' Gladys mimicked. 'The police can find out, can't they? Haul us all in and get the thumbscrews out? And that includes the Red Queen up in his old palazzo. Where's that Giovanni? It could have been him did it.'

'It seems,' Felix said glumly to Paul, 'you'd better escort Miss Masters to the police, since you speak fluent Italian.'

Jonathan Vale spoke for the first time. 'You'd better go too, Felix.' Seeing Felix's look of surprise, he added, 'Annie's right. If there's any suspicion that his death was not an accident, as trustee of the tontine you're involved, aren't you?'

Felix stood up glumly. 'Yes.'

A knock on the door – Gemma was back in her room after having booked everyone back in. Paul didn't stop to be invited before coming in. 'What a mess!' He sank down on the bed. 'Annie's still pretty well hysterical.'

'Should I go to help?'

'Keep out of it is my advice. Felix and I will calm her down, as we take her over to the police. We're going to have at least another twenty-four hours here, that's for sure, and probably longer by the time they've sorted out next-of-kin. It doesn't seem right anyway to go home and leave poor old Stan's body in limbo. It would be nice to take him back to England with us, but I don't see that being possible. There might be an inquest, I suppose.'

'Inquest? So you think there's something wrong?' She thought her voice was neutral, but it couldn't have been, for Paul looked at her sharply.

'You think there is, don't you?'

'I only know that John Peacock died too, and at least one person, Victoria, didn't think there was anything accidental about it.'

'But it was very specific – not food poisoning after all, but a mix up over bottles and one of those strong cleaning detergents. That's what the inquest decided.'

'Perhaps so, but two of the five survivors are dead. That's a big percentage in the course of a few months.'

'They are all around eighty, Gemma,' Paul reminded

her. 'In normal circumstances, that's a pretty good age. Illnesses happen, accidents happen. Victoria is on her way out too. That leaves you and me in the ring.'

'That sounds very callous.'

'I don't feel callous, Gemma. I'm sorry if it sounds that way. Perhaps we've been too much apart when we should have been together. I thought you knew me better.' He looked suddenly very tired. 'Once again, it's the lawyer in me speaking, separating the facts of the situation from my feelings about it. I can speak dispassionately if I need to, regardless of what I feel about it inside me. That do?'

'I'm sorry. You're right. We've got off to a bad start.' She put her arm round him, held him to her.

'It is only the start though, thank heavens. Not irredeemable, is it? In fact, we could redeem it right now if Felix weren't waiting downstairs – and if circumstances weren't as they are.'

She shivered, cold inside. Time enough for themselves. Push through the tangled wood first, and then seek the golden land.

'You don't think,' Gemma said after a moment, 'that Annie could have been right about Giovanni being a hit-man?'

He considered this. 'Unlikely on the whole. After all, neither he nor Ted could do anything about the rest of them, could they? Victoria and Gladys will be beyond his reach even if Ted does fancy himself as a Borgia.'

'Victoria's ill – that really just leaves Gladys.'

'Gladys is the healthiest of the lot. If Ted was going to have a go at one of them – she'd be the one to tackle first, surely not poor old Stanley with his heart condition, who might have popped his socks at any minute. And what about John Peacock? If your theses are correct, there'd be two murderously inclined orphans.'

'Or sponsors.'

'True.' He grimaced. 'Even so, the odds would be long.'

'Unless Ted had a private motive for wishing to kill Stanley.'

'Like what, for instance? Stanley and Ted in a duel of love? Stanley on the trail of the lost Pomona?'

'I suppose that is ridiculous. Oh, Paul,' Gemma said, 'that poor old man. The only harm he probably ever did in his life was to withdraw an overdraft facility.'

'It's tough luck. I liked him.' He thought for a moment. 'So let's take your sponsor idea and think about it. Annie wouldn't nobble her own horse. And, apart from us, who are whiter than white, there's only Jonathan Vale. The gent who must have gone deliberately to meet Stanley, took him out to lunch, then back to the hotel – waiting for opportunity to strike.'

'No,' Gemma said flatly.

Paul raised an eyebrow. 'Suddenly Jonathan Vale is in favour?'

'I can be objective too, Paul.' Gemma was slightly irritated. 'If Vale had in mind to diminish the number of contenders for the jackpot, he had every chance to do so before we were ever drawn into the tontine affair. He had fifteen years' start to track these folk down and bump them off without anybody suspecting anything.'

'True, oh devil's advocate. Except,' Paul added as he got up to go, 'you've forgotten two things. One: in those fifteen years there were *other* orphans alive. What did they die of?'

Gemma was taken aback. 'And two?' she asked slowly.

'Two: Victoria Ireland has only a short while to live, so

243

his time, like hers, is definitely running out, and that information has only recently reached Mr Vale.'

Gemma had to escape from the confines of the hotel. She needed to get away from the noise, from the surroundings that were now imbued with the horror of what had happened. She needed not to see anyone to do with the tontine. She needed the emotional solitude, if not physical.

She walked quickly through the city centre to the river, then, reluctant to dive further into tourist land, turned west along the river bank, past the square in which lay the cloister which she and Paul had visited the first time they had come, and then plunged into the anonymous sprawl of roads lined with tall grey buildings and small shops on the street level, with residential quarters above them. One of them contained the Orvino family. Quickly, she turned and turned again, through streets punctuated by narrow alleyways offering tantalising glimpses of artistic stone or ironwork. Occasionally an open communal door would reveal inviting-looking courtyards beyond, old frescos on the walls. This was a city of hidden secrets, of which the Palazzo Tositi was only one.

She turned up yet another side street, which brought her to an open piazza with a garden in the middle, in which a few tourists and Florentines and pairs of lovers were wandering. But all Gemma could take in was the magnificently beautiful Gothic church before her, its colourful marble façade perfect in its discipline, glowing serenely in the late autumn sunshine. She consulted her map – the church of Santa Maria Novella. How had she missed this in her previous ramblings? She walked into it just as they were reopening the doors after the siesta, welcoming the cool embrace of its high columned nave. Here she might sit and think, pray perhaps for Stanley, for her grandfather, for guidance in sorting out fact from the products of an over-fanciful mind.

Outside might lurk death and mystery, but inside was order, calm and timelessness, as the vast columns led the eye to the high altar. On each side of her in the aisles were masterpieces of the Renaissance; but here in the nave there was the grandeur of God. She sat down in a pew, and wondered at the dedication and genius of those who designed and built such glories. The majesty of this nave was caused partly by illusion, for the space between these enormous columns grew less the further one progressed towards the altar. But was the achievement any the less for its being planned so? Gemma sat there for perhaps half an hour before at last she got up to wander round the church.

She put a coin in the lighting box in the transept, and sat to watch as the Filippo Lippi frescos danced into life around her. They were five hundred years old, she supposed, at least, and must be faded, but could anything rival this for sheer vitality and confidence? Could fifteen million pounds produce its like today? Of course not. There had to be a robustness of belief, and money could not provide that. When she left the transept, she noticed more frescos behind the altar and, interested now, went round into the gloom to view them. Once in the sanctuary, she felt at home, cocooned in a sense of family warmth that the grand nave had lacked. Here too only a coin was needed to bring the frescos surrounding her on all sides to life. There were only one or two other people here and they were already moving out of the sanctuary.

With an odd sense of excitement, Gemma pushed lire

into the light-box – and there was light. The sanctuary wasn't empty, however. It was full of life; she was surrounded by a world that harmonised in its Renaissance pride, Florentine men and women of the fifteenth century observing and partaking in scenes from the life of the Virgin Mary and John the Baptist. Spiritual and secular combined in a graceful, pleasing, everyday detail. But there was something else too. Another human presence, for not all the visitors had left. One had remained to cast a shadow in the light around her.

It was Jonathan Vale.

He nodded at her, as she recognised him and fought the ridiculous urge to turn tail and flee. She was not going to run away – not from here. This was a chapel dedicated to birth and hope, not to death which they had both so recently witnessed. Jonathan walked across to her, stood by her side. For a moment she dreaded that he would talk of Stanley, but he did not.

'A glorious Yes to life, aren't they?'

She did not reply immediately to his quiet comment, but followed the direction of his eyes towards the series of frescos dominating, but not overpowering, the walls. These were the scenes from the life of the Virgin, set in the rich houses of the artist's patrons; each one of these Florentine ladies must obviously have been identifiable with some notable of the day: the Virgin's birth, the Annunciation, her presentation at the Temple. On the other wall were scenes from the life of John the Baptist, Florence's patron saint. Common enough themes, but it wasn't that which leapt from these frescos. It was the delight in everyday life, and the care and loving attention to small household details, to the architectural detail of the buildings, to the faces and expressions of those the painter saw around him. God lived amongst these fifteenth-century Florentines. Five hundred years later, He had been rehoused on the outskirts of life.

'*This* is the Renaissance,' she said slowly. Not familiar masterpieces of Leonardo and Michelangelo, geniuses who burst forth in individual and dynamic vigour, but the age that had allowed them to do it, their fellow artists on whose shoulders they stood.

'It's achievable still.'

She looked squarely at him. 'The Lakenham Folly?'

'Folly? I think not.'

'Dream, then.'

' "Or what's a heaven for?" Have you seen his house?'

'The Brownings?' Leaping after him effortlessly.

'Yes. The Casa Guidi. To us it's small, just another Florentine apartment, but to them, to Elizabeth and Robert Browning, one of heaven's mansions.'

'Like this one?'

'Like this. Look at this.' He took her by the hand, walked her over to the Birth of the Virgin. 'Look at the way the woman who's taken the baby in her arms is smiling at it. Look at the love in that face. And look at the way he's drawn attention to it, by placing that window above, the only source of light in the room, taking the eye down to the Light of the World. Yet do you appreciate all that at first? Is that why people look at it? No. It's simple happiness coming across. Ghirlandaio was thought to be old fashioned in his day, but his was the most popular school in Florence. If old fashioned, how could these frescos still have such timeless appeal? They're not admired as relics, they're *loved*. I've seen that look in Lakenham village when young mothers are queuing up for family benefits, haven't you?'

'Yes.' The style reminded her of something or some-one. She searched in her memory, but it had gone, as elusive as the thread that held her here with Jonathan Vale.

'Domenico Ghirlandaio. Michelangelo was apprent-iced to him for a year or so while he was engaged on these frescos. He was fifteen or so, I think. He helped Ghirlandaio with them as all apprentices did, but there's a legend that this figure,' the grip on her hand tightened, as he pointed up, to a half-naked man sitting on the Temple steps, 'is Michelangelo's work. Ghirlandaio got the praise anyway, because it was rare to paint semi-nudity then. Ghirlandaio is said to be the first chap who ever painted anyone in glasses, incidentally.'

'Then if I ever find an Old Master of a man nude save for a pair of horn-rims, I'll snatch it up,' she told him gravely.

A squeeze of the hand was his only reply.

'Have you seen the head outside the Palazzo Vecchio which Michelangelo is rumoured to have done for a bet, sculpted with his hands behind his back? Anywhere but in Florence it would have an armed guard round it. Here there's so much else hardly anyone looks at it.' He broke off. 'Do you mind my talking to you like this? You might have a PhD in art history for all I know.'

'I don't, you must know that, and I don't mind. But I don't know why I don't.' She wasn't even making sense.

'Don't you?'

He took her other hand in his as well. She felt the touch as if his hands were caressing her naked body. She felt her response stabbing through her, followed by a dizziness that left her feeling that his hands were supporting her, preventing her from drowning in this womb. If only he'd stop looking at her. If only these calm frescos did not enclose them so closely. If only he would let her go. But he didn't, he was still holding her hands, the Ponte Vecchio between them. The frescos seemed to be forcing her into some kind of decision, or rather to acknowledge it as if already made. Reason might be wringing its hands in despair, but her body was dancing with desire, and whatever clouds of glory it might trail after it. This chapel of the Renaissance was a rebirth for her, Gemma. She tried to tell herself sex could – should – have no part to play before these scenes of spiritual and religious love, but knew she was wrong. It was all one. His grip was hurting now. Then, as she looked more closely she saw the grip was hers, not his. He knew what she was thinking, wanting. He must do. It was written on her face, pouring out through her hands. He smiled slightly, then leaned towards her and whispered in her ear: 'Not here. We'd be arrested.'

'Ghirlandaio would have understood.' Could cool careful Gemma Maitland be saying this? Part of her scrabbled for the high clifftop, but it scrabbled in vain. She took her hands away, but he was still walking beside her, through the nave and out into the autumn sunshine of the piazza. He stopped in the centre of the garden of the piazza, now full of strolling people, turned her face to him, cupped it in his hands and kissed her. If clasped hands had aroused, lips did more. Presently – soon? she didn't know which, he broke away.

'Now?' he asked gently.

'How can I?'

'How can you not?'

In anyone but him it would be arrogance, but a denial would be something this reborn Gemma could not manage. An integrity, woman to man and man to woman, that she thought had died in her with Bill. She had only to walk beside him back to the hotel, back to his flat, and she would be in his arms. He was right. There was no option.

Whatever Gemma had expected it was not this. Jonathan Vale had still held her hand firmly in his as he unlocked the door of the third-floor flat near the Pitti Palace. Had she expected something dark, withdrawn, with something of its owner's mystery perhaps? Not here. This flat wasn't merely a pied-à-terre of convenience for occasional use. It was loved, used, and welcomed as a home. Books jostled chaotically in shelves, lay in piles on the floor, a huge table had one end clear, presumably for eating, the other bearing word-processor and ancient typewriter cheek by jowl, and papers piled everywhere. Yet it was this very aspect that froze her; outside she was still free, here in this flat the man, not just the body, would claim her. To avoid the moment, she casually walked over to study the prints on the walls.

'St Hilarion in North Cyprus. Know it?' he asked her, after a moment, coming up close – too close – behind her. 'Breathtaking to look at, breathtaking to consider the engineering. I suppose it doesn't look much to you from that.'

It didn't. It was a ground plan with small sketches surrounding it.

'It's perched on the tip of a pinnacle, a Byzantine castle, of interest to us since Richard the Lionheart captured it. With tremendous exertion of brainpower he had the bright idea of putting his captor's daughter right back into the castle as a hostage so that it wouldn't be recaptured.'

'And this one?' she asked, pointing to a plain print of an arched gateway.

He glanced at her. 'The Gate of San Giorgio, here in Florence. Machiavelli was sent to inspect the fortifications early in the sixteenth century. Unlike most people sent to inspect, he actually listened to what he was told by the man on the spot – and gave him credit for it. In this case it was the captain of the fort. Machiavelli was told ditches are always the best defence, and among other things the captain suggested broadening and lowering a nearby tower so that it could carry heavy guns. His idea was to attack the enemy in strength in front and not on his flank. I'll show you what I mean tomorrow.' There might have been a faint interrogation in his voice.

She ignored it. Before tomorrow came the night, the evening and the *now*. The *now* meant commitment, it meant a giant step into the unknown. In the open it had seemed easy, her body shouting out the answer, but here it was muted, waiting. If he touched her but once, she knew the choice would instantly be made for her, like a match to a firelighter, but he made no move. He was standing there as if demanding she should make the first move. He said nothing, did nothing, just stared at her with his enigmatic eyes, as she turned at last to him. The magnetism was so strong she felt it like a physical wave washing over her. Too strong.

She dug her ditch. 'What's this?' she asked blindly.

'Uccello's *Rout of San Romano*. Copy, of course, but a good one. War depicted as a tournament – a far cry from Paul Nash, but it makes his point nevertheless. He has a fine line in knights on white chargers.'

'No wonder it looks so unreal.'

'Why do you say that?'

Her light comment had pushed her headlong into face-to-face combat. Gemma looked at him steadily. 'Grandfather was an infantryman after all, and he brought me up the same way, to fight on my own two feet.'

'Until today I thought you and Paul Shane were fighting as one.'

She could fight him now he was in the open. Anger gave her strength to resist the battering ram.

'I have only once been "as one" with anyone, and certainly am not now. Not with Paul, not with you.'

'Your husband?'

'Yes.'

'Do you still blame him for dying?'

'Blame?' she repeated unbelievingly, cursing herself for being led to fight on alien territory. Of all the words that people had used to her over Bill's death, blame was not one. Love, loss, grief, even guilt had been thrown at her and she had passed by them untouched. Not *blame*, but she would not accept it. Instinctively she turned away, but he caught her arm.

'I would have done,' he said. 'I might have felt cheated. Cheated of my life, cheated of children.'

Hate flooded through her. Hatred of anyone who dared get so close, seek out the secret places she had so securely locked away she had forgotten they were ever there. No, that wasn't even true. They *weren't* there any longer. She pulled herself free.

'Gemma, forgive me. It had to be said sometime, but not now.'

'You – how can you . . .?' She was incoherent with emotion. 'Let me go.'

'I'm not touching you.'

He was, he must surely be. Otherwise why was she still standing here, facing him, hating him, bound to him? But he was right. He wasn't touching her. She was free to go and couldn't move. 'How did you know that when I did not know myself?' she asked bitterly.

'It's written in your life.'

Surely she made no movement, yet she found herself in his arms again. Somewhere outside was the noise of traffic, the far-off sounds of people shouting and laughing. No, she would not be enclosed. She would be free. She disengaged herself, went to stand by the window, looking blindly down into the street where people were free. 'How did you know?' she managed to repeat at last.

'You really want me to tell you?'

'Yes.'

'Very well. You had had your life with Bill, your career, you might have thought about remarriage and children but instead you turned your back on them all. Especially Bill. And now you're trying to do it to me as well. You came back with me here to make love. Now you no longer want to. Or, correction, your body still does. If I took you in my arms, kissed you, held you against me, ran my hands down your body, far down, slipped them over your breasts, then inside your blouse, put my lips—'

Damn him. He wasn't even touching her, he hadn't moved, and yet she felt her body stiffening, wanting, leaping, even as her mind closed against him, against what he demanded. And that was the surrender of the fortress. The price was too heavy and would not be paid.

'Don't worry,' he told her matter-of-factly. 'Your

cloistered virtue is in no danger.'

She felt the blow almost physically, as he had meant.

He continued gently, but it did not remove the sting of the words. 'I don't fancy making love to a backside, to put it crudely. Physical or emotional.'

'You wouldn't be able to. I'm leaving – or would you say that's turning my back?'

'No. I'd say that was nasty temper.'

Eventually battering rams succeeded. Trembling, she snatched her coat and shoulder-bag, opened the front door on to a saner world of shabby, impersonal stairs. He made no attempt to stop her.

Sanity returned with Paul. She heard the click of the lock from the room next door and went to knock on his door. It was unfair. She had just come from the arms of another man, and instead of sorting out just what the hell she thought she was doing, she had managed to persuade herself she needed to talk to Paul. Talk, no more. Anything more was a quicksand, no matter who was beckoning her forward.

'How did it go?' Odd how natural her voice sounded, as she followed him into the room.

Paul grimaced. 'A lot of shrugging, a lot of shouting and a lot of vague promises about taking statements. We've all got to report this evening, but I can't think they're particularly concerned. Can you blame them?'

'How's Annie?'

'Still hysterical. Hardly surprising. I suppose I would be if I saw my chance of fifteen million disappearing under a bus.'

She was thrown back into the world of tontines and nominees, which this morning had seemed a fantasy world. Now it seemed practical reality compared with what had happened since.

'That's tomorrow out. We won't get home before Thursday, if then.'

Gemma jumped guiltily at the thought of home. She would have to ring Loretta and make arrangements for cover for another few days. Arthur was not going to be pleased, however delighted Pam Wallace might be at the increased pay-packet. Gardens required attention this time of year, especially with harvest-time upon them.

'That's if we can get a flight, of course,' he continued. 'Lord, I'm tired.'

He flopped down on the bed and stretched out a hand to her. She sat down on the edge beside him, ignoring the hand. She wanted to take it but could not. Today the body had not been merely consulted, it had taken control. Terra firma was much the safest place.

'We haven't been together much, have we?' he asked after a moment.

'No. But how could we, here?'

Another pause. 'You mean loving time is loving time and tontine time is just that. Never the twain should meet.'

'Yes,' she agreed with relief. She was cheating him, she was less than honest, but she needed time. And the heart must pause to breathe. Well, Byron should know – he had enough complications in his sex life. Did he ever feel like this? Hedged in, pulled at from all sides, fighting to retain control of what would not be controlled?

'Perhaps you're right. But I miss you.'

'Me too.' She meant it. She missed the easy companionship that came of satisfying sex, the warmth and the anticipation. But after Paul had come first the deluge, and now the guilt. Paul didn't like Jonathan Vale, and had all but warned her off him, a warning she had blithely ignored. And Jonathan didn't like Paul either – obviously not, she supposed. *Until today I thought you and Paul Shane were fighting as one*. His words came back to her. Until today? What about today? Until Santa Maria Novella? That must be what he meant – mustn't it? She forced Jonathan out of her mind. It was the madness of a moment caused by high tension after Stanley's death, and must be disregarded.

'Where's Annie now?' She spoke more abruptly than she intended in her deliberate change of subject, and Paul looked at her quizzically.

'Gone to her room, I suppose, poor kid. I haven't got her hidden in the wardrobe. She could be running round the Boboli Gardens naked with our Mr Vale for all I know,' he said lazily. 'No, that's unfair of me,' he added immediately. 'She's had a rotten deal. We all have, but her particularly. We'd better look after her tonight. We'll take her out to dinner after we've been to the police station, shall we?'

In the event they avoided this awkward trio. Felix and Victoria joined them – and Jonathan at the last moment.

'The police seem satisfied.' Felix looked drained nevertheless, and the fact he had raised this hostage to fortune at all showed how tired he was.

'I'm not,' Annie retorted flatly.

'Without witnesses—' Felix began once more.

'I don't need witnesses. I know what happened as well as you all do.'

'Felix, did Stanley talk to you after he came back at lunchtime – before it happened?' Gemma kept her eyes steadily on him, aware of Jonathan's eyes on her from the other side of the table. She glanced at him only to find she was wrong. He was talking to Annie, soothing her down.

'No.' Felix looked surprised.

'When Stanley returned, he asked whether you were around because he had something to say to you, but you were out summoning taxis.'

'Probably it was only about whether he should leave a tip,' Felix said uneasily.

'Did he tell you, Vale?' Paul intervened. 'You walked back with him.'

Annie's sharp face was suddenly interested. 'Well, did he?'

'No.' Jonathan did not elaborate.

'It might have been something Parsons said to him.'

'Possibly. Or nothing at all, as Felix says,' Jonathan replied dismissively.

'He certainly looked anxious,' Gemma said, remembering, 'as if something had upset him.'

'If you think it's worth it, I'll go and ask Parsons,' Paul offered.

'I'll come with you,' Felix said, somewhat glumly.

'There's no need—'

'On the contrary, there's every need,' Jonathan said so firmly that it could have been a gauntlet thrown down. Gemma took it as such in any case.

'Are you implying Paul can't be trusted?'

'Thanks, Gemma,' Paul replied easily, reducing the matter to common sense, 'but Vale's right. In this affair, with such allegations as Annie is making, I'm very much an interested party. As are you – and you, Vale.'

'We'll all go,' said Felix quickly. 'After all, Gemma at least should be there to protect her own interests.'

It was an unfortunate choice of word. 'I should have

protected mine better. I hadn't realised quite what I was up against,' Annie said bitterly.

Felix looked even more worried. 'I'll have to report this to my board. Miss Masters, are you still serious about these allegations?'

'Sorry, Felix, I'm not withdrawing them to make life a picnic for you. I'm going right on stirring up all the dirt there is in their mucky little pool. I'll be watching very carefully to see who wins the big trout.'

Gemma felt the threat behind Annie's flat statement. She shivered. 'Wins?' she retorted sharply. 'I don't see it as a win – I see it as a responsibility.'

'Oh yeah?' Annie sneered. 'Fifteen million to spend as you like?'

'*No*. To have to decide how to fulfil the tontine's aims.'

'With just a tiny bit left for yourself maybe.'

'That's theft.'

'That's my girl,' Paul said enthusiastically. Jonathan said nothing.

'Oh, very sanctimonious. Paul, what would you do with your ill-begotten gains?'

'I've told you, Annie,' he replied levelly. 'I'd set up a complementary medicine centre.'

'I suppose I could go for that. I'll help you run it.'

Gemma glanced at Paul to see how he would treat this generous offer.

'Thank you, Annie. I'll remember that.'

Oh, the diplomat, Gemma thought, amused.

'What about you, Jonathan?' Annie asked, managing to look feminine and fragile suddenly. For a moment Gemma thought he would not answer. But he did.

'I don't think this is the time or the occasion to discuss it really, but in brief, I don't see any option. The money was left to raise a memorial to the Lakenham Set, and raised it shall be, if I have anything to do with it.'

'Irresponsible,' Paul said curtly.

'On the contrary—'

'Gemma, did your grandfather specify his wishes in his will?'

'No. He absolved me from that, leaving the decision to me.'

'And what would it be?'

'I don't know,' Gemma replied frankly. 'I should try to resolve their aims with the needs of today.'

'Playing God,' Jonathan said dispassionately. 'Do you think you're equipped for the role?'

'No, but I have no choice.'

'You're simply fence-sitting,' Paul said impatiently.

'Nothing wrong in that, if there's a minefield either side,' Gemma retorted.

Even the excellent food and wine in the trattoria failed to break through the tension of the ill-assorted party, and she went back to her hotel room with relief. It occurred to her that Paul might try her door, in order to restore harmony between them. But he did not, and she heard no sound from his room. From the other side, from Annie's, she did, however. She heard Annie being consoled by the oldest method known to man, and the sound of the man's voice. Who it was she had no idea, and she didn't care, she told herself, burrowing beneath the duvet and pulling it up over her ears. It could be Paul, Felix or Jonathan – or one of the waiters for all she cared, she told herself. After all, who was she to cast stones? She who had turned away from commitment and intended to remain that way. All the same, sleep did not come until all sounds had died away from her neighbour's room.

★ ★ ★

To Felix's transparent delight they were greeted not by the Teddy-boy outfit or Superman in the palazzo. This time Ted appeared in a long silken dressing-gown affair, complete with hat and gold chain, and in golden silk. Underneath Gemma was almost sure she could see tights. The journey as usual had been surrounded with over-secrecy, with all eight of them squeezing sideways along the edge of the garden and through the hidden door. Once again Ted greeted them in the tapestry room and Gemma's eyes strayed to the mysterious doorway. When she finally gave her full attention back to what was going on, she found Jonathan's look fixed on her in curiosity.

'Well, old Stanley got his. Poor Stanley.' Ted examined his fingers affectedly.

'He's dead,' Bert put in helpfully.

'I know that, me old fruit.'

'What did you tell him to upset him?' Gladys demanded, regardless of Felix's attempts to take control of the meeting.

'Me?' Ted looked innocent. Or was it alarmed, Gemma wondered? 'Never said a word. Nothing. Cross me heart and hope to die.'

'Don't say that, darling. There's only three of us left now.'

'So there is.' Ted giggled. 'I'll have a bit of a wait till little Vicky's gone, and then just you and me, Glad.'

'That's right.'

Victoria looked furious, but did not say anything, merely puffed furiously on a cigarette.

'Stanley came back and told Gemma he wanted to speak to Felix, but he never did,' Paul began. 'We wondered—'

Giovanni, entering with bottles of wine and glasses, burst into a rush of Italian which Jonathan translated deadpan: 'They think I rushed out and killed him. Me, Giovanni, never!'

'He couldn't hurt a fly,' his employer offered. 'Not even a Spanish one.' Ted guffawed loudly.

No one else did, except a sycophantic Bert, and he relapsed into silence after seeing his mother's face.

'Why don't you laugh?' their host shouted pettishly. He flung open his silken gown to reveal what were indeed black tights, topped with a gold doublet. He posed theatrically, head thrown back proudly. 'I am Tositi,' he boasted to the ceiling.

'You're Ted Parsons,' Victoria corrected sweetly. 'We've already agreed on that.'

The head was lowered, the gown closed, the face relapsed into cunning. 'So we have, darling.' Ted guffawed again. 'On the other hand, I might not be. How do you know?'

'Here we go again,' muttered Felix in Gemma's ear. 'I have a strange feeling I'm never going to see my wife and home again.'

'Or come to that,' Ted continued, '*you* might not be little Gladys Smith, eh?' He chucked Gladys under the chin, a familiarity she obviously did not appreciate.

'Come off it, Danny La Rue. You know who I am all right, don't you?'

He stared at her, then waved a hand at Giovanni. '*Vino*, Giovanni, presto.'

'*Sì, sì*.' Giovanni scurried round with murky-looking glasses full of even murkier-looking wine.

'My name,' Ted informed them genially, 'is not Danny anything. I am Lorenzo.'

261

Annie groaned audibly. 'Can't anybody shut the old fart up?'

'De' Medici,' he shrieked, dancing up and down in rage at being thus rudely interrupted.

'The chap who designs birthday cards?' Bert asked, inspired.

'Lorenzo de' Medici owned this palazzo,' he shouted. 'It is his legacy to me.'

'I wonder if there's anything about nominees not being of unsound mind in the tontine trust rules?' Paul whispered to Gemma.

'His mantle has fallen on me,' Ted roared, disconcerted when his announcement brought forth no great response of awe.

'Looks more like his dressing gown,' Gladys retorted scornfully.

'It belonged to Lorenzo!'

'The dressing gown?'

'The *palazzo*.' His voice was almost a sob. '*And* the gown. He wore only black and gold.'

'Tell us, Ted,' Gemma said quietly, seeing he was genuinely upset. Genuinely? How could she be sure of that? Of anything – here.

'Yes, do tell us, Ted,' Paul said straight-faced.

'Is true, signor,' Giovanni said indignantly, rightly interpreting the note of mockery.

'They tried to bump the Magnificent Lorenzo off in the cathedral during High Mass.' The great Lorenzo's putative descendant relapsed into the accents of his youth again. 'Fourteen seventy-eight that was. His brother Giuliano got his come-uppance, but Lorenzo escaped, nipped into the sacristy, slammed the doors and was saved. He never felt quite the same about churches after that. San Lorenzo was the nobs' regular church, and Lorenzo didn't fancy a second round, so he built a private means of escape if someone took it in their head to have another bash. He didn't fancy running round the cloisters chased by a load of cats—'

'*What*?' Gemma asked faintly.

'Cats,' Ted repeated innocently. 'So he built this escape route to the outside world, and halfway there decided a nice private fortress might not be a bad idea for when he wanted to chat unseen – or entertain the ladies. The Medici Palace and the Palazzo Vecchio were what you might call too public for a cunning old devil like him. And me,' he added modestly.

'And where do the cats come in?' Gemma inquired, resigned to the tangent and diverted by the thought of Lorenzo look-alike Jonathan Vale rushing around cloisters with cats on his tail. Inadvertently she glanced at him and wished she hadn't. Immediately she felt protective hackles rising in her as instinctive as in any of the basilica's cats.

'The cloisters got overrun with them years ago. One or two came in, liked the place, and decided to settle down. Well, St Francis is big around these parts, so the canons couldn't do anything nasty to get rid of them. Nor could they let them starve. So they found an old lady to come in and feed them every day, and soon there was more shit than grass. Hundreds of them. Don't know how they got rid of 'em in the end. Imported someone who didn't mind too much about upsetting good old St Francis, I wouldn't be surprised. One gets in every so often still. We got one, ain't we, Giovanni?'

'*Sì*.'

'Sounds like bullshit not catshit, Ted,' Gladys told him

scornfully. 'If this was old Lorenzo's palace, he'd have done himself a bit better than this.' She looked scathingly round the room, shabby for all its tapestries.

'You don't believe me?' Ted grinned. 'Giovanni, *la cassa, per favore.*'

Giovanni scuttled obediently from the room, apparently unsurprised, while Ted stalked round complacently refilling glasses. He had something up his sleeve. What though? Taking advantage of his distraction, and reminded of her earlier puzzlement, Gemma inched her way over to the door in the far wall, unable to resist the opportunity to make quite sure of where she was. So much had happened she had pushed her question about the layout of the palazzo to the back of her mind, half convinced that on her first visit she had been deluded. She opened the door and walked through the archway, aware that Ted's eyes were on her. He made no attempt to stop her, however. Once inside, all was as it was on her last visit. Shabby plain walls bore a few nondescript cheap prints of Uffizi masterpieces, the same rugs were scattered on the floor, the graceful pillars and beams were the only relief to this uninteresting room. The slit windows in the far wall were the one source of light in the room, since one larger window almost at floor level had a shutter over it. She gazed all around her, as if a domed painted ceiling might appear at any moment.

'What do you find so fascinating in here?' Jonathan was standing right behind her.

'Nothing.' Defensively she advanced further into the room.

'I see.' He followed her, then strolled over to the far wall, peering through the glass at the shutter of the tombstone window. He opened the window, heaving at the ancient iron bars that controlled the shutter to raise it. She joined him to look out on the narrow balcony or passageway whose safety rail, if it had ever had one, must have rusted away years ago. Jonathan remarked. 'Curious.'

She had to ask him. 'Why?'

'Nothing.'

'I suppose I asked for that.'

'You did. Look, there's a courtyard down there, and up above us are arrow-loops for archers, and crossbow men, plus embrasures for artillery men with harquebuses. There're even signs of where the platform was for the men. Yet this is an inner wall; it's the outer wall that's the thick one. Why should the inner one carry fortifications while the outer one is unfortified with just that shuttered window space opposite this one?'

'To shoot people when they were in the courtyard in an enclosed space?'

'If they expected the enemy to get so close, why not build a more solid wall than this? Odd. I wonder if there's anything in what he says—'

'Ted's story of Lorenzo de' Medici's owning it?'

'It makes a pretty story.'

'Like the Pomona,' she said unguardedly.

He cocked an eye. 'Do tell,' he said softly.

'Just a piece of nonsense. Forget it.'

'Leonardo's missing Pomona?'

'Not now.'

'Is that the art fraud you spoke of?'

'*Not now!*'

Quickly she walked back into the tapestry room, annoyed with herself, and pointedly went to stand by

Paul. Jonathan had a way of making one unguarded of tongue. Giovanni had returned, and had placed a small chest on the table; wooden, old and bearing something that Gemma recognised: a Medici escutcheon. Seven balls appeared on Cosimo's, six on Lorenzo's. This one had six.

'Maybe we both underestimated him, Paul,' Gemma said.

Ted lovingly, carefully, opened the lid as they crowded round, all curious to see the contents. Jonathan had somehow managed to get into the front, she noticed.

Inside, the gilt paint was flaking, and the contents were dull with age. In an upper layer lay a tarnished chain, and in a small wooden tray a ring, its beauty discoloured, but which seemed to be gold with a triangular diamond set in it. Underneath were two short swords, and between them a large discoloured gold seal with a base with embossed ornamentation, and above an intricate network of delicate silver feathers round a ring which contained a triangular diamond-shape in gold.

'Those are Medici emblems, and the blades of the swords are late fifteenth century,' Jonathan said sharply. 'Where did you find this?'

'Here,' Ted informed them airily. 'In the cellars. There was more – pictures, silver, Roman vases – I've sold it all but this.'

'Junk,' Gladys pronounced, picking up the chain and flinging it round Bert's neck. 'Here you are, Bert. How do you fancy being a Medici?'

'Ma?' he asked, puzzled, fingering the heavy discoloured metal with some distaste.

Gladys cackled. 'Ted reckons he's Lorenzo de' Medici's

descendant, don't you, me old darling? Well then, Bert, let me introduce Ted Parsons, alias Ned Williams, alias Lorenzo Tositi, alias Lorenzo il Magnifico, alias King of the Con Mob. Otherwise known as your dear old Dad.'

Chapter Nine

Ted perked up. Captain Maitland was coming over
to have a word with him, like he always did. He
vaguely supposed the Captain was the only reason
he kept coming to these dos. Not his style. In
Lakenham House he was out of his depth. There
was something odd about these parties. He always
had a fleeting hope the something odd might turn
out for the benefit of Ted Parsons, but it never had
yet. This was going to be the last, though, and he
was going to be in at the kill. Fifteen bleeding years
they'd been holding them, ever since the war, and
the old codgers turned up year after year. It was
free, at least, even if you had to put up with old
Dukey there, short of a bob or two on the brain
side, and that stiff-necked bugger Lakenham.
Shane was a rum one, too, but Maitland was all
right. They must all be over forty. What the hell did
they do it for? Perhaps they were all pansies.
They'd never made a pass at him if so. The food
was pretty good too. Never knew with the upper
classes, they never seemed to get no fun out of life.
That wasn't the way Ted Parsons intended to live,
that was for sure. All he needed was opportunity.

And fat chance of that here with the Depression grinding on, and dull faces everywhere.

'How are you, Ted?'

'Very well, sir.' Ted drew himself upright, and spoke heartily. *Maitland always took a special interest in him, and one day it might pay off, you never knew.*

'Job, have you?'

'Oh, yes, sir. Chauffeur.' (Not precisely true – he drove a rag-and-bone cart and did odd jobs for a posh family in Mayfair.) 'Looking out for something better.'

'Well done, Ted.' Reggie Maitland hesitated, aware something more was expected of him, knowing that he probably had no more to give. *The Lakenham Set had gone, and with it the memory of that crazy day as war broke out.* Then someone else claimed Ted's attention, and Reggie turned away.

'Fancy seeing you 'ere, Ted. Quite an honour, I'm sure. Ain't been for the last two years, 'ave you?' Gladys looked up at him with her large pert eyes.

'Glad you've bin counting. I suddenly had an irresistible urge to see you, darling.' Ted leered, making an unmistakable gesture.

Gladys shrieked with laughter. 'Ain't you going to ask me to dance, then? You always were a lovely dancer.'

She pressed her thin, mobile body up to his.

'Do you know, Glad, I never knew you cared,' he murmured over her head, watching Victoria dancing with Dukey and wondering whether she'd ever make it with him – that's if he knew what it was for.

'Oh yes, Ted, ever so.'

He looked at her sharply, aware of the demure note in her voice. 'What are you doing now, Gladys?'

'*Well now, that's telling.*'

He grinned. *No change in young Gladys. The rest were going nowhere fast. He was never wrong about people. Take Stanley – he looked eighty, but he was a month younger than him, and not yet twenty. So far as Ted was concerned, if Glad fancied him, why not?*

'*Wot d'yer say we nip outside, Glad? How about a bit of a talk in that old ruin?*' *His hand caressed her bottom in case there was any doubt about his intention.*

'*You're a one, Ted. Talk about a fast mover.*'

'*None of that, Gladys. We know where we are, don't we?*'

'*Oh yes, Ted. We do.*'

Gloomy old place, Ted decided, as he pushed open the door to the Folly. Stuff lying about, yet looked as if it was never used. All the better. Unlikely to be disturbed. He remembered from earlier years there were bedrooms upstairs. They weren't made up, but for a quick one, who cared? Not Gladys, that was for sure.

'*I know a pub,*' *she began briskly, buttoning up her dress half an hour later.*

'*Oh yeah?*' *Ted lay back on the pillows watching her. She'd a body like a jack-in-a-box, all coiled up, all springs. Not bad at all.*

'*They're looking for a couple to run it.*'

Suddenly he was all attention. Couple? Run it? There were lots of things you could do when you ran a pub. As well as having it off with Gladys.

'*We'd have to be married, of course,*' *she told him.* '*It's a respectable pub.*'

'*Where is it?*' *he asked cautiously. After all, she*

might have weird notions about going to the country.

'Bermondsey.'

'Bermondsey?' he echoed in astonishment. He burst out laughing.

'Ever so respectable,' Gladys murmured innocently.

'I bet it is. Mr and Mrs Parsons will be ever so respectable too, won't they, Glad?'

'You bet, Ted. We'll get spliced then?' She sat on the bed, inching her skirt up over her knees again.

''Course,' he said easily. After all, you could always get hitched abroad – harder to prove – and then scarper after you'd made what you set out to.

In fact, he stayed three years before he scarpered.

'He never even knew he was a dad, did you, Ted my dear?' Gladys jeered.

The former Lorenzo the Magnificent cowered back as Bert lumbered up to him. 'Dad?' he asked, puzzled. 'You my dad?'

'So I am told. But I am not. I am Tositi.' The voice rose to a painful shriek. 'Giovanni, *aiuto!*' he cried pitifully. For once, however, Giovanni looked as if events were overtaking him, and he pretended to be busy cleaning glasses.

Bert was not easily put off. He walked all round Tositi several times, then stopped in front of him, seizing his hand. Was he going to kiss it or shake it? Gemma wondered, fascinated. Neither, apparently. He simply looked at it, rather touchingly, and dropped it, staring at him. Ted retrieved it and hitched his golden robe defiantly closer to him.

'So love of money found you out after all these years, Ted,' Gladys said sardonically. 'I've been looking for you for fifty years or more. You got into a good thing when you left me, didn't you, old cock? And when I tracked you down, thinking you might like to share a bit of the ready with your nearest and dearest, you scarpered again – straight into the army, like the true little patriot you are. And after that, when I got a sniff of you at last, blow me, you vanish again. Quite a little magician, aren't you, Mr Ned Williams? And then Mr Ned Williams 'as gorn. Quite the heartbroken widow I was, telling the War Office you must have wandered orf 'cos your mind weren't what it was after your terrible experiences in PoW camp. Just you leave it to us, Mrs Parsons, they said. I did, for four bleeding years – and all of a sudden Ted Parsons, they regret, is dead. I should have known better than to believe 'em. You got your price, I'll say that for you. It took three-quarters of a million to smoke you out, you bastard.'

Ted said nothing, but his eyes flickered malevolently towards Gemma, obviously blaming her for this torment.

'I didn't know, Ted,' Gemma told him quietly. 'I had no idea.'

Gladys cackled. 'Did you not, missy? Did you not? Your boyfriend did though, didn't you, Paulie boy?'

'I did not,' Paul replied patiently.

Gladys cackled again scornfully and Gemma's face burned.

'We had fun, Glad,' Ted said suddenly. 'Didn't I give you fun?'

'Oh you did, Ted. You did,' she said softly. 'Till you scarpered. Then I had fun managing the pub and the kid on my own.'

'You weren't on your own, Ma,' Bert said reasonably. 'There was Charlie Norman – you married him when I was a nipper, and Uncle Vic—'

'You be quiet.'

Ted's eyes were sharp. 'You did all right then?'

'No thanks to you, or to Charlie Norman, or to Vic Thomas. To me, mate, thanks to *me*.'

'You married me so you could get your hands on the pub,' Ted burst out, stung with indignation. 'You was in the landlord's bed more than mine. How do I know this is my nipper, eh?' He broke off as Bert, gathering the drift of this, lumbered towards him in a definitely menacing way.

'Delightful though this family reunion is,' Felix broke in firmly, 'I fear I have to leave.'

'You can't leave me,' Ted shouted in sudden fear. 'Not alone with her.'

'You'll be quite safe, dearie. Giovanni can chat with Bert. Bert will help him get a spot of lunch in the kitchen while we have our twosome. After all, he made me a bigamist all those years. Words have to be spoke,' she explained virtuously.

Bert brightened at this prospect of lunch, and set off towards the kitchen with Ted shouting helplessly behind him. Giovanni departed speedily in Bert's wake. Gemma wavered before leaving, seeing Ted's agonised look, but after all, Gladys and he were man and wife – of a kind.

'When the hell can we go home?'

A twosome with Annie in the hotel lounge was the last thing Gemma wanted, but it seemed to have been thrust upon her, as Felix and Paul set out to see the Consul, and Victoria disappeared to lunch accompanied by Jonathan.

'It's all very well for you, but I've got a job to do,' Annie continued crossly.

'Quite,' murmured Gemma soothingly, thinking guiltily of Loretta and potential lost business, and a hundred and one things that would undoubtedly be awaiting her. Like the VAT return, for example. 'We should know as soon as Felix and Paul get back.'

'It's all very well for you, Gemma,' she grumbled. 'At least you are still in with a chance. And if it hadn't been for you, Stanley would still be alive.'

'Just what do you mean by that?' Gemma retorted dangerously.

Annie had a grace to look somewhat abashed. 'I mean your digging up the old fraud here set the cat among the pigeons, and started everyone thinking they'd better speed the game up.'

'Fraud?' Gemma pounced.

'I reckon he is.'

'His wife doesn't seem to think so.'

'She wouldn't, would she?'

'I don't follow.'

'If she identifies him as her husband,' Annie scoffed, 'she doubles her chances of getting her hands on the loot, and Bert would come in for the lot as their heir. It only needs Victoria to pop her clogs and there you go. That's just what they're cooking up now. And incidentally, what proof is there they were married?' She blew smoke in Gemma's face.

'Felix will sort things out.'

'I'm sure he will. But once the old poof is identified as Parsons, there you are. He hasn't denied having married our Glad. Good old Ted's just seen his way to the main chance, hasn't he? Even if it means taking on Gladys and

275

darling Bertie. Ted's a crafty old devil.'

'Perhaps you see too many black devils, Annie. Life is not that complicated.'

'And you see a sight too many white knights, lady,' Annie sniggered, as though she had scored in some way. 'Ever stop to think it might not be your fantastic sex appeal that has both Paul and Jonathan sniffing round you?'

Gemma flushed with anger. 'My private life is no business—'

'Private life? You're really dumb. There's no private life where fifteen million is concerned.'

Gemma mentally tried to count to ten, telling herself that Annie was merely young and overwrought. She did not convince herself. How did Annie know about Jonathan, for example? Only if he had told her. And where did that conclusion lead her? That she'd made a fool of herself, one hot emotion-ridden day, that's where. She had been drawn by his undoubted sexual magnetism, carefully applied in her honour. Or was Annie merely guessing, in order to make trouble? She merely looked bored at present, though, not gloating.

'What kind of a job do you have, Annie?'

Annie cast a glance at her. 'I work in a doctor's surgery. That's why I've a lot in common with Paul.'

This madam really took your breath away, Gemma thought. She and Paul had as much in common as Henry VIII and Saint Francis. Before she was called upon to comment, though, Felix came in with Paul. Gemma was interested to see the change on Annie's face, from boredom to youthful vivacity and concern in one easy move.

'It's sorted out,' Paul told them with relief. 'In theory we can leave tomorrow.'

'Theory?' asked Annie sharply.

'Stanley's dead wife's nephew is coming to take the body home. I suppose one of us should remain.' Felix looked worried. 'I've got to get back – to make sure my desk's still there, apart from anything else.' Nobody smiled at the weak joke. 'There's room on the flight tomorrow afternoon for us all otherwise.'

'I should go back too,' Paul declared. 'Otherwise the firm will think I've opened a Florentine office.'

'Who stays?' asked Gemma. 'We can't leave Gladys and Bert to look after the poor fellow.'

'No use looking at me,' said Annie. 'I only took three days' leave. I can't stay longer.'

'I suppose I'd better then,' Gemma said without enthusiasm.

'No,' Paul said instantly.

'Why not? Gemma asked.

'You have a business too. Besides—'

'Besides what?'

He did not reply, but was obviously annoyed, though for the life of her Gemma could not see why.

'One of the pleasures of being self-employed is the right to starve,' she observed lightly. She did not mind staying too much. With both Jonathan and Paul distanced from her, she might begin to judge what was happening to her, work out how she could forget the madness of Santa Maria Novella and start afresh with Paul.

'I think that's much the best plan,' declared Annie enthusiastically.

'I'm sure you do,' Gemma thought ironically, watching Annie begin to talk animatedly and exclusively to Paul.

Loretta took the practical view. 'Fine. Send me back the

hunk and you stay where you are with the man.'

'I'm sending them both back to you, with compliments.'

A pause. 'Is that entirely wise?'

Once she had waved the party off in their taxis to catch the London flight the following day, Gemma found herself pleased at being alone in Florence once again. True, Stanley's nephew-in-law would soon be arriving at the railway station after having taken a Pisa flight, but after that her duty would be done. She played her usual game of picking out which one he would be, as she held the name-board high above her head. A correct guess won her a Scotch at home when she went off duty. 'Don't let it be the one with the poky little trilby,' she pleaded with fate. It was kind to her. It was the nervous-looking one with the copy of *A Year in Provence* sticking out of a shoulder-bag. A traveller manqué then.

'I don't understand what he was doing here,' he told her somewhat querulously.

Straight in. 'Two of the people he was with were at the orphanage with him. They used to meet regularly and they came here to see another of their former childhood friends.' Friends? Ted, Gladys, Victoria . . . The saddest thing about it was that Stanley probably thought so.

'My mother wants the body back,' Robert Wickham explained, as they climbed into the taxi for the short ride. 'She thinks it ought to lie with my aunt's, or at least his ashes ought to. I didn't mind coming. I've only been to Spain before. It looks better, more respectful somehow.'

'Yes,' she agreed, adeptly following his switch of subject.

'The police just said a road accident.' Was there a faint question in his voice, she wondered? 'But they said too they had investigated all other possibilities. Did they think he committed suicide?'

'No.'

'Oh. I just wondered because my mother had a phone call from a woman who was claiming he was murdered. It seems very unlikely. Who'd want to murder Uncle Stanley, unless it was a mugger?'

Gemma's heart sank. Damn Annie Masters. She tried to keep her tone as light as possible. 'Your uncle had a life interest in some money,' she told him. 'Someone in our party suggested your uncle's death was intentional.'

Quick enough where money was concerned. 'I never knew about any money,' Wickham said sharply. 'Life interest, you say?'

'Yes.'

'Not bequeathable?'

'No.'

'Oh.' A pause. 'Even if he was murdered.'

'I think not. I'll give you the name of the trustees, of course, in case you wish to check.'

A pause. 'Do you mind me asking who benefits now?'

'No. In your case I'd ask the same,' she replied frankly. 'All of us in the party had an equal interest and benefited indirectly.'

'But the police are satisfied it's an accident.'

'Yes.'

'Are you?'

Back into shadowland. 'The police can find no one who says it was other than an accident, and in a crowd such as that surrounding him, who could say otherwise?'

'Suppose you all did it?'

'I'm sorry?' She was startled.

'For the sake of argument,' he repeated patiently. 'If

there was a group of people round him at the time – all of one party – perhaps they all did it together. There's a detective story about that.'

She stared at him. 'Impossible,' she said flatly. 'You don't know the others involved. They'd never cooperate on something like that. They're too suspicious of each other.'

'Of course. Forgive me. I have a weakness for detective stories.'

Why on earth did she feel guilty when there was nothing to be guilty about? And how could she say now what she intended about his uncle, how she had liked him, and wished he had received his money to retire to Spain? It would be put down as hypocrisy.

She settled Robert Wickham into his hotel and then handed him over with relief to the Consul, whose ear was no doubt being well and truly bent. By three, she was free. Tomorrow she planned to go to see Ted one last time, so her first call was to the Orvinos to request an audience – she had come to think of it in those terms. For once, she suspected, Ted would have no objections. This afternoon she was free though, and she knew just where she would go. To Fiesole, following the age-old tradition of Florentines fleeing the hot dryness of their city for an hour or two in the land of El Dorado.

Once she had discovered the right café in which to buy a bus ticket, figured out the correct bus and climbed aboard, she was more than ready for escape, and the shadows lifted slightly as the road wound out of Florence up the hillside past huge villas shrouded by cypresses. The sky, though sunny, held the threat of storm. Like everywhere else it had not been a good summer or autumn in Florence, but by the time she alighted in the central piazza of the village, the air felt clearer. She had an espresso at a café, then decided to see the Roman ruins first. She knew Fiesole had once had an importance it now lacked, and had traces of many civilisations including Etruscan. Back in the midst of their ruins, she could perhaps get her thoughts in order. She passed the museum and headed for the theatre. The auditorium was well preserved, and she stood on the top step looking down to the stage area.

Away from it all? What a hope! That back in front of her, the man sitting on the steps, was surely unmistakable, or at least the lurch in her stomach told her so. Why had she rashly assumed that Jonathan had gone back to London with the rest of the group? Fortunately he hadn't yet seen her, and she had time to escape if she moved quickly.

'Gemma!' He didn't even bother to turn round as he said her name.

'Do you have a periscope with you?' she asked.

He did turn round at that, but he didn't bother to move. 'No. Are you coming to join me in the dress circle?'

'No.'

He stood up, and ran up the steps to where she was. 'Then I suppose I had better come to you, and try not to feel as though I'm five years old again, trotting behind the sophisticated seven-year-old Miss Maitland.'

'I thought you'd gone home.' So she *had* met him at Lakenham House and that had been the 'insignificant detail' he'd confessed to lying about. Sophisticated? *Her?*

'As you see, I haven't.'

'Why not?'

For a moment she thought he would not answer her

blunt question, for it was, she knew, out of bounds.

'A few unanswered questions I thought I'd look into.'

'Stanley?'

'No.'

'His nephew has arrived to claim him.'

'It was thoughtful of you to stay.'

'Not really. I needed to be on my own.'

'And now I'm here and you're not.'

'I could walk away.'

'Why don't you?' he agreed, sitting down on the top step.

She laughed, caught out in her childishness. 'The nephew had heard about Annie's allegations.'

'And what did he say?'

'He suggested we'd all been in it together.'

'Impractical.'

'That's what I thought.'

'Who comes next, after all?'

'You mean, the conspiracy would have to close ranks in ever decreasing circles.'

'Even now Gladys and Paul could be plotting an attempt on Victoria.'

'Don't joke,' she said sharply.

He laid a hand on hers. 'Believe me, Gemma. No joke.'

'You're serious?'

'In general, if not the particular.'

'John Peacock?'

'John never had a day's illness in his life until the one that killed him.'

'Stanley?'

'All too easy to push an old man none too steady on his feet.'

'Not Paul,' she said steadily.

He did not reply, and she rose to her feet to go. Anywhere but here. He didn't try to stop her.

She concentrated hard on the Roman temple, then on the baths and the Etruscan remains. As she passed the theatre on the way back to the museum, she noticed he had gone. It was in the shaded square by the Church of St Francis she found him again, at the top of the cobbled path which wound steeply past the church of St Alexander, past the memorials and the old cottages, into the quiet peace of the convent square. And there he was. At her side, even in this quiet place.

Below them in the valley lay Florence, spread out in panoramic view. She braced herself. If this was Armageddon, so be it. Apparently not, however; it was merely no man's land, limbo.

'Can't you imagine Lorenzo here?'

'Tositi?' she asked, deliberately obtuse.

'The other one.'

Was he aware of the resemblance between them, she wondered. Or did it not exist? Was it merely her imagination which seemed to work overtime here?

'Yes,' she answered. 'I can see why the Medicis built villas up here. Above the politics and machinations. Here Lorenzo could see Florence laid out like a map, the raw material of his Renaissance. Not quite what our Medici claimant aspires to. What did you think of Ted's story about the palazzo?'

'I'm not sure. I'd like a closer look. I'll ask Orvino to book me in for a visit tomorrow.'

'I'll come too—'

She had been going to explain that she was going the following morning, but he interrupted her, laughing.

'Very flattering. Do you think I'm going to knock him on the head?'

'No. Oddly enough, I felt I ought to say goodbye to him before I leave. He was hardly in a state to pay much attention to me yesterday. And, as you say, the building is interesting.'

'A sudden interest in medieval defence?'

She hesitated, but there was no reason she should not tell him. 'There seem to be two identical floors above the ruined ground floor.'

'No, there aren't.'

'Then how,' she asked, nettled, 'do you explain the fact that when I first went there, I saw a room beyond the tapestry room that isn't there now?'

'Mistake?'

'Kind of you, but if I made mistakes like that I'd be out of a job.'

'Very well. Explain.' He drew her by the hand to the stone bench. 'We've all the time in the world up here.'

No escape now. 'The first time I went there, Giovanni tried to pretend *he* was Ted Parsons, and I was so angry I rushed straight for the far door we went through yesterday, and in the next room I found the real Ted Parsons. I'd taken him by surprise.'

'And?'

'It was a different room. It had a domed ceiling, with light coming in from the top. No windows, and all the walls *and* the ceiling were painted.'

'Painted?' he repeated sharply.

'That's not an adequate description. It was like stepping into a chamber peopled with colour. Almost three-dimensional it was so vivid. I don't mean the colours were vivid in themselves, but that the scenes were so *part* of the

284

room they were alive. I didn't – couldn't – stop to look closer because I was so eager to beard Tositi, who was cowering on a gilded throne—' She thought he would laugh because it sounded so crazy, but he didn't.

'Go on.'

'That's it really. He was sitting on this in grubby white satin splendour. I rushed up to him and he jumped off and hid behind it.'

'Was it on a dais?'

'I don't think so.' She swept this irrelevancy aside, following her own train of thought. 'You see, it *happened*, so it follows there must be two identical tapestry rooms, on two different floors.'

'A splendidly rational deduction,' he said gravely. 'But there aren't.'

'There must be.'

'We'll find out tomorrow.' He paused. 'What do you think of Tositi, Gemma?'

'A frightened poseur.'

'A clever one. What drove him into that palazzo?'

'Fear.'

'And of what? You know, don't you?' And when she did not reply: '*Tell* me about Ted Parsons and this interesting Ned Williams, Gemma.'

'I can't.'

'Do you think I'm in league with these people, whoever they are – Gladys, perhaps – who want to kill him?'

'No. I don't know what you are, or what you want of me, but I don't think that.'

'What I want of you?' He laughed. 'That's simple. I'm following up a debt of honour, to keep an eye on your welfare. No more. After all, your grandfather had wanted us to marry, after Bill died.'

'*What?*'

'Careful, don't fall off the seat.'

'I don't believe you. He wanted me to marry Paul. Anyway, I notice your enthusiasm for the idea did not exactly send you rushing to my arms. I saw neither hair nor hide of you till Stansted airport.'

'One is straightforward, the other could be remedied.'

'Save the hide for Loretta.'

'Who?'

'My assistant.'

He reflected. 'Large, blonde, sexy and lively?'

'The same. She thinks you're a hunk, but before you get over-excited, let me tell you she uses hunks for flooring practice; she tends to feel more motherly towards wimps.'

He said nothing, leaving her feeling put down, even though she knew Loretta would be applauding if she were here, despite the fact her own word would not have been motherly.

'He really wanted you to marry Paul?' he asked at last.

'Yes. But it won't influence me.'

'I'm sure not. Tell me about the Pomona, Gemma.'

'I think you must be descended from the Medicis,' she said feelingly. 'Or Machiavelli. Your thumbscrew politics are good.'

'The Medicis actually. My mother is descended from some obscure branch or other, so she claims. Mind you, so does most of Tuscany. Tell me about the Pomona.'

Was there anything to be lost? No, for that, after all, was not what she had come for. She would have to ask Ted about it tomorrow anyway – if at all, and Jonathan Vale would be present. She related the story, rather enjoying the opportunity to talk of Rosalind, and the whole Wandsworth story.

He listened intently. 'What do you think now you've met Ted?' he asked. 'Bearing in mind there might never have been any such painting.'

'So much has happened, I'd put the Pomona to the back of my mind. I can't forget that Ted is a trained forger, and that confidence tricks were his stock-in-trade. And yet, there's still a question-mark in my mind.'

'The kind of question-mark that sent men to their graves in gold-fever days. The oldest confidence trick of all is feeding people what they want to hear.'

'I know.'

'Ted Parsons specialises in illusion too. All these costumes – he'd have made a good member of the magic circle. I wonder if that room you thought you saw is anything to do with that?'

'I *did* see it,' she said coldly.

'People can see empty cabinets when the magician is still hidden inside. All done with mirrors. No, that wouldn't work here, because we walked *inside* that empty room. Perhaps the paintings you saw have just been removed, and the ceiling covered.'

'Why? It's not a room we were likely to go into.'

'But it wasn't locked yesterday, which implies there can't be anything to hide.'

'This room is on another floor – as I told you.'

'So you did. And to think the Medicis came up here to find peace.'

'You're right.' She swallowed her anger. 'This isn't a place to fight in.'

'No.'

'Then why are you protecting yourself against me, Jonathan?'

'Am I?'

'Your arms are defensively crossed and you wear the Medici scowl.'

'I'm not sure I can answer that.'

'Or you don't want to.'

'Perhaps.'

'You've stopped being the maypole.'

'Very symbolic, even if your meaning is obscure.'

'The man in the middle, who calls the lasses to dance around. First Annie, then me.'

'Annie?'

'Paul told me you were seeing her.'

'Did he? Did you believe him?'

'Yes.'

'Do you always believe everything you're told?'

Prickles rose. 'I do not.'

'Sex can get in the way.'

'It can, but it has not.'

'Are you sleeping with him?'

She trembled with anger. 'By what right, by what *right*, do you question me?'

'This right.'

For a moment she thought he'd kiss her, but he didn't. He pulled her towards him by putting an arm round her shoulders, so that she could not escape, and pointed down towards Florence. 'Here we're above all that makes life tick in the city, in *any* city: the day-to-day wheeling and dealing, the machinations, plots, intrigues. Here it can or should make sense.'

'A high clifftop?'

'If you like. *That*'s the city where Leonardo walked,

where Michelangelo was born and worked, where countless surges of electrical creative power called upon came
together under the leadership of one man and turned
itself into the Renaissance, which propelled Europe
forward with a life force for five hundred years. Beside
that, it seems insignificant who's sleeping with whom,
doesn't it? Me with Annie, you with Paul. All that
matters is the dynamo that turned that rebirth on, and the
truth that drives it still.'

Gemma had counted on breakfast as a period of respite
to prepare herself for the morning ahead – what to say to
Ted, and, she was uncomfortably aware, what to say to
Jonathan. She was conscious that she regarded Ted as
'her' private domain. However irrational, the thought of
his intrusion upon it was unsettling. Last night she had
given up trying, leaving it until the cool light of day to see
her way. Now it had come and it was all the more
disconcerting when Jonathan materialised in the breakfast room at nine o'clock instead of at San Lorenzo at
eleven, as they had arranged. When she saw the expression on his face, however, she realised it was no idle whim
had brought him here.

'What's wrong?'

'I had a phone call from Orvino. Someone's tried to kill
Ted.'

'*What?*'

'Poison apparently. Household turps in his food – wine
most probably.'

'How is he?' Hurriedly she pushed her chair away from
the table, ready to leave.

'Steady. Finish your coffee. I'll have one too.' He
looked at her as shakily she battled to come to terms with

this new development. 'He's all right, Gemma. Really.'

'In hospital?'

'Not even that. He didn't drink enough, obviously: vile though his wine is, he tasted something odd. It all happened late last night.'

'An accident?' she asked without hope.

'I doubt Giovanni would be pleased to hear that suggestion.'

'Who then?'

'Any of us presumably. In theory, anyway. He was finishing up an old bottle. Any of us could have spiked it before we left. It seems rather hit and miss, though.'

'It hit.'

'Partly,' he amended.

'Has he had other visitors?' she asked, knowing the answer.

'No one but us, Orvino says. Visitors are rare fish, as you can imagine.'

'Unless Giovanni were bribed,' she said doubtfully.

'I think that's unlikely, don't you?'

She grinned. 'I don't think he'd know a bribe if he saw one.'

'Then it's one of us – by which, I mean of course, one of the larger group, including ourselves.'

'Can we see him?'

'That's why I came. Ted's asked to see us as soon as possible. Maybe he suspects me – I've no idea. Do you?'

It was a light enough question, but serious. 'How,' she asked flatly, 'can I possibly know?'

He stared at her. 'Of course not. You know, Gemma, I wish I'd never started this caper. Your grandfather was right in the first place. It should have been left alone, buried with the Lakenham Set. I've known about it for fifteen years, but what has it achieved? Two deaths and an attempted murder.'

'My grandfather decided he was wrong,' Gemma replied steadily. 'He wanted the Lakenham Set to have what they had paid for. Nothing has invalidated that.'

'There must come a point when it's questionable. How to balance it? How much blood before the ideal is stained?'

'Now who's playing God?'

He put out his hand, touched hers. 'Let's go, Gemma.'

Giovanni met them on the steps of San Lorenzo and immediately set off towards the side-street entrance, babbling, wringing his hands and gesticulating, incomprehensibly as far as Gemma was concerned, while Jonathan put in an occasional *sì* or *no*. As they went through the passageway, Jonathan took the opportunity to précis the exchanges for her benefit.

'Apparently it is all the fault of the Great Outside. They were happy until we came, his late wife, Sophia, he and Tositi, in a cosy little threesome. He's worried about what will happen to him when Tositi dies.'

'But how *is* Ted?'

'Weak but much better. He still wants to see us.'

'A grand audience,' she tried to joke, but she found to her surprise that she was relieved. Was it relief for a crazed old man? Or relief that yet another life had not vanished during this affair? Or was it even that her own chances in the tontine were not diminished? No, that at least she could discount. Every time she thought of the responsibility of the future of the trust being laid on her, she found herself ducking the problem.

'He is in bed, signora,' Giovanni told her.

'Will he mind my coming in?'

'No. He wish it.'

The bedrooms lay where she had guessed, on the top storey. Evidently Jonathan was right. There didn't seem to be two identical floors, yet the layout was so confusing it was impossible to be sure. Giovanni led them to the right at the top of the upper staircase, through an empty room, then another and, finally, Ted lay in a worn four-poster with threadbare linen. On the wall above him the unmistakable Lorenzo de' Medici six gilt-coloured balls gleamed from faded green paint. Elsewhere were old tapestries, as in the downstairs room, a chipped bust of a girl's head, and nothing else save a minimum of shabby furniture.

Ted Parsons watched them intently, his gnarled hands clutching the bedclothes in apparent agitation. A commode stood by the bed, and a carafe of water. Gemma put down her offering of fruit and magazines, watched by a carefully scrutinising invalid. But his pallor wasn't feigned.

'How are you feeling?' she asked sympathetically.

'Please, you no tire him,' Giovanni exhorted instantly.

'What d'yer think? Like Van Gogh's old boots.'

'Can we do anything for you?' Jonathan came to stand beside her.

'No.'

'Why did you want to see us then, Ted? To tell us how the turps got into the bottle?'

A spasm of retching, real or feigned, seized him, and Giovanni rushed protectively to his side, basin at the ready.

'Are you afraid of someone?'

There was no answer from Ted, only from Giovanni. 'Si.'

'Gladys?'

'*Sì.*'

Ted Parsons shook his head crossly. 'Nah!'

'Who then, Ted?' Gemma dreaded what might come, ridiculous though the thought even was. Paul of all people would not put turps in a bottle. If Paul were to do something, it occurred to her, he would make sure it worked. She caught herself quickly, amazed at the topsy-turvy ideas that came to her in this crazy fortress.

'Who, Ted?' Jonathan pressed.

'Little Vicky.'

Gemma felt Jonathan flinch at her side, as she did herself. *Victoria?* Who only had a year to live? Yet simultaneously the thought flashed through her mind that it had been Victoria who had urged her to seek out whether Ted Parsons was still alive, despite the evidence to the contrary – and she had unquestioningly obeyed. But if it *were* Victoria – where did that leave Jonathan?

'I don't believe that, Ted,' Jonathan said easily, dismissively. 'Why should she? She doesn't have half your strength.'

A weak giggle was the only answer, fingers plucked feverishly at the sheets.

'Is there some private reason you should think this?' ventured Gemma. 'An old love affair?'

Ted nodded eagerly. Too eagerly? Surely it couldn't be Victoria.

'Go now,' Giovanni almost commanded on cue. 'Signor Tositi tired.'

He looked remarkably bright to Gemma, but they could hardly stay on against Giovanni's wishes.

'Be careful, Ted,' she told him. 'I'll be back to see how you're getting on.' Inane clichés but she did not want to add anything more before Jonathan. She intended to talk to Orvino about money, for one thing. There was precious little here, and she owed Ted something for her grandfather's sake.

Giovanni led the way out. She followed him down the narrow staircase, assuming Jonathan was behind. But when they reached the first room, Giovanni stopped abruptly. '*Dov'è* Signor Vale?'

'I don't know.' She'd assumed he was behind, but he wasn't.

Giovanni uttered a shrill scream and rushed off like the White Rabbit back the other way. She followed, and found him already returning, with Jonathan in tow like a prize trophy.

'I just wanted to look at the tapestry room again,' he told her amiably. 'Giovanni, I think the signora and I will leave by the other exit into the church. More convenient, and more – educational.'

'*No.*'

'Why not?'

'Closed.'

At that moment came the sound of Tositi's voice and Giovanni disappeared, with an agonised look and injunctions to wait. Jonathan had no intention of doing any such thing. 'Come on.'

'Where to?'

'I want to walk that church exit-route again. You can satisfy yourself there are only the three floors: the ground, this main one and the one we've just come from. Hurry. I've a notion Giovanni is going to be most displeased.'

She followed quietly up the staircase again, along through the kitchens and down the far staircase.

'What do you think is odd about this?' she asked as they found themselves stumbling along the dank, dimly lit ground-floor passageway and through the heavy doors. Once she fell against him as he tripped up a step, twice she cannoned into him as he stopped, apparently to test the ceiling with his hands.

'This is a fine time to indulge hobbies,' she muttered.

'Work,' he reminded her.

'Of course.'

She was relieved when they reached the short flight of narrow stone steps circling up to the linking corridor, linking the palazzo to the San Lorenzo complex.

'Is that how you remember this route?' he asked as they reached the door at the top of the steps. There was an excitement in his voice that stone walls and stale air could not possibly account for.

She hesitated. 'No, but I can't think what's different.'

'Try, Gemma,' he urged.

And then she knew.

'We didn't pass a courtyard, Jonathan, the one we could see from the room beyond the tapestry room. I'm sure I saw it through an archway last time I came this way. *And* it seemed even darker in the corridor this time.'

He expelled a sigh of sheer pleasure. 'I thought I was dreaming. Look.' He raced her back down the steps and into the corridor. 'This arched door here – this must have been where you saw the courtyard, but it gives way only to another door.' He pushed through it and disappeared into complete blackness. A smell of fetid air met her nostrils; to her relief he quickly reappeared. Standing alone surrounded by silence and darkness was distinctly unnerving. 'It seems to be an almost completely enclosed room, empty. There's a gap in the inner wall, though,' he told her. 'Interesting.'

'Frantically,' she agreed.

He grinned, then strode up to the door at the end of the first stretch of corridor. His hand was on it, ready to open it, when the sound of Giovanni's pounding footsteps reached them. 'Back,' he hissed. Obediently she ran up the steps again, and stopped in the bridging corridor, questioningly.

'What now?'

For answer, he held her back along the inner wall as Giovanni reached the door beneath them.

'Am I in the *Prisoner of Zenda*?' she hissed.

'Unfortunately I left my broadsword at home today,' he whispered back. 'Let's hope he assumes we've gone, and doesn't lock the door.'

'Why?'

'We're going back in.'

'*Why?*' she asked again, exasperated, as the sound of the footsteps receded.

'Darling Gem, there's a disappearing room and a disappearing courtyard. Don't you want to know where they are?' When all was quiet, Jonathan shot back to the lower corridor and felt its inner walls. 'I think it's thick enough,' he said, apparently to himself.

'For *what*?'

'Brick and tile. It's substantial enough, but not too much so. It's rotting. But not at the bottom.' His voice rose in excitement. 'This floor's been repaired and it's comparatively flimsy.'

'Do you mind telling me what this is about?'

'Do you mind giving me two seconds of quiet while the Great Man thinks. Then I'll tell you. Truly.'

'As quiet as a particularly unliberated mouse,' she said through gritted teeth.

'Gemma, you don't know how right you are. We're *in* a mouse, a medieval mouse.' His voice rose in excitement, and he hugged her, then swung her round.

'I presume,' she observed drily when he finally released her, 'this palazzo is where the Medicis put prisoners they wanted to go slowly mad.'

'Quiet. This time Giovanni *really* mustn't know we're here or we'll not find that room.'

Jonathan set off back along the corridor into the palazzo. He halted abruptly at the first doorway, so that she cannoned into him again. He examined the ceiling once more with great interest, and began to grin infuriatingly. No way was she going to ask why. He set off again, then stopped. 'There must be another door,' he muttered. '*Yes*! Here. Do you see, on the right here? It's painted out – a *trompe-l'oeil* to deceive the eye.' He pushed and it opened, revealing a dark and smelly interior with a few steps leading down.

'I'm not going down *there*,' Gemma told him, peering round his shoulder.

'Where's your spirit of adventure?'

'Cowering behind my fear of rats.'

'A mouse is what we're looking for.'

'Not without a torch.'

'I have a small one in my pocket. Sorry, I forgot about it. Did you think, in Mae West's immortal words, I was just pleased to see you?'

'Down here, believe me, Jonathan, I *am*.'

Cursing all absent-minded historians, she stumbled down after him and the pinprick of light, and once down in the cellar clutched at him, feeling ridiculously like a child alone in the dark, but not caring.

'It's a workroom,' she said, as he shone the dim light around.

'Nearly.' The satisfaction of one proved right oozed from his voice. 'It's a huge engine room that goes right under the house. Correction: two rooms at least. There's a small one there, controlling the corridor. Medieval engine rooms, Gemma. Look!' He started to move in his enthusiasm, and she found herself shrieking hoarsely.

'Don't go without me.'

'Sorry,' he grabbed her arm. 'Hold on. Keep close to me.'

'Delighted,' she said savagely.

'I hate to puncture your ego, but down there there are things even more exciting than your lovely body.'

'To you perhaps. To me the latter seems rather important.'

'Gemma, just look at this.' He squatted down by one of the half-dozen or so huge capstans, with iron ropes round them. 'They're run by powerful motors now, of course. Don't you see, this place is *used*, Gemma. When it was first built, teams of men would haul them in by hand, now two old men do it by pressing a few switches. Oh, there was money around when Ted Parsons first moved in here.'

'But why are you so excited?'

'How would you feel if you looked on the Pomona for the first time? If you found a crock of gold? If you looked on the completed memorial to the Lakenham Set? To me this is the most exciting thing I've ever seen in my career.'

'But what are they?' she asked, bewildered. 'What do they draw in? Some kind of drawbridge?'

'That's part of it.' He flashed the torch. 'I think we'll

find those smaller capstans there operate mini iron gates, like lock gates, to the bottom level of the palazzo. At the far end, under the bridging corridor, there must be some reverse machinery, I suppose. Those even smaller capstans controlling the corridor in there must open to let the mouse in—'

'And what's a *mouse*, damn you?'

'A medieval machine of war, well, Roman, in fact. It was used in a siege. The idea was you built a huge tower or belfry on wheels, from brick and tile, and made it as resistant to fire as possible. It had several storeys and held men to defend the mouse as the whole contraption was wheeled closer to the walls. The mouse was a long gallery built out from its ground floor, which would be run right up to the enemy walls. Under its cover you could dig away at the enemy fortress's foundations, while up above your archers and stone-chuckers kept the enemy busy. You know what I think, Gemma? This must be Lorenzo's own special version of the mouse. It's separate from its tower and its objective was the reverse. It was a defensive measure, not offensive.'

'Explain, O Great Master.'

'I *think*, merely a humble "think", Gemma, that it was his escape route from the church, just in case another attempt was made on his life. The quarry, i.e. Lorenzo, would come dashing along the bridging corridor and leap into the crenelle—'

'The what?'

'We took it for a deep window with a shutter, and the corresponding space in the outer wall for a window. It wasn't. The outer wall hole was an embrasure, covered with a door, painted as a *trompe-l'oeil* of stone, and giving way to the shuttered crenelle – they were still

used in fortresses for quick escape on behalf of the
besieged as well as for pot-shots at the enemy. As soon
as Lorenzo had hopped in the inner wall, the shutter
would be dropped more quickly and more securely than
any door could be bolted, after killing any assailants
they could see. The rest of the hunters would turn
down the staircase and find themselves in the mouse,
which would begin to trundle off into the palazzo
proper under a small portcullis.'

'So that's why you gazed so enthusiastically heaven-
wards?' she asked resignedly.

'Yes. There was definitely one there at some time. I
suppose those who didn't make the mouse would dash
through the side arch into the courtyard where they
would be impaled by an arrow from the receding tower,
or blown apart by a harquebus.' He cocked an eye at her.
'You do see, Gemma,' he continued, 'why I'm excited?
This one is still *working*. I'll do a monograph—'

'You'll do some more explaining to me first, please.'

'What, for instance?'

'I see the mouse explains the disappearing courtyard,
but where does the *tower* go – oh!' She smote her
forehead.

'Precisely. It goes into the building and presumably fits
into the room you first met Ted in. I wonder what they
did about floors – the room I saw must be fifteen feet or
so wide. What happens to the—'

'*Why?*'

'I need paper,' he said abruptly. 'I need to think this
out. Do you have any?'

'I could produce a petticoat in true heroine fashion.'

'Later. Not the time,' he said absently.

The darkness was beginning to get to her. Jonathan

prowled round the engine room leaving her looking at his dark shadow in a pinprick light. Suppose Giovanni returned? Suppose he slammed the door on them? Claustrophobia began to envelop her. 'Can we go?' she asked stiltedly.

He came up to her and peered at her. 'Yes.' He took her arm, and then they were through the door onto the staircase. What had once seemed dark now struck her like fresh air. She breathed it in gratefully.

'All right?' he asked.

'Yes.'

'Can you take more? Your painted room should be visible if we're right.'

She was tempted to rush away, back to sanity, but the lure of the solution of the puzzle won. She hurried up the steps.

'Gently, we don't want Giovanni on our track,' he warned her. 'They've gone to some pains to make sure we don't see that room.'

There was no sound from the house. Thankfully Giovanni was not in the kitchen, and they were down the staircase without alerting him to their presence. The tapestry room was empty. The far door stood closed against them; it was a magnet drawing them both towards it. The knob, one push – and all would be revealed. He gestured for her to go first. 'Yours, Ali Baba.'

'Let's hope I don't get the boiling oil.' She put her hand on the knob, smiled tentatively at him, now as excited as was he. Her hand, sweaty with excitement, slipped on the knob and she tried again, pushing the door open. She stepped over the threshold and he came quickly in after her.

'I wasn't wrong,' was all she could say. 'It *is* here and – it *is* alive.'

He said nothing, just stared transfixed at what surrounded them. From all four walls medieval Florentines jousted, rejoiced, celebrated. Round the dome with its central light the saints and the Virgin Mary reigned over them. On the rest of the painted ceiling, pagan gods and goddesses riotously illustrated the changing of the seasons. A glorious medley of theme and colour, which crazily harmonised into a whole. But it was the frescos that held Jonathan's attention.

'Haven't we seen something like this before?' he said eventually, as she came to stand by him.

'Yes. Santa Maria Novella. The Ghirlandaio frescos.' And, she realised now, the fresco of the Last Supper in the refectory by the Cloister. 'But surely these can't be – '

'Why not?' he asked quietly. 'We've found Lorenzo's infernal machines. Why not his treasures? Look at the grouping and the architecture, the background, landscape. Faultless. Who else but Ghirlandaio? And above all, look at *it*. The soul, if you like. The infinite grace. The *rightness* of it.'

'You remember the figure sitting on the steps, that you showed me in the Santa Maria Novella frescos?' she began, wondering whether excitement was making her imagination leap too far ahead of reason.

'The one attributed to Michelangelo?'

'Look at this.' She led him to the opposite wall, and pointed to two of the figures in the crowd: an old man applauding the tournament, and a mother holding a baby. 'Don't you think those faces are in the same style? They stand out so boldly, almost in a three-dimensional effect. You found your medieval mouse preserved. Why

302

not Michelangelo too?' It was out, she had said it, ridiculous or not.

'Glad you like my work, duckies.'

Ted Parsons, supported by a livid Giovanni, stood in the doorway, complete with black velvet dressing gown over a purple nightshirt.

'Yours, Ted?' she asked blankly.

He sniggered. 'My restoration, I meant, young lady,' he amended. 'Purely restoration, of course.'

Chapter Ten

Jonathan's unexpected deep laugh greeted this statement, bringing forth a scream of indignant abuse from Ted. He let go of Giovanni's shoulder in his agitation and shuffled forward menacingly. Jonathan parried this with an amiable, 'Go and sit on your throne, Ted, while we have a closer look. Then you tell us about it – as much or as little as you like.'

Rather surprisingly, Ted did as he was told. Nevertheless Gemma was conscious that, as he took possession of his throne, Ted Parsons seemed imperceptibly to change into Lorenzo Tositi. He and Giovanni watched suspiciously as she and Jonathan studied the frescos more closely.

The fresco covering the wall nearest to them was of a young woman in exquisite blue Florentine dress, presenting an ornamental helmet, obviously an award, to a young man in a velvet coat and cap studded with precious stones, whom she recognised as Lorenzo de' Medici. At his side stood another equally splendidly clad youth, and behind him a page bearing an exquisitely painted standard, bearing the legend *Le Temps Revient*. On the flanking wall was the joust itself, Lorenzo in silver armour, his helmet surmounted with plumes and the horse covered with a cloth of blue and gold. On the outside wall, the roles were reversed. The second youth was receiving the award from a different woman and Lorenzo and the first woman stood watching. Behind the throne, painted panels brought the couples together: four stylised portraits, the two men kneeling on the inner panels, the young women receiving their homage on the outer. To balance earthly love, above them shone its sacred form, an Annunciation scene and the Birth of Jesus, and that of John the Baptist. To balance them, around them the classical gods and goddesses disported themselves in lusty fertility.

And yet, was her immediate thought, against all reason, the whole room in its disparate elements of pagan, secular and holy *gelled*.

'And you say you *restored* these, Ted?' Jonathan asked quietly.

'Certainly.'

Jonathan went up and deliberately examined the frescos, watched uneasily by Tositi.

'Come off it. Define what you mean by restoration. You're a craftsman – Ted.' He added the name deliberately. 'Be specific. Do you mean cleaning or restoration? You can still see the plaster joins here where one day's work finished and the next day's began. Any cleaning work would have to have been done pretty carefully in order not to ruin any parts painted later by the artist in distemper with an agglutinant which dissolves in water. Yet look at the ultramarine on this man's sleeves – that's one of the colours that must be in distemper, yet it's showing more wear and tear than the faces. Did you omit to clean all the parts in distemper? If so, why do the frescos look so uniformly harmonised in tone? The same goes for restoration. How would you have matched all the subtle tones of the original fresco paints? These are all faded with age, grown old together. And look at this patch of mildew, and the corner where it's flaking. Did you throw up the job halfway? Was it too difficult?'

'I did not,' Ted shouted, taking this as personal insult. 'They were whitewashed over, were they not, Giovanni, when we came here? I, Lorenzo Tositi, cleaned off the whitewash. I took the very crumbs from my mouth to spare the distemper. I *saved* them.'

'A remarkable job,' Jonathan said politely. 'So these aren't fakes, they're the originals?'

'Naturally,' Ted replied with dignity.

And the Pomona, Gemma longed to ask. And the Michelangelo drawings? Are they all genuine? And where are they?

'What about the mouse? And the tower, your moving room on wheels? That's fifteenth century too? Restored, of course.'

Ted looked relieved, as if they had moved to safer ground. 'Lorenzo's little idea. Ingenious, isn't it?'

'I don't see what purpose the tower serves,' Gemma asked.

'It hid this – ' Ted waved a lordly hand – 'from prying eyes.'

'And that's all?'

'Nah. They're a couple of mousetraps, see? Lorenzo figured he would come along at the double, straight through the window into the tower packed with archers and gunners. Hey presto, he was conveyed straight into home-sweet-home, the villains would rush down the steps into mousetrap number one, and they'd run through the side arches into the bottom of the tower

and find themselves in mousetrap two. The upper
tower moves forward in here, the iron gates open down
below, and the lower wall of the old tower passes
through.'

'The gap presumably slides past a central retaining
pillar?' Jonathan asked, intrigued, sketching busily in a
pocket diary.

'Yeah. Clever, ain't it? If they stay in mousetrap one
they're taken on, the doors are whipped open and they're
greeted by some jolly gents with arrows and guns. And if
they *miss* both buses, they can only go one way – into the
courtyard, where the archers and harquebus gents knock
'em off from the back of the tower. Clever.'

'Whoever designed it must have been,' said Jonathan
feelingly. 'I suppose . . .' A sudden thought seemed to
strike him. 'Who *did* design it?'

Ted grinned. 'Lorenzo,' he replied mockingly. 'Of
course.'

'You seem to know a lot about Lorenzo's life,' Gemma
observed.

'Signor Orvino's a bit of a historian,' was the bland
reply.

'How does the tower get in?' Jonathan was concentrating on his own passion. 'It slips between the iron gates on
the ground floor of the main palazzo. But how do the
gates close again; to support the weight, how does the—?'

'They don't, old chum. Lorenzo had the pillar added and
the walls strengthened down below and the floor up here
ain't that wide, eighteen feet maybe. See for yourself.'

'Even so, to get the upper part of the tower over the
floor of this room must take some doing. I presume the
tower has no floor of its own, Ted, or it would be
impossible?'

Tositi visibly wavered, and then obviously saw that nothing further could be lost; he made an impatient sign to Giovanni, who reluctantly swept aside rugs to reveal a complete floor.

Jonathan stared. 'How?' he asked.

Ted shrugged modestly. 'The tower walls run along grooves, and the floor has beams underneath that rest on the real floor.' He made it sound breathtakingly simple.

'But how on earth does the upper part of the tower support itself then? It can't just hang in space until the palazzo floor slides under it.'

'The front of it rests on that shelf outside,' Ted told him, 'snug as a jam jar in a larder, and the middle and back have got four hangers and brackets, them pretty pillars to you. Underneath there are legs, propping it up on the lower walls. Lovely little legs, just like Gem's. And nice little knees – hinges to you. The tower slides in, they hinge back and let the old palazzo floor take the weight of their poor old feet.'

Gemma tried to puzzle this out, but in vain. 'I may be dim, but how does it get past the wall behind you, Ted?'

'Can't reveal all my secrets, love.'

'I can. Illusion, isn't it, Ted?' Jonathan asked hopefully. He strolled confidently up to the painted panels. 'See – this painting is all in tempera, not fresco; there's no plaster. The walls are of wood. And here's another *trompe-l'oeil*, Gemma. You see this painted pillar here, between the two men? There's a crack in it; it looks like the fluting of the pillar. But the man's hand that extends so gracefully over the pillar is the knob to open up the panels. It looks painted; in fact it's three-dimensional. It presumably pulls the panels back to rest parallel with the side walls as the tower glides in.'

Giovanni beamed, reconciled at such perception. '*Sì, sì.*'

'Ingenious. Your idea too, Ted?'

'Lorenzo's,' he replied airily.

'Just when did you move here, Ted, and why?' Gemma asked curiously.

Ted clutched Giovanni's hand. 'I'm not feeling too good,' he declared weakly. 'I think it was after Helmut died. I took that hard, very hard.' He leant against Giovanni, breathing theatrically loudly.

'And how did you live?'

No reply this time.

'Shall we guess?' Gemma asked gently.

'Take me away, Giovanni.' He clutched his heart.

'You lived on the proceeds of the Pomona?'

His answering glare confirmed her belief. 'You sold it, didn't you?' she went on. 'Once Helmut was dead, you could keep all the proceeds. Where is it now, incidentally? It hasn't surfaced in any art galleries apparently.'

'I may have told 'em to keep it out of sight,' Ted said faintly. 'It was pinched from the Eastern bloc's state heritage.'

'But Helmut got it from Austria.'

He looked vague. 'Did he?'

The terrible suspicion came to her that Helmut might have been helped on his way to the afterlife, or did she have murder on the brain? Gemma forced herself to go on. 'How could you part with it, Ted?' she asked gently.

This time he didn't answer.

'Or did you sell another fake?'

'Dear lady, who do you think I am?' Ted, suddenly restored to indignant, vigorous life, laid hand on heart virtuously. 'I am, or was, a most respectable restorer.'

'Who did the fake Leonardo for London then?'

'Helmut.'

'I'm not sure I believe you.'

'Then I can't help you, love,' Ted told her regretfully.

'All these frescos are real, the Leonardo Pomona's real, so were the Michelangelos. You're a lucky chap, Ted.'

'I think so,' he murmured modestly.

'But not a businessman. You should be living in a real palace, not in poverty.'

He glared, caught in a trap of his own making. 'I was. The money ran out.'

'Then why not produce more fakes?'

'*Fakes?*' he shrieked. 'That was Helmut.'

'So you know about them. Tell us, Ted. We're not going to turn you in.'

There was clear deliberation, then Tositi vanished and Ted Parsons was back with them, as chirpy and slippery as he must have been forty years ago. 'It started when I left the old bag – Gladys, that is. I'd gone in with a partner, nicking. Small time, but I learned the trade OK. One day we turned over this old house at Southend. Me mate were after the silver, he wouldn't let me touch it. I grabbed a pile of old junk from the cellar. Laugh? I thought he'd split his sides. Junk it was. But there was something there took my eye. I flogged the rest, but I kept this thing around. Didn't look much. It was an old piece of wood in a sort of round, shield shape. Old pub sign maybe, I dunno. But it had a dragon on the front, breathing fire and fumes like it was bonfire night in the gunpowder factory. Startling, it was. Not nice, says Gladys. She chucks it out one day. I left her there and then. Know what it was?'

'Um. Not,' Jonathan asked politely, 'the famous shield Leonardo is supposed to have painted as a youth, and on which his father exercised some acute commercial acumen, by switching between artist and purchaser with a plain bit of wood with a daub painted on it?'

'The same, mate.' Ted was clearly annoyed at having his thunder stolen. 'I never did track it down again. Burnt, most like. But I was right. Soon as I saw Leonardo's Medusa, I thought, that's it, Ted my lad. The same hand painted that. I've got a nose that can sniff right from wrong. Though with pictures it's different. You *sees* and you *feels*.' He looked soulful, and staggered against his trusty companion, who led him tenderly to a glass of restorative water, which was impatiently waved aside.

'It got me interested like,' Ted continued. 'Then the war came. You don't see much in the way of Old Masters in the Eighth Army.' A cough to remind them of his delicate condition due to war service. 'In PoW camp it was different. I picked up a lot from one fellow.'

'He's a famous painter now.'

'Is he?' Ted showed no interest.

'And you taught forging, I gather.' Gemma pinned him down.

'A useful service to my fellow prisoners.'

'And to a future career?'

'You gotta learn all you can about the trade, ain't you? Old Masters are heads, fakes are tails. All part of the same penny.'

'That's one way of looking at it,' Jonathan agreed.

'Then I met Helmut. Now Helmut knew what we were up to. Gave us a few tips. A rare one was Helmut. And he had contacts. He'd been in Colditz and other camps, where there were aristos from all over. He treated them

312

OK, got friendly. He could see which way the wind was blowing in the war, and it weren't towards the Reichstag. After the war – there wasn't no Berlin Wall yet – he kept in touch and found all these aristos desperate to flog the family jewels – those that still had estates to go to or had hidden the old assets well enough. Those that didn't – and this was where Helmut was a shrewd one – he didn't drop them like maggoty plums, he kept them on working for him.'

'*Working?*'

'Of course. One great big Mafia, the aristos. They'd flog stuff to their own when they wouldn't even trust Helmut.'

'And you were the London end, to sell them.'

'Got it in one. I mugged up on the act, went round the museums. Refined my eyes to see proper. Course, the stuff we were dealing in was genuine. And then Helmut got wind of the Pomona. This was the big one. It took years to track it down, and in the end she lay down for us like the plump little beauty she was.'

'The real one?'

'When you look at something like that, you don't need to ask, do you? You know. It's glory, mate.' A soulful look came into his eyes. 'She, with her veils floating around her and a face like an angel; only a hint of fruitiness, if you know what I mean. Helmut and me was almost crying, I can tell you. Could we part with it? We could not. So I said, why need we? We'll do a fake – we've been giving them genuine stuff so long, they'll think it genuine.'

Put that way, it sounded eminently reasonable. Gemma was almost persuaded she'd have done the same herself.

'Then how did you force yourself to let her go in the long run?' Jonathan inquired, obviously not convinced.

'We had to live. The good thing about frescos,' he looked round lovingly, 'is they stay put.'

'You could sell them if you wanted to,' Jonathan pointed out. 'They could be moved if someone was prepared to pay – if, as you say, they're genuine, of course.'

'Nah. This is where they live, this is where they stay. Why, it would be like betraying old Lorenzo,' Ted said hastily.

Something you'd never do to an old friend, Gemma thought, amused.

'You realise how unique this is, don't you? Secular art mixed with sacred, when secular subjects were only just beginning to be acceptable. And look at this . . . this . . . pageant.' Jonathan seemed lost for words as he indicated the tournament and the portraits.

'Old Lorenzo's love-nest,' Ted commented with relish. 'Not too erotic, but the best they could manage in them days. He built and fortified this place after the assassination attempt in '78. But he didn't commission old Domenico to paint these till the year his wife died, 1488. I reckon he'd gone maudlin and decided to dedicate a room to his first sweetheart, Lucrezia Donati: he always carried a torch for her, although she was married to someone else. He put on this tournament supposedly to celebrate his own betrothal in 1469, but he made little Lucy Queen of the May or whatever and asked her to present prizes to the victor. No expense spared. He wasn't too hot at the old jousting lark, but guess who the victor was? Our Lorenzo. *What* a surprise, eh? A few years later he did the same for brother Giuliano and his

314

current girlie, Simonetta someone. You've got a bit of her look about you,' he told Gemma approvingly. 'Nice little bird by all accounts, but she died the next year.'

'And you keep all these frescos to yourself. Why?'

'Because I sold the bloody Pomona, that's why,' he said piously. 'I had to atone. It's my penance. Anyway,' he added more practically, 'if people knew where I lived, that scum in London would be after me.'

'It's nearly fifty years ago, Ted. Do you really think they'd come racing over here?'

'Gladys did. And Victoria. And look what's bleeding well happened,' he told her querulously.

'Very well,' Gemma soothed him. 'But if we assured you there'd be no danger, wouldn't you let an expert in just to *see* them?'

'I *am* an expert.' Ted began to giggle hysterically.

'You tire him. He is sick, sick. They try to kill him,' Giovanni pointed out yet again. 'Lorenzo, *Lorenzo, il mio signore.*'

How beautiful the words sounded in Italian. There was genuine affection there, thought Gemma; she could not determine its source, but its existence could not be doubted.

'*Sì*. Victoria tried to kill me.'

'I can't believe it,' Jonathan said flatly.

'Then who? You, Johnnie? You, Gem? My own wife? My own son?'

'We'd better go. You need rest,' Gemma intervened quickly. 'Could we come back just with Signor Orvino to see the frescos again? And perhaps someone he might vouch for who is experienced in fresco work?'

'No. *No!*'

'But why not?'

'No! Roberto, you. No one else. I'm off.'

'Why not, Ted?' Jonathan blocked his path. 'There's some other reason.'

'They would say – because it suits their purpose – that they are fakes,' he said sulkily.

'But why should that worry you if they are real and you want to keep them?'

'You don't understand. Fools, fools, I am surrounded by fools!'

'Make us understand, Ted.' Jonathan held Giovanni easily off, while he still blocked Ted's passing.

'No, Jonathan, no,' Gemma pleaded. 'You're pushing too far.'

'I'll push to the truth,' Jonathan said grimly. 'What *is* it, Ted?'

'I painted them.' It was a whisper, barely audible.

'You mean they *are* fakes?' Gemma asked uncertainly.

'Art,' he corrected sulkily. 'By me.'

'When did you do them?' Jonathan demanded.

'Twenty, maybe thirty years ago.'

'And if we don't believe you?' He glanced round the room.

'Time will prove me right. After I am gone.' He was regaining confidence now, grandiose.

'Fortunately time as yet has not laid his icy hand on them,' Jonathan said, looking at them, marvelling. 'Odd if they are fakes. They'd have shown themselves as such by now.'

'Blimey, do you think if they were not fakes, I'd live like this? My penance,' Ted mimicked himself, giggling.

'I don't know,' Gemma answered him after a moment. 'With you, Ted, I don't think I can begin to guess.'

'Do you think I'd risk me life, even for the sake of

three-quarters of a million quid, if I had Lorenzo's frescoed room to sell to a grateful public?' he mocked. 'Michelangelos and all,' he added as a throwaway.

It was an unanswerable argument.

'If they're fakes, why bother to add the Michelangelo touch?' Gemma asked. 'And if they're *not*, is it possible they're real too?' Ted had made his exit on his grand line, and they had promptly been shepherded out by Giovanni. An espresso in the Piazza della Signoria seemed a good idea.

'It's possible. It fits. Michelangelo was at Ghirlandaio's studio the year these frescos were commissioned, and when Ghirlandaio was in the middle of tackling the Santa Maria Novella commission for Lorenzo's mum's family. As an apprentice, Michelangelo would have a small hand in both commissions. The following year he broke his apprenticeship – or Ghirlandaio agreed to let him go – and went to work in Lorenzo's sculpture garden under Bertoldo. Normally apprentices grouped colours, prepared plaster and, if very, very lucky, did minor parts of the painting under guidance. The master did the faces, the apprentices the draperies sometimes. But the story about Michelangelo is that even Ghirlandaio acknowledged the boy's genius as superior to his; that Michelangelo took every opportunity to do as much as he could on the frescos, with or without permission,' Jonathan paused. 'Do you fancy lunch before you depart?'

She was catching an afternoon flight. 'That would be nice.'

'At the flat or restaurant?'

'A trattoria would be nice.'

'So it would. You're very distrustful, Gemma.'

'After this morning, can you wonder? Trust and truth seem to have movable goalposts. I don't believe a word he says. Do you?'

'Stand up the real Ted Parsons?'

'I'm not sure there is one,' she said, as they went into the nearest trattoria. 'I think he's lost touch with reality and forgotten the truth himself. It's all one big con.'

'Can't be,' Jonathan pointed out. 'The frescos are real enough, whether he painted them, or Ghirlandaio, or Michelangelo.'

'How do we know which?'

'In support of the Michelangelo theory, one could say it might be the answer to something scholars have never been sure of – just how he came to Lorenzo de' Medici's attention. If he were playing a significant part in the work here, it's easily understandable. In support of Ghirlandaio, I think undoubtedly they're his overall style. There's a rather horrid red he's rather keen on that popped up in those portraits – ever seen his *Virgin and Child* in the National Gallery? Fortunately he spared the frescos, or they'd lose a lot of subtle tones.'

'And in support of Old Master Ted?'

'The sheer unlikelihood of undiscovered Florentine masterpieces. Anyway, there's a school of thought which believes it doesn't matter *who* painted what, that what the eye sees and the brain interprets are the only criterion.'

'But isn't that a con if you paint in the style of someone else?'

'Not necessarily. Diamonds are beautiful whether they're worth millions or tuppence. It's the value placed on them that is the arguing point.'

318

'Try telling that to the art market. Or to Rosalind Chambers.'

'Anyway, it's not really relevant. Let's concentrate on lunch. Or even the tontine—' Suddenly the latter seemed uncomplicated by comparison.

'Suppose it's linked?'

'Lunch and the tontine?'

'Idiot. I mean the tontine and who tried to kill Ted.'

'We don't *know* it's to do with the tontine, do we? It could be Gladys's long-hankered-for revenge. It could be Bert's. Or suppose this is *all* a con, Gemma. Thought of that?'

'I don't understand.'

'How do we *know* Tositi is Ted Parsons?'

She looked at him aghast, feeling ground slipping under her feet. 'He's convinced Felix.'

'Ted Parsons was a con-man, so was Helmut. Tositi *is*, I reckon. Remember the old philosophical chestnut: Empedocles the Cretan declared that *all* Cretan men were liars. Where does that leave truth?'

'I *feel* he's Ted Parsons. Jonathan, I meet a lot of people in my work, especially the big assignments. It's like biting the bad sovereign. With con-men there is an infinitesimal pause before the answer comes back. It's like speaking over an old transatlantic phone line, only the pause is much less discernible. The answer is rushing through a brain computer before it's given to you. You don't always realise it at the time, but afterwards, summing somebody up, you do.'

'And you get that with Parsons?'

'With Parsons, perhaps, but not with Tositi. He *believes* in Tositi, Jonathan, and Ted is far in the past.'

'They're one and the same, Gemma. Your nose, as Ted

would say, is letting you down rather badly in this case.'

'You don't *know* about Ted.'

'I had in mind Paul Shane.'

The spaghetti suddenly looked the less inviting. 'Did you?'

'No need to get over-excited. Just be careful.'

'Because of fifteen million pounds? I'm sick of being told that. Don't you think I take it into account? Anyway, why should he threaten me in any way? Gladys is surely going to outlive Ted.'

'No harm in having a safety net. And Victoria's not got long to go.'

'Why did Paul fancy me and not the gorgeous young blonde then?' she asked belligerently. 'I had no idea at first if Ted was alive or not.'

'What makes you think Paul didn't?'

She almost choked over her spaghetti. 'If you're trying to tell me he was chatting up Annie as well as me, I simply don't believe it. He's too serious and straightforward.'

'Where was he that evening I came to your cottage?'

'At the office,' she snapped.

'Working late, no doubt.'

'Yes.'

'Tell me, when you both thought Ted Parsons died in 1957, did Paul still seem as keen?'

'Of course.' Had he? She had a sudden doubt. It was all so long ago now, and so much had happened since. Uneasily she recalled Paul's lack of contact. But there were reasons for that. Good ones. Weren't there?

She left Florence with relief, glad she was leaving Jonathan behind, glad to escape from what seemed one

vast city of illusion and doubt. There seemed new glories
in Britain's solid, down-to-earth grime. As a result she
found she was embracing work eagerly, welcoming all the
dull routine she had so often rebelled against. So much
for Gemma Maitland, Special Agent. This assignment
she should write off and let fate decide the outcome, but
at the back of her mind she was dissatisfied. There were
so many unanswered questions, and nothing she could do
about any of them. Or rather, there was one thing she
could do, compromise though it was. She arranged a
meeting with Felix, Paul – and Charles. Charles, not
Jonathan. Too many sudden deaths, too much coincidence, and this was not her problem alone, it was a joint
one.

Felix chaired it at his office. 'An attempt on Parsons'
life? Are you sure?'

'Certainly.' Gemma looked at Charles. 'Your son can
confirm it.'

'Is there any other proof?' Charles asked mildly. 'A
doctor's evidence, for instance?'

'One was called and Ted was obviously in great pain.
Don't you think it's a big coincidence, three of them out
of five?'

'Yes. But to be practical, Gemma, what can the bank
do? The Italian police have investigated and put Stanley's
death down as an accident. Even if the nephew wants to
kick up a fuss, it's nothing to do with the trust now
Stanley's dead, callous though that sounds,' Felix pointed
out. 'So that leaves John Peacock. Accidental poisoning.
Body cremated.'

'But there must be *something* we can do? We can't just
sit by and do nothing if one of the others is threatened.'

'What do you suggest? The police can hardly put an

armed guard on the remaining three for the rest of their lives. The most we can do is to warn them of putative danger. We may deter a crime that way.'

It had got her nowhere. On the way out, Charles hesitated, obviously wanting to talk to her, but Paul forestalled him, appropriating her with a, 'I'm sure you don't mind, Charles.'

'But *I* do,' Gemma muttered crossly. She had no wish for a tête-à-tête, but by that time Charles had given up and was talking to Felix.

'You're avoiding me, Gemma. Why?'

'Am I?'

Was it just her annoyance that set up this barrier inside her, this reluctance to share her experience in Florence? Or had, terrible thought, she been influenced against her will by Jonathan, or by desire and the treacherous body? Paul had shared the tontine problem with her since the beginning. He had been the one to help her through her grandfather's loss. She wasn't being fair to him.

'Did you find the Pomona?' he demanded lightly.

'No.' An easy one that, particularly as Paul probably imagined he was skirting round the chief issue.

'Has Ted admitted it existed?'

'No. He says it was a fake.'

'Then it's Vale.'

'What is?' she stonewalled.

'He's flourished his special magnet, and managed to put you off me.'

'Do you think I'm so easily led?'

'Anyone is by an expert like Vale.'

'I'm tired of people telling me what I should believe and not believe,' she countered vehemently. 'Just leave me alone to decide my own beliefs.'

'Then he has been trying to put you off me. By harping on about Annie Masters, no doubt.'

'Yes.' She was relieved to have it in the open.

'Has it not occurred to you that darling Annie would prefer a coronet to accompany her fifteen million? True, Gladys is a better bet than Victoria, so Annie likes to keep her options open, though not conspicuously so far as I'm concerned, thank goodness.'

'It's all very childish.'

'Marriage is when you boil it down to the essentials. Updated fertility rituals, that's all, plus hard bargaining.'

'You think I'm part of it?'

'I think you're confused, not seeing things clearly.'

'And as a solicitor you are, and thus entitled to warn me off Jonathan.' Why was she getting so defensive about him, it occurred to her. Pig-headedness probably.

'Is this – ' he swallowed – 'why you don't want to go to bed with me?'

'No,' she cried, anguished. Some small part of her mind was wondering whether Moorgate Station usually hosted conversations like this. 'I *do*. Oh, Paul, I do.' She hugged him, but he remained tense, unresponsive. 'Don't you see, I'm fighting through my own personal jungle. If I get sidetracked, I might never get things straight.'

'And how long is that going to take?'

'When I'm ready, I'll know.'

'And if I don't choose to wait?'

'Then you must go. But I hope you don't – '

'Only if I can't stand the image of your cavorting in bed with Vale. He's conning you, Gemma. Cleverly, I grant, but he is. He's sized you up, judged what you want to hear and tosses it back to you like a gift. Vale doesn't abide by rules where women are concerned. Or anything, come to that.'

'That's enough – stop.'

He did, white-faced. 'I'm sorry, Gemma. I'd better go.'

She watched his back disappearing from the station down Moorgate until engulfed by the lunchtime crowds. She was alone, and suddenly she felt lonely.

Loretta perched on the back of the chair, feet splayed on the arms. With her build it required a delicate balancing act, but she always managed it. Loretta was like that; Gemma envied her.

'Don't mention hunks *or* men, if you please,' she stated firmly.

'Certainly not. In fact, you look as if you could do with a dose of non-stop hen parties to set the world in order, before a masculine gender crosses your path again.'

'You're so right. Anything on, or do you fancy a drink? Kirsty can bleep us if anything comes in.'

They were glad to see the fire lit in the Green Knight, cheering after the drizzle outside. No Indian summer this year, the weather gods seemed to be declaring.

'How happy could I be with either, were t'other dear charmer away?' carolled Loretta. 'That it?'

'No. I feel like abjuring men for ever.'

'Drastic measures. Not for you.'

'Do you think I'm the dependent sort?'

'No.'

'Why then?'

'There are lots of reasons men can come in handy.'

Gemma cautiously touched the nerve. 'Children?'

'Even more basic.'

'That needn't involve all the heart.'

'With me no, with you yes.'

'Not after Bill.

'*Because* of Bill.'

'Oh, Loretta.' Gemma put her glass down on the table. 'Am I such a fool? How can I be attracted not to one man but to two?'

'Or perhaps none at all. Perhaps your little heart has bounced back unhurt.'

'Now that's an encouraging thought. Another drink?'

'Yes. And here's another encouraging thought. You can always pass the hunk over to me.'

'I have an idea hunk may require more than either of our sweet loving selves. Fifteen million might help.'

'Getting cynical, are we?'

'I have to be.'

'No, you don't.'

'Wary then.'

'Wrong. You'll know when it's right. The fake will show up, given time.'

'That's the second time someone told me that – not about the hunk, though.' The hunk. Calling him that distanced him, distanced Florence and the frescos. Distanced, if she admitted it, desire.

She had a sudden urge to tell Loretta about the frescos, but something held her back. She knew there was no problem over confidentiality, for that was the first rule of their working relationship, but somehow she knew if she once voiced mention of them here, of anything other than was strictly essential about Florence, then back would come the cloud of confusion, back she would plummet into the whirlpool, with danger only to be avoided by grasping a helping hand. But whose?

★ ★ ★

This would be the first Christmas she'd spent alone, without Bill, now without her grandfather. She had not expected to mind, but she did. The prospect of sharing a turkey with Launcelot failed to have much appeal as the weeks rolled by. Paul had told her he was spending the holiday – a long one, of course, to make matters worse, with his mother in Scotland; he had invited her to join them, but she found she was glad of the excuse of business rotas not to accept. Her relationship with Paul was still delicately planted in no man's land, and too close an intimacy might tip it over – pushed by either party. What was she waiting for? She couldn't define it herself, save as a disinclination to leap off her clifftop into the quagmire that might be waiting – or not, of course.

She had heard nothing from Jonathan Vale, save a formal note telling her Ted was restored to full health: this she knew, for she'd heard direct from him, asking, to her surprise, if she would visit Florence again. She'd replied suggesting the spring, and had heard no more. Late November in Britain made the thought of Florence tempting, but in her business the busiest few weeks of the year lay ahead, the run-up to Christmas, and there was no way Arthur was going to be able to cover for that. He'd be too busy driving a fourth car.

The Saturday post brought a surprise in the form of a letter from Charles, inviting her to join his family for Christmas Day. Her first reaction was sheer pleasure at the kind thought behind it, and the wording convinced her it was no mere offer for form's sake. Christmas at Lakenham House was tempting. The way the weather was shaping up suggested a white Christmas was on the cards at least, and she imagined the Folly covered with snow. Her second reaction was more guarded. Jonathan would probably be there. The churning in her stomach began once more, until she pulled herself together. 'To hell with it,' she told herself. 'I'm going.'

The day darkened and she was glad to get back from an airport run without meeting bad weather. No sooner had she come off duty at ten than the phone rang.

'Gemma? Paul.'

'Hello—' She broke off in surprise. His tone was cold and clipped, something was definitely wrong. Badly wrong.

'Are you alone?'

'Yes.'

'I'm coming down.'

'Not tonight.'

'Tonight, Gemma. I'm nearly there. I've reached Canterbury.'

'No.'

'You'll have to see me. Gladys is dead.' And then there was only the buzz of the telephone in her ears.

She put the receiver down and automatically went to draw the curtains across. Outside soft snowflakes insidiously pattered on the windows, illuminated by the outside light, blown by relentless winds. Gladys, dead? Accident? Heart attack? Or were they back in the nightmare?

It took Paul twenty minutes to reach Bishopslee. By the time he arrived, the snow was blowing harder, beginning to settle with a vengeance, resting on his light coat, melting in his hair as he came in to the cottage. His mouth was set tensely.

'I've got hot cocoa ready.'

He hardly seemed to hear her, plunging straight into what he'd come to tell her, confirming her worst suspicions.

'She's been poisoned. She died on Thursday night. Bert said it was a fit, but the post-mortem showed otherwise. Cyanide. They're holding Bert,' he added, almost offhandedly.

'But that's crazy. He'd *never* poison his mother.'

'You know that, I know that. The police don't.' He covered his face with his hands in despair.

'I know you were fond of her, Paul,' she said gently. 'I was myself. She was a character. I'm so sorry.'

He sat up, his face full of misery. 'I'm not going to pretend to you, Gemma. I can't. Not to you. Yes, I liked her very much. But it's not that. It's the centre. Gone. I really thought I'd be able to build it. Create something worthwhile, *do* something to help put right the mess this country's in.'

She laid her hands on his. 'I understand. I really do.'

'You don't think the worse of me for it?'

'How could I? If I had a life's ambition, a good one, and saw it snuffed out by a whim of fate, or,' she plunged, 'by someone else's hand, I'd feel the same. Desperate.'

'It could have achieved so much. I saw it all. I practically lived there in my own mind. The centre would be at the hub of a huge web, county-wide, eventually even country-wide.'

Gemma let him talk on, sometimes incoherently, sometimes rationally, while he tried to work out his frustration. When at last he stopped, he was able to give her a weak grin. 'At least this affair will have one good effect, I suppose.'

'And that is?'

'You must realise I was right about Vale.'

'You believe Jonathan is behind this?'

He sighed. 'Gemma, you presumably don't think I did

328

Gladys in myself? Or that Bert did? Who else? It's either you, Victoria, or Vale, and I know who my money's on, as I suppose I can take it that it isn't you.'

She forced herself to think logically. Jonathan, who had accompanied Stanley back to the hotel before he was killed. How had he come to meet him so conveniently? What had Stanley learned that morning that he was so anxious to pass on to Felix? It must have come from Jonathan or Ted. And she had been so caught up over the frescos she had not pursued this line. Jonathan, on whose father's estate John Peacock had worked. All circumstantial. Nothing else.

'No,' she told him flatly. 'I can't accept he's a murderer.'

He shrugged. 'You have to, Gemma. There's no other explanation.' He wandered to the window, drew aside the curtains, glanced out at the falling snow. 'Gemma, let me stay tonight, please. I need you so much.'

So easy to say yes. She held herself back with great effort. 'You can stay,' she forced herself to say, 'but not—'

'Don't tell me. The sofa,' he said bitterly. 'Or do you have the luxury of a spare room. Don't worry. I'll go . . . find a hotel in Canterbury and drown my sorrows.'

'You can't. Look at the weather. The lane out to the Canterbury road may already be blocked,' she cried with genuine alarm.

'I'll get through. I'll ring when I get there, if you're worried.'

'Paul, I'm sorry.'

'Are you?'

'Yes.'

'Perhaps you are. But it doesn't change things, does it?'

She could not reply, for he was right.

She watched from the upstairs window as he managed to get the car moving, and gradually it disappeared from sight, two lights, then nothing but driving snow. She turned her light out, so that she could see the quiet woods, blanketed in white, silencing doubts in their stillness, calming in their completeness, and hugged the solitude to her as the friend it was.

'Jonathan?'

His voice over the phone sounded detached and cool. It helped. Paul had telephoned as promised to say he was safely in Canterbury, but it had made her determined to tell Jonathan the news herself, to gauge his reactions, she told herself.

'Yes, Gemma?'

'Have you heard about Gladys?'

'What about her?' Instant sharpness in his voice.

'I'm afraid she's dead.'

'*What?*' His horror sounded genuine enough. Then he fell silent.

'Are you still there?'

'Yes.'

'She was poisoned. You realise what that means?'

'Not straightaway. It needs thinking about. Does Bert need help or is Shane rallying round?'

She avoided this. 'Bert's being held by the police for questioning, but it's impossible to think he had anything to do with it.'

'As I said, it needs thinking about. Thank you for letting me know.' There was finality in his voice that spelled the end of the conversation. Not yet, if she had anything to do with it.

'I want to see Victoria, Jonathan. Do you mind?'

'No. Why, though? You don't think *she* put cyanide in the cider?'

The handset was suddenly clammy. 'À la Inspector Clouseau, I didn't say it was cyanide.'

A pause. 'So that's the way the wind blows, is it? Shanewards. Just a phrase, Gemma.'

'Of course. But it *was* cyanide.'

He dismissed this. 'Gemma, I can trust you not to go accusing Victoria of murder, can't I? She's not very strong.'

'Of course.'

'And only you go, not Shane.'

'You make yourself so charmingly clear.'

'Good.' He put the phone down.

If Victoria was surprised at Gemma's visit, she did not display it. The snow had iced up on the ground, making business often impossible, but trains equally inaccessible for her. By Friday, she managed to get to Kensington, however, and Victoria fussed and flapped round her as though she were an honoured guest, rather than a woman whom she could only associate with trouble.

'I expect Mr Vale has told you,' she began hesitantly, 'that Mrs Norman is dead.'

'Yes.' A fluttering hand flew to her face in stage expression of sadness. 'What a tragedy. And poisoned, too.'

'Yes.'

'They don't know how it was administered, apparently.' Was there a distinct note of relish in her voice? 'So they have had to release Bert.'

Why hadn't Paul told her that? Gemma felt unreasonably annoyed.

'Do you think it is to do with the tontine, Gemma?' she asked.

'It looks too much of a coincidence not to be.'

'That's terrible,' Victoria said warmly. 'It means either Mr Vale, yourself, or *me* – if we discount Bert. Or,' she added, with a sweet smile, 'Ted. That man, Gemma,' Victoria jabbed her finger warningly at her, 'is capable of *anything*. Do not be fooled,' she said darkly. 'Tea?'

'Thank you.'

Victoria looked pitifully towards the kitchen and Gemma took the hint.

While waiting for the kettle to boil, she looked round the assorted photos and trophies adorning even Victoria's kitchen. Victoria receiving an Oscar for her cameo role in *Sunset At Three*. Victoria pictured in *The Importance of Being Earnest* at Chichester, Victoria in the British megafilm of *She-Wolf of France*. There was even an old wartime publicity pic. But nothing earlier. Nothing from orphanage days or her early career. It must say something about Victoria that only her successful years were to be remembered. She dragged back in her mind and dredged up that Victoria had had her first big success in a Hollywood film in the early forties. Susie in *The Running Waters of Blue Creek*.

'How did you get to Hollywood?' she asked Victoria curiously when she returned with the tea.

'I was in a B-picture here, and they talent-spotted me. So long ago. So many more worthwhile things since.' Subject closed. Evidently she was not proud of it.

'Did you see Gladys after you returned from Florence?' she asked as casually as she could.

'I did not.' She gave Gemma her sweet smile again, but the voice did not match the warmth. 'If I had, I would hardly tell you now, would I?'

Gemma laughed. 'No, I suppose what I meant was that I'm curious about the effect of your all meeting again after so long. Do you still feel a bond between you?'

'I can't say I ever did,' Victoria informed her. 'It was an unfortunate start in life. I had no close friends at the orphanage and so feel no *bond*, as you put it.'

'Not even Ted?'

'Especially Ted. He is an evil old man, Gemma. We women *know*, don't we? He will stop at nothing to stir up trouble. He always did and always will. He's always *there*, you see. That's why I was so sure he was still alive. You can never get the better of Ted. Never,' claimed the woman whom he had accused of trying to murder him. Interesting.

Jonathan's flat was a ground-floor one in a converted Victorian house in Hampstead. Gemma had come straight there from Victoria, even surer now of her ground.

'I didn't upset her,' she told him coolly as she followed him into the living room, half-work, half-relaxing room, from the look of it. A television and video stood side by side with computers and printers.

'Good.'

'I think she could have stood it, even if I had.'

'Do you?'

'In the five or so months I've known her, she looks no different. Remarkable for someone with a year to live.'

'Not unusual.'

'She's no iller than her years produce by themselves, is she?' Gemma pressed.

'Frail, but not ill,' he conceded. 'I'm afraid it was my

doing, as was the suggestion later that Ted Parsons might still be alive which she passed on to you. I suggested to Victoria this might not be a very safe world with so much money at stake. It might therefore be as well if she seemed to be out of the serious running.'

Thereby also making yourself seem out of the serious running was her instant, unspoken thought. As he had said, this was a dangerous world.

'In view of everything that's happened, Gemma,' he continued, 'it seems to have been a wise precaution on my part.'

'Very well. Now I want to know how you managed to track the orphans down.'

'Why?'

'Because there might just be something that's relevant, you never know.' Relevant to what, she wasn't yet ready to discuss with him.

He frowned. 'All right. I'll tell you if you wish. On one proviso. Shane hears none of this. And particularly about Victoria.'

'Very well,' she managed to reply.

'I'll get you a drink first.'

'Small, please.'

He disappeared, presumably to the kitchen. Soon she heard the chink of glasses – and then the sound of something else. It didn't register immediately for what it was. And then it did and she froze. It was the sound of Jonathan whistling. Back it all came, unbidden, her animal terror at the cottage that evening before all this had begun. And then the tune changed. *Daisy, Daisy, give me your* . . . Blindly, she rose – just as the doorbell rang, blocking her escape route. Jonathan came past the door, glanced at her standing there and went on by.

Surely her imagination – wasn't that the same spicy aftershave she'd smelled that night? Then another voice she recognised. 'Darling.'

Unsteadily Gemma went out to see Annie Masters in his arms; he showed no signs of objecting to it, or to its being the first time. Civilised behaviour vanished as she pushed by them, ran down the steps to the front gate. Annie's car was outside; as she paused, she saw a large hold-all on the back seat. A weekend bag.

Chapter Eleven

Buttering sandwiches at speed was never Gemma's forte in the culinary field, but she had offered to do something to help Bert, and the offer had been accepted. She had only just finished her task by the time the funeral procession arrived. The service at the crematorium on a wet autumn day was an ordeal, and the gathering afterwards at Gladys's Sunshine Café boded little better. She was mistaken, however. Gladys had been a popular local character, and the café and the living quarters behind and above were all crowded with a lively group of assorted people intent on remembering Gladys at her best. Her recent best. There seemed few from her past.

Bert moved through them with a glazed look, as if seeking the mother he knew must be there somewhere if only he could find her. He had been sent home by the police, free for lack of evidence, Paul told her. Was he his solicitor, she had asked. 'No,' he had told her without further comment. There was still restraint between them.

Bert flourished a plate under her nose. 'I've got gypsy tarts,' he told Gemma proudly. She gathered these were Gladys's favourites, and thus a special treat for her. She took one in order not to offend him. Or was it Gladys she did not want to offend? Gladys's personality was still so strongly imprinted everywhere that Gemma would not have been surprised to see her materialise. She was grateful for the crowds on her own account as well as Bert's, for it gave her an excuse for anonymity. She could, in short, avoid Jonathan Vale. She had not heard from him since the Annie Masters' fiasco, hardly surprisingly; and besides, her own behaviour did not encourage scrutiny. Running away like a frightened child – not that he would know of her fear. He would think – quite naturally – that she was jealous of Annie. And wouldn't *that* have given him a kick, she thought savagely. It was instinct that had sent her flying from his house, and now instinct had pointed the way, it was up to her common sense to keep going on the same path.

'And huffkins.' Bert pointed to a tray of cakes that might taste better than they looked. 'Mum was partial to them ever since we used to go hop-picking. Regular every year we went, her, me and Uncle Charlie.' His eyes were moist and he looked like a stricken spaniel.

'What are you going to do now, Bert?' Gemma asked gently. 'Will you run the café alone?'

'I don't know.' Panic shone briefly in his eyes. 'I thought I might ask Dad.'

For a moment she thought she'd misheard. Dad? *Tositi?* Then she realised he was quite aware of what he'd said, and was looking at her for approbation. She had to go gently here. 'Do you mean, ask his advice?'

'He might like to come and work here,' Bert muttered.

'I don't think that's very likely, Bert. He's a very old man.'

'Ma was old too.'

'He's been a recluse for nearly fifty years.'

338

'Eh?'

'He's lived shut away from people, and in another country. It would be difficult for him.'

'I've written to him. He ought to know about Ma. He's my dad, you know. He was very fond of her. He told me, did my dad.'

Gemma was grappling with the implications of this, wondering what on earth to reply, when Paul came up to join them, and Bert lumbered off.

'Need a hand on sandwiches?' he asked. 'Vale's on the drinks.' Gemma must have shown her surprise, since Paul added, 'He's been making himself helpful apparently for quite a time. Nosing around, both before and after Gladys's death.'

'Before?' she asked unguardedly.

'Ask Bert. He looked in a couple of times. Very neighbourly of him, I'm sure. *Now* do you wonder at my warning, Gemma? He protects Victoria like a mother hen – look, she's standing with him now. What does she think you're going to do to her? Bash her over the head with a cheese sandwich?'

'Me?' she asked, surprised.

'Sorry. Not in good taste. I'm being practical, Gemma. As always. The orphans are down to two now. If I were Ted I wouldn't sleep easy at nights. Our friend has made one attempt, after all.'

Gemma remained silent, and he raised an eyebrow. 'Why no impassioned defence of Vale this time, Gemma?'

'Should there be one? After all, as you point out, it's Charles Lakenham or me, now.'

'What's happened?' he asked sharply. 'You've gone into your shell.'

'Nothing's happened,' she white-lied. 'I'm trying to keep an open mind.'

'It's open both ends, believe me. You're letting facts march in and march right out again.' Paul looked worried. 'How can I convince you that this *is* serious? That you might be in danger?'

'Nobody has any reason to hurt *me*.'

'Who's your heir?'

'Three old schoolfriends at the moment. Do you think they might be lurking in the bushes with a machete?'

'That's an odd thing to say.'

'Just a phrase.' Her eyes fell away. 'I did have a scare some months ago,' she added slowly.

'You didn't tell me.'

'It was before I met you. Just a peeping tom, I expect.' *Daisy, Daisy* . . . A whistle on a summer's night. 'O whistle and I'll come to you, my lad . . .' Not this time, *not this time*, my lad.

'Brave man, to tackle the virgin queen. That's my role. There's only one problem.'

'My armour?' she asked drily.

'I can rip armour off. No, more down to earth. If I press my suit, as they say, now, Vale would claim I was after your millions. I prefer the Hollywood approach of walking in gentlemanly fashion away – temporarily. Until Gladys's murderer is arrested anyhow,' he added meaningfully.

'And when will that be?'

'I'm working on it.'

'Drink?' Jonathan Vale materialised at their side with a bottle.

'Thanks.' Paul held out his glass.

A terrier and a bulldog, planted foresquare, animosity

quivering unspoken between them. Red Knight, White Knight. But there were no white knights, so Annie had said, and she might be right – save for the chessboard sort, and they moved in mysterious ways, not straightfor-wardly. To forestall them you had to see round corners. Gemma had thought she could, but in this particular game, she had the distinct feeling she was caught in constant checkmate.

'You've never told me the details of Gladys's death, Paul,' she said clearly. Jonathan paused, checked as he was about to leave them.

'No. I've only just gathered them myself. She died on the Thursday night. It was her birthday, and she and Bert were going out to celebrate. He found her dead. I gather you were in that day, Vale?'

'I was.' He gave no sign of agitation.

'It acts quickly, doesn't it, cyanide?'

'Very. But they haven't said – if they know – whether she took it by mouth or skin.'

Gemma shivered. 'So it would have been planted.'

'Quite. The police have been crawling around this place like flies. It hasn't done Bert's business any good at all – not because of the possible contamination of food, I hasten to add – but because of the police presence.'

She smiled; it might lighten the atmosphere, as Paul obviously intended. With Jonathan Vale standing there silently, yet – creepily – dominatingly, that was necessary. She addressed herself to Paul. 'We're assuming her death was to do with the tontine, because it's so much on our minds. You don't think someone else might have had a grudge against her?'

'Not the sort that would call for cyanide in the soup.'

'Poison isn't that easy to come by,' Jonathan pointed

out with the air of a disinterested observer.

'The police are checking to see if they can track down any link with a hospital or chemist laboratory.'

Annie flew into Gemma's mind, Annie the doctor's receptionist. She guiltily pushed her out again. Doctors' receptionists did not have easy access to bottles of poison; surely not cyanide, anyway.

'But the fact remains that she died,' Paul concluded bitterly. 'It's a two-horse race now.'

Jonathan made no comment, simply nodded in agreement or valediction, and left them.

Paul insisted on seeing Gemma to the Tube after the gathering broke up – save for a hard core of regulars obviously intent on making a night of it.

'It's not necessary, Paul. What do you think Jonathan is going to do to me, for heaven's sake. And *why*?'

'Have a go at hurrying up his inheritance, I should think. I can think of a couple of ways he would achieve it, too.'

'I would only pose a threat if I personally protected Ted. But he's a wily old bird. Bert says he's written to him about Gladys, so he'll be well aware of the dangers. Anyway, I must go now. I'm on duty tonight. Christmas party time again. Oh joy!'

Reluctantly he let her go, kissing her goodbye. How easy it would be to respond, go back to the relationship that had begun so promisingly, been consummated so successfully – and was now on hold. Until she could go to him with the whole of herself, heart, mind and body, it would have to stay that way. However hard.

Christmas now loomed ahead as an ordeal, she told herself. Jonathan might be in Florence, he might even

342

bring Annie to Lakenham, or he might – blessed thought – not even be there at all. Be damned if she was going to make an excuse not to attend, though. Why not dine in the lions' den, after all? She would go dressed to kill as many lions as possible – and enjoy it.

As the BMW slid over Lakenham Bridge, she was still glad she was coming. Visiting Lakenham meant something, even if it did bring problems. What could happen? A few unpleasant words at most. Words could never hurt her though, and his 'sexual magnetism', as Paul called it, wasn't going to work at long distance. Surely she could stand the proximity of Jonathan Vale for a few hours – provided no one mentioned the tontine, and surely, on this day of all days, no one would. The village of Lakenham, spared its white Christmas, looked peacefully still and serene, with the special feel that Christmas morning lent to everything. As the car nosed up the drive, she remembered her last visit and was doubly glad she'd come, for his sake. Jonathan might be an enigma, but Charles was, in an odd sense, 'family'. She headed for the private wing, but saw Charles standing on the front steps of the main house waving at her.

'Happy Christmas, my dear.' He kissed her and led her inside, where those residents still here for Christmas were in full and noisy swing, opening presents and sipping sherry. 'We're here for the loyal toast, and then we can retire,' he whispered to her. Fortunately, she had anticipated this, and had come well supplied with bottles and chocolates, which were well received. Maria was elegantly clad in a little black number that made Gemma – who thought she'd left home looking as much like a fashion-plate as possible – feel more like a schoolgirl. Her welcome was warm and genuine, though, as she kissed

Gemma on both cheeks. 'After the sherry we go back and open the champagne, yes?'

'Champagne, no.' She laughed. 'I've got to drive.'

'Ah, here there are plenty of beds, and plenty of time to sleep a little. You are not driving your taxi this evening, are you?'

'No, we closed down at twelve o'clock today. Not very public-spirited, but we decided to be lenient with ourselves this year.'

The private party was not large: the Lakenhams, their daughter Charlotte, her husband, Mike, and three teenage children, four family friends – and Jonathan. No Annie. It all went much more easily than she had expected, as though a Christmas armistice had been declared in the trenches. Jonathan spoke across the table as though she were merely a pleasant acquaintance, Charlotte chattered on about her garden and flower business, and Charles chatted about Gemma's grandfather and his father, unostentatiously and warmly. No one spoke of the tontine, although surely most people in the room must be aware that in the not-too-distant future either she or Charles would receive fifteen million pounds and the other would lose it.

Lulled by the excellent food and wine and unprovocative conversation, time passed quickly, and she was suddenly aware that the children were no longer present and that the light was rapidly fading.

'I need a walk,' Jonathan pronounced. 'Charlotte?'

'Count me out. Sleep more like.'

Gemma knew what was coming next. The slow smile, the cat and the mouse. 'Gemma?'

Why not face the lions after all? 'A short one. I'll have to be getting back soon.'

'But why?' cried Maria. 'Tonight I have made manicotti.'
Charles groaned.

'Take no notice of him,' Jonathan said. 'Mother's manicotti are delicious. Father just believes if it's got a foreign name it can't be good. I sometimes wonder how he and Mother got together.'

'It had nothing to do with food, *mio figlio*,' his mother assured him blithely.

Gemma laughed. 'It sounds wonderful. I can't miss it.'

She was disconcerted to find they were the only ones going on the walk. She'd counted on Mike at least. Talk, Gemma, she told herself; she must say something to break this silence as they walked side by side. 'I'm sleepy enough now. After the manicotti the car will have to drive itself.'

He smiled slightly. 'You can always call a taxi. Or sleep here.'

'That's what your mother said. Did she mean it?'

'Old established Italian custom to extend siestas all night. Go to bed and leave the guests on the sofa.'

Damn him, he was doing it again, the will-o'-the-wisp, leading one to quicksand. Not this time.

'I'm only sleepy from smoke, not drink.'

'Of course. A brisk walk then. To the Folly?'

That's what he'd planned all along, wasn't it? And how could she say no – particularly when she wanted to see it again? He knew that, he must do. He sized up what she wanted and gave it to her. That was the con.

It was growing dark now, and the trees surrounding the Folly and its garden looked forbidding in the half light. Impossible now to conjure up the summer's day when young Reggie Maitland had wooed Ellen Shane by the tennis court.

'I've got a torch, don't worry,' he said as she stumbled, and he caught her arm.

'You always have.'

'It's no bad thing to have a lamp to light the way.'

Goodness knows what he meant, and she didn't care as she fell against him again, thanked him stiffly as he steadied her. Once he caught his own foot in trailing dead bracken, and she gripped his arm, felt the wrench as she took the jerk of his body. He nodded at her and they set off again. Don't let him whistle, she thought. The trees shrouded them overhead. She would be all right so long as he did not whistle. She thought of the old Kentish legend of the Seven Whistlers, harbingers of ill-fortune. Seven? She needed only one to send her into blind panic, and he was right beside her. Walk into my parlour. Santa Maria Novella had vanished. This was December chill, where one saw things clearly, not seduced by the warmth of Florence.

The door swung open as he unlocked it, and he stood aside so that she could enter. Six months ago she had come here with her grandfather, and how much had happened since. Perhaps here she would gain the strength to face the responsibility of the decision that might lie ahead. A fifty-per-cent chance of that now.

'How does your father feel about this place?' she asked hesitantly. 'And what would he do with it if . . .' She did not need to finish. The words lay starkly between them.

'Not as I do,' he answered after a moment. 'Gemma, I'm going to tell you something you are not going to like. That's why I wanted to bring you here today, so that you can get used to the idea while there's still time. It's mine, not my father's.'

'The folly? But he can't make over what's not his.'

'No. That's not it. If Victoria outlives Ted, the tontine pool and the decision on what to do with it are mine legally. You all thought – and we deliberately let you – that I was my father's representative at some of the meetings and during the investigations. It was the other way round. He was mine.'

'Does Felix know of this?' she asked levelly.

'Obviously. There were good reasons he agreed to the slight deception.'

'And they were?'

'Pointless, as it happens. They've been outstripped by events. Does it change things?'

'Why?' she asked, avoiding the question. 'Why not Charles?'

He wandered round the room, touching things. 'You know, when we were small the place fascinated me. Father would rarely let us come in, but I stared through the windows endlessly. Charlotte didn't care about it, but I set all my fantasies here. It was a time-warp, another world. Can you wonder I took up military history? That last day before they set off for the orphanage, when war was certain and the tontine planned, it's as if it were imprinted on this place. Like the theory of ghosts, an event so significant took place that it could not be expunged by time, particularly if the air is not disturbed. And the Folly has been so very rarely disturbed. I didn't come here again until my grandfather died, but I could describe what had taken place here on that Saturday before war broke out to my grandfather, and he told me that's much as it had been. Since then, I've come here a few times – not too often, in case I grew to think of it as mine.'

'You talked to your grandfather about what *he* wanted for the memorial?'

'Oh yes. That's why he wanted me to have it. He talked it over with my father, of course, and he was only too happy. He could see it becoming a prize pain in the neck. How right he was.' He paused. 'Do you mind, Gemma?'

'It's not up to me to mind.'

'No. I mean, about my not telling you before.'

'Logically it makes no difference.'

'And other than logically?'

'I don't think I can answer that. Not here, anyway.'

'Even though it's you or me? One of us will have the decisions to make. Unswayed by others, I hope,' he added.

Impossible to mistake his meaning. She wanted to yell out Annie Masters' name, but the impulse fled as quickly as it came. It was too petty for their surroundings. Jonathan was standing close to her. He was not close enough to justify her shouting 'offside', yet she was as much in his aura as outside the cottage that night last summer, drawn inexorably by an invisible lasso towards the peeping tom of her nightmare. The other side of desire was fear.

'I say, Thomas, who's that new girl of yours? What a stunner. Let's toast her. Tell us her name.'

'Not done to mention ladies' names here,' Thomas said loftily.

'Sisters aren't banned though,' teased Philip. 'A toast to Ellen Shane, eh, Reggie?'

Reggie's first impulse was to blush; it was too new, too sacred to be bandied about. But, after all, these were friends. He lifted his glass joyously. 'To Ellen!'

'Mind you, you can do better than old Ellen, old chap,' Philip said mournfully. 'Sorry to see a good

chap like you throwing yourself away.'

'I challenge you, sir,' Reggie shouted.

'What to?'

'A drinking contest?'

'Done.'

Honour was satisfied after three glasses of claret.

'How about you, Jack?' Thomas said. 'As leader of the Lakenham Set, I demand to know whether your intentions towards the fair sex are honourable.'

'Certainly not,' Jack declared in horror. 'A poet can't be married – what can he write about? I need a harem. A dozen mistresses at least.'

'Anthony?'

He was soberer than the rest. 'We're going to war. It makes one think.'

'Of what pray, Mr Plato?'

'Of all I might miss. Of all I need to fight for.' *He looked round quietly.* 'And the chief of them is love. And for all our boastful talk, I daresay there are a few of us in this room who, like me, haven't lain with a woman yet. We've written poetry, we've painted, we've composed, we've dreamed. But we haven't loved, haven't lived.'

There was instant quiet.

'We'll be back,' *said one suddenly.*

'And if we're not?'

'All the more reason to toast love, you fellows,' *Thomas proclaimed stoutly.* 'What else is art, after all, than love? What's death, beside love? Love lives.'

'Well said, Tom. A toast to all the little Lakenham Sisters we can manage to leave behind us. And their lovely mothers, God bless them. The ladies.'

'The ladies,' *nineteen voices chorused after him.*

Reggie thought of the flower in his blazer pocket, and drank.

'I can't bear it,' Gemma said sadly.

'Bear what?'

'This place.'

'Haunted?'

'Yes.'

'By a poppyfield?'

'And withered rose petals.'

He moved.

'Don't touch me, *please*,' she cried.

'Once for the roses.' He only kissed her on the cheek. His body didn't even touch hers, but she felt the kiss tingling down her body, treacherously, with an electricity that called out in the night with its siren song.

She watched his back as he lit another lamp. 'Annie,' she began.

'Not now.'

She stopped. He was right. The Folly was not fighting territory. It was not theirs. It belonged to the Lakenham Set.

'What will you do for them?'

He didn't need to ask of what she spoke. 'What they wanted. What else?'

'But how? Their ideal is a dinosaur.'

'Look how many flock to see resurrected dinosaurs in every shape and form.'

'Fifteen million is a lot to spend on one.'

'All right. How will this do? I see this as the hub, the control room if you like, of a network of tentacles. The tentacles will carry spurs to endeavour in every form: scholarships, theatre, scientific invention, whatever. But the priority will be the Folly. If the electrical load is right to kickspin the tentacles into mobility, then the whole operation will be right.'

'How do you know what's right for this hub, though?' She looked round the old room, caught in its poignant memory of the past.

'I'll know when it happens because, like the frescos, it will be *right*. Gemma. What of you? Are you still sitting on the fence?'

'Yes. Heart pulled one way, conscience the other.'

'And which is the stronger?'

She looked at him. 'Like you, I'll know when it happens. It will be *right*.'

This way from the enchanted wood. Twenty young men marched from it in 1914. Now he and she were caught in the middle, waiting.

The early New Year brought miserable, damp weather. Gemma had a few days in New York on an inquiry in an industrial espionage case, and returned at the end of the first week of January, head dizzy with computer data but triumphant. She also returned to a pile of post, including one with an Italian stamp. She didn't open it right away. She poured a drink, stroked Launcelot, indignant at having been left in Loretta's care, assured him that she still adored him, and braced herself for problems. She was not disappointed. She was precipitated back into the middle of the tontine problem again.

The letter was dated before Christmas, so she must just have missed it when she flew out. It was from Orvino's son, the 'linguist', written in broken English. But the message still came over loud and clear. Signor Tositi wanted to see her as soon as possible. He was not ill, the letter assured her with Italian practicality, but wished to discuss something with her. She told herself this was fine by her; she had something, after all, she wanted to discuss with him. There was only one problem: Paul.

He usually came down when she had a free weekend and was due on the morrow. Next weekend she might well not be here. She looked forward to his visits, selfishly perhaps, since he stayed in the spare room and she was aware she was being escapist in her decision to mark time. It wasn't easy, especially in a cold, miserable winter. But she had the measure of temptation after all. She'd been tempted by Jonathan, who had used sex and attraction for his own ends. She and Annie. Paul was not like that, but still she needed objectivity. The rest of the country was snowbound. In Kent it was merely bleak, and rainy. Never-ending rain, flooding fields, crops and roads.

'Next weekend,' Paul remarked when he arrived on the Saturday, 'you can come to London.'

'No, I can't I'm afraid.'

'Why not? Duty calling?'

'In a way. I'm going back to Florence.'

'For heaven's sake, *why*?' His voice sharpened. 'Tontine business?'

'A courtesy visit to Ted,' she replied evenly. 'It doesn't seem right to ignore him, now we've found he's alive.'

'I'll come. How long are you going for?'

'There's no *need*, Paul.'

'I believe there is. Vale's still involved in the affair.'

'He always will be. He's the legal heir, Paul, not Charles.'

'I wondered when he'd condescend to tell you.'

'You *knew*?'

'I got it out of Felix after Gladys's death. Don't look so annoyed. It's the professional nose.'

'You didn't tell me.'

'Professional secrecy. Felix was adamant. I wanted to, though.'

'Thanks.'

'I'm most certainly coming. I don't trust Vale an inch.'

'Nor he you,' she wanted to say, but discretion prevailed. She needed tact for what she had to say. 'You make things very difficult for me, Paul. It's a private visit, not for long, and it's *business*.'

'*We're* not business, are we, Gemma?'

'No longer. I shouldn't have upset you by reminding you of the tontine. I suppose I should have said I was going to Timbuctoo on a job for my firm.'

'No, you shouldn't.' He regained equanimity. 'Openness is first and foremost between us. There's been too much secrecy without our adding to it.'

She felt for him deeply; he was able to be concerned for her when he had lost so much. Concerned for her feelings.

'Come on, let's go down to the pub,' she grinned.

'Compromise?' Paul said at last, seated by the Green Knight's fire and watching the rain running down the windows. 'I'll come with you to Florence, but you can see darling Ted alone. No fuss. OK?'

'You bet.' She flung her arm round his shoulders. 'You're very understanding, Paul.'

'It must be the man in me,' he murmured, lips briefly against her hair.

It was strange to be back here again, back in the central hotel she'd already stayed at with Paul. She was glad he was with her after all. She began to wonder why she had made such a point of seeing Ted alone, as the ritual of meeting Giovanni began. To her slight surprise he took her by the church route; when she found herself glimpsing the courtyard through the arch, she realised why. It was as good a hint as any that the fresco room was not on view today. Not to her. The tapestry room was once again the audience chamber. Despite the red satin cape outfit Ted had chosen today, his face was not painted, nor was he wearing a wig. An 80-year-old man with thin wispy hair – and a red satin outfit.

'Where have you been?' he demanded querulously as soon as she came in. 'I've waited and waited.'

'Blame the Christmas post. Then when your letter came I was in New York on business.' It occurred to her belatedly that Ted could have no concept of what this meant. When he left London, New York was a matter of days and days on a boat, not nipping on to the nearest airbus.

'Well, finished staring at me, have you? I'm still here.'

'And you look well.'

'No, I don't,' he snapped. 'I'm never well.'

'Better than when I saw you last,' she amended.

'Ah. Now you know how right I was. So old Gladys is dead. When's the next attempt on my life going to be, eh?'

'No one could get in here without bribing Giovanni or Signor Orvino, and that's not very likely, is it?' She hesitated. 'I shouldn't let *anyone* in if I were you, not to do with the tontine. Except me. You're safe enough with me.'

He looked more cheerful. 'I'm a widower,' he announced. 'Got to look after myself.'

'You've got a son, too.'

'Yes. Wanted me to come to London. Me! Do you think he's in with them?'

'Them?'

'Them who's after me.'

'There's no one . . .' She stopped. Stupid thing to say when there was patently one at least. 'Were you fond of Gladys, Ted, in the old days?'

'She were fun, I'll grant you that.' Ted's eyes gleamed as memories of the 'fun' obviously came back. 'I've been thinking about them. Yeah. We had some good times. Poor old Glad.'

'So why did you leave her?'

'Matter of business necessity.'

'The police were after you?'

'Nah. Might have been, though. We were doing all right in the pub, but I had some sidelines, as you might say, that I was interested in developing. They didn't go with a fixed address and wife. So, Ted me lad, I thought, why not leave her to be licensee in her own name. Otherwise we might both have been chucked out with nowhere to go. I did her a favour.' He looked virtuous.

'She didn't seem to think so.'

'Women always see things wrong.' He pondered. 'You got nippers?'

'No.'

'Missed out, have you? You look all right.' His eye ran up and down her appraisingly, though not lasciviously, so it amused rather than irritated her. 'No good holding out for marriage too long. After a while, no one wants what you got. That fair one's got his eye on you.'

'Paul?'

''Specially now Gladys is dead, eh? Suddenly you must

be looking a much plumper little chicken.'

'Oh yes,' she agreed readily. 'I'm such an innocent little chick I'd fall for the first man who asked me to marry him.'

'What about the other one? Vale. Young Johnnie.'

'He fancies young Annie.'

'I see his point.' Ted looked quite concerned, and she burst out laughing, rather to his surprise. 'I don't see nothing to laugh at. If you loosened up a bit you might not be a bad-looker. Getting on a bit, though.'

'Shall we stop talking about my marital prospects?' she asked patiently.

'It makes a change,' he explained. 'I ain't seen a woman, not *seen*, if you know what I mean, since Sophia died. No harm in speculating. Reminded me of Rosalind.'

'Me?'

'Sophia.'

'I met Rosalind.'

'Did you now? Nice little figure, eh?'

Not now, she thought. Not at nearly eighty, sprawled on a sofa with a parrot for company.

'Anyway, it turns the tables, me sizing *you* up. Look at all the time you lot spent judging us kids like horseflesh.'

'Did we?' she asked with concern.

'Not you, maybe. Some of the others.' He did not specify. 'Still, now Gladys is dead, what I want to ask is, how you going to stop her before she has another go?'

'Who?'

'Little Miss Victoria.'

'You think *she* murdered Gladys?'

'Tried to do me in, didn't she? She went home and decided to have a go at Gladys then. A very determined lady, that. She'll be back. I don't know why you leave me alone, I don't.'

Gemma drew a deep breath. Careful, Gemma, careful. 'What did you tell Stanley that morning he came to see you, Ted? You never answered our question when we asked before.'

'Did I tell him anything?'

'Yes, and then he was killed.'

He said nothing.

'I think I know, Ted,' she went on. 'Or rather, I can take a wild guess which only you can confirm.'

'And what might that be, me love?'

'That she's not Victoria Ireland at all.'

'Well, well, look who's here. If it isn't young Vicky. Thought I recognised your lovely body on stage, darling. What you calling yourself Gloria Rose for, then?'

Through the smoke-filled haze of the Windmill Bar the two girls stopped with drinks in their hands. 'Hello, Ted,' Vicky said warmly. 'They dragged you into uniform, I see.'

'Dragged? I was the first to volunteer.'

'Not married, then.'

'Not me, darling. Fancy me, do you, or got your eye on better things now? I heard you was a film star. All on account of your natural talent I was admiring just now, eh?' He leered at her well-rounded bosom.

'That's right. My natural talent, and, come off it. Star? It were a B-flick and I had twenty lines. But it got me where I wanted. Look, Ted, I got a letter from Hollywood today . . .' She opened her bag and flourished it. 'Come over and do a test and see what they

357

can do for me, they say. We're off to celebrate, me and my room-mate. Come with us, eh, Ted? Celebrate the old orphanage turning out such talented kids.'

'Yes, why don't you?' chimed in her companion, smiling at Ted.

'Hands off, Sally,' said Vicky amiably. 'He's mine this evening. I'm paying. I get the man.'

Ted sized up the opposition. Pretty, fair-haired like Victoria, but slighter. Not so generous in the boob department. Still – 'Don't worry, girls. I can satisfy both of you.'

'None of that lip, Ted. Sally's a respectable girl, ain't you, love? We share a room down St Martin's Lane, so I know.'

'You never got Dukey then, Vicky?'

'Tell you the truth, there weren't a lot to get, poor devil. He's dead, did you hear? He wanted to marry me honest, but the family stopped it. Politely warned me off, you might say. Let's go then, Sal. You coming or not, Ted?'

'Might as well.'

'Big of you. Go to the Café de Paris every night, do you?'

Ted was impressed. No, he didn't. It would be a lark. He patted Sally's bum appreciatively as they went out into the cool March air. She couldn't be that respectable, because she didn't object. For all her little shriek, she liked it. He could always tell.

Victoria was a trooper with the champagne. You got used to it, working at the Windmill. But she didn't put on side. This wasn't bad either. Mostly officers, but they couldn't stop him coming in. He was a guest, even if he was a private, and intended to stay one. No sticking his neck out. After this war he was going to enjoy the good life, see if he didn't. He knew how it was done now – he just needed the means. Shouldn't be too difficult one way or another.

'Come on, Vicky, fancy a dance?' He winked at Sally. 'Don't go away, I'll be back for you, love.' Vicky felt good in his arms. He'd always liked Vicky. 'Remember the day behind the bicycle sheds, love?'

Her giggle caused heads to turn.

'If you knew how much that'd cost you now, Ted. I keeps myself to myself.'

'In Hollywood, love?'

'Sure, I'm going to marry Clark Gable. He needs someone to look after him after his wife's death. Sad, wasn't it? Or Jimmy Stewart. Is he married?'

'What about home-brewed? Leslie Howard for starters.'

'Reminds me of Dukey. Too aristocratic. I like them earthy. Like you, Ted.'

'What are you doing later on, Vicky?'

She giggled again. 'I told you. No fancy stuff for me – and keep your hand off me leg. This is the Café de Paris.'

'Even they must have bicycle sheds somewhere, lovely.'

The dance ended and he returned to the downstairs restaurant to join Sally. Ah well, he thought, a different kettle of fish from Vicky. He needed time here, and wasn't sure if it was worth it. Still, why not? He asked her to dance with a broad wink and she accompanied him up to the dance floor with alacrity.

'*What you aiming to do, Sally, when Vicky goes to Hollywood?*'

'*I'd go with her, but I can't. No contacts. Swiz, isn't it?*'

'*Pretty girl like you shouldn't have much difficulty. You at the Windmill too?*'

'*I am not,*' she said emphatically. '*I'm an actress.*'

And then the world went black. Ted was spinning through a huge black circle, arms and legs flailing. Quite nice until he stopped spinning and fell into a deep pit of blackness and nothing. When he opened his eyes again there was something on his chest – blankets? snow? Neither, and a girl – Sally something? – bending over him, pulling stuff off him, talking to someone. The air was full of smoke like fog. Smoke? No, dust.

'*I got him breathing again,*' *he heard her say to someone.*

'*Can you move, mate?*' *came a disembodied voice.*

He tried, he could. He sat up very cautiously. Sally started crying. What the hell for? He looked round. What was she howling about? He was all right. Blimey, where was he? Then he knew. It was a bleeding bomb. It took some time to remember this bombsite was the Café de Paris. It must have taken a direct hit. '*I gotta get out of here,*' *he declared with conviction. Ted Parsons had had another lucky strike and he wasn't going to stay around for his luck to change. The whole lot may come down.*

'*I'll help you up.*'

'*You do that, sweetheart.*'

On his feet, he looked around. Bodies, arms, legs, and nothing but rubble where the band had been.

People going out, others coming in with stretchers. His leg hurt, he staggered and held on to Sally. She supported him, still howling her eyes out. He looked at her curiously.

'You got me breathing?' he asked her hoarsely.

'Yes.'

'Thanks. You're all right, Sal. I'll see you're all right one day. Where's Vicky?'

More howls. Blimey, she'd been downstairs. Still, might be OK down there. 'I'll go,' he said in a rare fit of chivalry. Anything to get away from that dis-embodied arm lying there.

'No,' cried Sally, 'I've got to see.'

'All right.' Ted's first instinct was to leap at the opportunity of escape, but then he felt obliged to go with her. They hobbled down the stairs together with the heavy rescue mob who'd just arrived. Once down there, he swore to himself. Bodies, nothing but bod-ies. Sally was screaming at his side. There was a light still on, so they weren't spared.

'Over there, she was sitting by that door.' Only there was no door. Just a heap of bodies, plaster and wood. They arrived with the stretcher-bearers, only there wasn't much saving of life to be done. Sally gagged as she saw what there was of Vicky was dead. He looked the other way, but she went right on staring. There must have been two bleeding bombs. One got them up by the band, the other came straight through down here.

'This her handbag?' He picked up the dusty, torn object. But Sally was rushing outside now. He hobb-led after her, still holding the bag.

He caught up with her just as she was sick in the

gutter, and he dragged her into a side road while she coughed up. 'All right? There's a First Aid Post somewhere. Want to go there?'

'In a minute.'

'Drink?' He was suddenly inspired. He pushed his way into a pub, through the flocking crowds come up to see what was happening. 'A brandy for this young lady. We was in that lot.' He pointed. It was enough to ensure free drinks.

'How many gorn?'

'Hundreds, mate,' Ted replied. It won him another free round.

He sat Sally down while she drank the watery brandy. Then she managed to giggle. 'You do look daft with that bag.'

'This?' He looked in surprise at the bag. He hadn't realised he was still holding it. 'It's Vicky's, ain't it?'

'We ought to hand it over,' she said vaguely. 'They'll need it.'

'Who?'

'The . . . next-of-kin.'

'That's me, darling. I met her in an orphanage. No one closer.'

'We still ought to hand it over. Poor Vicky.'

Ted opened it, there might be money. There was. With great restraint he handed it to Sally, who recoiled, so he stuffed it into his own pockets. 'Here, here's that Hollywood letter. Pity no one's going to be using it,' he added thoughtfully, glancing at her. 'After all, you turn up and they won't ask no questions. They won't ask to see identification, will they? Not as if she was Vivien Leigh, after all. Her stage

362

name's Gloria something, but you can turn up as
Victoria Ireland.'

'Me, Ted?'

'In a manner of speaking.'

There was a pause. 'They'll know.'

'Sally died, remember. Poor little Sally, in the
bomb alley.'

'But—'

He cut her off. 'Listen, she's got a passport, ain't
she? And here's her identity card in her bag. Get me
the passport.'

'What did you have in mind?' she asked slowly.

'Never ask a gent that. I owe you a favour – Vicky,'
he said deliberately. 'How about a nice new passport
and identity card for Victoria Ireland?'

'But—'

'Trust me, Vicky. I think tomorrow we'd best find
the ARP Controller, don't you, and identify poor
Sally?'

'It's callous. I liked her,' Sally declared passion-
ately.

'So did I, love,' Ted said softly. 'So did I.'

The room in St Martin's Lane was hardly big
enough to swing a couple of kittens in, and Sally
started bawling again as soon as she entered. Ted
spent the time looking round. He'd need to get a move
on. Forgery took time. And he needed sleep. You
needed concentration for that job. But it had to be
done to pay back favours. He didn't like obligations
left. Made him feel uneasy. He didn't feel too good
anyway. Sleep first. Here. Sally wasn't so bad, if she'd
only stop crying. He needed a wash and a pee. And,
he was surprised to realise, something else. After all,

she might not have Vicky's curves, but she had that bum. 'Where's your bathroom, love?'

'Along the landing. It's shared.'

'That's just what I had in mind.'

Funny old thing, sex. Just when you think it's furthest from your mind, there it is. Unavoidable. Like it was balancing off tension up above. And how she liked it. More please. And more. But he didn't owe her that much, so in due course, after she went to Hollywood, he scarpered.

The new Victoria Ireland didn't give a damn.

'Very sharp of you, duckie,' Ted Parsons told Gemma approvingly.

'A guess. It's not often one sees such a complete lack of photos of one's early life. Either she was paranoic or there was something odd. It explained a few things I'd registered but not added up. She was so nervous about coming here, she hung back when meeting Gladys and Stanley, she wanted me to find out if you were *really* dead. I see it now. So that's what you told Stanley.'

'Might have done.'

'And he told Jonathan who . . .' No, there was no proof that Stanley's death had been other than the accident it seemed. But Jonathan had denied Stanley had told him anything. Taken all together, it looked damning. She fought off nausea as she reasoned it out. What to do now? 'Do you have proof of what you're telling me?'

'Inside here.' He tapped his head.

'Your word?'

'Good enough.'

'There's no one to support you now Gladys is dead.'

'I need that money, love.'

The *money*. How could she have been so dim? If the real Victoria Ireland was dead, Ted was the sole survivor. She'd scooped the tontine pool.

'I thought you should know the truth,' Ted said meekly.

'I'll have to tell Felix and discuss it with him. But I can't see his accepting it without written proof.'

'There'd be ways. And hurry up. I don't want to be murdered in my bed,' he told her querulously, and then went straight on: 'Like to see the bedroom, would you?' He saw her face and giggled. 'Don't worry. You ain't my type. No bum. Now if it had been Annie—'

'I'm sorry to disappoint you.'

'Better a head on your shoulders than bare shoulders in a bed,' he said encouragingly. 'To a eunuch, any road. Come and have a look. You never know, you might see Pomona.'

Curious, and glad to get away from this oppressive room, she supported him back to the staircase and upstairs. He leant on her shoulder, breathing down her neck, like the duchess in *Alice*, getting heavier and heavier. He opened the door. 'Go in,' he said.

She obeyed, expecting the room to be as she had seen it before. The bed was the same, nothing else. The far wall and that to the right now seemed to be wallpapered with drawings, close up against one another, secured so fast to the wall they might indeed have been pasted on. As she stopped to look more fully at them, he shuffled in past her to the far corner – and swung out what she thought at first was the whole wall. It wasn't. It was a shutter – rather like those she had seen in London at the Sir John Soane Museum. This fitted back neatly across the wall and doorway from which they had entered, to complete two more walls papered with drawings. It was a box, without a door, a box that enclosed her. She fought down momentary uneasiness. He was trying to alarm her, well aware of what she must be feeling, but she wouldn't give him the satisfaction of seeing he'd succeeded.

'Neat, ain't it?'

'Lorenzo?'

'No one got in Larry's bedroom without permission.'

'But what if he needed, or you need, to get out in a hurry?'

'There's a way. Giovanni knows it. You just interfere with one of those gents' private parts. It's three-dimensional. One's the handle, or tug a ball and Giovanni trots in.'

Fine, Gemma, you asked just what he wanted, she thought, amused. Which one, she wondered. There were plenty to choose from. Nudes of young men, old men, studies of form, complete figure drawings. Some were just of heads, or muscles taut in terror, some just feet, or torsos. There were a few women too, not so many. And some weren't anatomical. There were sketches of fortifications, a turret, gateway or bridge. A few were of faces, of angels, of devils, of love or of hate. All was conflict and struggle on one wall, harmony and love in various forms on the other. A mother gazing down in love was side by side with an erect phallus, a saint's head gazed lovingly at a Rodin embracing couple. Some were in black chalk, some red, a few in pen. They all had one thing in common: power. She wandered round.

'That's a Rubens bum,' Ted helpfully told her of one squatting rear view of a man.

'And this?'

The youth seemed to be leaping out of the drawing,

head thrown back in effort, feet rushing for some ever-unreachable goal.

'My, ain't you got good taste? Michelangelo. And this plump beauty is Rembrandt.'

'No Leonardos though?' she said.

He giggled. 'No Pomona after all, darling. But play your cards right with Uncle Ted and you never know your luck.'

'You don't have the Crown Jewels tucked away in this palace too?'

'Only fakes.'

'The jewels are fakes?'

'These are all fakes.' A casual arm encompassed the room.

'I don't believe it,' she told him. 'They're shouting out genius, most of them.'

'I did 'em.'

'All right, Ted. Scribble me another one. *Now*.'

'Oh, I can't, love. I have to wait till the muse comes, and me not being so fanciable as I was, she don't come as often as she used. A very quiet life I lead here.'

'Aren't you going to spin me the line that the master speaks through your hand?'

'Nah. There'd be too much of a jumble, if so. I don't fancy Leonardo and Michelangelo fighting it out over my bed. Course, I could always tell them who's going to be the lucky one today.'

Gemma sat down on the bed and looked at the drawings again, wall by wall. Why, she asked herself, had he brought her here? He had some purpose and he wasn't into self-glorification. Or was he? Her attention was caught by one sketch that looked familiar, of something slightly familiar. She studied it for some time, trying to make sense of the artist's scribbles at the side. At last, she got there.

'It's of the mouse and its tower, isn't it?' she declared triumphantly.

'My little mouse. Clever little lady. The original design for it.'

'But that's familiar writing, Ted.' She'd seen it in so many reproductions and in the Uffizi drawing gallery.

'So it is,' he agreed.

'Fake?'

'Now would I presume? Found it here, didn't I?'

'You mean the mouse and tower were designed by *Leonardo*?' She almost shrieked.

'Well, it weren't me, love. I weren't around in them days. Wish I had been. Look at them . . .' He pointed to the prominent genitalia of a handsome youth. 'What do you think of Giovanni then? Has he a classical figure, would you say?'

Was this deliberate linking? 'He's very devoted to you.'

'Think we're pansies, do you?'

'Pansies?' She took a second to get this. 'It's called gay now. And I've no idea, to answer your question.'

'Gay? What's that when it's at home? Nah. It were Sophia we both fancied. Never thought she'd be the one to die and leave us together. Nice little thing, she was.'

'Another *menage à trois*?'

'Or more of a roundabout. What do you think of that?'

He was obviously testing her again. There was no such thing as truth with Ted, she realised with some depression. He had covered it with so many veils and gauzes that the real Pomona of truth had long since vanished. He might even have forgotten it himself.

★ ★ ★

She found Paul waiting for her in San Lorenzo, as arranged, and was glad to be out of this home of secrets. How many more? And how much could she now tell Paul? That Victoria was not Victoria, that Stanley must have passed this on to Jonathan, and that Jonathan had then kept the information to himself? Jonathan, who did not yet know the possible origin of his beloved mouse.

Paul was standing in front of a Nativity scene altarpiece. 'Ascribed to the School of Ghirlandaio,' he told her as she arrived. 'Remember the fresco of *The Last Supper*? That's who painted it.' How could she forget it now? And how not feel herself a Judas sitting apart. Later painters than Ghirlandaio mixed Judas in with the group so you couldn't tell who he was. Was it Jonathan? Paul? Or herself, by keeping the revelation of Ted's frescos from him? Who the traitor? Who the betrayed?

'The book says Ghirlandaio was overfond of this red,' Paul told her. And so had Jonathan told her that. Oh, yes, this red overshadowed the gentleness of the faces, the delicacy of the background. It shouted at you, as truth should. Yet she had failed to hear it – until she had heard about Victoria Ireland, with whom Jonathan's hopes of the tontine were inextricably linked.

She linked her arm through Paul's. 'Let's go and have lunch.' It was a statement of some sort, if only to herself.

Chapter Twelve

'I cannot but feel,' Loretta remarked thoughtfully, 'that your heart is not entirely in driving Mrs Francis to her old girls' school reunion in Tunbridge Wells.'

Gemma laughed guiltily, and tried to look busy at her desk. 'Am I that obvious?'

'You are.'

'To the customers?'

'Merely to us, your long-suffering lieutenants.'

'That's all right then.'

Loretta threw her magazine at her, but it was skilfully fielded. 'What's wrong?'

'Moral dilemma. Love of money being the root of all evil.'

'Sounds worth the risk to me. Tell me?'

Gemma hesitated. 'I'm not sure I can explain. It's a question of suspicion without proof.'

'À la tontine presumably. Have you talked it over with the Man or is it to do with Hunk?'

'Only indirectly, and no, I haven't talked it over with anyone yet.'

'Since the Man's direct involvement in the tontine is now over except for you, it's—'

'Except for me?' Gemma interrupted sharply.

'Don't be a starry-eyed nincompoop. Liberated we may all be, but the time-honoured method of acquiring wealth by marriage hasn't entirely been outmoded.'

'That's what Paul warned me to be wary of in the Hunk.'

'Percipient, isn't he?' There was a certain dryness in Loretta's tone.

'You don't like him, do you?'

'You're wrong in fact. I do, very much.'

'So do I. That's what makes life difficult. There aren't heroes and villains, there are only people.'

'Doesn't that apply to Hunk too?'

'I suppose so.'

'You don't sound sure.'

'You're right. Villains are created by imagination and hindsight, and I was beginning to think of him as a great big Snark, to be carefully hunted down.'

Loretta laughed. 'If he "softly and silently vanishes away", you know where he's gone. Or come rather. To my lovin' arms, baby. Seriously, has he actually appeared in villain's guise?'

'Yes.'

'Threatened you?' Loretta asked in astonishment.

'Not physically.' Not in the way Loretta meant anyway.

'Then how?'

'By being there.'

'Oh, sex.' Loretta dismissed this.

'No – well, yes, but more than that. He's been hanging round my cottage.'

Loretta frowned. 'I don't like the sound of that.'

'Nothing happened. Nothing at all, even though he had ample opportunity. It was creepy.' She shivered at the memory. 'I didn't even see him. But I know it was him.'

'That's all?'

'Put that way, it doesn't sound much. But it was, at the time. Launcelot didn't like it.'

'That proves it then, to judge and jury.'

'You may laugh, but cats have an instinct and so, somewhere, do we. It's wise to acknowledge it.'

'In that case, I should definitely talk your dilemma over with the Man.'

'I might just do that. Thanks, Loretta.' She rose to leave to pick up Mrs Francis.

'Not at all. On your way back from dropping Mrs F., you can do my school run for me.'

'I suppose healthy walks are good for me?' Paul inquired, leaping with aplomb but some disdain over a slushy part of the footpath, where the thin covering of snow had melted into sludge. 'Playing squash doesn't get me quite so soggy.'

'They're frightfully good. Especially with a pub at the end of them.'

'I suppose there's no use shortening the path and getting to the pub earlier?'

'It wouldn't be the same as a walk in the snow. Anyway, you'd miss Caesar's camp.'

'I could bear the omission,' he said plaintively, as a magpie took off with a clatter of wings in front of them.

'You're supposed to take your hat off and say, "Good Morning, Mr Magpie".'

'I'm not wearing one.'

'The bird isn't looking.'

'What happens if I don't?'

'It's bad luck.'

'Then I won't bother. I've had all I need, thanks.'

Wham. Straight into it, with both clumsy boots. 'Now I come to look closer, I can see his mate,' she said, repairing the damage. 'That rules out the bad luck.'

'Good luck?' he asked hopefully.

'I'll ask them.'

'You look so glowing today, I'm almost inclined to think they'll agree. Certainly the ice is thawing.' He put an arm casually round her, then slipped in a rut and fell unceremoniously against her.

She hauled him upright. 'I need your advice, Paul, or, to be accurate, I'd like to throw some thoughts at you.'

'Man or solicitor?'

'The latter, I think.'

'Ah. Your neighbours playing Prince till four a.m. at top volume? Rap parties?'

She laughed. 'The only Prince my neighbours have heard of is called Charles, and even then their first thought would be his predecessor in the post, the Duke of Windsor. No, it's to do with the dreaded tontine.'

'Out with it,' he told her briskly.

'Confidentially?'

'What else are solicitors for?'

'Ted Parsons suggested to me that Victoria Ireland is not in fact who she claims to be. The real Victoria died during the war.'

'How many magpies did you see?' he cried out delightedly. 'It must have been dozens. That's wonderful news, Gemma.' He hugged her and laughed, shaking his head in disbelief. 'Incredible.'

'We don't know it's true, or whether we can prove it true. Ted is not a great believer in truth. It may be his idea of mischief.'

His face clouded. 'You mean, he has no proof?'

'He just says he *knows*, and that Gladys realised it too. They had the same general characteristics, hair colour, eyes and so on, and after fifty years or more it can't have been easy to be sure.'

'Knowing is no proof, not even if Bert confirms Gladys told him. Damn. There must be a way. I'll see Felix. Give me the details, and I'll start burrowing immediately. I take it you haven't tackled Victoria on the subject. Or our Mr Vale?'

'I have not – and hold hard here, Paul. I haven't asked you to do any burrowing, and most certainly don't want you to tackle Victoria.'

'But we have to. It's too important not to. You do realise that, if it's true, you've won the tontine?'

'Yes.'

'And you can stand there calmly in your gumboots telling me to do nothing about it?'

'Victoria's an old lady and she's ill, for heaven's sake. She may only have a few months to live.' Stall, Gemma, stall.

'I saw no signs of illness in Florence. I wouldn't put it past Jonathan Vale to have made that up to keep the heat off her.'

'No . . .' she said involuntarily, guiltily.

He sighed. 'Don't you think you should at least jump off your comfortable fence, in this one thing at least, and acknowledge Jonathan Vale presents a real threat to you?'

'I don't want to get ahead of myself here. There's no proof that there's anything in this story at all.'

'Not *yet*. What's her real name?'

'So far as I know, Victoria Ireland,' Gemma said deliberately.

'Is Ted proposing to talk to Felix?' Paul demanded.

'Nope. He's leaving it to me.

'He'll have to do it himself if it's true, and, after all, he's only told you because he wants the money *now*. Gemma, don't you see, that's why he grabbed the opportunity to get you to do his work for him. Only for you, read me.'

'For you, read nothing, Paul,' Gemma said quietly. 'I said I wanted to throw a few ideas at you. I have and I'm grateful, and I'm sure you're right. But I'll go and see Felix myself.'

He grinned and caught hold of her hand. 'What an obstinate lady you are, Gemma. Can I come too?'

'I'd rather not,' she told him frankly. 'But you can take me out to lunch afterwards and I'll tell you all about it.'

'Done.'

'February never was my month,' Felix told her ruefully. 'I can't say you're improving this one, Gemma.' She had never seen him look so shaken.

'I thought you'd merely tell me to run away and bring you proof.'

'I could, but it's more complicated than that. Time is not on our side, or on theirs.'

'Whose?'

'Miss Ireland's and our Ted's. There could be a nightmare scenario in which Ted dies, Victoria inherits, and then dies herself. Her tontine money would go to her heirs and the tontine pool would remain with Mr Vale. If she is then proved to have been an impostor, there would be a pretty pickle. Ted's heirs and you would have to sue to get it. Not an appealing prospect. I wish you hadn't told me,' he added ingenuously.

376

'Why?'

'Because I have to take note of it. The position will have to be frozen till we get to the bottom of it, since the tontine is at such a delicate stage.'

'Paul offered to do any delving necessary.'

'Did he?' Felix brightened. 'We'd pay him, of course, but it would help, since he knows the background. If you've no objection, that is – and I'd have to notify Mr Vale of course.'

'I don't want Victoria upset,' Gemma said quickly. 'He might well want to cross-examine her. Let's leave it a little until we can try to get a line on any of Sally Rich's family. Then at the point we approach them, you tell Jonathan.'

'Fair enough. But I'll have to interview Ted formally at the same time.'

'Here? He won't come. I know Ted.'

'And in my business,' Felix said smugly, 'I know people and money make a fatal combination. If he needs to come, he will.'

'Is that necessary at this stage?'

'Courteous.'

'That doesn't bother him too much. Can you leave it till Paul's done a preliminary check on Sally Rich's background?'

'I suppose so.' Felix looked worried.

'Her name was Sally Rich, according to Ted.' She had met Paul as arranged in the Italian restaurant near his office.

'Did he tell you anything else?' Paul asked. He seemed to have a knack of doing two things at the same time, ordering food and wine while not losing the thread of the conversation. The dynamo in him driving him on, she supposed. Did she resent it or welcome it? She ought to be doing this herself – after all, weren't special assignments her job? – but distaste for this one made her glad Paul had offered.

'Victoria was working at the Windmill when Ted met her on the night the Café de Paris was bombed. Sally shared a flat with her in St Martin's Lane, and she was a walk-on in a comedy at the Granville Theatre nearby. What are you going to do? Try to prove she isn't Victoria Ireland, or that she *is* Sally Rich?'

'Both, I suppose. The latter would be the easier, I suspect. We know Victoria Ireland can't have family, but Sally might have. The Granville – I can kick off in the theatre museum. And dear old St Catherine's House; there can't be that many Sally Riches born around 1914.'

'We don't *know* Sally was.'

'They must have been somewhat of an age.'

'True.'

'As for Victoria not being Victoria,' he grinned at her, 'I suppose you couldn't call on her and have a subtle scout around?'

'No.'

'I thought not. You're far too honourable to be a solicitor's wife, Gemma.'

'I'll bear that in mind. And I don't want *you* to call on her, either.'

'How did I guess you'd say that?'

Paul came down to Waynings two weeks later. It was a Saturday and a busy one, and it was not until she handed the reins over to Lisa that she could spare time to listen to a patiently waiting Paul.

'A certain amount of progress,' he told her. 'I tracked down someone who worked with Vicky at the Windmill. Hard to think of her as a former stripper, I must say, poor old soul. She told me folks used to pay for her to take her clothes off, now she has to pay the Social Services to do the same thing. Anyway, I showed her a picture of Victoria Ireland today which she hadn't connected with the Windmill girl, who worked under a pseudonym of course. She didn't recognise her, but pointed out it was fifty years ago. She did lend me a snapshot or two which I've had copied. Pretty non-conclusive, but it might help in a dossier.'

'How about St Catherine's House?'

'I paid a researcher to do that. He's come up with two possibilities: one born in Lancashire, the other in Essex. I've plumped for Essex girl, since it's nearer, and I'm going to see a surviving brother on Monday.'

'Do you still have a practice? You must be spending a lot of time on this – it's good of you.'

'Revenge,' he said lightly.

'On me?'

'Of course not. But someone killed Gladys, and if I can put a spoke in someone's plans, so much the better.'

'Seriously.'

'Some truth in it. The rest of the truth is that I want you to have the money.'

'I'm not sure I do.'

'You'll face it when the time comes. And talking of the time coming . . .'

She ought to have foreseen it, idiot that she was. So set on her one-track mind where the tontine was concerned, she had overlooked that sooner or later a reckoning must be made. A Saturday evening sitting in front of the fire on a dreary March night. They had been lovers once – *had* been? Would be again, surely, once the path was clear, and not blocked by the shadow of Jonathan Vale. If that had to be removed, some might argue that to commit herself to the man who was looking at her now from the hearthrug with obvious desire in his eyes was the easiest way of doing it. They would be wrong. For she could only do things her way. And her way entailed clearing the path by herself.

Unexpectedly he reached out ·for her, caught her, pinned her to him, kissed her. She felt the floor beneath her head, and Paul half on top of her, herself beginning to respond, and then rebelling. *This was not what she wanted.* And almost immediately, *But how could she stop him now?* But automatically her arms were shooting up, toppling him off balance, off her, and she was free, scrambling up, turning to face him.

'You weren't so frigid before,' he said shakily.

'No.'

'It's Vale.'

'No. It's me. It will come right, Paul. I know.'

'I hope so.' Perhaps he managed a forced smile. 'Are you *sure* you saw two magpies the other day?'

On the Sunday, when she was prowling round the cottage, feeling both guilty and somewhat stupid, Jonathan Vale rang.

'I have a message from Signor Orvino, Gemma. He says Signor Tositi is tired of waiting for you to come up with something. He's travelling here himself.'

'*What? When?*' She could hardly take it in.

'Next Thursday, the tenth. He's coming in to Stansted. What's all this about, Gemma?'

'Is he coming alone?'

'So I gather. They want you to meet him and look after him.' A pause. 'Do you need London accommodation?'

'I'll have him here,' she told him quickly.

'From the palazzo to the wild woods of Kent might be quite a culture shock.'

'I can look after him better . . .' She stopped, uncomfortably aware of the interpretation that could be placed on this. 'I mean feed him better than a hotel would.'

'Of course. What else could you mean?' he replied equably.

Protect him from *you*, were the words that lay between them. Protect him from the man Stanley had confided in, perhaps to his own cost.

Her hands were clammy, both from the effort of speaking to Jonathan, and at the realisation of what lay ahead. It was easy enough to say: Ted Parsons would be returning to his native land. Yet it was over forty years ago, and thirty-seven of those years had been spent more or less as a recluse. The shock of emerging might kill him. Then she comforted herself by realising that Ted was mentally resilient, for all his posing. Yet why had he suddenly decided to come when he was in such fear of vengeance after his post-war misdeeds?

'Thank you for letting me know,' she said, injecting a note of finality into her voice.

'Why's he coming, Gemma?'

'He hasn't told me. He's probably going to flog the frescos,' she told him, and put the phone down with some satisfaction.

What was the sight of modern London going to do to a man who lived with oil-lamps? There must be electricity somewhere in the palazzo to run the machinery below.

But had Ted ever seen television, for example? Surely Giovanni and Sophia must have had some such contact with the outside world? All in all, Ted's visit did not promise to be problem-free. And one of them was letting Paul know about it. She might as well get it over with.

'*Ted?*' his incredulous voice came over the phone. 'Good grief. How did you achieve that? Where's he staying?'

'I didn't. His choice, and with me.'

'Is that wise?'

'I think so.'

'With your martial-arts skills,' he said feelingly, 'it's as good as having the SAS installed. But I'm still worried. Does Vale know?'

'He passed the message to me, but he doesn't know about Ted's reason for coming, so far as I know. I didn't tell him, and I doubt if Felix would without letting us know first.'

'I think he'd be better staying in London.'

'With Bert?' Gemma suggested politely.

Paul laughed. 'I think not. Not at first, anyway. With me, I was thinking.'

'That's good of you. Perhaps when he's acclimatised.'

Paul's flat was in Belsize Park, which was about as big a leap from a decayed Medician palace as Waynings.

'I've got a stage further in the Victoria hunt. I struck lucky with Essex man – Sally Rich's brother, to be precise. Now living in Saffron Walden. He lost touch with his sister, would you believe, during the war, heard she'd gone to Hollywood so wasn't too surprised, and since he worked in Africa for thirty years after the war, missed the dazzling career of one Victoria Ireland who bore a remarkable resemblance to his sister. His parents lived in

Ireland and both died in the sixties.'

'It could explain it.'

'I've got a letter written from the young Sally Rich to her brother. We could compare it with Victoria's hand-writing.' There was a hopeful note in his voice.

'*Felix* can compare it with Victoria's,' she replied firmly.

Paul laughed. 'I must be in on this visit. Is Ted bringing Giovanni?'

'I gather not. Orvino is seeing him off.'

'In red satin?'

'I trust not,' she said fervently.

This disconcerting thought once planted, she watched with some trepidation as passengers cleared customs at Stansted and came through to the concourse. She didn't recognise Ted at first, perhaps because she was subconsciously looking for satin. When she eventually picked him out, he was much smaller and slighter than she'd thought, perhaps stemming from her impression of his towering in his palazzo home territory. Here the monster was reduced to size. He hardly blended into the landscape, however. No satin, no paint on his face, but an elderly mafioso appeared, clad in a suit somewhat too large for him. It was reasonably smart, even though cream linen on a cold March day was going it some. So were the dark sunglasses and bright green shirt. Nevertheless, it was a brave effort, although she was glad she'd packed an old overcoat of her grandfather's in the car. Trolleys appeared to be beyond his capabilities, for he carried a battered brown suitcase, which looked suspiciously as if it might be the one that had accompanied him to Florence in 1952. He marched along bemused, as one swept by an extremely unwelcome tide.

'Ted!' she called.

He stopped, saw her, and waited, people pushing past him as he stood in the middle of the wave. She fought her way through to rescue him, with some difficulty.

'Hello, me old china.'

'We'll wait till they disperse,' she promised, getting to the heart of the problem.

'Right-o.' There was a certain carelessness about his tone which conveyed vividly his inner panic.

'This Heathrow then? I heard it was crowded, and they meant it, didn't they?'

'Stansted. It's north of London.' She didn't add, 'A small airport.' 'I'm taking you back to Kent, and then we can go to London tomorrow after you've rested.'

'Darenth, eh?' He cackled. 'Back to the nest.'

'No. Not near there. Come and have a coffee before we go.'

He agreed eagerly. Obviously the airport had replaced the plane as a womb before the real world outside need be faced. He surveyed the crowds from a café on the concourse, and Gemma wondered what he was seeing. His chair was very close to hers, as if for protection, as he watched groups of backpackers, businessmen and early holidaymakers wandering around. 'Dressed funny, ain't they?' he said eventually.

Coming from him, that was rich, she thought, then realised how much clothes had changed from formal to informal in the years he'd been away.

'I'd have been arrested for that,' he said wistfully, watching goggle-eyed as two teenagers sensuously clung to each other in an embrace. 'Cor, look at that!' He watched a black-legged, short-skirted girl in a black leather jacket wandering by. 'You can see her legs disappearing right up her bum. Tart, is she?'

'No. Girls dress like that now.'

'I've bin away too long,' he said feelingly.

She brought the BMW up to the front entrance, and he scuttled into the back seat with relief, as if fearful he'd be stranded here alone. The front seat would be too much for him, she had decided; the motorway would be bad enough without giving him a head-on view. Fortunately the electric windows fascinated him and took his attention from the main A-road.

'You're not going to like this,' she warned him, as they edged on to the motorway. She was right. He fell very silent, and she was aware he was slipping further and further down in the seat, so that his head was below window level. When she next glanced back, he was curled along the seat like a baby, hands in front of his face. The only time he perked up was when they crossed the Dartford Bridge, when he peeked cautiously out, and screamed.

'It's like a blooming bird,' he yelled. 'Where d'yer say we were?'

'Dartford.'

'That's further down from Woolwich, ain't it? So up there's the East End, and over there's Bermondsey.'

'Vaguely,' she agreed. 'Your old haunts?'

'I didn't stop long enough to have haunts.' He slid down again, as if to indicate that the discussion was over.

'Do you want to visit Gladys's café while you're here?'

'Nah.'

'Bert's your son. He'd want to see you.'

'Listen, darling, how do I know he's my nipper, eh? Does he look like me?'

'No.'

'Does he look like her?'

'No.'

'Well, then.'

'Point taken. All the same, I think you should see him.'

Ted did not reply, and after a minute or two she heard him snoring. Just as well. The M25 followed by a dose of M20 was no place for faint hearts. Monster lorries towered above her on either side, seemingly lurching towards far-off destinations that would never be reached. They would circle round the M25 for ever, the Flying Dutchmen of the modern world.

He was still asleep when they got back to Bishopslee. She had put the central heating on full blast, and already laid a fire as well. Gently she woke him up.

'Blimey,' he remarked somewhat nervously, 'trees.'

'Don't you like them?'

'Prefer houses. Trees are nasty scary things.'

She knew what he meant, but knew they could also be friends. Hers were. She led him down the path to the cottage, but he didn't seem too impressed with Waynings.

'I ain't been in a place this small for sixty years. Can't you afford nothing bigger?'

So much for ancient beams and legends, she laughed to herself. Ted scuttled inside like a rabbit, all the same. That settled it. They'd be eating at home. No pubs for Ted, not yet anyway. Nor was she sure that Bishopslee was quite ready for Ted Parsons.

Inside, the biggest hit was definitely the bathroom. The toilet did not impress him – Stansted had been better, she gathered. But her green bathroom was a different matter. He decided he needed a 'barf' straightaway. He was in there so long, she thought he'd fallen asleep, until she heard him carolling out: ' "How would you like to be;

Here in the bath with me",' to the tune of 'Under the Bridges of Paris'.

She grinned. At least something here met with his approval. 'I got a loverly bunch of coconuts' was Ted's next offering to the musical world, and she didn't wait to hear if he had any improvements to the lyrics of that. She realised she had never investigated the sanitary arrangements at the palazzo, probably because subconsciously she had always preferred not to. An earth-closet? A hole in the cellar? A tin bath? A watering can for a shower? Next time she went she'd— It occurred to her with a jolt there might not be a next time. That she might not even see the fresco room again, and found herself dismayed both at that thought and by the fact that it made her realise just how involved she had become with the tontine.

She was intrigued to find next morning a small pile of clothes outside Ted's bedroom door. Part of Giovanni's job no doubt, only unfortunately Giovanni was not here. She picked it up, thanking science for the washing machines that no doubt the palazzo did not possess. She was relieved to see that Orvino must have obliged with some of the clothes, though the longjohns smacked suspiciously of having descended from the 1950s. She decided to dry them over the radiators rather than treat her Bishopslee neighbours to the sight. If she was going to be put down as a scarlet woman, she wasn't going to have this image linked with longjohns.

She gave Ted the choice of travelling by train or by car to London to see Felix, and he chose the former. He was to stay in London overnight in a hotel, after seeing Felix, and she planned to stay with him. He obviously needed a perpetual guardian, or nanny might be a more accurate word.

Fortunately, the trains did not appear to have changed at all. They probably hadn't, in fact. Ted stared out of the window, obviously feeling safer behind this grimy British Rail glass than in her BMW. Perhaps after all it had been a mistake to treat him to the M25.

'I recognise that,' he said suddenly.

She looked out. 'You're right. It's the Darenth Valley, Ted, where your orphanage was, and where the Folly is.'

'Folly?'

'In the grounds of Lakenham House. It's where the Lakenham Set used to meet, and where they met the night they decided to set up the tontine, on the eve of the Great War.'

'Yeah. We had the parties at the House.' He continued staring out at the dull, bleak countryside. There was only the occasional sign that winter was nearing its end – catkins in the banks, crocuses and brave early daffodils in the gardens bordering the railway line as they neared London.

'Lots of roads, ain't there? Big 'uns,' he said approvingly. 'That's what I like. Not all these fields. Houses. This is more like it.' His excitement rose as the suburbs thickened and the standard degenerated the nearer they got to Victoria.

He walked up the platform slowly, leaning on a stick. Then stopped as he saw the crowded concourse ahead. 'Hell's bells,' he said simply.

'Come on, Ted. Hold on to me, and we'll make for the taxi-rank.'

He fidgeted in the queue and she was glad when at last they could get in. Ted promptly closed the door and the window, as she directed the driver to Felix's office.

'I'd like to see Piccadilly,' he told her.

'Via Piccadilly,' she told the driver resignedly.

As they inched their way round, he goggled at the sight, swarming with lounging youth even in March. 'Look at all them kids. What they doing out of school?' he muttered. He was disappointed.

'They don't go to school.'

'How did they get to be so bleeding lucky?'

'They just play truant, or many here are young unemployed, or runaways.'

'Scarperers, eh? Not the Piccadilly I knew,' he said dismissively. 'And wot's more, it ain't London.'

'What do you mean?'

'This place is different.'

'How?' she asked curiously.

'The people. Look at them. And the whole *place*.'

'The London you remember in the fifties still had rationing; it was dowdy and down at heel. Now it's affluent compared with that.'

He stared at her. '*Affluent?* Effluent more like.' He sniggered. 'I thought they was all beggars. Hardly a suit to be seen. Look at them, half dressed some of them. I like that hair though.' His attention was caught by a pink punk hairstyle marching by. 'Think I could get a haircut like that?'

'I do not.'

'I could get a wig.'

'Perhaps.' Gemma began to feel more like a headmistress than a nanny now.

'This is more like a shanty town,' Ted continued disapprovingly.

Gemma gazed blankly at the shops lining the streets.

'Here today, gone tomorrow. Now, you take my place,' Ted said proudly. 'Built in the fifteenth century, lasted ever since.'

'London had quite a few buildings like that, but someone thought it was a good idea to knock them down for modern buildings, not long after you'd gone.'

'They knocked the guts out of the place, if you ask me. You knew where you was in those days, right or wrong. All this place says to me is, "you're on your own." Perhaps I'm getting old,' he finished mournfully.

'Changing times, Ted.'

'Then give the old wheel a spin, darlin'.'

Felix had asked to see Ted alone, and she waited down in reception till he appeared and she was able to sweep him off to lunch to find out what had happened.

'Call this fish and chips, do they? On a *plate*? Where's the newspaper? Blimey, Giovanni could do better than this with a dead rat, and he's no Rosa Lewis.'

'I thought you'd enjoy it.'

'Oh, I do, I do,' he assured her.

'What did Felix say?'

He took another large mouthful and delicately managed to convey that a gent would not speak with his mouth full.

'About young Vicky, you mean?' he asked eventually, innocently. 'He needs more proof.'

'Are you sure you have none?'

'I told him straight – proof? There's me, and I want me money. He said that weren't enough.'

'That's rather vague, Ted.'

'He said he'd got some stuff from relations – you know about that – but needed more. There's probably some around. Why not ask Vicky, I said? She'll come clean. He

390

said, why not wait, she's going to die soon anyway. We all are, mate, I told him. It's coming right down the road, but some of us are in the advance guard, that's all. Young Vicky, I said, she's not going to die. You ask her. Poppycock. It's me you gotta worry about, mate, I said. I don't want to have young Victoria getting her hands on me again. She's had one go. So I told him to haul up this flock of young Sal's relations, and lay on a nice party for her. A surprise one. Won't that be nice?'

'It's cruel,' Gemma replied horrified. 'You can't face her with that without warning. Was what she did so terrible after all? No, not till the tontine reared its head. She's behaved no worse than you, after all; you pretended you were dead.'

'Maybe, but I got my money to think of. You too. You're too blooming soft-hearted. Think Victoria would worry about you? No, she's got her reputation now; she's probably forgotten all about Sally Rich.'

'As you did about being Ted Parsons.'

'Believe me, with money at stake, memory comes back awfully quick.' He grinned at her. 'Still, I might not be Ted Parsons, eh? Tell you what. Let's get moving. Take me to see Rosalind again.'

'But of all the people you're so scared of, surely she's one of the worst? You've got very brave all of a sudden. What's changed?'

'Ah well, that were Tositi,' he replied easily, smacking his lips in relish at the apple pie and cream. 'Ted now, he'd argue his way out of anything. *And* into anything.' He sniggered. 'I want to see her.'

'But suppose she tells Joe's relations?'

'They don't know where I live, do they? You wouldn't tell 'em, would you, ducks?'

'Of course not.'

'Come on then, you wouldn't keep old sweethearts apart, would you?'

'*Old* sweetheart is the word, Ted,' she said as gently as she could. 'She's not twenty any more.'

'Inside she is, ain't she? She's still my Rosalind.'

'Yes, she is.'

He roared with laughter. 'Haven't lost me touch, have I? Women always fall for that line. Listen, luv, you take me to see the old trout: I bet you she still likes a tickle.'

'Not with me there surely.'

'You don't know Rosalind. Don't tell her I'm coming, though. We don't want the heavy brigade there.'

'Are you up to going now? It's quite a way,' she said doubtfully.

'One of those taxi jobs will do.'

Sure, all the way to Blackheath, she thought resignedly.

Ted was beginning to gain confidence now, and the journey was punctuated with his catcalls and wolf-whistles at each short skirt passing by, to the blank astonishment of the young driver.

'That's against the law now,' Gemma laughed.

'What is?'

'Sexual comment like that. That's why you don't hear them any more.'

'You don't hear 'em,' he said judiciously, ''cos none of them skeletons are really worth it, 'cept for the legs. They're not women like they used to be. Not like—'

'Rosalind?'

'Nah.' Having reached their destination, Ted fidgeted at her side as she banged on Rosalind's door.

This time a voice did call out, or rather bawl. 'Come in.'

Immediately Ted seemed to have second thoughts, for he pulled back; Gemma gripped his arm firmly, feeling it bony under hers.

Rosalind seemed not to have moved from her sofa since Gemma was last here. The peroxided blonde hair still shrouded her face, and surely the same cigarette dangled in just that position from her lips. The parrot let out a squawk as Gemma entered and bounced up and down on its perch.

'Who's that?' Rosalind asked sharply, craning her head to see past Gemma.

'A friend from the past,' Gemma said brightly, too brightly.

Very slowly the friend emerged from the shelter of her back.

Rosalind's eyes narrowed as she ran her eyes up and down. 'Stone the buggering crows,' she said at last. 'If it ain't Ted himself, walked into the lions' den.'

He cleared his throat. Gemma might not as well have been there, for all the notice this couple took of her.

'Back from the dead, eh, Rosie?'

'You certainly are, you thieving crook.'

'Now, now, Rosie.' Ted was hurt. 'Those ain't nice words to greet an old friend.'

'OK, tell me what you got to say for yourself.' The parrot burst out with an invitation to leave forthwith.

'If he don't want me here, I'll go,' Ted announced with dignity.

'Oh, you're not going, Ted. I got the phone here. You walk out of that door and I'll put a call through to Joe's son before you've touched the pavement.'

He shook his head sadly. 'You're harder than you used to be, Rosie.'

'Experience, luv.'

'Everyone makes a mistake.'

'Some are bigger than others, Ted. As in all things, eh?'

He chuckled. 'Mine was real enough.'

'Your cock might have been. It's your Pomona I'm more interested in. The only bleeding mistake I ever made was to be taken in by you. Just like poor old Joe. It won't happen again, that's for sure.'

'You're a fine-looking woman even now, Rosie.'

She snorted. 'I'm a crock, and so are you, so none of your lip. Time's treated us both the same, I'll say that.'

'I mean it, Rosie.'

'I can't walk much, that's all. I'm stiff as a wooden post.'

'How far up?'

'How far . . .' She stared at him, then burst out laughing. 'I can't walk, that's all. Thinking of old nooky, are you? Your usual way to get what you wanted.'

'Who's old nooky?'

'Where you bin? Locked up in a bottle like a genie?'

'If I had, I'd grab you with all three wishes,' he said promptly, with soft eyes.

'I only need one, chum. I want to know where the real Pomona is.'

'The what?'

'Don't give me that.'

'Ah, the Pomona,' he said, striking his head theatrically. 'Of course . . . I seem to remember—'

'Let me remind yer,' she jeered. 'Go in there and have a look.' She jerked her head towards the only other room, presumably the bedroom.

He went in and there was silence.

'Can I go?' Gemma asked, afire with curiosity.

Rosalind shrugged. 'If you like.'

Ted was standing at the foot of the bed, leaning on his stick. No wonder. Before him on the wall an oil painting dominated the room, fading all else into insignificance. It first seemed all darkness. Then, as Gemma stared at it, she saw the dark colours glowed vibrantly, as one single shaft of light, shining through the trees, lit the face. There was blossom on the tree, fruit at her feet, and in one tender hand. Tendrils of flowers curled around her. Behind her in the shadows was a man, and perhaps the suggestion of another whose back was turned. The woman's draperies were flimsy veils, whirling round her dancing figure. It was returning spring, life resurgent. The draperies were light, but partly shadowed, leading the eye upwards without detracting from the beam of sunlight. But at first Gemma saw none of these things. She saw only the face, the face that was unforgettable. It was the face of the Virgin of the Rocks, the face of Pomona.

Ted cleared his throat. 'Listen, ducky, run away, will you?'

Gemma followed him as he shuffled slowly back into the living room.

'Rosie, let's do a bit of art studying, eh? Admire the lady together?'

She didn't even bother to look at him. 'Liven up the day, I suppose. Might as well.'

'Come off it, Rosie. You were never backwards. Here, you – ' he beckoned to Gemma – 'give us a hand before you go. Help me with the lady.'

Gemma Maitland, Special Agent – surely this was her oddest assignment yet? Somehow they managed it, she and Ted between them, but mostly her, supporting

Rosie's dead weight as far as the bed.

'The chair?'

'I'm a bit past them sort of acrobatics, luv,' Rosalind snorted.

'The bed, ducky,' Ted said patiently. 'Right under old Pomona's nose, eh, Rosie?' He looked at Gemma. 'Now hoppit.'

She 'hopped' to the café opposite for three hours, until he appeared, imperiously waving at Rosalind's front door. Obediently Gemma paid up and went. Was it the real Pomona? And was this the real Ted Parsons? Did the real ones exist? And how important was it that they did? For herself, she had seen Pomona.

'Looks my sort of place,' Ted said grandly. Obviously he had decided to be paternal, having somewhat grudgingly given way to Gemma's pleading and agreed to visit the café before returning to Kent. 'Can't have changed since the forties.'

Already, Gemma noticed that the name had changed, though. It was repainted 'Bert's Sunshine Café'.

The proud owner beamed. 'I'll show you round inside, Dad.'

He walked with his ponderous stride through the curtain into the cramped rooms behind. Ted looked round in silence.

'I'll take you upstairs,' Bert offered.

'Thanks, but no, son.'

'But you got to.'

Ted shrugged.

'That's my bedroom.' Bert opened a door. 'And that's yours,' he said proudly, displaying a dingy room, ill furnished.

'I beg yer pardon?'

'I said that's yours. You're coming to live here, ain't you?'

'Not me, old son.'

Gemma inwardly groaned. Tact was not on Ted's menu.

'But I thought it was arranged. You don't have to work. You can stay here and I'll look after you. I wrote to you, told you.' Bert was bewildered.

'Nice of you. I appreciate it, son. But I live in Italy, where I gotta sun what shines every day.'

'I shine every day too,' Bert muttered.

'I'm sure you do, mate. But stale rolls and bacon and eggs ain't my kind of life any more. I'm getting old. I gotta think of myself,' Ted told him virtuously.

'I'd call it "Bert and Ted's Sunshine Café",' Bert's desperate voice floated after his disappearing father. This noble offer was ignored.

Downstairs again, Ted walked past Gemma, tapping his stick pathetically; he hobbled straight through the café making a beeline for the street.

'Where are you going?' Bert rushed past Gemma to reclaim his father.

'Me?' Ted's voice floated back from the street. 'I'm scarpering, son.'

Chapter Thirteen

'Tell you what!' Ted deflected his eyes momentarily from the television quiz show. 'What about this Folly then? I'd like to see that before I push off.'

'I'm sure I could arrange that. Charles won't mind. It's going to be cold, though.' The coldest March for years, and this was the time Ted had chosen to come out of the seclusion of sunny Florence and revisit his native England.

Ted considered this. 'Yeah. Well, I'd still like to go. What about this Lakenham Set then, what's the angle on them?'

'There's no angle, Ted. The tontine money was left to establish a memorial to them in the form of the achievements of the twentieth century.'

'Pretty good from what I can see.' He nodded at the quiz show.

'Some might think it's turned out more like the Dark Ages. Anyway, it's my problem if Victoria is proved to be an impostor.'

'Nice little lady, that.' He gazed thoughtfully at the plump girl in the overtight skirt, on the point of making the fateful decision that might award her a holiday in Greece. 'Yeah, I'd like to see the Folly. That where your grandpa and the others met, ain't it?'

'What are you planning to do with your life, Ted? You're twenty now, aren't you?'

'I've got a good job, sir. I'll find a little wife, and settle down, couple of kids.' He trotted it out automatically, for he knew what was expected of him from these old-school types. He knew what they liked to hear, so why not supply it?

'I doubt that, Ted, very much. I think you have quite different ideas in mind, don't you?'

Ted was taken aback. 'Maybe,' he said cautiously. Where was this leading?

'You've got brains, Ted, and you've got ability. You'll get what you want, but I believe you should think out carefully just what that is.'

'What I told you, sir.' He was beginning to feel uncomfortable with those gimlet eyes boring into him. Then an idea came to him. 'Of course,' he added regretfully, 'I could do better if I had a bit of cash to start me off like.'

Captain Maitland laughed. 'No, you couldn't, Ted. I'm not falling for that one. You and your chosen way of life don't depend on my purse.'

'That's all very well, sir,' Ted said indignantly. 'It's different for you, if you don't mind my saying so.'

'You mean because I was born into a family that gave me what I wanted. Sometimes that's just as constricting as having nothing. It's our own decision, not our birthright that should guide us.'

What was the old geezer on about? Ted made another stab at it. 'What do you think I ought to do with my life, sir?' he said seriously. That was the other line that always went down well.

'You don't need me to tell you. You'll find it.'

'Do you think I'm cut out for the army, sir?'

'No, Ted.' Maitland tried to keep a straight face. 'Look, I'll tell you what I'll do. I'm going to write you out a cheque for fifty pounds. Do you have a bank account?'

'No, sir.' Bank account? Him?

'Good. I'll leave instructions with my bank that this is to be cashed when you come in with it. But that, Ted, is to be when you need it, when you've discovered what is your path in life. Understood? Not before.'

He didn't quite know why, but he did keep the cheque. He didn't claim the money for three years, by which time he'd almost forgotten about it. It was the first time that he had ever received something without wheedling for it or stealing, and for some reason he decided to honour it. He kept it to prove the old codger wrong about him, he supposed. But, almost by mistake, he was proved right . . .

'There's a load of stuff in tonight,' Max whispered to him as he tossed down the mild and bitter.

'Where from? Thanks, mate,' Ted added out loud for the benefit of his other customers – and Gladys, who was born with twenty ears, he reckoned.

'Pimlico way. Not much quality, but worth your picking through, Ted, before you move it on.'

Ted's role was to store the goods in the old workshop in the yard behind the pub. Gladys did not know about it – or, if she did, she pretended she didn't. He had to make sure it reached the right destinations: fences for quality stuff, the market for the junk. Jewellery, furniture, wirelesses, even books. Most of it usually went down the market and disappeared within a couple of days. He found to his surprise he had a good eye. Perhaps his dad had been a fence. Or a nob. After closing, he wandered outside when he was sure Gladys was occupied, and took a squint at it. Usual stuff. Few wirelesses that would fetch a bob or two. China, he grimaced, nothing much – a pile of old pictures. Ladies tripping down cottage garden paths (to the privy, he always thought to himself realist-ically), a few dead pheasants, and one mucky old picture that, when he'd blown the cobwebs off, he saw was a woman standing by a wooden box on legs, with a window behind her, and a picture above her head of a naked man and woman leaping around in the woods. It took his fancy. So when he went to Whitechapel next, to the fence they used for the art stuff, he produced it at the last minute. He kept it back, found himself reluctant to take it down, kept hiding it at the bottom of the next pile and the next . . .

'What's this?' he asked casually. 'Picked it up at my aunt's – thought I'd bring it along.'

Harry Jones took it, carried it to the light. 'Not bad,' he said at last. 'Dutch. Might be after Vermeer. He had a soft spot for ladies sitting, standing, and doing the highland fling on the virginals.'

'The what?'

'The virginals.'

'Blimey. It's not bad though. I'll keep it.'

'You bleedin' won't, mate. Your old aunty don't wash with me.'

'I'll pay you.'

'How much?'

Ted stared at it. He liked the look of that woman.

402

She was a goer. He must be off his rocker, but when he got an idea in his head, it stayed there. The trouble was, this one was going to cost money. Then he remembered the cheque. 'I'll give you fifty quid.'

Harry goggled. 'You ain't got that kind of money.'

'I will have tomorrow.'

'Knocking off a bank tonight, are you?'

'Something like that.'

The next day Ted cashed his cheque and handed the money over.

Harry burst out laughing.

'What's so funny, mate?' Ted asked suspiciously.

'It's a fake. Don't say I didn't warn you. After Vermeer, I said.'

Ted didn't know what that meant then. He didn't go for Harry though; he looked at the picture and decided it still looked the same. The woman still had that 'Come here, Ted' look on her face, that light coming in the window showed up her behind nicely, even if it was covered with brocade. That couple up in the woods were still having a high old time. Nothing had changed. He liked it.

'Not to me, it ain't, mate,' he said jauntily.

He kept it under the bed. It was nice to think about when he woke up, that look in the woman's eye, her plump fullness. Then Gladys found it, and started asking questions he couldn't be bothered to answer. So three days later he scarpered – with his Vermeer.

'Do you still have it?' Gemma asked him sweetly.

'Yeah. Daft, ain't I?'

'Does it look like a fake to you now time's gone by?'

'That depends what you want to see, Gem.'

'But sometimes one has to be objective. After all, I could point out that the Vermeer seems to have replaced Leonardo's shield in your moving story of how you came to Art.'

He wasn't even thrown off track. 'The rose-tinted glasses of memory, Gem.'

'One or the other, then – is that how you got into faking?'

'Me? Not *me*,' he said virtuously. 'Just gave me an eye for the good, just like your grandpa said. Good fake, good Leonardo, what's the difference? Vermin or Vermeer, what's in a name? Either way, your grandpa put me on the path to the promised land, you might say.'

'The faking of the frescos.'

He giggled. 'If you say so, darling. Let's go and see this 'ere Folly, shall we?'

Cold it might be, but daffodils, violets and primroses were beginning to emerge rather cautiously in the hedgerows, more vigorously in the gardens of Lakenham House. Ted snorted in some disgust as they made their way up the Darenth Valley. 'All the same, ain't it? I ain't been here for sixty years and it hasn't changed a blade of bloody grass. A few more houses, maybe, and bigger roads. It's a bit more civilised, I suppose.'

'I'm glad you think it's an improvement,' Gemma said, straight-faced.

'What are we stopping here for?' he asked, as she drove up outside the main house. 'Dining with the Queen, are we?'

'No. Just getting the key. The Folly's not mine yet, you know.'

'I know, dearie.'

She hoped it would be Maria who opened the door, but

as usual the worst alternative materialised in the form of Jonathan Vale. He nodded coolly and came out to join them. 'I'm coming too, if you've no objection.'

She could hardly say yes. She supposed she should have expected his presence, for it was Mother's Day, and there had probably been a family luncheon. 'Do you need a wheelchair for Ted?' he asked. 'We've got plenty around.'

'You're not getting me in one of those.'

'Then I'll walk and you take Ted by car, Gemma. The drive goes up to the edge of the Folly grounds.'

She almost touched her forelock.

Like the pantomime devil, Jonathan somehow managed to be at the Folly first, nevertheless. Did he shoot up through some secret star-trap? He was on the steps to meet them, running down to give Ted a hand up.

'Time someone cleared out all this muck,' Ted announced disapprovingly as, having painfully made his way through the overgrown garden, he walked into the dusty littered rooms that the Lakenham Set had bequeathed.

Gemma caught Jonathan's eye and tried not to laugh, both thinking of the palazzo and its lack of amenities.

'I'll get round to it,' Jonathan promised gravely.

'Let her do it,' Ted told him. 'It's woman's work.'

'You've been away too long,' Gemma retorted amiably. 'Things have changed in that direction.'

Slowly Ted walked round on his tour of inspection. 'Like a blooming Roman temple, ain't it?'

'That was the idea, I gather, when it was built,' Jonathan told him. 'There were quite a few Roman villas built round here anyway.'

Ted looked knowledgeable. 'Yeah, I read there was

one dug up at Lullingstone just before I had my spot of trouble.'

Spot of trouble? One way of describing a fake Leonardo, she supposed.

He looked down at the mosaic floor of a Bacchanalian feast in the entrance hall. 'Ghirlandaio did them.'

'Mosaics? He didn't pop any into your palazzo, did he?'

'Larry didn't order any.'

'Or maybe you're not good at mosaic, Ted.'

'*Me*?' his eyebrows shot up in innocent surprise. 'Why me?'

'Let it pass,' Gemma laughed.

He looked round the room, peered into bookcases, examined the pictures on the walls, opened cupboards, while they watched. She was conscious that in so doing she was still avoiding the real issue: Jonathan. Sooner or later the tension within her had to be sorted out. How could he stand there so unconcernedly while she wrestled with the fact that between him and the tontine pool stood the life of one person, Ted Parsons? Or was the *real* issue buried deeper within her even than that?

'When are you going back, Ted?' he asked – casually enough, but she was immediately suspicious.

'Soon as possible, mate. I've had enough of country, enough of London, and enough of this stinking weather.'

'What about Bert?'

'What about him?' Ted asked cautiously.

'Are you just going to leave him alone there?'

'You bet, chum. What's this 'ere?'

'The library. It was the baths.'

'Bathroom? With all these books around? You seen Gem's bathroom, mate?'

'No.'

'You should, and her in it and all.'

'Have you been peering through the keyhole?' Jonathan inquired politely.

'The window, down the garden; you can see right in. Quite a nice little—'

'Ted,' Gemma interrupted, suppressing irritation since she realised full well he was deliberately winding her up. 'That's enough.' Nevertheless the idea, true or false, she'd been spied on, reminded her uncomfortably of the night outside her cottage last summer, and the man at her side.

'You oughtn't to be so shy,' Ted assured her. 'He fancies you rotten, don't you, mate?'

'Of course,' Jonathan agreed quickly, though with almost deliberate lack of enthusiasm. 'However, unfortunately for me, the lady is spoken for.'

'I am not,' she told him angrily, and he laughed, having succeeded where Ted had failed. 'Paul is merely—'

'Did I mention him?'

'Who else then?'

'Claimed by the past.'

Safer ground. 'The only past that concerns me is this Folly.'

Ted, bored, hobbled upstairs; when he returned he had clearly been disappointed, for he went back to the large semi-circular room that looked out over the gardens. 'Romans,' he said at last. 'They did things right. It needs a bit of thinking about.'

'What does, Ted?'

'My Vermeer.'

'I don't like it.' Paul sounded worried over the telephone.

'You mean Vale knows Ted's movements?'

'There was no way of preventing it. Anyway, what can he do, and why should he do anything?'

'Because Vale isn't stupid. If he suspects Victoria isn't Victoria at all, he's got to move quickly now he knows Ted's been here. Ted is our only evidence. And we know he bumped off Stanley probably for the same reason.'

'Just a minute,' Gemma interrupted angrily. 'We don't *know* that. You were the one who told me he was keeping an eye on Annie with regard to the marriage stakes. You were right enough there.'

'The situation has changed since then. He's a loner, Gemma. You and I have been married. He hasn't. Ever asked yourself why not?'

'He's gay?' she asked sweetly.

'You should know.'

'Why should I?'

'He's kissed you, hasn't he? Made love to you? You've come back from him with that satisfied look on your face. How you—'

'Stop, Paul, please.'

A pause. 'I apologise. Out of court.'

'Way out.'

'Nevertheless,' he rallied, 'the threat remains real. Ted's in danger, and if you're with him then you are too. For all Vale knows, he might have handed evidence over to you.'

'There is nothing concrete.'

'So Felix said. Nevertheless, I'm going to keep a careful watch on Master Vale. I'll come down, stay in the cottage, and sleep on the floor.'

'It's not necessary.' Her voice was curter than she'd intended, but the thought he'd been hob-nobbing with

Felix behind her back annoyed her.

'It is.'

'No, Paul.'

Ted announced he wished to leave on the Wednesday, and by Tuesday she was grateful. The responsibility of having an elderly child in the house was getting too great. There was one snag, however. 'You can see me home, Gem,' he announced grandly, as they returned home from the Folly.

'I'm driving you to the airport, as we arranged.'

'Back to Florence.'

'Ted, I can't. I have a business to run.'

'Lovely Lisa says she can spare you for two or three days.'

Gemma's heart sank. Thanks, Lisa, she thought crossly. Loretta terrified Ted, but Lisa he had found manageable. He had pawed her at first meeting and she brushed him off like a fly. He had taken it well, apparently highly delighted and approving of her womanly qualities. Lisa was not so impressed, and this was doubtless her revenge.

'Can't Signor Orvino see you home?'

'He's not there. He's away.'

Gemma found this hard to believe.

'You got me into this, you and your grandfather, so you can see me out of it.'

'Very well.' Three days wasn't the end of the world, she supposed.

The time crawled by until Wednesday. She wasn't used to being unpaid companion, housekeeper, carer and cook to eighty-year-old men, and found herself counting the hours to his departure. Jobs, even routine, were welcome diversions, though she feared what he might do if she left him too long at a time. She had booked herself off duty from Tuesday evening, but annoyingly found herself called out. As soon as she returned she knew something was wrong by the way Launcelot yowled at the door. The light beckoned in the darkness as she rushed up the path, unlocked the door and hurled herself inside just in time to see the back door slam. She rushed to it, opened it, and stared into the darkness, but the intruder had already disappeared through the back gate into the forest. He must have a torch, she thought at the back of her mind – *that* torch? – even as she grappled with the greater fear.

Heart in her mouth, she turned back and ran into the front room, fearing what she might find. To her relief, Ted was alive at least. He was lying on the sofa, croaking, staring at her with startled eyes.

'Ted! Thank goodness you're all right.'

'Tried to strangle me.' An attempt at his usual insouciance.

'I'll ring for the police and ambulance.'

'No,' he shouted more vigorously.

'I must, Ted. Who was it? Anyone you recognised?' Fear made her hoarse.

'No rozzers.'

'So it *was* someone you know. Was it – ' her lips were dry with tension – 'Mr Vale? Or someone sent by Victoria?'

'Yes,' he whispered.

'Which?'

'Victoria's geezer.'

She didn't believe him. 'I'm sending for the police,' she said dully.

'No.' He struggled to his feet. 'I'm orf if you do.'

'All right.' She gave up. 'Then I'll call my own doctor here.'

'All right. And give me a whisky.'

'Not till the doctor's been.'

The doctor pronounced him not seriously harmed, but ordered him off to bed, a suggestion he took amiss until the doctor agreed a whisky might accompany him.

'He'll be all right?' Gemma asked after he'd departed.

'When he's leaving, Gemma?'

'Tomorrow. I'm going with him.'

'Good. Don't let him leave a forwarding address, will you?'

'Another two days in sunny Florence. Lucky you,' Loretta said without envy. 'Hunk going?'

'Hunk not,' Gemma replied briefly.

'Oh. Free for me?'

'It's not advisable. Someone attacked Ted last night. I only just got home in time.'

And how safe would Ted be in Florence? Perhaps he would be less open to attack from Victoria, but for Jonathan Vale the situation was all too easy. She realised she would have to warn Signor Orvino, and with this decision she felt much happier. She rang Paul from the airport.

'Are you going to say I told you so?' she asked him after she'd finished.

'Just read my lips in future, honey child. Gemma, when you're back I've a good mind to take Ted's place as lodger.'

'Lodger?'

'Yes, I did say lodger, not lover. That too, if you insist.'

'Paul, when I've fought my way through this suffocating plastic bag of a tontine, maybe I'll be fit company again. But not now.'

'I'll be waiting.' He rang off.

So much for Ted's credibility. Papa Orvino was there to meet them at Florence airport. He greeted Ted with cries of joy, and much earnest conversation in Italian followed. Ted in some odd way had metamorphosed into Lorenzo Tositi again, now back on Italian soil. Ted the chameleon. The shoulders swelled back, the strut was more pronounced, sunglasses were donned. The side-street entrance was beginning to look like home even to her now, and she had come to accept the crabwise crawl along by the garden as being entirely normal. The house door was firmly locked behind them, and Giovanni threw himself forward for a repeat performance of Orvino's; he clasped his master in his arms as though he was welcoming him back from the dead. As indeed he almost was, Gemma thought wrily.

'Tonight,' he told Gemma firmly, making it clear she should not accompany them further. 'Supper,' he said somewhat shyly. An invitation to dine at the palazzo? She was intrigued; something had clearly been planned to celebrate the safe return of Lorenzo Tositi.

She had no difficulty booking into the central hotel at this time of year, and for once Florentine faces and motor scooters outnumbered coaches and tourists. She lay on her bed for half an hour and then decided to go out in search of culture and tea – not necessarily in that order. She wandered about at random, thinking over her visits to this city of secrets: with Bill, with Paul, and with Jonathan. Of all Italian cities, it was the one her countrymen were most drawn to, and yet it retained its individuality, almost an isolation, from the world around. It lent generously of itself to others, and yet remained distinct. Like the perfect marriage, she supposed, and the thought of Jonathan's accusation came straight in the wake of the thought.

Reluctantly she acknowledged the partial truth of his accusation. Bill who'd made her laugh, like and then love him, until she'd assumed there could be no other route to happiness save through another just like him. Only there never would be another Bill, and for that she had blamed him. To find these things now she had to find another route or abandon the hunt. Of the two paths offered she had to avoid the blind alley of sexual attraction, which led nowhere save to delusion. That was the fake path. The other was there to be chosen, when she felt able to face the journey.

Giovanni had told her to come to the San Lorenzo entrance and she was glad of it, as she walked through the majestic basilica in the early evening, to find the serene cloisters for once empty of tourists. It felt like a familiar path now, to take the twisting corridor to the palazzo. The tower was out, for no courtyard was apparent as she hurried down the steps. The smell of damp caught at her nostrils, and she shivered in the light dress she had daringly put on for this festive occasion. At least, she hoped it was festive. It was a palazzo, after all, and she would dress for dinner, no matter how odd the occasion. Her high heels clicked on the stone as she hurried up the stairs to the upper floors, and through the kitchen where she found Giovanni. Primitive his equipment might be, but the smells were magnificent. He even managed a smile when he saw her. His delight at seeing Ted returned must have spread into general bonhomie, she decided. With great ceremony, he led the way down to the first floor. Would it be the tapestry room, or the fresco room? To her pleasure, the tapestry room was empty and Giovanni flung open the far door.

It was indeed a celebration. Huge candelabra on the long table lit the room, revealing Lorenzo's throne pulled up to one end of the table, and Ted adorning it in full glory. In the middle of the table was an ornamental vase – surely of some precious stone, which commanded attention by its grace and proportions. Ted and Orvino were already present. She made a third, and presumably Giovanni was the fourth. Lorenzo (odd how difficult it was to think of him as Ted now they were here) was dressed in a long golden robe, sword strapped incongruously at his side, Lorenzo the Magnificent's chain round his neck, and a black wig, a Medici wig if ever she saw one. He lacked only Il Magnifico's face: from under the wig leered the wrinkled painted face of Ted Parsons.

'Like it?' he grinned.

'It's superb, Ted,' she said truthfully. With the candle-light flickering the frescos glowed into life, the figures so lifelike they seemed almost part of the celebration. Orvino struggled to his feet on seeing her, and collapsed gratefully again as she took her place. She was doubly glad she too had dressed up. Clearly they were to celebrate in style.

The superb smell turned out to be osso buco comple-mented by mellow Tuscan red wine, cheese, salad and fruit; Giovanni was pulling out all the stops, no doubt about that. There was plenty of red wine, so that when the conversation was in Italian, Gemma felt her eyes closing in the comforting shadowed warmth of the candlelight. She jerked awake at the touch of a finger on her neck, the feel of something cold, glanced down to see Ted's seat empty and round her neck the red glow from a ruby falling on her white dress.

'That's for you, Gem,' Ted said, shuffling back to his seat.

'But—'

'It ain't mine. It's Lorenzo's.'

'*Bellissima!*' Orvino clapped approvingly.

'But you can't just give me this, Ted.'

'Why not? Won't suit me, will it?'

'Bert's wife, if he marries,' she said ridiculously.

'Blimey, she won't need rubies,' Ted said succinctly. 'She'll need a dildo.'

'*Buonasera*, Roberto, Ted.' Even though the candle-light shadows hid the face, the voice was unmistakable. It was Jonathan.

'I let myself in, I hope you don't mind, Ted.'

Ted leapt up, one hand clasped to his throat, as he gave a cry of animal terror, gazing hypnotised at the new-comer. A torrent of words poured forth from Orvino, replied to in calm, measured tones by Jonathan.

'I'm sorry to have startled you,' Jonathan said to them all. 'I dislike being quite such a spectre at the feast. I gather, Gemma, Ted thinks I tried to murder him. Roberto is nobly defending me. Giovanni apparently wants to lynch me. Might I ask where you stand?'

'Someone tried to kill Ted at my cottage when I was out. He says it was you or, to be correct, a hit-man hired by Victoria. He knows which, of course, and now he's made it clear to me.'

'What nonsense is this, Ted? Victoria wouldn't hurt a

415

fly, let alone you,' Jonathan asked curiously, apparently not perturbed.

'Some fly,' Gemma retorted. 'Look.' She went up to Ted and showed them the marks now fading on his neck.

Jonathan's face changed. 'You think I did that?'

He was good, she'd say that. He looked completely appalled as he walked up to them.

'Don't touch me, not again!' Ted waved his hands protestingly dramatically. Too dramatically.

'*Did* you see who did this to you?' Jonathan demanded.

'Yeah.'

'Then you *know* it wasn't me. For one thing, Gemma,' he turned to her coldly, and his eyes went to her neck and the ruby, narrowing speculatively, 'much as I hate to spoil your theory, I wasn't even in England yesterday. I was here. In Florence, as Roberto can testify, can't you?'

Papa nodded vigorously.

For a moment she was shaken. Surely Signor Orvino would not lie. Then, insidiously, doubt crept back. Oh, but he would. Had he not denied all knowledge of Ted Parsons? It had been for good reason, but nevertheless he had at best evaded truth. He was willing to lie to protect his friends – and Jonathan was among their number. Perhaps his allegiance was split between the two of them. In any case, there was a relationship here she could not fathom, and nothing, but nothing, could be accepted at face value.

'Why are you here?' she asked politely.

'Work – and you.'

'Me?'

'Felix mentioned you'd be coming back. I thought a friendly eye in Florence might do no harm.'

Lame, Jonathan, lame, she thought. Out loud: 'That's

416

very good of you.' And left it.

Swords merely withdrawn until the next bout, but he obviously thought he was the victor.

'May I join you at the table?'

Ted theatrically cowered back.

'It's all right, Ted,' Gemma told him angrily. 'He won't harm you. I'm sure Signor Orvino will vouch for that.'

Ted muttered sullenly to his friend, who from his body-language was obviously still defending Jonathan. Jonathan took Giovanni's seat as the latter went in search of a further chair. Orvino poured him a glass of wine and he held it aloft. 'To Lorenzo's safe return to his fortress.'

Lorenzo? Jonathan was the one who in the dim candle-light seemed the embodiment of the palazzo's designer: strong, set features, generous, cool – and the master of ruthless political cunning.

'No thanks to you, mate,' Ted informed him.

Jonathan set his glass down. 'Look at this room, Ted, these frescos, this table. Is this the time, is this the place for games?'

Ted sat up straight in his chair, and his hands gripped the throne's arms in lordly pride. He made one last snatch after the disappearing Ted. He giggled. 'What you come for then?'

'For one reason only when I heard from Mario that you and Roberto were together. Gemma is, of course, a bonus.' A slight nod that turned studied compliment to indifference.

'What's that?' Ted asked suspiciously.

'I want to see the workshop.'

Roberto gave a strangled gulp, and wine slopped from his glass; Giovanni muttered a curse, and tears filled his eyes. Even Gemma sparked with curiosity. Only Ted remained unmoved.

'What workshop, mate?' he asked with interest. Ted had obviously speedily replaced Tositi.

'The one you and Roberto ran in this palazzo. The fakers' factory.'

'Sounds a bit of all right,' observed Ted. 'Wish we'd thought of it, eh, Roberto? What you been telling him?'

Papa was beyond telling anyone anything; he was gazing at Jonathan like a hypnotised rabbit.

'He told me nothing. Ted. It wasn't, after all, very hard to guess – and if I had any doubts, you've just set them to rest.'

'You mean it's still here in the palazzo?' Gemma asked eagerly. Of course it was. Why had she not realised it herself? The first and second floors were the shop, the fakers' factory lay hidden elsewhere.

'Not active, of course, or no doubt Ted would not be needing his three-quarters of a million.'

Gemma turned to Ted. 'So *that's* what you were scared of – a come-back on your faking activities here. It was nothing to do with Pomona and the Leonardo forgery.'

'Fake,' he corrected indignantly. 'It'd only be a forgery if I'd got the original, wouldn't it?'

And have you? she longed to ask, but Jonathan's eye on her warned her not to let Ted deflect her on to golden side-paths.

'It didn't take much imagination,' Jonathan continued, 'to work out how you two made your living, and where it was pursued. It explained, for one thing, the installation of electrical machinery for the tower and its mouse. I take it you're not claiming *that* was put in by Lorenzo the Magnificent?'

'Garn,' Ted informed him, 'what d'yer think? That we was all cavorting around with bows and arrows ready to play Robin Hood when the villains came hunting for us?'

'No, but my hunch is that when the tower was in, there was an admirable and impregnable storage space between its wall and the palazzo wall.'

A silence.

'We could,' Jonathan suggested, 'pop down and see since the mouse and its tower are at present out of their hole.'

Orvino fidgeted with his glass; Ted was sulking.

'I could of course,' Jonathan continued offhandedly when there was no response, 'ask Florentine art dealers if Helmut Muller still lives near here. Or if it's true Ted Parsons is still alive in the old Palazzo.'

That drew a reaction. A screech from Giovanni.

'It's not safe. Walls are crumbling,' Ted countered.

'The palazzo has stood for five hundred years,' Gemma pointed out. 'It's good for another twenty minutes.'

'Or is the whole castle a fake too, and only made of marzipan?' Jonathan asked. 'Like that throne, for instance. Lorenzo de' Medici would have had no truck with thrones; I think that's a good old Parsons fake.'

'Fake, young man, is not a word to be taken lightly,' Ted shouted, no fear in his voice now. Temper had taken over, Gemma realised.

'I'm sure it wasn't,' Jonathan agreed. 'Are you going to show us?'

A rapid consultation in Italian, ending in a resigned shrug from Orvino. Ted, or rather Tositi, rose ceremoniously to his feet, and the procession began. Ted was in the lead, followed by Giovanni, bearing a candelabra, then Roberto, herself and finally Jonathan, who slipped into last place deliberately.

First Ted slowly walked upstairs – to the bedroom? No, the kitchen? Apparently so. A larder door was pulled open to reveal not preserves but another concealed door which Ted thrust open. It was dark but the candlelight showed a long, slim room, or rather a studio, with windows looking out towards the San Lorenzo domed roofs. Below her lay the answer to one question, a flat roof where the soft coo of pigeons answered for her the question of how Orvino contacted the palazzo. Beyond rose the dome of the Chapel of the Princes, here around her were benches and easels with the paraphernalia of painting and drawing lying scattered around as though its users had walked out yesterday. Quills, oils, brushes, golden varnishing paints, chalks, inks, all scattered and mixed up, even a few pieces of broken eggshells. The smell of the paint still hung in the air, as though work were merely suspended.

'Here?' Jonathan said. 'There's more, isn't there? This is a studio, not a workshop.'

'Patience, my son,' Ted told him reprovingly, and led the way down the stairs once more. This time they were led to the ground floor, through the dark and cold of the machinery room.

'That'll teach you to wear a thin white dress,' Jonathan whispered in her ear, his hand brushing her thigh; whether it was accidental or intentional she could not be sure.

'I was expecting dinner,' she retorted, 'not a trip to the underworld.'

On each side of the machinery room was an archway;

stumbling in the dark over cables, she followed Orvino through the far one. To her surprise the next room was not so damp, nor so dark. Windows let in the late evening light to reveal a ghostly workroom. Then suddenly it was flooded by light. Of course, being next to the machinery room, it carried electricity, she reasoned, and indeed it would be essential to work by down here. She surveyed the room. To her it was a dusty, disused relic from past industry. To three of these men, it was more than that. There were, she saw with surprise, tears on Papa's face, as he said something to Jonathan.

'He hasn't seen it for fifteen years,' Jonathan translated for her. 'When they retired.'

'If they painted in the upstairs studio, what went on here?'

'The work, I suspect. The ageing, the retouching, the preparation of paper and its ageing, the fake framing, all the scientific techniques behind the forging.'

'Restoring,' Ted said airily.

'You need peroxide for restoring?' Jonathan inquired politely. 'And gelatine? Marouffe glue?'

'Stop nosing around.'

'Well, well, here's a Vasari battle scene. Or is it School of Parsons?' He dived at an old canvas lying face down on a bench.

Ted giggled.

'You're an old crook, Ted,' Gemma informed him. 'How many people did you employ?'

'Five painters, three technical,' he replied, somewhat to her surprise. 'Roberto did the selling, Lorenzo Tositi was King of the Workshop, eh, Giovanni?'

'Sì, signor.'

'When did you operate it?'

'When poor old Ted died,' Ted informed her simply. 'Tositi took over.'

'And Helmut?'

Ted jerked a finger. 'Him. Roberto became Helmut – not in Florence, naturally.'

'*Ja*,' Roberto replied proudly, if somewhat nervously.

'The Florentine School of Parsons,' Jonathan said wryly. 'Why give up?'

'We got old, that's why. Time to hand on to the younger folk, trained by us, of course.'

'Now try the truth,' Jonathan suggested.

'They got too smart for us,' Ted said, aggrieved. 'Them and their science. They don't play fair. Whatever you do now they can find a way round, them and their computers. Couldn't shift the stuff any more. The fifties and sixties now, that was different. Artists like us could work then.'

'I will show you,' Giovanni said. 'Come.' Waving the candelabra about dangerously over his head, he led them back to the far side of the machine room, not to the archway through which they had entered, but to the further one. Beside it at right angles was a shuttered door, set about two feet from the ground. Giovanni helped Ted and Orvino through. No such offer for Gemma, but Jonathan provided an unsought-for heave at her rear. She did not thank him. She found herself in a narrow corridor, lit and cooled only by slit windows set in the thick walls. Mouldering canvases were stacked face on to the wall. Gemma turned some over. 'A Canaletto,' she remarked with amusement.

'Yeah. Popular, they were.'

Ted had order, she'd say that for him. Each pile represented a different artist or school. Dutch, Italian,

German, even a heap of Constables and Gainsboroughs.

'Is everything a fake, Ted?' she asked sadly. Everything, even the frescos, she wondered?

'Yeah,' he answered readily. 'The lot.'

'I'm still not sure I believe you, Ted,' Jonathan told him amicably.

'You come and have another look at them frescos then.'

Back in the fresco room, Gemma wandered around the frescos once more, stared up at the painted ceiling, and marvelled. How could these be fakes, when they spoke so clearly across the centuries to her, when she could return to them again and again, each time seeing them more beautiful, with more depth, more meaning, and yet more layers of mystery. The art and the colours of painting in pure fresco had now been all but lost. Why on earth should Ted fake them, not for sale, but merely for his own amusement?

'My masterpiece,' Ted announced grandly. 'Roberto helped, didn't you?' Sidelong look between the two men.

'*Sì.*'

Jonathan did not comment.

'If they're fake, then there really is no reason,' Gemma pointed out, 'for your not allowing an expert to come in and confirm it to us.'

Then Jonathan did speak. 'That's sacrilege, Gemma. This is a room to be loved, not analysed. As one loves a woman.'

She wondered of whom he was thinking.

'My thoughts exactly, chum,' Ted confirmed, highly pleased. 'Ain't it nice to be on such matey terms with my murderer?'

'Cut it out, Ted,' Jonathan retorted.

'If you say so, young man. Wouldn't like to offend you.' To Gemma, watching, it seemed as if there were some unspoken conversation going on between them from which she and even Giovanni were excluded.

The moment passed, and as if by silent assent the rest of the evening passed agreeably enough, till she could see Ted visibly tiring. She rose to go.

'I will take you to your hotel, signora,' Giovanni insisted.

'Thank you.' This was a surprising courtesy from Giovanni, and one she'd accept – if only to avoid the same offer from Jonathan.

Giovanni made his point clearly enough. 'The ruby, signora.' There was a note of reproach in his voice, as though she were underestimating the importance of the gift. She expected a demur from Jonathan, but none came, and he walked off in a different direction to herself and Giovanni.

She should have known it was too easy. On the other side of the hotel door, waiting for her, when Giovanni departed, was Jonathan Vale.

'Did you don red cloak and wellington boots to fly here?' she asked crossly.

'I know the short cuts.' He dismissed her irritation as irrelevant. 'Can we talk, Gemma?'

'No.'

'We need to.'

'Tomorrow then.'

'Tonight please. If you still think I'm a murderer, we can take a stroll through Florence; there are masses of people still around. We could go down by the river; the parapet is high enough to occasion comment if I decide to try to heave you over.'

'It isn't funny.'

'It is to me, for I have the benefit of knowing I'm harmless.'

As well now as tomorrow, she thought. She was tired but not so tired she couldn't be on her guard with Jonathan. It turned out to be strangely enjoyable walking through the dark streets towards the floodlit piazza and then down to the river. Even with him, there was a magic in the night air. There were few people about, for all his claims.

'What did you think of the workshop?' he asked.

'I'm glad we saw it – the palazzo's last secret.'

'That I doubt. There's no such thing as the "last" with Ted. If you find him out one way, he'll rear up in another blind alley.'

'What was that odd look Ted gave you for?'

'You don't miss much, do you?'

'It's wiser not to in my job.'

'Do you really think I carried out that attack on Ted?' he asked.

'My dear Jonathan,' she retorted, exasperated, 'he *says* you did. He should know.'

'Does it ever occur to you that you can't rely on a word Ted says about *anything*?'

'Not over this sort of thing. In art, perhaps.'

'Life is art. You can't separate them. It's the same outlook on life; two windows to the same view.'

'He says you did it.' She clung obstinately to this one unassailable fact, and plunged recklessly on. 'Stanley, as well. And what about Gladys?'

He stared at her. 'Who the hell do you think I am? Are you crazy, Gemma? You seriously think I've carried out two murders and an attempted one?'

'He says Victoria carried out the first attempt on his life. Very well, between you you could have decided to strike again.' Stupid to tackle him head on. With no one else would she have done so, but she had to clear this from her mind. She didn't know what to expect, tensed herself for physical attack, or verbal abuse. Neither came.

'You're raving, Gemma,' he said at last. 'Think, think, *think*.'

'I have, and every time it comes back to you.'

'Of course. Why? That's what you have to ask yourself.'

'Because you did them.'

'That's falling into heffalump pits built to trap.'

'Then haul me out if you can,' she challenged him.

'I don't have to. What I tell you three times is true,' he replied grandly.

She was well aware she was being deflected from her path, but she laughed all the same. ' "The Hunting of the Snark." I *told* Loretta you were a snark.'

'It's a very respectable profession.'

'I'm still the Bellman though.'

'Understood. So I'll tell you who attacked Ted: Bert.'

'*Bert?*' The idea was so crazy she laughed.

'It isn't funny, to quote your words.'

'He's Ted's *son*,' she exploded.

'Quite.'

'You mean he was so upset at Ted's refusal to live with him and his scarpering again, that he tried to kill him? *Bert* found his way down to Kent all alone to attack him at Waynings? Bert couldn't find his way to Victoria Station, let alone Bishopslee.'

'With help he could.'

'Whose?'

426

'Leaving that aside, no, that isn't the reason he tried to kill Ted, in my opinion.'

'Then what is?'

'Because Ted killed his mother.'

'Oh, for heaven's sake! Ted was in Florence, Jonathan.'

'To be more accurate, he was the means of her death. Lorenzo de' Medici actually did the deed. I doubt if I can prove it though.'

This was just not funny; this was real fantasy. Suddenly Gemma was aware she was alone with him at the river's edge; she had to get away, back to the hotel and safety. She turned casually round, ready to dash across the road, and yawned.

He sensed her tensing up and caught her arm. 'I'm not barking, Gemma. I mean it. You remember the box of tricks he showed us at the great reunion? There was a ring in there. Lorenzo's ring. I saw it again a few days after Gladys's funeral.'

'What were you doing there?'

'I looked in to see how Bert was faring on his own.'

She wasn't going to ask why – it would lay open the path for him to score a point. She waited.

'It was on their mantelpiece, which started me thinking – and I suspect Bert for all his slowness had been working on the same lines. The Medici were paranoid about assassination, rather like Ted. Lorenzo, after all, had seen his beloved brother killed before his eyes and, according to our maestro, that had driven him to building the mouse and the tower and fortifying the palazzo. The Borgias were the real specialists in poisoning, but later the Medicis came a close second. I think Lorenzo saw the possibilities early on and had a poisoned ring ready as a "gift"! A needle shoots out when the hand is shaken in the right spot and injects poison. I think Gladys put it on for her birthday, and someone hit Ted's jackpot for him.'

'And the poison remained there for hundreds of years, still virulent?'

'We'll probably never know. It could have done. Cyanide has been known as a poison for centuries. Either Ted put a fresh dose on it and gave her the ring, or he left it to chance to see if she'd pinch the ring. Or he was completely innocent. But Bert blamed him anyway.'

'But why should he want to kill her?'

'I know I'm villain Number One in your books, but I suspect the reason is that Ted knew Gladys had bumped off Stanley. She might even have told him. Victoria is ill, so she thought, so Ted was the next practical objective for removal, and into the bargain it was a pretty good thank-you for the way he'd treated her. Ted, I suspect, was afraid he would be next on the list, knowing Gladys of old, so decided to forestall her.'

'Then who, mastermind, made the attack on him? Was that Gladys's first shot, or Victoria, as he claimed?'

'I think he did it himself, Gemma, knowing that Gladys was about to die and thus deflecting suspicion from himself.'

'But what about the other night? You can't tell me Ted tried to strangle himself. Or did I do it and then decide to blame you?'

'No. As I said, that was Bert.'

She sighed. 'It's the wine making me go in circles. I'd forgotten we'd several murderers on the loose. Don't forget John Peacock, though.'

'Oh, I'm not. I think that was Gladys too, and that she boasted to Ted, putting the idea in his mind of spiking his own drink. I think she paid Peacock a visit, popped something like a chloride cleanser in his coffee – probably one of the strong ones they'd use in the café – and provided a suitably unlabelled bottle of it to be found, then emptied a tin of fish, and neatly washed it clean, leaving it as "evidence" of food poisoning into the bargain. I can see you don't believe me, but I'm sure I'm right. These cleansers are hard to identify in the body. Now, I'm going to shoot a few questions. What's so fascinating about Ted's bedroom? I presume it's not the lure of the flesh?'

'In a way,' she replied guardedly.

'He's melted your icy heart?'

'Don't be idiotic,' she said shortly. 'Because I don't fancy you, it doesn't mean—'

'Leave it. I'm more interested in the bedroom. He didn't attack you, did he?'

She shook her head. 'He hasn't lost interest in sex, but there's no serious intent – not towards me, anyway.' Amused, she remembered Rosalind.

'I'm relieved. What then?'

She hesitated. To tell or not to tell. 'It's a treasure trove of drawings, nudes mostly, and presumably fake. Some are erotic, some just anatomical; there are a few trees, windmills and so on, and some—'

'What?' he asked sharply, as she stopped.

'And so on,' she finished meekly.

'I see. Some anatomical sketches, trees – and something else. What might that something else be, presumably in Renaissance work? Gemma, you're holding out on me. Deliberately. Therefore – ' he thought for a moment – 'it's buildings, no – military buildings.'

'The river looks very calm tonight.'

'It won't in a moment, when I toss you in. *What* buildings?'

'Did I say buildings?'

'Come on, cough up.' Then he suddenly looked taken aback. 'Gemma, you're not scared I'll go rushing back to bump Ted over the head if you tell me, are you?'

'No. I'm just enjoying power.' But there was an element of truth in what he said, wasn't there?

He picked up the hesitation. 'Look, my Doubting Thomas, let me show you.' He fished around in his jacket pocket, producing a crumpled airline ticket. 'Does this convince you? An Apex ticket for Monday night. Return this coming Monday. Gemma, it was Bert, you idiot.'

'It was of the mouse and tower,' she said clearly. Sometimes you had to jump. It was as much of an apology as she could give.

'Oh, glory.'

'It's a sketch in Leonardo style.'

A sigh of pure happiness. 'You're still holding out. Style? School of? Fake? *You* think it's genuine, don't you?'

'How can I know?' she asked reasonably. 'One genuine sketch in a house of fakes? I'd like it to be, though.'

'Would you?' A sudden spark in his voice. 'Did you know Leonardo was a military engineer before he was known for anything else? They were the whizz-kids of the day, of course, so he naturally pushed it, and that's why the Duke of Milan hired him and he left Florence. Gemma, do you think your sudden thaw towards me would extend to trusting me not to turn into Bluebeard – would you come back to my flat now? I've got to look it up in the books straight away. I can do it alone, but you might like to be there.'

430

'You really think the tower could have been designed by Leonardo?'

'Why do a drawing of something already in existence? Of course, there's a chance – if you're right. And we *don't* know everything else is a fake.'

Oh, the cunning of the man. She knew she was a fool. Ten times a fool. But she was going. How could she not? What after all would he gain by murdering her? Nothing. And rape? Not him. He was too arrogant, too much pride, to feel force was needed on a mere woman. He would rather wait till she fell at his feet and pleaded with him to take her. He'd be waiting one hell of a long time.

'Help yourself to a drink and pour one for me. Or do you want coffee?'

'Neither, thanks.' He could whistle for his drink.

'Good. Now, let's get working.' He ran to his book-shelves, snatching books eagerly, piling them on the table. Then he started in on them, feverishly hunting down index references. 'Here. He was in Florence until 1483, then he went to Milan. That would fit. Giuliano was assassinated in 1478. The year afterwards the chief assassin, Bandini, was caught and hanged. Leonardo sketched him in the process. Suppose Lorenzo saw him at it and promptly got hold of him to help in the building of his private fortress? Leonardo was a young man, he'd have leapt at a commission from Lorenzo, even a secret one. It's often been commented on how odd it was for Lorenzo never to have commissioned Leonardo to carry out work – he was well known then. Here's the answer. Oh frabjous day, he *did*!'

'Your theory could even,' Gemma said excitedly, 'fit the Pomona.'

'How?'

'When I saw Rosalind's Pomona I thought her face was like Mary's in the *Virgin of the Rocks*, though not the same pose. So I went into the National Gallery and had a look at the cartoon. I was right, it was, and the contract for the *Virgin of the Rocks* was 1483. Suppose Leonardo had just carried out a commission for Lorenzo for Pomona, and decided Pomona's face would be just what he'd want for his altarpiece. He didn't get round to painting it for years, but he'd still have the drawings I suppose.'

'I thought you told me Lomazzo claimed Leonardo painted Pomona in Milan some time between 1507 and 1512.'

'Yes, but he was writing from what he'd been *told*, so he's not a hundred per cent reliable. It's the kind of subject Leonardo would have liked when he was young and experimenting with painting draperies and flowers and so on. Besides, Pomona herself is a young man's subject.'

'A young man's fancy in spring?'

'Don't mock me. It's much more likely. And suppose Ted found Pomona *here*, not in Austria. Damn, he didn't come to the palazzo till the fifties. So suppose Leonardo did it at the same time as the face for the virgin, about 1507, and—'

'Equally, suppose Ted faked Pomona, basing her on the *Virgin of the Rocks*?' Jonathan pointed out drily.

'Then your mouse drawing is a fake too,' she retorted.

A pause. 'Why should he make up such an elaborate fiction?' Jonathan asked hopefully.

'He's a fantasist. Don't be too ready to believe what you want to believe is truth.'

'And you, Gemma,' he threw casually back at her, 'don't you realise the reason you're so keen to believe I'm a murderer is that that absolves you from feeling anything else?'

'No,' she said abruptly, forced back into fields she had no wish to enter. 'That's got factual basis.'

'What?'

'You whistle.'

'I do what?' He burst out laughing. 'You can't be serious.'

'I can.' She shouldn't be saying this, rushing ahead into uncharted fields. 'You were outside my cottage last year, before the party. I was terrified.'

'Me?'

'You were whistling "Daisy, Daisy". I *know* it was you. I heard it again at the MoD, *and* when you went to answer the door in your flat to Annie Masters.'

'And why should that scare you?'

'You were an unseen presence. Just there in my garden in the darkness. Threatening me.' It sounded ludicrous as she haltingly put it into words.

'In your garden?'

'I nearly ran into you. Just a presence, Jonathan, just a threat.'

He stared at her. 'Gemma. I'm going to touch you, *now*. Just hold you.'

'No!' She backed away.

'Kisses don't harm. Not physically anyway. You, my doubting lady, are going to know once and for all whether I'm true or fake.'

She backed against the bookshelves until she could go no further. He reached out for her and took her in his arms. She almost screamed, as if victory from that night at the cottage was now complete. She forced herself not to, but held herself back from relaxing against him, then found it impossible as his lips travelled her hair, her eyes, her cheeks and then found her mouth, which treacherously responded. She heard him swear. Why did he object, she wondered, as she felt his hands travelling down her, holding her to him, and then, the sensation hitting her like a cold shower, she was free.

'I'll see you back,' he told her flatly.

They walked almost in silence back to the hotel, more apart than ever. Stupid, she thought, stupid to part now. The waste; oh, the passing of precious time.

'Fake?' he demanded as they reached the door. 'Shall I softly and silently vanish away like the Snark I am?'

She did not, could not reply. The words would not come.

Chapter Fourteen

His voice was still drowsy on the other end of the phone.
Perhaps he too had been late for an appointment with
sleep. There might, however, Gemma thought, amused,
be just one difference between them. Jonathan's thoughts
would have been charging around in pursuit of Leonardo;
hers had been obsessed by Jonathan. The night had that
effect, liberating feelings that hurtled on like high-speed
trains, unchecked and unexamined. The morning clari-
fied; it removed doubts and focused on resolutions.
Reason was outstripped now; it wasn't being hurled
headlong into the hall of mirrors called love that caused
this dizziness, it was emerging again into clear daylight
and seeing the simple shining signpost that shouted: THIS
WAY.

'Do you have plans for the day?' she asked clearly,
casting her dies without hesitation, though her hand
round the handset was clammy as a teenager's.

'You've postponed your flight?'

'Yes.' Dive in with both feet. That was the way it had
to be, for there was no other way with him – and no other
way, she now knew, for her.

'Come round.' The click of the phone was as gentle as
the purr in his voice, which half amused, half irritated,

and completely wooed her. She could hardly begrudge him his conquest, she told herself. 'Oh whistle, and I'll come to you . . .' How right she'd been. Light-headed with relief, now the step had been taken, and slightly sick with anticipation, she took longer than usual burnishing her hair into submission, even if her crackerjack heart would not accept the same discipline.

She strolled across the Ponte Vecchio, the old bridge spanning the Arno river, deliberately keeping her pace slow, savouring every moment, pushing down bubbling excitement. Here Byron and Shelley had walked, here Robert and Elizabeth Browning doubtless stopped to window-shop as she did, at the displays of jewels and silverware in the windows of the small shops, and at last she plunged into the narrow road that would lead her to him.

He opened the door immediately: he must have been standing right by it. Behind each door in Florence might lie some secret treasure; the trick was to know which one. Behind this one was Lorenzo the Magnificent, or so he appeared to think from the smirk on his face. Dark blue cords and sweater, and fifteenth-century Florence still poured from him. She went without a word straight into his arms. He smelt of morning, of aftershave, of coffee and fresh bread, a hug and kiss of homecoming. He eased away from her, and there were two of them once again.

'You look,' she said shakily, 'very pleased with yourself.'

'With life,' he amended. 'Shouldn't I?'

'Me too.'

'Now tell me why, Gemma?'

'There was no longer a choice. Florence seems to be a one-way city.'

'No compromises?'

'Not now. Nothing here compromises. I suppose that's why Ted fits so well. He doesn't compromise either – in his own way.'

'You wanna wear make-up, you wear it, even if you are an eighty-year-old man supposed to have been dead for forty years. Florence makes only one proviso: it has to fit her spirit, whether it's true or fake.' He pulled her to him again, and whispered lovingly, 'Tell me more about the Leonardo, Gemma.'

'I thought you wanted me, not the Leonardo drawing,' she breathed in mock hurt.

'Leonardo is merely to pass the time.'

'Till when?' she managed to say.

'Till now.'

This time the kiss had nothing to do with coffee and morning. This time his kiss wooed, paused, then claimed; his lips touched, caressed, and aroused, then, as hers responded, shot throughout her body the rays of a piercing sun. Something seemed to be slipping, and she realised it was her skirt, which he had undone and pushed down. She reacted slightly, and sensing the movement he relaxed his hold, studied her.

'I love that slow smile you give,' he said. 'Is it saying "But . . ."?'

'I think it's saying "Now?" '

He put his arms round her again, pushed down the skimpy slip and ran his hands over her briefs. 'That's the easiest question you've ever asked me.'

He was hugging her so close, he was lifting her clear of her clothes; one arm was behind her back, the other hand, she was all too well aware, was claiming what she'd imagined she could control for ever. He walked her backwards, as excitement and desire made her shout out in combined laughter and happiness. She saw his surprise, then the grin coming, as he sat down on the bed, reached out to her before him and removed her briefs, reached out again and, as she gasped, pulled her down beside him and took off the rest of her clothes.

He looked at her until eventually she had to turn away.

'I'm sorry,' he buried his head in her lap. 'It's just that I've seen so much of your rear view all my life. I was evening the score.'

'You could do that some other way,' she said gently. Goodbye for good, practical Gemma Maitland. She preferred the other one, kneeling nude on the bed, stripping off a man's clothes as he lay back, dodging his hands which had other intentions, laughing at him, playing, until finally, as she leaned over to push the last of his clothes on the floor, catching her, sending spasms of mingled love and desire through her. Yes, it was her. *Much* more fun.

'Sure?' he asked, as he came to her.

Amazed he had asked, till she realised it was for himself he needed to know. She ran her hands down his body, stopped and kissed. 'Yes.'

He quivered as she put out her arms to hold him. His kiss started at her mouth, then travelled down, taking her heart with it, until it rested achingly, demandingly where he was.

'Gemma?' Jonathan finally stirred at her side.

She lay on her back, listening to the sound of the Florentine world, distanced, hurrying by in the street below. Where were they going, all those people? Did they even know where – as now she did? Jonathan's hand shot out and closed on her breast. 'It's like the first look at a good painting.'

No need to ask what he meant by 'it'.

'All impressions and ecstasy. The greater the painting, the better and better it gets. More depth, more hidden beauties. The fakes you only want one bite at.'

'What about Ted's frescos, then?' she murmured. 'He claims they're fakes.'

'I'd like to see them again. Those faces have stayed with me, especially the woman.'

'Lucrezia Donati?'

'The other one even more. Simonetta, Giuliano's love. She reminds me of you. If you had that long white ornamental dress on, and your hair braided as hers—'

'A far cry from what I'm wearing now.'

'I'd prefer to paint you as you are now. Glowing. And clothes don't do your breasts justice.'

'What did you mean by having seen enough of my rear view all your life? I can't believe you treasured the memory of a five-year-old boy,' she asked lazily.

'Is this the time for pillow revelations?'

'Yes.'

'Very well then. No, I didn't. Not precisely. But some images remain in your memory, even as a child. And somehow that day did. Partly because it was the first time I'd seen the Folly, and partly because of you. There you were in a yellow coat, and ankle socks, busily clip-clopping away from me. I was crying, because I couldn't keep up, and you came back for me. But you got impatient and went on to the Folly with your grandfather. By the time I got there with mine, you'd seen it all, and I suppose I felt excluded. Not exactly love at first sight. Insecurity, I suppose.'

'And that was all?'

'No, I forgot it. Then you came again when you were about ten or eleven, I suppose. I was eight or nine. And it brought it all back, explained my dream. You played with me. We played hide and seek with my brothers and sisters, and you found me. I was huddled under the bushes, and found I was staring up at your knickers. I regret to say, when you bent down to say you'd found me, I made a grab at you and them.'

'Charming.' She hesitated. 'Did I oblige?'

'No. You replied with perfect dignity. You kicked me and ran away.'

She laughed. 'Serve you right, you precocious monster.'

'We were all born with original sin. We don't get it handed to us at puberty.'

'And this made you bitter and twisted and made you determined to get your revenge on me?'

She watched his hand coming, touching her lightly, lovingly.

'Yes.'

'Liar.'

He laughed. 'I forgot all about it, except that you stuck in my memory as a stuck-up little girl, who was far too prim and proper, i.e. you ran away from *me*.'

'And you still remember the insult.'

'I hate to puncture your vanity yet again, but I would have forgotten all about it once more, except that I did see you later. I didn't repeat my earlier misdemeanour, but it reminded me of our earlier contact. Or lack of it. I saw you with Bill.'

'Did you?' Shock at hearing his name while lying in bed with Jonathan vanished almost as soon as it struck. 'When?'

'I was about twenty. I arrived at your grandfather's just as you two were leaving. You can't have been married long, and you didn't see me. Your back was of course towards me. I remember the look on your face, though, as you turned and said something to Bill. That was the face of love, I thought; full of laughter, hope and optimism.'

She could say nothing.

'Have I hurt you, Gemma?'

'No. Because you've given that to me again.'

She heard his intake of breath, felt the clasp of his hand on hers. 'Me, not just this part of me,' he glanced down.

'No. Though I don't think the word "just" is relevant.'

'You gave me a salutary lesson that day in the bushes. I've been improving my technique ever since.'

'I didn't notice a lot of beating about the bushes when I came in today.'

'Ouch. If you're going to make bad puns, I'm going to make the most of sexual equality and demand payment for my sexual prowess.'

'How much are you charging?'

'The admission price to see that Leonardo drawing.'

'You didn't have to drag him along, did you, Gem?' Ted asked disapprovingly. Then he grinned, as though something were amusing him.

'I'll vouch for him, Ted. You're not really scared of him, are you?' she asked curiously. 'I simply don't believe it was Jonathan who attacked you.'

'Not if you say so, Gem,' he said munificently.

Jonathan was fidgeting beside her, trying to restrain his excitement as they followed Ted who was deliberately slowly hobbling up the stairs and through to the bedroom, and going through the ritual of folding back the walls. For once it was not the fortification of the room that held Jonathan's attention, but the drawings. Ridiculously, she felt her knees go weak as he paid almost too much attention to the erotic drawings. Was he delaying coming to the drawing of the mouse, or was he genuinely intrigued? She watched him look at the sketch of Rodin's *The Kiss*, and felt him inside her again. She flushed as though he could read her thoughts, and then did not care if he could. She glanced at Ted to find him eyeing her speculatively, as Jonathan moved on to the mouse at last.

'Like it?' Ted asked, after Jonathan had stood plumb in front of it for several minutes.

'The jewel in your crown, Ted.'

'Yeah, I made a good job of that.'

'You?' Jonathan asked politely.

'My Leonardo period, you might say.'

'Have it your own way. I'd like to compare this with the real tower and mouse again if you've no objection. Giovanni can take us.'

'You can go – Gem stays with me.'

Jonathan cocked an inquiring eye at her, which Ted noticed. He cackled. 'It's all right, mate. We'll go back downstairs, all nice and proper.'

Gemma laughed, glad to see Jonathan disconcerted for once. 'Enjoy your mouse.'

'I got another present for you, Gem,' Ted said mysteriously when they got back downstairs. He opened a drawer in the long table and produced an ill-wrapped parcel. 'Don't unwrap it now. You wait till you're safe at home. Away from your new cock in the roost. You be careful. He tried to kill me, you know.'

'I don't believe it, Ted. It's another nonsense of yours.'

'Don't you, miss? Sun shines out of his cock, eh, now he's had his oats?'

'You're going too far, Ted,' she told him warningly.

He took no notice. 'What about the other one?' he asked querulously.

'He's a good friend.'

'Oh yeah? I reckon he's still hoping to get in your—'

'Ted, shut up!' she said firmly, and this time he did.

He grinned. 'You take this, keep it to yourself, promise? And come back and tell me what happens. I want my money, remember, and *he's* not going to help me get it, is he? You remember that when you're rolling in the hay.' He pointed his finger downwards, presumably towards Jonathan, as though he were the devil incarnate. His direction was misplaced, as at that moment Jonathan came back in the room. She felt her face flood with warmth at the closeness of him. He began to whistle lightly as Ted chatted on. With some difficulty she identified the tune: 'How Little We Know . . .'

'I think it's genuine, Gemma.' Jonathan sat back at the table in his flat, pushing the book over to her. 'Look at this one of a continuously cooled still, and this of a bridge across the Bosporus. Why should Ted fake a drawing of the tower of all things? The writing and everything else looks right. I'd like to whip it away from the palazzo and let the experts run it through the tests.'

'That would spoil the point.'

'That palazzo could do with a little of the cold light of day.'

'It might collapse, dissolve away.'

'My, my. Are you becoming a romantic, Gemma?'

'Perhaps I always was.' She had just needed to be reminded of it.

He was not deflected. 'Did Leonardo do the design, and Lorenzo build from that? Or did Ted fake the drawing, copying the installation he found at the palazzo? Or do you favour Ted building the actual tower and the mouse?'

'That I'll never believe.'

'Look at this reproduction of one of Michelangelo's designs. In the 1520s he fortified Florence against imminent attack from the Prince of Orange. One of his bright ideas was the hilltop fortification of San Miniato. He shoved in a few more guns but realised that would make the tower even more of a target against a cannonade. So he built on an enormous cornice on the vulnerable side – and what do you think he did?'

'Built a mouse?'

'Way out, lady. He suspended thick mattresses to take the force of the shells. Simple, isn't it?' He paused. 'Talking of mattresses, did you know your left breast was brushing against my arm?'

'I'm afraid I did.'

'I'm mentally in bed with Leonardo at the moment, but there's room for one more.'

'To hell with Leonardo.'

'And Paul?'

She cried out in shock. 'That's not fair.'

'I'm sorry, but it is.' He leapt up and put his arm round her as she moved away, trembling.

'I thought he was important,' she said stiffly. 'I thought he was an answer. Now I know he wasn't. And Annie?' she hurled at him.

'A figment of Paul's imagination.'

444

'Some figment. She threw herself into your arms.'

'Precisely. Did you see me encourage her? I was curious to know what was going on between her and Paul, and if the way to find out was not to discourage too severely her come-on approach, it seemed worth it. Do you believe me?'

'About you and her, yes.'

'That's enough for now. I believe you, too.'

She laughed shakily. 'Now what?'

'Easy. We carve our initials on the old oak tree.'

'Have you carved yours deep before?' Would he reply, or was she pushing too far?

'It would be strange if I hadn't, wouldn't it?' he replied after a moment. 'I'm thirty-five, after all. You have to plunge in the wood to recognise the path. So yes, I have. I lived with someone for eight years.'

'You did not marry?'

'No.' He did not elaborate. 'Three years ago, she left me for someone else. A not uncommon story in itself, and a forgivable one. What made this not so forgivable was being left not for the breakdown of love, but more down-to-earth reasons. Money. Another common story you might think. But not in her, or so I had thought. She had ambitions in the art market, but needed either extraordinary talent or money to fulfil them. Acknowledging finally that she lacked the first, she decided to follow the second course. Betrayal Number One. Herself. As I lacked both the money and the desire to underwrite her, hence Betrayal Number Two. Of me. End of story.'

'Lewis Carroll's mouse's tale.'

'Are you gently reminding me, Gemma, that I am still an optimist, that I still believe in happy endings and genuine Leonardos? That I still think the Lakenham Set's ideals can and should be achieved?'

'I believe in happy endings.'

He was very still. 'Is your left breast still feeling companionable?'

One could get vertigo in love, she discovered, that could hit you even in the morning, even doing something so mundane as checking out of an impersonal hotel room, paying bills and dispensing tips. How had this love hit her so suddenly and completely? She didn't remember how it had happened with Bill, but it wasn't this way. Perhaps it had slipped unobtrusively up one night and declared itself acknowledged. This time it was more like a hot jacuzzi, battering itself at her, knocking her off balance.

On her final room check she stuffed her sponge-bag in her hold-all – and found Ted's package, which she'd forgotten about. She supposed she should open it now. She tugged impatiently at Giovanni's ill-tied knots of thick string, flung off the wrapping paper, and found a collection of documents, letters and passport. She stared at them, taken aback. What had she expected? Another necklace? A fake painting? No. This was the proof Felix needed. Victoria Ireland's passport. Not the Victoria Ireland she knew, even as she would have been in 1941. This was a fresh-faced girl, with a rounded face who looked as if a smile was never far from her face, even if it had been banished for the occasion of the passport photograph. Victoria Ireland, brown eyes, five foot two inches, actress. And her signature. Nothing like the signature of Sally Rich's discarded passport. This Sally looked a descendant of the woman she knew today as Victoria Ireland.

The shock of being catapulted back into tontine-land again made her feel sick, and she went to the minibar and drank some mineral water before tackling the rest. Letters from home, snapshots, all the memorabilia Sally Rich would have had with her in her London lodgings. She must have handed it all to Ted to destroy and left him with all the proof Felix would need to face her with for a confession and, if need be, a court case. In her hands lay the evidence that would lose Jonathan the money to fulfil the Lakenham Set's ideals – and win it for her. She could still give him his heart's desire, his happy ending, if he would accept it. But how could she do it, when she didn't know yet what she, Gemma Maitland, would decide?

She was tempted to destroy the material, and let fate decide which one of them should get it, but there was only one thing in the way: Ted Parsons, waiting confidently for his three-quarters of a million pounds. He trusted her to give it to Felix, and so she had no choice. Desolate, she picked up the wrapping paper and saw tucked inside an odd piece of packing material. She was about to throw it away when she realised it might possibly be part of an old painting. She examined it, and realised it was indeed darkened paint on one side. One of his old fakes? She looked at it more closely. Holding it against the light she saw shapes of dark colour that might just possibly be a bowl of fruit and, resting on it, possessively and lovingly – if she were being fanciful – a hand, draped sensuously over the rounded shapes. As she stared at it, it became more obvious, with a certain familiarity she could not for the moment place. Preoccupied as she was on the journey home with the horror ahead of her, it did not come to her till she was back at Waynings. Those fingers in their soft gentleness, in their imperceptible movement from light to shade, their cloudy mystery, reminded her of the hands of the *Mona Lisa*.

'Good time?' asked Loretta innocently, cocking an eye at her.

'Very.'

'You look well. In fact, you look very well. If I didn't know your nunlike habits, I'd say—'

'Better not.'

'Oh good. I won't be jealous, I promise.'

'I'm relieved. Kirsty!' Gemma yelled down her staircase, and Kirsty appeared beaming, in her own time. 'Give Mr Johnson my compliments and tell him Loretta is taking him to the Rotarians today.'

'I'll do my penance like a saint,' Loretta told her meekly, and departed. From downstairs her voice wafted up, as she bumped into Lisa. 'Gemma's back.'

'Good.'

'She's glowing, very glowing.'

'Glowering, in fact,' Gemma yelled again, irritated this time.

'Don't worry, Boss, I'm history,' Loretta carolled, vanishing out of the front door. Lisa rushed upstairs.

'Did Loretta tell you your swain has been calling night and day? We told him you'd be back Friday.'

Hope hurtled up like a weight on a fairground trial of strength and crashed ignobly to the bottom as she realised it was not Jonathan of whom Lisa spoke. 'Paul?'

'The same,' Lisa said cheerily.

At least she'd played for time in staying away at the weekend, Gemma thought thankfully. 'I'm afraid I haven't been pulling my weight,' Gemma said ruefully.

'You've had a special assignment,' Lisa said seriously. 'It's understood.'

Gemma felt even guiltier, since the special assignment was Jonathan. The phone rang and she jumped.

'It's not a snake,' Lisa grinned. 'Who is it, Kirsty?' she shouted.

'Mrs Pretty,' she passed on to Gemma.

'Thank heavens.'

'And you've never said that before,' Lisa pointed out. 'Things are *serious*!'

Paul didn't ring till the evening, and then Gemma was out. She played the message back, and dithered over whether to ring back immediately. She did, heart beating, but he wasn't in. Thankfully she replaced the receiver, wondering why she felt so reluctant. It was, after all, something she had to face, though she wanted to tell Jonathan what had happened before she told Paul. There was, however, no reply from Florence, none from his London flat, and no luck at Lakenham House, though Maria told her he was expected there the following Sunday. 'Why don't you come?' she invited Gemma cordially. 'I'll tell him to ring you if he gets in touch.'

'That's very kind of you.'

'Come to lunch.'

Gemma made an excuse. She'd arrive later. How could she break bread with the Lakenhams before telling Jonathan about Victoria Ireland? On a sudden resolution, she rang Paul. The relief in his voice at hearing from her faded quickly. 'Next time you go off to the South Pole, do let me know first, will you? It was the South Pole, I take it?'

'Florence.' No reason to conceal truth.

His voice sharpened. 'Not *again*. What the hell for?'

'To see Ted.'

'You *are* conscientious. Or did he give you the low-down on Victoria? If not, it's about time you saw Felix and agreed to tackle the lady head-on. I'm getting on nicely, but it's all circumstantial, hearsay.'

'I'll do it in my own time, Paul.'

'Your time could be running out.'

'What on earth do you mean?'

'I don't have to spell it out again, do I? Danger, Gemma, danger.'

She sighed. 'I'm quite capable of coping.'

'Obviously not, as Vale attacked Ted in your house.'

'Paul,' she attempted, struggling hard, 'I know you mean well, but I'm a grown woman.'

'That I dimly remember.'

Fury rose in her, but guilt made her defensive. 'Paul, I'll contact you. I'm very busy.' And I don't need advice from you, was what she managed not to add.

'I quite understand, Gemma. I won't crowd you, but I'll be looking after your interests, don't worry about that.'

She rang off abruptly, furious with him, more furious with herself. She had not behaved well, but perhaps she'd had no choice. She had thought she loved him, and had found out that she was wrong. Sooner or later she had to tell him, and however she wrapped up the words, the task was not going to be easy.

She had to see Jonathan face to face: she could hardly break the news over the phone. In any case, he didn't ring, a fact that alternately relieved and perturbed her. The Sunday was sunny; she had lunch in the pub, and then drove on to Lakenham. Perversely for what lay ahead, the day was beautiful, with all the hesitant promise of spring and the optimism of budding green to be seen here and there. He opened the door himself, and she was swamped with instant pleasure at seeing him again as he drew her inside. The touch of his hands merely taking hers brought up such sharp physical desire, that she almost stumbled.

'I'm sorry not to have rung,' he was saying penitently. 'I had to rush off to Troyes and got rather absorbed in an orillon. Forgive me?'

'Yes.' She tried to make it sound natural, she with the much greater reason to ask understanding and forgiveness.

'Shall we go to the Folly?' he continued. 'You told Mama you had something you wanted to talk about.'

'Why not?' Why not wallow in unhappiness. It was, she supposed, only right to face the problem there. It might even make it seem more of a business problem and less of a personal one. There were tests in all relationships, but the prospect of one this big and this early was daunting. The lawns were sprinkled with clumps of daffodils under the trees, and in the overgrown gardens, spring herbs pushed their way through in places.

'A touch of the famous Roman central heating wouldn't come amiss inside,' he said ruefully, as he pushed open the door.

She drew back and he looked at her in surprise.

'Don't let's go in,' she said, trying to sound natural. She couldn't. It seemed a betrayal of all it stood for.

'If this is bad news, let's have it quickly.' He followed her to the stone seat in the central arbour, and kissed her lightly. 'Something *is* wrong, Gemma, isn't it? You're stiffening up and not for the right reasons. What is it? Is the Leonardo a fake?'

'Not Leonardo.'

'What then?'

'Victoria.'

He sat down and pulled her down beside him. 'Tell me,' he said slowly.

'She's a girl, or rather woman, called Sally Rich. The real Victoria died in 1941.'

Jonathan looked out at the gardens, not at her, and said nothing for a moment.

'Ted told me,' she rushed on.

'You believed him?'

'He made me believe him, and Felix too.'

'And I wasn't told.' No hint of the degree of his feelings.

'How could we? Not until we had more proof.'

'And you have it?'

'Ted gave it to me in Florence.' She glanced instinctively towards her shoulder-bag and he followed her glance.

'Will you show it to me?'

'Of course. Jonathan – what else could I do? How could I tell you or tackle Victoria if it were nothing? We *had* to have proof.'

'And now you have.' His voice was detached.

'Yes,' she replied bleakly. 'Look.' She passed him the passport and the letters, and told him the story of what had happened.

'Yes,' he commented at last. 'I'm no expert, but I can see it adds up.' He glanced at the Folly, then away again when he saw she was watching him.

'I'm sorry, Jonathan.'

'What for?'

'Dashing your dreams for the Folly.'

'I was thinking of Victoria actually.'

'There's no reason for it to be made public,' she said quickly. 'I'll make sure of that.'

'I'm sure you will.' Distance, great distance between them. 'Are you going to take this stuff to Felix?'

'I have to.'

'Why?' Again that detachment.

She looked at him, startled. He asked *why?* 'Because of Ted, of course. You can't think *I* want the money, and the decision of what to do with it. You know how I feel.'

'No, I don't.' Some warmth was creeping back.

'Look.' She tried to make amends. 'See this scrap of painting? Look at the hands. I think Ted put it in the parcel for a purpose. I think it's either a failed fake or—'

'Or?'

'Or a scrap of the true Pomona.'

He burst out laughing at that. 'The romantic.'

'Look at the fingers, don't they remind you of the *Mona Lisa*? The same curve, the same rosy tint.'

'Of course. That's precisely how Ted could fake them for the Pomona.'

'Oh, come on. We've got it here – you can take it to experts if you like.'

'No.' He pushed it quickly back to her. 'It's yours. You must do as you wish.'

'Please, both of us.'

He picked up the passport. 'This too?' he asked ironically, waving it high above his head. He was testing her. She stared at the dark blue rectangle of board and paper, which hinged her whole relationship with him. What to say? What to do? She felt like a caged rat; pressing the right lever brought manna, the wrong one nothing. The gardens around them, the Folly looming before them, seemed to retreat, concentrating her world in the two of them and that passport. Slowly, but surely, Jonathan was slipping beyond her reach, seeing in her face the answer she would have to give. She would lose him either way, and both of them knew the risk: to take it to Felix might betray the Lakenham Set, to suppress it would betray herself.

'Gemma!'

An agonised shout at first did not register with her. Then another, and as she saw Jonathan turn, turned with him to see, unbelievably, Paul leaping down through the undergrowth from the far boundary, and now rushing across the path towards them. She could make no sense of his presence, and looked at Jonathan, as taken aback as was she. She managed to say, weakly, inanely, 'What on earth are you doing here, Paul?'

'It's just as well I am, isn't it?' He ostentatiously looked at the passport which Jonathan still held in his hands. As Jonathan rose lazily to his feet, he shouted, 'Give that back, Vale. It's Gemma's.'

'Oddly enough, I'm aware of that,' Jonathan replied. 'More strictly, it belongs to Sally Rich, or in the case of Victoria Ireland's passport, to the Passport Office. However, I cede Gemma's *de facto* claim.' He handed it back ceremoniously to Gemma, and turned to Paul. 'Now would you mind removing yourself?'

'Not quite yet.'

'As present custodian of the Folly, I can formally request you do so.'

'As incoming owner, Gemma can decide.'

'That's easy, Paul,' she interrupted, stepping forward. 'Just *go*. I'll get in touch later.'

He flushed, but stood his ground. 'I'm afraid I won't. You need someone to protect you, Gemma.'

'I'm hardly flattered,' Jonathan said quietly.

'You don't really think he'll let you get away with that material you've left on the bench, do you, Gemma? Why do you think he brought you down here?'

'We came here,' she said coldly, emphasising the '*we*', 'so that I could tell Jonathan about Victoria Ireland, before I rang you to tell you I had the documentary proof Felix needs.'

Paul laughed angrily. '*Tell* Jonathan? Gemma, you fool. He's known all along, haven't you, Vale? Did you think it was going to be a great big shock to him?'

'That's not true,' she retorted angrily. 'He heard it all for the first time just now. You're—' She broke off, uneasily aware that Jonathan was edging away from her, back to the bench, aware that suddenly the atmosphere had changed. What had seemed a squabble between two jealous men suddenly took on a new dimension. The wooded gardens seemed darker now, the air charged with a menace she could not identify, but which grew stronger. Not between the two men, she realised at last, with a throb of fear, but between them and *her*. Both of them were still, staring at her; Jonathan blocked the path leading from the Folly back to the estate; Paul the one to the boundary path, down which he had come.

'If you're right, Gemma,' Paul's voice rang out with deadly precision, 'why did Victoria inform me she had told Jonathan herself she was an impostor? Why did Felix tell me when he asked me to look into Victoria's background that he'd put Vale in the picture over what was happening? You must trust me, Gemma.'

Words, words, they didn't register. But the look on their faces did. Instinctively she moved away – back from both of them and picked up the bag. Useless. In the dense undergrowth behind her there was no hope of escape. The only chance lay forward towards the terrace and Folly. Once inside she could slam the door, open a window at the rear perhaps, before they realised her intention. There was at least a slim chance. Then, *then*, she could fight her way through this terrifying spider's web enmeshing her both emotionally and physically. Sheer instinctive panic was beginning to pulse through her. She forced reason back to her aid. 'Do you have any proof of this?' she asked Paul coldly.

'I imagined you'd ask that. You can see this letter Felix sent me if you like.' Paul waved a letter. 'Come and look. I'm not coming to you. Vale might misunderstand my motives.'

'I'm not coming near you.' It was a childish reply and one that Jonathan must have taken as encouragement, for he moved towards her.

'Stop,' she yelled.

He froze. 'If you want to, Jonathan,' she continued steadily, 'you can go and read the letter yourself.'

He just stared at her. 'I won't bother, thanks, Gemma. He's quite right. I did know.'

The pit of her stomach seemed to freeze. The lover she knew was suddenly turned into a stranger. She *did* know him, loved him, she couldn't have made a mistake. Yet from his own lips came the damning words; it was the lover she had abandoned who had spoken the truth.

'You can trust me, Gemma,' Jonathan continued. His voice suggested he didn't care if she did or not.

'Gemma, would I take all this trouble if you weren't truly in danger?' Paul's voice was anguished.

She turned from one to the other, bewildered. Reason was of no use here. Instinct, animal instinct was her only chance. Paul, face twisted in tense agony, waiting to pounce on Jonathan. Jonathan, distant, mocking. On either side of her was danger from one or the other; behind her certain capture, in front lay an open path with a slim chance if she outran them – with the evidence she did not want but was responsible for. If she ran to Paul, Jonathan would overpower him – and would she even now have the moral strength to fight him? If she ran to Jonathan, she sacrificed her integrity and self-respect. He might have done so, but she would not. There was only one way, as there had always been. Not passion's slave, not reason's tool, but her own way.

She put the parcel back in her bag, aware they both immediately tensed up. There was silence until Jonathan's mocking voice broke it:

'For the Snark *was* a Boojum, you see.'

That did it. With a cry, she went to turn to Paul and, as they reacted, doubled instead up the short path to the terrace, taking the steps in bounds and hurling herself towards the door of the Folly. If only she could reach it, some hope of safety lay beyond. Hope? Pounding footsteps behind her, shouting. Jonathan's voice, Paul's – the words made no impression. As she reached the door, she was violently wrenched round, the bag was snatched from her hand, and Paul's manic eyes looked at her for a moment before he tore round to the side of the house dropping the bag as Jonathan pounded up the steps the other side of the terrace. He halted just for a second, looking at her, fury exploding in one word of bitterness:

'*Why?*'

Numbly she followed him, shoulder bruised from Paul's grasp, then realising Jonathan might need help quickly, dumped the bag. What use now? She jumped down the steps to see Jonathan tackling Paul; they crashed to the ground, rolling over and over until Jonathan clambered to his feet and dragged Paul up. Paul delivered a vicious punch to his groin on the way, sending Jonathan reeling backwards, and Gemma in to tackle him instead. Then Jonathan hauled her unceremoniously out of the way and delivered a punch that sent Paul reeling to the ground, where he lay still.

She knelt down by his side.

'Don't waste your sympathy. He'll be all right,' Jonathan said dismissively. But she stayed there through shock. In bending over him, the pungent spicy aftershave that had assailed her nostrils nearly a year ago did the same now. Not Jonathan, Paul. There, in unconsciousness, truth was revealed as in sleep. What she had thought good-looking was merely mean, what she had looked upon in love was shuttered, the face of a cat who sees prey in the springtime. The prey had been her.

Only a songthrush incongruously split the silence now, as Jonathan walked back on to the terrace. She followed him, and saw him picking up her shoulder-bag. She watched his hands, hands that had loved her, now bruised from the fighting, handing over the parcel that had divided them.

'Take it to Felix.'

He turned and walked away. Stunned, she watched his rear view hurrying up the path out of the Folly. Out of her life.

'Jonathan,' she called in agony, scrambling after him. 'Take it, please, take it for Felix or keep it. Either way.'

'It's your money now, Gemma. That's what you chose. Not me.'

'No. *No!*' she cried. 'You don't understand.' But how

458

could she say, it was not the money. It was that she had doubted him. Not through his fault, but because of her own fears, she had trusted to the path of reason, not the unaccustomed call of passion.

Felix's office. This is where it all began and ended. With money. Whatever happened, whatever private miseries or joys come to one in life, money, like washing-up, had to be dealt with. At least Felix made the process a little more enjoyable, and at least this time she knew where she was going and what she was doing. His shirt this morning was a mere plain lilac, but this restaurant was simply to show off the jazzy purple stripes of the tie.

'The tontine pool is yours, Gemma, bar the cheque. That takes a bit longer. The last hitch has been sorted, and Victoria and Jonathan have both signed quit forms.'

She had expected nothing else. It wouldn't be Jonathan's style to delay proceedings by fighting – whether the fighting were for the tontine or for her. All or nothing for him. She did not comment, merely: 'Can I take you to lunch to celebrate, Felix?'

'Several, if you like.'

She did her best. Felix had worked hard, he had done nothing to deserve other than at least a token celebration of his efforts in winding up the albatross tontine, and for the space of a lunchtime she could share the celebration. She succeeded so admirably that by the time coffee had arrived, he did not re-raise business matters. Instead: 'You know, Gemma, this sounds a cliché, but if I wasn't married, I'd make a pass at you. And, before you mention it, *without* the tontine.'

'You do my ego good, Felix. Especially the last bit. I'm beginning to feel distinctly mixed up about that.'

459

'Ah, I thought I caught a whiff of ice around some-where. Jonathan's quit claim had a touch of the frozen north about it. What's wrong, or doesn't that fall under the terms of our relationship?'

'In a way it does. I misjudged him.'

'Not a hanging offence, on either side.'

'It is in this case.'

'Not the money, then? He's not doing the decent thing and keeping out of the way now you're a rich woman?'

'If only it were that simple. I hurt him, that's all, and at a certain stage of a relationship that's fatal. You break off the fruit-bearing shoots.'

'Sap,' commented Felix judiciously. 'I'm a bit of a horticulturist.'

'Good heavens, I'd have put you down as a golfer. Sap?'

'You grievously misjudge me too then. I wanted to point out that sap comes up the trunk, not from the end of the shoots.'

She laughed. 'You're very comforting, Felix, but that doesn't help with Jonathan. He took an axe to the trunk.'

'What's Ted going to do with his money?' Felix switched topics. 'Have you discussed it with him?'

'No. I thought I ought to see him.'

'Splendid. Ted may be an old rogue, but I imagine he's good at sap.'

'I can't imagine why he should be. He doesn't strike me as a tree man.'

'He knows when to scarper.'

'You think I'm scarpering?' she asked, startled. 'You're wrong. It's Jonathan who's scarpered.'

'Is it, Gemma? You may be right, but as your financial adviser, think about it.'

'*Are* you my financial adviser?'

'Certainly.'

'Then I'm afraid, Felix, we'd better go back to your office. I've something to tell you.'

'It was good of you to come,' Paul said quietly.

'No,' she replied. Honestly, for she deliberately arranged to see Felix earlier on the same day, and at this time of the evening it was too early for the hotel bar to be crowded. She sipped the white wine. Now she was here, things slipped back into place. No heroes, no villains. This wasn't the monster that had in nameless guise haunted her, intangibly threatened her, and finally materialised. This was Paul, whom she'd liked, once loved, and now, to her surprise, found she still did like, despite his blind spots. Some blind spot, though. She had to remember that.

'I have to apologise,' he continued, 'for the way I treated you.'

'As a means to an end?'

'You believe in bluntness, don't you? Yes, but it was a good end.'

'We all use people in some way or another.'

'It wasn't just that.'

'No?'

'We'd have made a good team running my medical centre. I could see it all so vividly in my mind. I still can't believe—'

'I'm not good as part of a team any more,' she interrupted gently.

'No.'

'You don't have to agree quite so quickly.'

He laughed, as she had intended, and the tension

461

evaporated. 'Have you seen Felix yet?'

'No need to make it quite so obvious.'

'Unintentional.'

'I've a thin skin at present. It'll harden up and realise dreams are only dreams.'

She laid her hand briefly on his, then withdrew it.

'I can't say I approve your choice though,' he continued.

For a moment she was almost startled into saying that choice was no choice at all, that Jonathan had vanished from her life. Then prudence reasserted itself.

'But I'm going to make partial amends to you,' he went on, 'and tell you the *whole* truth. Vale did know about Victoria Ireland, as I told you, but not at first. He reported her to Felix in all good faith as one of the orphans still surviving. Then he realised that John Peacock's death might not be what it was cracked up to be, so he suggested that she pretend to have a limited lifespan – perhaps in his own interests, perhaps in hers. Who can tell?'

She could, now, too late.

'She told him the truth about herself only when the question of the great reunion was mooted, because naturally she didn't want to go to Florence and face Ted Parsons. Jonathan insisted she went, for the reason, I gathered from her, that he wanted to be at hand to protect your interests. I realised even before your grandfather's birthday party that he must be somewhat keen on you.'

'*Before* the party?'

'That's my other confession. The legal profession is not so large that whispers can't circulate reasonably speedily. I found out about the tontine long before the party – at roughly the same time that Vale tracked down Gladys. I wanted—'

'Go on.'

'You're not going to like this. To see all interested parties. Not only Gladys's fellow orphans, but their sponsors. Gladys told me of your grandfather, and I knew of you through him – my family kept up a vague contact. I wanted to see you to—'

'See if you could double your chances?'

'It doesn't sound good, does it?'

'No.'

'But now I've eaten the bitter pill, and taken the truth drug, I'll go on. I lurked outside your cottage one night.'

'Yes. I thought it was Jonathan.' Fool that she was.

'He was somewhere around. He had cottoned on to what I was doing, and decided to keep an eye on me, he told me later. We didn't exactly hit it off.'

'He implied to me that you and Annie were lovers.'

He grimaced. 'The biter bit. Like me, Annie knows what she wants, only her ideas are not exactly geared for the welfare of the world, only for that of Annie Masters. Annie decided Gladys was a better bet than Victoria or Stanley, so I became instantly more attractive than Jonathan, especially after Stanley died. Before that, we'd been neck and neck, so to speak. Annie likes bed and bucks, not necessarily in that order. Best of all, she likes the two combined, and, yes, I did go to bed with her. Why not, Gemma? If I had to play chaste knight to you, I needed something.'

'I suppose so,' she said, meaning it, but shivering inwardly at the sheer indifference.

'Annie came to the conclusion that Vale was gay, on the grounds that he didn't want to sleep with her. She couldn't think of any other reason. You didn't rate.'

'Thanks.'

'Don't mention it.' He hesitated, and appealed to her. 'Does that help at all, revealing the truth at the end, as in all good stories?'

She thought about it. 'Yes.' But it was too late.

'Are you in love with him?'

'Yes again.'

'He won't make you happy, money or no money. He's too uncompromising. You're more like me, practical.'

'Practical?' She foresaw a life now mapped out for her: twin guardian angels called Business and Money would escort her, blinkers called Duty shield her eyes from any temptation to leave the path on which she had set her own foot.

'We did it, eh, Gem?'

'Thanks to you.' It was a celebration day. In honour of it, the cloth of gold had made its appearance, but in deference to her, no wig and no make-up. 'What will you do with the money?'

'Give Giovanni more housekeeping,' he told her nonchalantly. 'Do this place up a bit.' He might have been talking about a semi in suburbia.

'Restore the other rooms?'

'In good time. I might touch up the frescos.' He gave her a sideways look.

'But they're fakes.'

'Course they are,' he agreed readily.

'Aren't they?'

A silence.

'Ted, *are* they?'

Another silence. Then, 'Want to look at them?'

'Isn't that a lot of work for Giovanni?'

'Nah.' He rang the bell – some kind of antiquated

464

system that Queen Victoria would have recognised. 'I can afford the electricity bill now.'

It took half an hour while a noise like an overhead thunderstorm reverberated in her ears and told her the mouse was going out to play with its tower. 'Does it ever break down?' she shouted.

'Got a friend who fixes it.'

A friend? She decided not to inquire further into the palazzo's underworld, curious though she was. 'Doesn't it harm the frescos?' she asked.

'Nah. The noise is the engines. Leonardo put it on rollers to carry it past the frescos smoothly, and the whole Mighty Mouse is designed to send the vibrations through the floor, not the walls.'

'Leonardo did?' she asked, amused. 'Haven't you got your dates mixed? He didn't know about those frescos. He designed the mouse in the early 1480s, and the frescos – fakes of course – weren't done till 1488, according to your original story.'

'Ah well. That's it, you see.'

'What is?'

'Leonardo saw his eye to the main chance. He were going to do the frescos himself. He did one of them, in fact. Then he got this job in Milan with better pay and scarpered.'

'Leonardo did one of the fakes,' she said resignedly. 'Is that the new story?'

'The true story, Gem. Honest.'

'Then you show me, Ted. Come on.' She helped heave him up from his chair, reflected that a washing machine might not be a bad investment for him, and escorted him into the fresco room.

'Which one, Ted?'

'It ain't here *now*,' he said, looking round the frescos. 'Don't you know *anything* about art, Gem? Leonardo was a bit of a spiv – always on to something new. Try this, try that. Bit of architecture, bit of science, how about inventing an aeroplane today, how about a new canal, anything to make money, that fellow. Same with his painting. Always new techniques, whereas Ghirlandaio here,' he slapped one fresco appreciatively, 'just kept right on with the old methods. But Leonardo's wide-boy techniques didn't work. Slap bang on the walls with his own method of oil-painting. Off it comes, quicker than a – ah, well, never mind. That's what happened to his *Last Supper* at the convent of Santa Maria delle Grazie. Nothing but a blinking patchwork now. You bin to the Hall of Five Hundred?'

'Yes, Jonathan—' she broke off.

'Never even got past the starting line there. Leonardo was going to do one of them frescos, but got it stuck in his head that oil was the thing. Sank right into the plaster. Same sort of thing here. Five years, and it was begging to jump off the wall. So Lorenzo called in our Ghirlandaio to do the other frescos, and touch up Leonardo's. Then this young spark Michelangelo comes along, sees the Leonardo fresco going home fast, promptly gets rid of it, plasters the wall up afresh for his master – and has a go himself into the bargain. Look at this,' he pointed to the old man in the crowd at the tournament which Jonathan had pointed out to her. 'Notice him?'

'Yes.'

'Old Domenico must have done his nut when he got back from lunch and saw what the apprentice had done. But that's nothing to what Leonardo did when he got back from Milan and found this fifteen-year-old prancing around, painting over *his* fresco. And worse, it was as good as, if not better than his. You know they hated the sight of each other, Leonardo and Michelangelo – well, where do you think it started, eh? Right here, in the palazzo. Probably had a punch-up on the spot, and Lorenzo decided to give the kid a rapid promotion to the sculpture garden. A diplomat was Lorenzo. Keep everyone on the books and avoid union trouble.'

'It's a wonderful story, Ted. But only one flaw. You said all the frescos were fakes. That you did them.'

He sighed. 'I'm getting old, Gem.'

'Are you lonely?'

'That's woman's talk, Gem. Men don't think that way.'

'Then what do they think?'

He looked at the frescos. 'You see that old fellow there? See the balance he gives the scene. Harmony. It does something to you.'

'Your sap.'

'Eh?'

'Felix said you were good at it?'

'Don't follow.'

'The life-force in trees.'

'Blimey, I was born in an orphanage. They don't encourage you to go wandering round trees, and Bermondsey weren't big on trees either.' He looked at her sharply. 'You gotta face like a mouldy windfall yourself, Gem. Something gone wrong with Lorenzo the Maggie?'

'If you mean Jonathan, yes. And incidentally, it wasn't him who tried to kill you, was it?'

He shifted uncomfortably. 'Nah. It was Bert. That proves it. No son of mine would do that to me. Gladys was putting one over on him, *and* me. Ruthless that woman was. I knew I was next on her list when I heard about Stanley, so I thought of Lorenzo's old trick, the real Larry. Gladys always had an eye for a ring. If she nicked Larry's ring, well, how was I to know if it were a poisoned one or not?'

'And who told you it was the ring that killed her?'

'Lorenzo.'

'In spirit form?'

'Don't be daft. *Your* Larry. You know you do look like Simonetta there.' He pointed at the huge fresco of Giuliano's tournament, and the portrait of the girl in the wooden panel.

She had to ask, even though she knew it was a feed. 'Why is that, Ted?'

'Ah well, Ghirlandaio went out to lunch another day, after Micky Angelo scarpered off to the sculpture garden. This time one of the models stayed here to have her ham sandwich. He was using her for Simonetta on account of her likeness to her. In marches Lorenzo himself to have a decko, sees this girl and promptly thinks an assassin has come in to knife him. Paranoid, he was. So he made her strip so he could check for offensive weapons. When she was starkers, he still didn't believe she hadn't come armed, so he came up closer to check further, if you take my meaning. She, being modest, wraps her hair round herself, and he was suddenly struck by her resemblance to Simonetta, whom they'd all fancied, also by the fact she was definitely a looker. I know a chap who'd like to paint you, he said. So he postponed the body search, not wanting to spoil this fresh innocence, and hauled in Botticelli – painters weren't highly regarded in them days; you hired them like carpenters – and told him to paint her. Up comes the *Birth of Venus*, the one where she's prancing around on a shell with no clothes on.'

468

'What's your point, Ted?' she asked patiently.

'The girl thought she'd got off lightly, but Lorenzo was so tickled by the good job Sandro had done, the next time she came in to model for Ghirlandaio, he hauled her upstairs and bedded her.'

'The *point*.'

'No use asking me.'

'I don't believe any of your stories, Ted.'

'Now that's a pity, Gem. You ain't lost faith, have you? Take another look at them.'

She looked at the frescos, the harmony of the colours, the calm serenity of fifteenth-century Florence. Fakes? How could they be?

'Go on, girl, have a bit of sap.'

Chapter Fifteen

Gemma drove steadily down the track towards the Folly. All around were the signs of a spring that was suddenly in earnest, encouraged by the unexpectedly warm weekend. May Day was supposed to be a turning point, in all sorts of ways. Returning sun, returning hope. All right, she'd scarpered herself, as Felix said. She hadn't trusted him. But now she was back – for good. Suppose he wasn't there, though? She banished the thought. She'd arranged with Felix that the keys should be handed over in person. And, she emphasised, from the present custodian. 'I see,' he'd said, 'and not Charles, I presume.'

Gemma purposely did not stop at the main house, but took the rough track to the edge of the Folly gardens, where a haze of colour told her bluebells were replacing dying daffodils.

Through the trees she could see the Folly, and surely there was a light inside? It seemed far-off, a romantic dream that perhaps, even now, should be left that way. Nevertheless, she drew a deep breath, got out of the car, and walked through the gardens up to the sunlit terrace. Someone had been working here to clear the undergrowth. Thoughtfulness, or another sign of renunciation? Suppose he sent Charles or Maria? What hope then?

Unable to stand the suspense a moment longer, she ran the last few steps and pushed open the door.

He was lounging in one of the armchairs, Sunday papers lying discarded at his side. His head turned to her as she entered, their eyes met, and he rose to his feet. The shock of awareness of love was all the more severe in that it brought her sharp up against a wall that said no entry. Here is the secret garden to which there is no key. Jonathan nodded slightly to acknowledge her presence.

'I've got it all ready, as you asked. The bills, electricity and so forth, and council tax forms and so on have all gone to Felix. I gather you just wanted the keys today.' *Why?* his suspicious eyes seemed to be asking. Do not touch me was the clear warning being sent by his body-language, even if there were still a Jonathan at home to be touched. The Judas was not to be forgiven. So be it. She had expected nothing else.

'Thank you,' replied Gemma Maitland's best business-like voice as she reached out and took the keys. 'Shall we take the inventory now?'

'The what?'

Good. She had thrown him, judging by his horrified expression. The businesswoman raised her eyebrows. 'The inventory,' she repeated patiently. 'Naturally I have to check what is to be left here – to avoid future misunderstanding in case inadvertently Lakenham Hall property is amongst it.'

'And also to ensure no doubt that I haven't made off with anything,' he added drily.

He really had been thrown. Excellent. She looked surprised. 'I'm sure you would not have done, and of course if there are any little mementoes you'd like as . . .' She managed to break off before uttering 'keepsakes':

that was going too far. He'd smell a rat.

'Thank you, no.' He was as brisk as her now. 'I prefer to hand over the responsibility of the Folly and the Lakenham heritage to you.'

So he was back in the ring of throwing punches – right in the groin. 'I appreciate that,' she replied. Keep your voice warm, she told herself. Allow no hint of sarcasm. 'Shall we begin?'

'Do you have to lug that thing around with you?' he asked impatiently, looking at her pocket-book computer.

'Why not? It's battery-run.'

'It's too – modern. I can't—'

'I have a notebook,' she interrupted, anxious to be helpful. 'If I write in biro, you can sign it when I've finished, and I'll photocopy it for you. If that would suit you, of course.'

'As you wish.'

'Let's make a start. I don't have much time. The glass ship's decanter. Yours or the Folly's?'

'The Folly's. It belonged to . . .' He broke off.

'This sketch of Oxford by your grandfather?'

'It came from the house. I brought it down to the Folly when—'

'Then you must have it back,' she interrupted generously.

'No.'

'Please.' She had to take it off the wall herself, and she laid it on the table beside him. She caught his eye by mistake and saw in his face anger, frustration – and hurt. It hurt him. So what? It hurt her as much as him. 'Let's tackle this bookcase next,' she announced. 'Are any of the books yours? How about this first edition of Rupert Brooke?'

'The Folly's.'

473

'And Donne's love poems?'

A silence.

'Donne?' she repeated. 'Look at this. "Sweetest love, I do not go for weariness of thee. Nor in the hope the world can show a fitter love—" '

'The Folly's,' he broke in sharply, to her relief.

'Are you sure? There are some lovely sketches by your grandfather. It seems to be a private edition. I didn't realise he did erotic—'

'It's the Folly's.' His voice was harsh. 'We've another copy at the House.'

'Oh. And the Alfred Noyes? "I'll come to thee—" '

'That's – oh, what's the point?' He turned away. 'I don't want *anything*.'

'I know it's tough, Jonathan,' she said, injecting concern into her voice. 'But it has to be done.'

'I don't care about all this stuff. It belongs to the Folly now. I thought you would see that.' Was there a note of appeal in his voice? She ignored it.

'And *you* must see I can't be put in a position where later on someone in your family might object.'

He closed his eyes, muscles in his face working in agony. 'You're right. Let's get it over with.' He cooperated snappily and speedily, speaking only when essential and relaxing only when, sensing the end in sight, he led the way upstairs.

'These Phil May cartoons.' She came up close behind him.

'The Folly's. I believe there's one up at the House. I'll bring it back.'

'Very well. I'll note that down.'

There was real hatred in his eyes now. Much better than indifference. Most of the bedrooms were empty, as was the bathroom. The remaining bedroom was the one her grandfather had slept in that last night in August 1914, the covers and blankets still pulled over it, the pillow still lying there.

'There's an old book here,' she said, picking it up, '*Military Architecture in England during the Middle Ages* by Thompson. Odd book to find here.' She opened it. 'Jonathan, it's my grandfather's copy. He's annotated it with all his comments.' She knew his eyes were fixed on it.

'It belongs to the Folly.'

'I'd like you to have it.'

He hesitated, obviously longing to turn down the offer and unable to do so. He managed to bring himself to the point. 'Thank you.'

'Now is there anything else here?' she asked briskly. 'Check the wardrobe, would you, Jonathan?'

He swung it open, obviously glad of the change of direction. 'Nothing but an old blazer.'

'Check the pockets and I'll list it anyway. There might be a valuable old watch.'

'No. Only . . .' He stopped.

'Only what?'

'Nothing.'

'What?' She made her voice cold.

'A few old rose petals.' He turned round, saw her face. 'You knew, didn't you?' he said flatly.

'Yes. It belonged to my grandfather.' Something seemed to have happened to the brisk note. 'It's the rose he gave to Ellen Shane that last afternoon. She died before he could marry her, and that's why he wanted me to marry Paul, I suppose.'

'Me, actually,' he said absently.

'No. Paul.'

'That's hard to credit. Are you *sure*?'

'Yes.' She racked her brains to recall the conversation. She'd certainly mentioned Paul; he'd commented – but on that? Or on what he was looking at? Military books – Jonathan Vale's books. 'You're right. It *was* you,' she forced herself to admit. Her plan had been crumbled into ruins by a few old rose petals. Her moral high ground had been lost.

'How little Reggie knew about you,' Jonathan said bitterly. 'So anxious to win the money you couldn't trust me. Despite everything.'

'It's not *me* you're seeing, Jonathan. It's that other woman.'

He slammed the wardrobe door shut, then he was storming past her and out of the room. She heard his footsteps hurrying downstairs before, stunned, she was able to move. Then anger hit her and exploded inside her.

'Come back. Come *back!*' she yelled down the stairs.

He shouted up at her from the lower floor. 'I wish you joy of this place. Why don't you tear the place down, for God's sake, build a supermarket? It's better than what would happen under your stewardship.'

Anger gave her speed, and she caught him as he reached the main door and lunged clumsily at his sweater to stop him in his tracks. 'How can you even think that of me? You can't, you don't!'

'I'm a historian. I believe in fact.' He didn't even turn round. 'You're sitting on fifteen million, you've got rid of Paul, now you've shaken me off. You've got the lover you always desired. A gentleman called Mammon.'

'You've got it wrong.' Tears of fury and frustration poured down her face as he pulled free, but she automatically reacted by getting him in an armlock. From behind, jammed up against the sweater, she hissed, 'Listen, you. I don't know who you're talking about, but it's not me. I haven't got fifteen million pounds, you ape. I've given it away.'

He stopped struggling. 'You've done what?'

'I've given the money to Paul for his medical centre. All, that is, but half a million to Victoria and some to Rosalind. The rest is his.'

'Why? Because of me?'

To hell with him. He couldn't even apologise and was making it worse. 'No. Because of *me*. It was tainted money, if that doesn't sound too melodramatic. Because of it, three people were murdered. It seemed only right that the money should go to help save lives.'

'Let me go, Gemma, please.' She released him, and he rubbed his arms. 'Remind me not to chat you up in a taxi late at night,' he said ruefully.

It was going to be all right. Not yet, tread carefully. But did she want it to be all right? After what he'd said?

'Do I understand you've given the Folly to Paul Shane for a medical centre?'

It wasn't going to be all right, but now she didn't care. Not after that. 'I could take everything else you've hurled at me, Jonathan,' she said quietly. 'All the harsh words, because I deserved at least some of them. But not this. You really think I could give this place away to be razed to the ground for a medical centre? How could you think that of me?'

'No,' he replied reluctantly. 'But what are you going to do with it?'

'I would have thought you of all people would know the answer.'

'Carry out what the Lakenham Set wanted?'

'Yes.'

'How, without money?'

'So even you link money and achievement. There'll be a way, somehow, it'll take time, it will take effort. But there are going to be people who'll want to help. I'll pour the proceeds of my grandfather's estate into—'

'A pittance.'

'So I did wrong to give the money to Paul?'

He smiled slightly, at last. 'You think you're trapping me nicely, don't you?'

'No, I want to know your answer.'

'There's only one, as you know full well.'

'Say it, Jonathan.'

'You did right.'

'And I'm not crazy, to think something can be done about the Lakenham Set?'

'Yes, you are, thank God.'

'And you too?'

'From the day I trotted after you into this place and you told me to sit on the floor while you explored to see if it was safe. I looked round and up at all those books looming over me, and began to cry. You were quite motherly, you gave me a cup of pretend orange squash, and I fell in love with you there and then. I just forgot about it for long periods.'

'It seems to have lapsed again.'

'It takes this place to remind me.'

'Sap.'

'Not very complimentary.'

'I mean Ted's sap. His theory of heightened awareness

bringing dormant spirits to life again.'

'It sounds rather abstruse for Ted.'

'He has a story about the Botticelli *Venus* that you'd like.' She related it, and when she finished asked, 'What are you staring at, Jonathan?'

'Mentally undressing you and seeing you as a Botticelli *Venus*. Would you put another armlock on me if I came closer?'

'I most certainly would if you go on looking as sinister as that.'

'Come outside, into the sunshine. You might feel differently.'

She followed him outside, and watched him as he picked strands of greenery and, twining them together, twisted them into a garland and hung it round her neck. He stepped back to admire the result.

'The May Queen,' he observed judiciously. 'There's only one difference between you and Botticelli's *Venus*. You're not dressed like her.'

'My hair isn't long enough, and there's a spider crawling down my blouse.'

'Easily remedied.'

Why did fingers take such an unconscionably long time to undo buttons, or was he doing it deliberately? Then he kissed each breast three times.

'Is this a May Day ritual?' she asked.

'A fertility symbol, which I've just invented, to greet the returning sun.'

'A sort of renaissance?'

'A Second Renaissance.'

Lying on the bed upstairs, later, her arm round him, she wondered if she could ever have dared to dream the day would end this way. Outside the window a larch tree waved in the breeze, the sun crept through its branches to shine into the long disused room. Next to her was Jonathan, and on the floor at their side lay one fallen rose petal.

Later she drove him back to Waynings, for the Monday was, after all, a holiday, and her long-suffering lieutenants had agreed to cover for her. They arrived after a pub dinner, when it was already dark. Launcelot yowled as she opened the gate but not, she thought, in protest. After all, she had made arrangements for his dinner-time to be respected. Jonathan picked him up.

'He normally doesn't let people do that,' she said, surprised. 'He has a neat way of digging his claws in, twisting up over your shoulder and adjoining himself like a hump on your back. You bend down like a servile idiot, and he jumps off without undue stress to his paws.'

'Very Machiavellian. Why Launcelot?'

'I thought Gawain, who's big round here, ought to have some competition.'

'Are you sure he won't see me in the same light?'

'Apparently not.'

She drew the curtains, made cocoa, plumped cushions while he watched her. The cocoa was his choice – an odd one, which reminded her they had much to learn about each other. But there was time, thank goodness.

'Are you sitting at my feet in womanly submission?' he asked presently.

'Yes. I want to ask you about the Folly.'

'What we can do with it?' The 'we' was a gift to her, accepted and cherished.

'We could live in it.'

'With a mouse? Turn it into another palazzo? Live there till we are old and grey and full of sleep?'

'Ted's not full of sleep.'

'Much as I love it, the Folly isn't quite a dream home in itself, is it?'

'No, nor does that celebrate the achievements of the twentieth century.'

'It depends what we achieve.'

'After being taken by surprise this afternoon, it might be a baby Lakenham. Would you like that?' *Do you still blame Bill for dying?* One swift lunge straight to the point, and it didn't even hurt as the knife slid in.

'Or a baby Maitland.'

He caressed her shoulders and she twisted round to look at him, to find him grinning at her. 'Just so,' he said softly. 'Millions of people find that their own renaissance. We don't even need money.'

'I think you'll find we do.'

'Practical as ever. Luckily, you have your taxi business. You can plonk baby Lakenham in the boot.'

'Seriously, Jonathan, what dreams for the Folly?'

'All right, I'll be serious. It's not large enough for a major museum, even if that was what we decided on. I think it has to be a nerve centre, a fixed root for something that reaches out to affect people's lives, to offer them something just as Paul's medical centre will do.'

'What? Scholarships?'

'Hope, perhaps.'

'*Hope?*'

'I'm not crazy. Look at them; between them the Lakenham Set offered promise for painting, music, poetry, history, science, even medicine. Now what has the rest of the twentieth century achieved: transport, medical advances, practical things chiefly, with a division

481

now between arts and sciences. So much for the twentieth century. What of the twenty-first? What will it want? Arts, science, medicine? We don't know what the world will want. Or need.'

'A complementary "medicine" centre, that's what we could have,' she said at last. 'Not Paul's sort, our sort.'

'And what's that, Gemma?'

'Perhaps an artistic medicine centre. Whether people want guidance and help on aviation or art, books or boojums, if they're seeking direction, or a different path, having difficulty getting recognised, losing confidence, there'd be the Folly and us. New paths for old. New achievements from old stock, the renaissance of a spiritual confidence to carry them forward into the year 3000.' She stopped. 'Am I making sense?'

'No, but there's something there, Gemma, something we can work on. Shall I toast you in cocoa, shall I toast you in milk, shall I dress you in diamonds, all sewn on to silk.'

She laughed delightedly as he hauled her to her feet and danced her round the room, then embraced her, kissed her. 'Gemma,' he said, sobering down, 'if I stay here in your home, it might seem to you I'm claiming some kind of possession. Do you want me to sleep in your spare room?'

Plummeted from height to depth. 'You're scared, aren't you?' she managed to reply gently.

'Of what? The big bad forest?'

'The forest of "I have been here before" . . . I was scarpering too, but I've scarpered back.'

He grinned. 'I suppose we could hold hands and plunge into the forest together.'

'I'd like that.'

★ ★ ★

He was right though. Lying there in the night, next to her, she listened to his steady breathing as she watched the shadowy trees shimmering in the moonlight outside. He was immovable, it was a *fait accompli*, and a kind of panic gripped her as she looked at this stranger by her side. Sleeping together was more than loving together. Asleep, one was off-guard, exposed to scrutiny, so was that why she could only sleep in fits and starts? Had she surrendered part of herself? She must have fallen more deeply asleep then, for when the strident tone of the telephone cut through her dreams she awoke with a familiar start. Jonathan groaned and drew the sheets over his head, muttering: 'I've changed my mind over the taxi business idea.'

'I'm off-duty,' she hissed at him. Her cordless phone was therefore not at her bedside, and she had to grope her way down to answer the call. In the darkness she stumbled, cursed and sent the phone flying by mistake. When she picked it up she expected to hear Loretta's voice and was ready to blast her.

It wasn't. It was Charles Lakenham's. 'Gemma, my dear, I'm sorry to waken you at this unearthly hour. I've bad news for you. It's the Folly. It's on fire.'

Its flames were still licking the sky. In the darkness, darker figures were moving around the building, the sound of water from hoses could still be heard. The Folly or its ruins stood starkly against the sky. Slowly the flames were eating away her life, remorselessly and relentlessly. Charles and Maria, clad in nightwear with coats thrown hastily over them, came up to her, seemingly unsurprised by the sight of their son at her side. 'It's nearly out,' Charles told her reassuringly.

'How did it start?' Gemma asked listlessly. It had been a nightmare journey, neither of them speaking.

'No one knows yet. Young Peacock saw it first, called the fire brigade and then us.'

Young Peacock. The story had begun with the Peacocks and now it would end with them.

'We'll go back to the house and get some hot drinks ready. Come back and stay with us, Gemma,' Maria said sympathetically.

'Yes,' Jonathan replied to his mother for her.

Spectators began to disappear, as they watched, drawing closer to the building as access became easier. In an hour and a half the embers had ceased to glow, and the firemen began their investigation. How long it took she did not know. Her eyes were fixed on the blackened ruins of the Folly. From here, with little light, it looked as if the walls still all stood and part at least of the roof. But what of the inside?

'What caused it?' she asked as the chief fireman came over.

'Offhand I'd say there's a good chance it was deliberate.'

She stared at him, speechless, as Jonathan said sharply, 'Why?'

'Petrol on the terrace and inside.'

Then, 'Let's go,' Jonathan said, as soon as the fire-engines had departed. The touch of his hand on her arm made her realise how desperately he wanted to get away.

'You've got a black streak across your cheek. It makes you look like a rather bad movie pirate,' she tried to joke.

'Just what I've always wanted to be.' But there was no heart in his voice.

'We'll tackle this mess tomorrow.'

'Yes. Let's go.'

'Just a minute, Jonathan.' The sharpness in her voice stopped him. 'Look at this.' Standing in the garden right at the foot of the steps was a petrol can. 'It's not even hidden,' she continued. 'It's almost as though whoever did it wanted us to know it was deliberate. Where . . .?' She broke off as she saw him pushing through the gardens, regardless of paths, trampling down his way to the central arbour. He must have been eating carrots to see so well in the dark, to see what she had failed to notice. One of the dark shapes was not vegetation, it was someone watching. Someone seated casually on the back of the stone seat, feet planted on the seat itself, perched on a throne in the hour of triumph.

It was Annie Masters.

Gemma rushed towards her in Jonathan's wake, but he was there long before her, dragging Annie down. But she broke free and, standing on the seat, jeered as Gemma came up. 'You thought you had everything, didn't you? Fifteen million quid and generous little you gave it away. Now you haven't even got this place and serve you right.'

'What for?' she cried. '*Why?* I don't understand.'

'Oh, I do,' said Jonathan quietly. Even in the darkness she could see the pallor of his face.

'I bet you do. You pushed Stanley under that bus.'

'It was Gladys,' Gemma yelled.

'It was darling Jonathan. I saw him, you stupid cow,' she jeered at Gemma. 'Why else do you think I made a pass at him? Not exactly Richard Gere, is he? If he was going to grab the money, he could damn well take me along with it. He owed me. And it might interest you to know, now Pansy Paul has got it instead, he doesn't want me any more than he fancied you. I'm surprised darling

485

Jon's still here. I take it you've told his nibs you've given the money away?'

'Have you quite finished?' Gemma said coldly, anger so concentrated inside her it felt like an iron cannonball. Anger on Jonathan's account, on her own – and for the Folly.

'Oh, I have *quite* finished,' Annie said mockingly. Then she burst into hysterical laughter. 'I wish you two joy of each other. He can hardly get it up, and you wouldn't know what to do with it if he did.'

'Get out,' Gemma shouted. 'Or do you want to wait for the police?'

'I'll go home to change, darlings. I've never had it with the lovely Bill. I want to look my best, especially if there's more than one. I reckon that's what turns him on too . . .' She shoved Jonathan aside as she left.

He did not even speak then. He waited till the sound of her footsteps died away, and in the distance came the sound of a car engine in the silent, smoky night. Then he spoke: 'Do you believe her, Gemma?'

Careful, she warned herself. Tread between lightness and concern. 'About your sexual powers? Hardly.'

He didn't laugh. 'About Stanley.'

'Of course not.' She stared at him, aghast. 'What's wrong, Jonathan? Besides what I'm feeling too?'

'Then you know already what's wrong. It's over.'

The chill of the night came over her. 'Us?'

'No. This.' He took her hand, pulled, almost dragged her up to the Folly ruins, pushed open the singed door and went in. All, it seemed, in one continuous movement, as though the slightest hesitation would lose him the courage he had scraped up from his last reserves. 'Books, glass, carpets – look at it!' It was a cry of despair.

'Pictures – all gone. And the Lakenham Set with it.'

She surveyed the wreckage and tried to be strong for both of them. 'Nothing's destroyed unless we let it be. Are you telling me you're going to let her win?'

'And are you seriously telling me *we* can? Now everything has gone up in flames?'

'I don't know. Not now. It's too soon, too late at night. But anything's possible if we believe hard enough.' She had to say something, anything to lift his mood.

'But not what we'd dreamed.' Even as he spoke there was a tearing sound followed by a crash, as obviously another part of the roof had given way and the ceiling fell with its upstairs room.

'The spirit is still here,' she tried.

'Don't be sentimental.'

'I'm *not*,' she flared at him.

'I'm sorry, Gemma, but I mean it. We'll find another dream, don't worry.' He summoned up the energy to smile, to try to comfort. 'The Folly isn't the only one around. I just can't compromise, faced with this ruin. I did compromise once, and look where it got me.'

'When was that, Jonathan?' And when he did not reply, 'Tell me, you can't stop there.'

'Pamela,' he said at last. 'I wanted to marry her, she wouldn't – for the sake of her career, so she said. It wouldn't be fair, since she didn't want children. I caved in and agreed to her terms. She left me. End of story.'

'If it were,' she remarked wryly, 'there'd be no problem. Come back please,' seeing him leaving the Folly. 'We can face it, we *can*.'

'No.'

'So what are you going to do? Sell Lakenham when you inherit, so you do not have to see it? Block off the windows facing this way? You're a coward, Jonathan. You won't take a chance.'

'On what?' His voice betrayed nothing.

'On hope, I suppose. The Lakenham Set did, but unfortunately their plans have landed on you for fulfilment, and you're running away.'

'On *you*, Gemma, not me.'

'It's no use to me unless we share it.'

'No.' He said it gently, but with a finality that closed the door as certainly as the one he'd clanged to after him.

She stood still, shivering, choked by smoky fumes, still not believing that everything could have changed so quickly, so disastrously. The paradise of the afternoon had turned into the disappearing back of something called hope. Paul had been right. She and Jonathan were not good for each other, for they were too alike, yet not so identical that there was a solution in that. He had a mole on his right shoulder, she remembered inconsequentially. She'd never see it again, unless she did the compromising, and that would mean her getting rid of the Folly, for she could never bear to work on it alone now. Perhaps tomorrow he'd see things differently, she wondered, but dismissed the hope. He wasn't like that. Yet how could she think clearly tonight in this inky blackness? He'd got the only torch, she remembered, and he'd left her alone in this darkness. Suddenly she could mentally at least see quite clearly. One sometimes woke up in the darkness with a thought of such shining clarity that in the morning it remained with you, a pearl gathered from some undetermined source. Perhaps from God, perhaps from instinct. Perhaps they were both the same thing and called truth. She knew what she had to do about Jonathan, about the Folly – and those two were the same.

She ran to the door, pulled it open, and then stood on the terrace and shouted. 'Jonathan!'

A small pinprick of light at the edge of the Folly stopped its wavering progress.

'I need you.'

'Why?'

Didn't he *ever* compromise? 'You are my light.'

A pause. 'Did you say "and" or "are"?'

'Both.'

The will-o'-the-wisp glow seemingly took for ever, but at least she knew it was coming towards her, not retreating. With a shout of laughter, half a sob of relief, she hurried down the steps, and along the path to meet him.

'Are you always so practical, Gemma?' as he kissed her sadly.

'Yes – no.'

'Here's the torch.'

He put it in her hand, and she threw it as far as she could. It fell among the bluebells and swelling spring ferns, where it shone like a glow-worm, a pinpoint of light too far away even to be recognisable as such. She could only dimly make out his face, but she could hear his breathing. He put his arm round her, as they made their stumbling way to the Folly's edge.

'I see my mother has tactfully made up a room for you,' he told her as they got back to the house. 'Do you want it?'

'No.'

'I've only a single bed.'

'Still no.'

'Shall we use this one for your reputation's sake?'

'Still no.'

'You're getting to be a no-compromise person yourself.'

'Perhaps.'

And later, just as she was drifting into exhausted sleep: 'Does this no-compromise attitude mean you'll leave me because of mine over the Folly?'

'No.'

'Why not?'

'Because I love you. This comes as part of the package.'

'You really want it rebuilt just as it was?' Felix asked incredulously, since the insurance was still in the trustees' names.

'We don't have any choice,' Gemma told him demurely. 'It's a Grade I listed building.'

'It *was*. There's a strong case for knocking it down, though, as you know full well. We're not talking about Horace Walpole and Strawberry Hill here, you know. Merely one old man's personal eccentricity.'

'I don't believe that's moral,' she told him sanctimoniously.

'I'll leave that to you to convince the insurance bods about.'

'Oh, I will.'

And she did, rather more easily in fact than the builders, who maintained grim scepticism to the end. Only the fact that the bank was paying the bill, not this crazy woman, kept them at work. In a way they were right in their diagnosis. She was crazy to have embarked on a path to which as yet she could see no ending.

'Wallpaper or plaster?' Bob Kemp, the head builder, demanded in her ear.

She jumped.

'The walls,' he explained kindly. 'Ceilings, that sort of thing.'

'Plaster,' she replied. 'Of course.' Why 'of course', she then wondered. Plaster . . . She looked round this empty mausoleum, devoid of atmosphere, of charm, of any vestige of the Lakenham Set, a mausoleum to their departure, a giant folly erected to commemorate her failure. For months she had watched its progress to nowhere, while Jonathan never showed the slightest sign of interest. Immovable woman meets immovable man. Lorenzo the Magnificent might have thought out a solution, but she couldn't. She needed her own mental mouse, and the design had stuck halfway on an empty folly. She tried to force herself to think of it, not as it had been, but of its potential for the future. Nothing came. Only, oddly, an old children's story she had once read in a book that belonged to her mother. The sick king would only recover when the Never-Green tree was green again. But the tree had been struck by lightning and so that could never happen. Could it?

'The builders are moving out today, Jonathan. It's ready.' She buttered the toast twice by mistake in her attempt to be nonchalant.

'I presume you mean the Folly. Women are supposed to foist their cunning plans on their prey on the bed pillow. You choose Tuesday morning breakfast, just as you're leaving to go back to Kent to drive a taxi. I suppose it's original.'

'Practical. I'm on duty the rest of the week and the weekend, so I won't see you. And don't stereotype me.'

'I'll come down to you at the weekend.'

'Thanks a bunch. I'd like you to come with me today.'

'You know how I feel about the Folly, Gemma. Don't break the rules, and don't spoil breakfast.'

'You really are a gent of no compromise,' she told him brightly. 'The Folly looks splendid.'

'No doubt. But it's not the Folly we remember, and stop *talking about it*.'

'Please come, Jonathan.'

'No.'

'In that case I shall sell it to a supermarket who'll raze it to the ground in the best military fashion.'

'You wouldn't, don't try to kid me, and they'd never get planning permission.'

'But I want to share it with you.'

'That won't wash either. You started this on your own, and you can continue it for your grandfather, not me.'

'I need your company today.'

'Give me one *good* reason.'

'You're my partner-in-love, if not in the Folly, and that alone means you owe me your company on very special occasions.'

'Blast you, Gemma.' He threw down his spoon in disgust. 'I suppose I'll have to come.'

'And not in cords.'

'Why the hell not? You are difficult sometimes, Gemma.'

'It's a kind of opening ceremony for the new Folly. The builder is going to ceremoniously put the last square foot of plaster on, and I've bought some champagne. It deserves dressing up for.'

He regarded her, bemusedly. 'You haven't invited the neighbours in for a nice little drink, have you? Anyway, I would point out you've got jeans on.'

'I'm going to change.'

'Are my parents in on this touching ceremony? Felix?'

'No. I thought today could be just for us.'

He regarded her suspiciously. 'Now I'm sure you're planning something. If you're hoping to get me to change my mind . . .'

'Nothing could change your obstinate mind save yourself. And all I'm planning is a bottle of champagne.'

'I told you you were sentimental.'

The gardens were full of Michaelmas daisies now, the trees and bushes beginning to show that summer was done. She could see the nasturtiums planted by her earlier in the year sprawling over the edge of the terrace, a bright patch in this sea of green. Jonathan stopped as they stepped on the path that led to the building.

'Do you have a magic touch with builders? It looks . . .' He broke off.

'Go on, say it. I dare you.'

'Just the same from here,' he finished obediently. 'Would you like a pound of flesh as well?'

'We used old roofing tiles and other materials. No flesh.'

'It's the inside that matters, Gemma.'

'Then you must come in.' She took his hand and led him up to the terrace, in at the door, into the shining empty whiteness that was the new Folly. The smell of fresh plaster filled their nostrils. She could see by the look on his face how horrified he was. This was the hurdle.

'It's ready, waiting for us, Jonathan.'

'For you,' he replied, sadly. 'I'm here just as your partner, remember?'

'So you are.'

'You took that remarkably lightly,' he said suspiciously. 'And where are the builders?'

'I'm afraid they left yesterday. But I've got the champagne,' she hurried on anxiously.

His face darkened. 'I didn't think you'd do this to me, Gemma,' he said quietly.

'I had to.' The sound of a car horn interrupted them. Thankfully she ran outside. Talk about being saved by the bell.

'Who's that?' he said as he followed her on to the terrace.

'You'll see . . .' The smile died on her face. 'No, you won't. Who is it?'

'Felix, probably. Look at that limo.'

'Perhaps, but why . . .' She stopped, dumbfounded. 'It's . . .' Out of the limo struggled not Felix, but an elderly woman, bottom first, and clad in a bright green skirt and bomber jacket, so far as Gemma could see. Surely – 'It's Rosalind Chambers,' she cried. 'Ted's old flame.'

Rosalind stood wobbling on two sticks while the chauffeur produced a wheelchair from the boot, planted her in it, and proceeded to wheel her towards them as she waved her sticks in greeting.

'And what,' Jonathan asked grimly as they walked to meet her, 'is the lady doing here?'

'I haven't the faintest idea,' she replied weakly but truthfully. 'It wasn't my doing.'

The wheelchair stopped in front of them, and Gemma greeted her, but her eyes were on Jonathan.

'Introduce me, Gemma.' She eyed Jonathan up and then down. 'Well hung, aren't you?' she told him approvingly.

'Thank you,' he replied gravely.

'Believe me, I'm an expert, young man.'

'What on earth are you doing here, Rosalind?' Gemma asked her.

'I've come to get married, love.'

The wheelchair swept imperiously past them, on its way to the Folly, leaving them to follow.

'You're *all* crazy, Gemma,' Jonathan said mildly. 'Quite, quite loopy.'

'But I didn't know she was coming, and what does she mean, come to get married?'

'She obviously saw your design plans for the Folly and thought it was a church.'

'Oh, Jonathan, don't you see . . .' She stopped. No point going on. Not yet. And not then if her timetable was going so disastrously awry.

The chauffeur had opened the Folly door and pushed her inside. He passed them on his way back to the car.

'You're not leaving, are you?' Gemma asked in horror.

'After I've got her suitcases, yeah.'

Jonathan's lips twitched. 'Not a church. A hotel.'

'Be quiet.' Gemma shot inside to find Rosalind in the chair in the middle of the empty room, staring around her.

'Where are you getting married?' she inquired politely.

''Ere, of course. Where d'yer think?'

'This is the first I've heard of it. Are you sure this isn't a joke?' Gemma asked faintly.

'I never joke about weddings, miss. Specially this one. It's my first. Where's the toilet?'

'Er – upstairs.'

'You ain't got no disabled facilities 'ere, I see. You'll have to carry me up, young man, or I'll pee in my pants.

You be careful of that.' She waved threateningly at the chauffeur staggering under a huge package.

'What is it?' Jonathan asked curiously.

'It ain't an "it". It's a "her". Pomona's the lady's name.'

Jonathan began to laugh and didn't stop. She stared at him crossly. 'Who you cackling at? And 'ow about getting me on that toilet?'

Jonathan obediently carried her upstairs, an operation she seemed to enjoy judging by her waving feet and cackles. Gemma followed him up and whispered while they waited outside the door.

'We could try telling her Social Services she's hallucinating, and they'll come and collect her.'

'I heard that, young woman.' Rosalind appeared, full of wounded dignity, at the door. 'He won't be pleased if I'm not here when he arrives.'

Jonathan shot a curious look at Gemma. 'Why don't you come up to the House, Mrs Chambers? It's more comfortable.'

'I'm not stirring till he gets here. And it's *Miss* Chambers to you.'

'Who is *he*?' Jonathan inquired, when he deposited his burden back in the wheelchair downstairs.

'Ted.'

'Just a minute, Gemma.' Jonathan's hand clamped on her arm as she tried to steal away.

'Ted's a bastard,' squawked the parrot, obviously eager to get in on the act.

'I'll have to teach him summat new,' Rosalind said lovingly.

'Never mind the parrot. I want to hear more about this wedding and Ted,' Jonathan told her, clamping Gemma to him.

496

'He's coming here,' Gemma admitted.

'Is he, indeed? And why, I wonder? Apart from the fact this wedding may not be quite the hallucination we thought.'

The bell saved her again, as another, longer horn-blast trumpeted out nearby.

'I'll go, Gemma. You wheel Rosalind out to the terrace.'

She heard his 'What the . . .?' but was no longer worried, since events were well and truly out of her control. 'Hurry up.' He rushed back in to help her, as excited as she'd seen him since Florence. 'This you must see.'

It wasn't a car, it was a coach. Panic stilled in her as she realised there'd be a lot of luggage. But it wasn't luggage that emerged from the coach after Giovanni, and a shuffling but jaunty Ted.

'First Snow White, now the Seven Dwarfs,' murmured Jonathan, entranced.

A group of elderly men in various stages of physical fitness shuffled, hobbled and limped their way down the path after Ted. She almost expected them to burst into song. Certainly they were on their way to work, for behind them, at the coach, Giovanni unloaded luggage and ladders, posts, trestles, boxes.

'*Ecco*,' Ted said carelessly, waving a hand. 'Where's Rosie?'

''Ere, Ted.' Jonathan wheeled her forward.

'Blimey, I ain't seen you look so sexy for fifty years.'

'I take it,' Jonathan inquired, 'that you gentlemen are the boys from the workshop?'

From their blank but beaming faces it was clear they did not speak English. Ted answered for them. 'Yus. All the old team to do up this place. Present and correct, as per order.'

'*You* ordered them, Gemma?'

Now for it, the watershed. 'I remembered an old story about the forest folk who could make a dead tree come to life again with a little thought— '

'Just a story, Gemma,' he told her gently. 'Darling, you know I can't.' He kissed her cheek. 'I'll see you later.'

'Where you going?' Ted asked in surprise. 'You got a part to play.'

'What's that, Ted?'

'You ain't forgotten about the wedding, 'ave you? You're the bleeding best man.'

Gemma couldn't help it. She began to shake with laughter, then found it impossible to stop, especially as she saw Jonathan looking completely nonplussed.

'But you're not getting married *today*, are you?' he asked feebly.

'Take a look at us, mate. Rosie and I ain't getting any younger, are we? We've waited forty years. What's the point of hanging around?'

'You've brought my dress, Ted?' Rosalind intervened.

''Course I have, luv.' He regarded her fondly. 'Where is it, Giovanni?' Giovanni produced a battered suitcase out of the pile. 'You pop up and put it on and we'll make a start.'

'But don't you need a priest?' Gemma asked hesitantly, reluctant to puncture dreams.

'Ah well, Antonio 'ere took holy orders when he retired from a life of crime. Lucky, ain't it?'

'You'll need a registrar though to make it legal—' Gemma began, but was interrupted by Ted and Rosalind's combined shouts of laughter.

'Cor, stone the crows, Gem. *Legal?* Us? Come off it.'

'Come on, you.' Rosie waved a stick at Jonathan. 'Take me upstairs. And that's the last time I'll be saying that to anyone but me bleedin' husband.'

A thousand questions raced round in Gemma's mind and were dismissed. She watched as Ted's men, the 'old team', hobbled around sizing the place up, talking amongst themselves and arranging paints, brushes and materials. Her idea – but now she was no longer part of it. The Folly's fate was in their hands, and she was alone – again. No sign Jonathan would yield in the slightest. There would be no use in whatever Ted might achieve, if he did not admit the necessity for sharing the creative impulse to set it going. She realised with dread what would happen. Jonathan would be moved by the wedding, play his duty and then leave. And as for her – well, women were always permitted to cry at weddings, weren't they?

She heard Jonathan's voice call out: 'Ready, folks. Here comes the bride.'

They formed themselves into a welcoming group as Rosalind appeared at the head of the stairs, not in Jonathan's arms, but leaning heavily on it, clutching the rail with the other. His arm was round her to support her as she half walked, half dragged herself down the stairs to her wedding. But Gemma registered none of that. She saw only the dress. Lilac blue, full length, low necked, long, and heavily ornamented with rich gold braid. An old dress, dusty, but unmistakable. It was the Verrocchio-designed dress of Lucrezia Donati, worn in the tournament given in her honour by Lorenzo the Magnificent. It was the dress in the Ghirlandaio fresco.

'Blimey, girl, you look a corker,' Ted said, fascinated.

'Something borrowed, something blue, eh?' Rosalind shouted. 'You can't come behind me. Me bum's probably showing. It don't do up.'

'*Ecco!*' Giovanni, obviously anxious to please his new mistress, rushed forward with a workman's denim dust-sheet which he placed round the bride's shoulders.

'Now ain't he a luv, Ted,' Rosalind said fondly. 'I could go for him.'

'You won't, Rosie. You won't.'

'Nah. He ain't got your looks.'

'Do you think it was real?' she asked Jonathan tentatively, after the group departed to the hotel they had booked into. (Poor hotel, they didn't know what was descending on them.)

'The dress? We could look at that two ways. First, I don't see Ted or his team faking a dress, do you?'

'No.'

'Then he found it in the palazzo. The Florentine climate preserves things wonderfully.

'You see where that takes us.'

'Quite clearly.'

'It means the frescos are genuine.'

'But, second, does it matter? The palazzo's a maze and there are two kinds of maze. The first is the puzzle maze with blind alleys and twists and turns. We assumed it was that kind. Suppose it's the other kind, though.'

'What's that?'

'The oldest maze of all. It doesn't allow compromise. The path to the centre is the only one. You just have to follow it round and round, and not fall by the wayside.'

'And you find what?'

'I found you.'

Epilogue

Gemma started to laugh first, then Jonathan. There was a horrified moment of blank incomprehension, perhaps even of concern, then the Seven Dwarfs carefully laid down their brushes, permitted beams to spread across their faces, and then allowed them to burst into laughter too. Only Ted refrained. 'What do you think, Gem?' he asked guardedly.

'What do I think?' She looked round at the Folly. Not the old Folly, but the new one created here. 'Ask me again in a year's time, and I might have had time to sum it all up.'

'Nah, that's no good. It's the first impression, ain't it? That's what counts. What does it shout at you, Gem, me girl?'

She tried to put it into words. 'What it shouts loudest is that the Renaissance has come to Kent.'

Ted looked gratified. 'You hear that?' he asked Rosalind, translating it into Italian for the benefit of his troops. Further beams of delight appeared, they descended from their perches, and glasses and bottles appeared to celebrate.

'Not over the top, eh?' Ted asked, still slightly worried.

'Gloriously over the top,' she assured him happily.

'Superbly over the top. Of course, it was the only answer, and I didn't see it.'

'It's not your true fresco, it's only your *fresco secco*,' Ted murmured modestly. 'But seeing as how you ain't got what you might call a sunny climate here, it might last longer.'

'Till the Third Renaissance,' she told him. And she meant it, for the Folly was alive again. Colour sprang at you from the moment you walked in the door, from ceilings, from walls, from the arches, the stairwells, the corridors, the bedrooms; every corner was painted. Not just a painted room, but a painted house. Observing it, judging the twentieth century perhaps, on the wall of the arch facing the front door was a Ned Kelly figure in Sid Nolan's style. Only this Ned Kelly had no tin box on his head, though he sat astride a horse. This Ned Kelly was Lorenzo the Magnificent come to judge this so-called Second Renaissance.

The huge semicircular dining room walls were devoted to that last evening, the eve of war, the Folly's last supper for the Lakenham Set. Twenty young men caught, laughing, drinking, one with his arm round a kitchenmaid, one dancing on the table, one striking a pose as he read mock-seriously from a book of poems. Only their eyes, and the poppyfields glimpsed through the windows, suggested this was no ordinary evening. She felt Jonathan's arm round her as he pointed out his grandfather, sitting next to a young, keen-eyed Reggie Maitland. Muted, soft tones, depicting an age that had gone, as surely as had Ghirlandaio's fifteenth-century Florence.

It was the only point of obvious harmony in the house. The rest of it seemed to be a medley in subject and artist, as if each of the Dwarfs had been given a wall to cover in the style of his favourite artists. Fragonard had returned to life with two mini-skirted girls on a swing, Toulouse-Lautrec's Jane Avril did rock and roll with Van Gogh's self-portrait, Pissarro painted Concorde, Brueghel Piccadilly Circus in the rush hour, Canaletto had condescended to paint the Folly, Claude dreamily to depict an Unemployment Office, Uccello on D-Day jostled Klee on something that might or might not have been her long-suffering Launcelot. Boucher had enjoyed depicting a nude that looked suspiciously like Loretta being chased by a satyr who undoubtedly bore similarities to Ted. Blake, Hieronymous Bosch and Vasari joined forces in one room to present war, while in the corridor outside, twenty portrait painters had gathered to paint the Lakenham Set. Van Dyck had taken Lakenham, Titian had chosen her grandfather.

'Nah do you believe me, Gem?' Ted asked offhandedly. 'The palazzo is one big fake – like this.'

'No,' Jonathan said firmly. 'This isn't fake, Ted, and you know it.' In front of him a Toulouse-Lautrec can-can dancer kicked a Degas on her frilly bottom. 'Individually, maybe. Together they unite into a whole – and that's not fake. What are these, Ted?' he asked suddenly, coming downstairs and taking in the two splendid frescos facing each other on the stair-well.

'Ah. Well, it's a Hockney, ain't it?'

'*This* one is. It's your wedding, to Rosalind. But what's this?'

'Touch of your Van Eyck's,' Ted said carelessly. 'Sort of companion piece.'

The man stood in a room which had all the order and shape of a Dutch interior, but which wasn't Dutch. It was the Folly. He held the hand of his wife, who stood at his side, heavily pregnant. She was wearing Lucrezia's gown, Rosalind's wedding gown – and a month or two later Gemma's own.

Ted coughed deprecatingly. 'Arnolfini and his wife.'

'How can you tell?' Jonathan inquired mildly. 'You've left the faces blank.'

'Yeah, well, like the cathedral builders, you always have to leave a bit to God to do Himself.'

Gemma laughed. 'You're quite right, Ted. I am pregnant.'

'There now.' Ted cast his eyes to heaven. 'Didn't I say He'd do his bit? And we ain't given you a wedding present yet.'

'What about this?' Gemma spread her arms wide, encompassing the grandeur of the Folly.

'That ain't for you. That's for old Johnny Vermeer.'

'And my grandfather,' Gemma added gently.

'Maybe,' he muttered. 'Anyway, I got your wedding present in this cupboard.' He led the way to the huge old wardrobe in one of the bedrooms.

'Open it,' he commanded.

She obeyed, and cried out.

'Lovely, ain't she?' Ted said approvingly.

'But this is Rosalind's fake Pomona.'

'Is it?'

'Watch it, Gemma,' Jonathan said warningly. 'Here we go again.'

'It's another fake. It must be.'

'I tell you, Gemma, honest, and I'm an honest man, as you know – that bit of old painting I asked you to bring with you?'

'The *Mona Lisa* look-alike hand. Yes. It's on the table.'

'When we found Leonardo's Pomona – and we did – don't doubt that, it crumbled into bits as soon as we got it into daylight. Not before I had a good look at it, though. That's why I *had* to paint it, you see, cos only I'd seen it after Helmut went and died on me. That's the only bit left worth having. The hand. Believe me?'

'How can I, Ted? I'd like to,' she replied gently.

'Quite right, Gem. I knew you'd say that. So here's your present. Either you keep the hand, or you keep this Pomona. *One* of them's genuine, and that's gospel. Make your mind up which.'

'Which one's genuine Leonardo or which we want?' Jonathan asked.

'Which you're gonna keep.' Ted chuckled evilly. 'The other's going on the fire.'

Gemma looked at Jonathan. He nodded slightly. 'This,' she told Ted firmly, looking at the Pomona in all her veiled glory. 'Whoever she is, whoever painted her.'

He nodded approvingly. 'You made a good choice, Gem. Now you can give me Mona's hand.'

Suppose it *was* part of the genuine lost Pomona? Surely he'd not burn it? She turned away, unable to watch as painfully he got to his knees and lit the pile of paper and wood already prepared in the hearth.

'On the other hand,' Ted remarked, 'I might have Leo's Pomona tucked away for me old age.' He placed the scrap lovingly, carefully in the fire, and heaved a theatrical sigh. 'You'll never know, will you?'

A selection of bestsellers from Headline

LAND OF YOUR POSSESSION	Wendy Robertson	£5.99	☐
TRADERS	Andrew MacAllen	£5.99	☐
SEASONS OF HER LIFE	Fern Michaels	£5.99	☐
CHILD OF SHADOWS	Elizabeth Walker	£5.99	☐
A RAGE TO LIVE	Roberta Latow	£5.99	☐
GOING TOO FAR	Catherine Alliott	£5.99	☐
HANNAH OF HOPE STREET	Dee Williams	£4.99	☐
THE WILLOW GIRLS	Pamela Evans	£5.99	☐
MORE THAN RICHES	Josephine Cox	£5.99	☐
FOR MY DAUGHTERS	Barbara Delinsky	£4.99	☐
BLISS	Claudia Crawford	£5.99	☐
PLEASANT VICES	Laura Daniels	£5.99	☐
QUEENIE	Harry Cole	£5.99	☐

All Headline books are available at your local bookshop or newsagent, or can be ordered direct from the publisher. Just tick the titles you want and fill in the form below. Prices and availability subject to change without notice.

Headline Book Publishing, Cash Sales Department, Bookpoint, 39 Milton Park, Abingdon, OXON, OX14 4TD, UK. If you have a credit card you may order by telephone – 01235 400400.

Please enclose a cheque or postal order made payable to Bookpoint Ltd to the value of the cover price and allow the following for postage and packing:

UK & BFPO: £1.00 for the first book, 50p for the second book and 30p for each additional book ordered up to a maximum charge of £3.00.
OVERSEAS & EIRE: £2.00 for the first book, £1.00 for the second book and 50p for each additional book.

Name ....

Address ....

....

....

If you would prefer to pay by credit card, please complete:
Please debit my Visa/Access/Diner's Card/American Express (delete as applicable) card no:

Signature .... Expiry Date ....